White Bane

ROBERT JAMES ALLEN

ISBN: 978-1-64314-812-0 (Paperback)
978-1-64314-813-7 (Hardback)
978-1-64314-814-4 (E-book)

Library of Congress Control Number: 2023905670

AUTHORS PRESS

AuthorsPress
California, USA
www.authorspress.com

January 5, 1797, the *Fray*, the northern regions which border the dark and ominous heart of these lands known as *Vilkswood*. Within these woods, we find a hunter vigilantly tracking his prey.

This is his tale.

CHAPTER 1

Winter's Reign

Oppressed by winter's reign, he stood, staring sharply through the wood.

The frigid air was still as my fervid heart raced. My eyes then widened at the sight of a ten-point beige buck, so prominently grazing on tall thickets of snow-laden sage. This opportunity was three hours in the making, and I couldn't falter. This kill would be vital in feeding my wife, Heather; my eight-year-old daughter, Audrey; and me through these unforgiving months. So I took aim. I now had a clear shot at the buck's majestic frame, peering through the snowcapped columns of spruce trees. I squeezed the trigger, and the shot thundered with a three-second reverberation. "Got him," I whispered, as I stared intently at the buck gracefully falling to the ground in a drawn-out descent.

I'd always had a longtime affinity for the hunt. I killed my first buck at the sanguine age of twelve. I would frequently go hunting with my father in those days. Of course, back then I wasn't as skilled of a marksman as I am now, for it would take me three shots minimum to bring down a fully grown buck. Time has a way of gradually purging one's weaknesses or, thus, exacerbating them. I was thirty-two years old now, and my marksman skills were unparalleled to any other hunters in the region. That single bullet lodged in the once proud buck's neck was the proof.

"Thank you for feeding my family," I said to the fallen beast of the woods. My commemoration was soon stifled, as I recalled the wolves have been uncharacteristically vicious these past couple of months. So I then skinned and gutted the buck within thirty minutes. I cut four shanks from each of its upper hind quarters and eight six-inch-long steaks from its belly. I stored the meat and hide in a large leather satchel, which I slung over my back, next to my rifle. I had killed every type of creature that dwells in this region of *Vilkswood* (Wolf wood) including wolves as well.

If a pack of ravenous wolves were to befall me on my three-mile hike back to the cabin, I would have to make one of two drastic decisions. I could give up the twenty-plus pounds of venison I had stored in my satchel, or I could fight for the provisions my family and I so desperately need to survive. All of these scenarios raced through my mind, as I walked. I remember a fortnight or so ago, when me and my wife and daughter were in a tavern in *Bleakton* (the closest town, from our cabin in Vilkswood.) An old hunter was ranting on and on about his last hunt and how his life hung by a finite thread. Gimdrick Corval was his name. He saw himself as a thane of Bleakton, and many other residents agreed with that declarative title.

*****

Due to my sweet Audrey singing in my right ear, I could barely hear Gimdrick's story. Gimdrick was surrounded by a huddled mass of drunkards, hunters, and even little children. I must admit, the man was enthralling.

Gimdrick Corval

"Let me tell you fine folks of Bleakton a story. I am Gimdrick Corval, and I survived an onslaught from a pack of wolves, four days ago, and have the scars to prove it! I was making the trek from *Vilksridge*, and I had no more than six bullets left in the magazine of my rifle and a small dagger strapped to my thigh. I heard Bleakton is renowned for their ale, like drinking liquid gold. Everyone's been telling me, but that's not why I ventured here. It's the journey, not the destination!

"So there I was climbing down the shear stone face of the ridge, when I heard those demons howling. I was still focused on making it to the woods when I saw two black wolves appear right below my feet, waiting for me at the bottom of the ridge. So with one hand, I pulled out my rifle and fired down at those grim beasts but did not hit either one of them. The recoil from the rifle made me lose my grip from the rock face, and I plummeted thirty feet. I have never been so grateful for snow because if it hadn't been two feet deep at that time, I would have surely broken my ankles. So I had four bullets left, as I hobbled through Vilkswood.

"A couple of miles had passed, and I felt more relieved as I crossed the wooded fringe into the vale. Then I heard the dreaded howling once more. Two black wolves, most likely the same ones from the woods, had tracked me down and were racing on either side of me. I took aim with the rifle and fired two shots.

"The fear started to grow inside of me with the loss of each bullet, especially the fact that I had not hit a single wolf. They were too damn agile for my sight to lock on to. They followed me like a shadow, a shadow bearing swift fangs that seemed to gleam brighter as the day grew darker. I couldn't outrun them, not by any earthly means. The growling seemed to double in its ferocity, and so did their numbers. When I looked back, I saw four wolves chasing me! I then tripped but instinctively rolled over on my back and took aim with the rifle yet again. At that point in time, I knew I was going to meet a most painful and agonizing death.

"With two bullets and four wolves, the outcome wouldn't play in my favor. I managed to shoot one wolf right in the chest, just as it was lunging towards me, but the other three had charged right past their fallen ally at breakneck speed. There was a part of me that wrestled with the notion of using the final bullet on myself, but I didn't want to die as a coward. I would fight to the last breath! I fired the rifle but missed all three wolves as they darted from side to side. So I pulled out my dagger and welcomed my impending doom. The three wolves then slowed down their pace, and they halted no more than a couple of feet in front of me. I didn't notice it before, but there was a slightly larger, ashen-gray wolf among the pack of three.

"This wolf's dominant glare and growl had frozen the other two in their tracks; it was undoubtedly the alpha male of the pack. So he and he alone would challenge me. My dagger was ready to strike, as were the alpha wolf's fangs and claws. It dove atop my weary body, clenching my arm betwixt its jaws. I made sure, at all cost, to cover my neck with my other arm, for that's where wolves attack you first.

"So with my left arm draped around my neck and my right arm being torn apart, it was nearly impossible for me to fight back. I managed to roll over, in turn freeing my right arm from the alpha male's grasp. It then proceeded to maim my right leg, but at least, then my dagger-wielding right arm was free to go on the assault.

"I cried out in pain. By this moment, I had bite wounds all over my right arm and right leg. So I switched the dagger to my unscathed left arm and stabbed the alpha male right above its left eye. It let out a shrieking whelp, and the other two wolves jolted back in astonishment! Those other two beta wolves had never heard their leader cry out in pain before, and it bewildered them to the harshest degree.

"I laid there in grimace as I watched the alpha male stumble away into the woods with its two subservient beta allies. I cut my rifle strap into strips to dress my arm and leg wounds and then gathered up what little strength I had left as I staggered the last couple of miles. I would arrive in Bleakton in the dead of night, half frozen and bloodied."

*****

"So there you have it, folks!" Gimdrick shouted, followed by an array of beguiled praises and inquiries by hunters, drunkards, and children alike. The remaining townsfolk where skeptic, but after he revealed his covered-up bite wounds, which riddled his body like leprosy, he then had their unwavering respect and admiration, along with mine.

"Hail, Gimdrick, the first man in over ten years, who crossed paths with a pack of wolves and then lived to tell the tale," the barkeep shouted in a forthright tone. By that time, there wasn't a single soul who inquired why Gimdrick came to Bleakton in the first place (if it wasn't for the golden ale).

"Hail!" I shouted back among the crowd, raising my tankard of ale to the battle-scarred hunter in jubilation.

*****

I'd never experienced an onslaught by a pack of wolves through three different levels of terrain before. I only shot and killed a total of two wolves in my entire life as a hunter. Both these instances took place atop the lookout tower that I built next to the cabin; I used it frequently as a sharpshooter's nest. So I would have nothing to tell the townsfolk of Bleakton, for I did not cross paths with any wolves.

I could still drop a deer from a hundred yards away, and I was an expert at it. Did that make me softer than Gimdrick with his tale of unrelenting courage in the face of almost certain death? In some ways, I believed that even though I live sequestered with my wife and daughter in a cabin on the south edge of Vilkswood, I still had so much to learn about the coexistence of man and wild.

I was fortunate enough to not come across any wolves on my hunt that day. When I opened the door of the cabin, I saw Heather reading to Audrey by the fireplace. "I'm back," I pronounced in a triumphant voice. I then scooped up Audrey as she ran towards me with a cherublike demeanor.

"Thank God, you're back. I was beginning to worry," Heather said, as her warm lips kissed my cold cheek.

"Daddy, what did you bring back?" Audrey inquired and then started searching me with her tiny hands.

"You need not worry, for I have enough venison here to last us a month. We can cook what we need each day and then store the rest in the ice cellar" (a two-by-three-feet steel box buried outside beneath the front porch of the cabin). It was filled with snow to preserve our meats and safeguarded by a lock and key to keep wild animals out.

"That's wonderful news—anything that keeps you here with us and not hunting in those godforsaken woods," Heather said in a timid tone.

"If a bear or a pack of wolves should ever enter this cabin when I'm away, you and Audrey should lock yourselves in the storage closet as fast as you can. Don't try to use the rifle, you understand?" I instructed in a stern tone. I'd given these precautionary measures to Heather and Audrey many times, and both their eyes seemed to freeze with distress at the mere thought of it.

"Yes, dear," Heather replied while holding Audrey close to her hip.

I then began to stoke the three fireplaces in our cabin, while Heather put Audrey to bed.

"Do you remember the last time we visited *Squire's Tavern* in Bleakton?" Heather inquired in a tone that seemed to complement her peaceful disposition as she rested her head on my chest.

"Yes, that old hunter Gimdrick Corval was captivating the townsfolk for hours on end," I replied.

"Besides that, I noticed Audrey playing with the other children in the tavern," Heather said.

"Sorry, I missed that, dear. I was focused on Gimdrick and his tale of trepidation," I said to Heather in a zealous tone.

"She seemed really happy playing with the other children. I've homeschooled her in this cabin since she was a baby, and I cherish every moment of it, but I want Audrey to grow up and make friends with children her own age," Heather said.

"What are you saying, Heather?" I inquired.

"Maybe we should finally think about moving to Bleakton in the spring, for Audrey's well-being. I know this cabin was passed down to you by your father, and I've loved living here as well," Heather said. Heather then went on with her docile persuasions while we huddled closer throughout the night.

"I've envisioned our life in Bleakton many times. I could work in the town market selling meats from my various hunts," I said to Heather.

"I could enroll Audrey and teach at the *Claymore House*," (Bleakton's school/orphanage) Heather said in a zealous tone and gave me a warm smile.

"Then it's settled. We will move to Bleakton at the first thaw of spring," I said to Heather.

"I love you, and nothing would make me happier," Heather said with a smile.

"I love you too," I said to Heather with a smile as I leaned in close and sealed our decision with a good night kiss.

CHAPTER 2

Gideon's Run

What wonders will spring foretell as the coldness bids farewell?

The tepid rays of dawn's first light shone through the bedroom window. I could hear the sizzle and hum of Heather cooking breakfast on the wood-burning stove/ oven. I was looking through the bedroom window facing the south border of Vilkswood when I noticed something. It appeared to be a gust of snow blowing through the woods, but there was something about its shape and speed that confounded my eyes.

"Daddy, come and eat breakfast," Audrey shouted from the kitchen.

"Coming, princess," I said to Audrey. Audrey would giggle every time I call her princess. When I looked back at the south border of Vilkswood, the white blur had vanished.

"Oh, venison steak and blueberry biscuits," I remarked at the hearty breakfast that lay in front of me.

"Look, dear," Heather said as she tapped my shoulder. I then turned around to the sight of her and Audrey standing next to each other with angelic smiles. They were both wearing matching lapis dresses with black stockings.

"I love it when my two ladies dress alike. Now which one of you two fair maidens is my wife?" I inquired with a smile while I stared at Heather. Audrey's smile began to widen.

"I can't tell you two apart," I facetiously proclaimed while shaking my head. "You must be my wife," I said to Audrey as I snatched her up into my arms. "You've always had your mother's elegant beauty," I said to Audrey.

"Your father is just as dashing as ever," Heather interjected with a flirtatious smile. "Daddy, are we really moving to Bleakton in the spring?" Audrey inquired. I could see Audrey's eyes light up as she inquired of our decision.

"We sure are, princess, but in the meantime, I have to settle our housing and job arrangements," I replied.

Audrey was a precocious and insightful girl. The very best traits of her mother had been passed down to her. Heather gave birth to Audrey when she was twenty-two years old. If you were a stranger, you would swear that Heather is Audrey's older sister. Even now (at twenty-nine years old) Heather had maintained her slender and elegant body. Heather's gentle disposition always had a way of culling a man's inner demons.

Heather's ivory-tone skin seemed to pop in contrast alongside her straight sable hair, which cascaded down past her shoulders, stopping at her lower back. Heather had the kind of eyes that you thought no woman could possess, so deeply sapphire and emotive. I'd never forget the first time I saw them staring back at me.

NINE YEARS AGO

It was springtime, and *Gideon's Run* was upon me. Gideon's Run was a annual hunting contest created by Gideon Bleak, the founder of Bleakton. Gideon had been long since dead, but his annual hunting tradition has lived on for nearly a century. I, along with dozens of other hunters, signed up for the hunting competition at Squire's Tavern.

The contest rules were as follows: the contest would be one week long; you were judged on the kind of portions you brought back from your kill (pelts, antlers, beaks, teeth, hooves, etc.); the size and quality of the kill portions were very important factors in scoring high points with the judges. There was also a list of animals; each animal had a point value to go along with its name: squirrel and rabbit (5 points), fox and boar (10 points), crow and pheasant (15 points), hawk and eagle (25 points), ram (30 points), deer (50 points), moose and elk (75 points), bear (100 points), and wolf (200 points). Hunters could bring in a maximum of three kill portions to be judged. Another, perhaps the most important, factor was the option of bringing in the entire animal carcass. In this case, you would score extra points based on the number and placement of your gunshots in the animal's body. One shot to the head, neck, or heart would score an additional 25 points to the animal's original point value. Many hunters did not choose this option of scoring points on any animal larger than a fox. All hunters were also issued the same model rifle and ammunition. Any hunter would be disqualified by the judges if they deviated from these rules.

The winner of Gideon's Run would receive a two-thousand-dollar cash prize, the title of number 1 hunter in Bleakton, and a trophy symbolizing it. Most of the hunters cared more about the title of number 1 hunter, posted throughout the town of Bleakton, rather than the prize money. I, for one, was excited about all three rewards until I stared closely at the sign-up sheet.

I scowled at the sight of Clayton's signature on the sign-up sheet. They say all hunters have an unspoken bond of feral brotherhood. Well, this wasn't the case with Clayton Hornsborough. This forty-five-year-old hunter was revered and despised by every other hunter in Bleakton. I came in second place to that man for the past three years of competing in Gideon's Run.

The other twenty-four hunters and I were counting down the final-ten minutes to the start of Gideon's Run. We were waiting on the south edge of Vilkswood (a couple of miles from my cabin). Suddenly, I saw Clayton stepping forward from the crowd of hunters.

"I just want to say that none of you impudent shits stand a chance at beating me," Clayton proclaimed as if the contest was already over. "Vincent, I never get tired of you riding my coattails each year. Why don't you go back to your cabin, boy?" Clayton said while cracking his neck and spitting on the ground.

"I'll go back to my cabin, Clayton, with the title of number 1 hunter in Bleakton," I replied with a scoff and smirk.

"You think you little upstart hunters would learn by now. This title belongs to me," Clayton pronounced. Clayton's pompous declaration was met by an array of obscenities from the other twenty-three hunters. "For this year, I will trounce all your menial kills when I present a wolf's head pelt to the judges," Clayton pronounced. A burst of laughter then resonated throughout the twenty-three hunters.

"Every hunter who has made that statement was never seen again," a random hunter shouted.

"They're probably digesting in the wolf's belly," the hunter beside me proclaimed with a snicker.

"Go ahead. If you want to go after the most dominant hunters in Vilkswood," (wolves) "then you have a death wish," I said to Clayton in a stern tone.

"I am the most dominant hunter in Vilkswood, boy," Clayton replied. Clayton's overuse of the word *boy* was his way of belittling everyone.

At dawn's first light, Gideon's Run had begun. Clayton was the first to enter Vilkswood, with the other hunters and I in tow. Within minutes, we had all dispersed from one another, as we preferred. I had a proximity advantage over the other hunters, for my cabin was located right on the south edge of Vilkswood. I wasn't obligated to campout in the woods at night, although I didn't fear it. The other hunters were much too hasty. I heard countless gunshots within the first hour of the competition. After a day had passed, the time between each gunshot had lengthened to two hours. I returned to my cabin near nightfall every day, as Clayton so scornfully suggested. Eighty percent of the hunters competing in Gideon's Run, including me, were not from Bleakton. Those foolhardy men camped out in Vilkswood no matter what harrowing fate befell them.

It was day 3 when I spotted a boar lumbering in a shady grove twenty feet in front of me. So I took aim and fired. I would take this boar's eight-inch tusks as my first portion for the judges. I wanted a clean cut, so I carved around the perimeter of each tusk with my knife. I then picked up a rock and hammered it against the edge of my knife, thus cracking the boar's tusks clean off. I stored the tusks in my satchel and then made my way back to the cabin. Just as I was crossing the southern border of Vilkswood, I heard a bullet careen right past my left ear. I then dived to the ground, slamming my head against a rock. When I pressed my hand against my head, I felt blood running down my ear. I then heard a barking laugh, resonating from the woods.

"Watch yourself, boy," a voice shouted.

I could see Clayton's head peeking out from behind a tree. That bastard was trying to intimidate me!

"Men aren't on the kill list, Clayton. If they were, I would have put a bullet in your head three years ago," I shouted. By the time I was done shouting in rage, Clayton had receded deeper into the woods. My head was aching with pain by the time I made it back to the cabin.

Clayton's intimidation shot had put me out of commission for a day, as were his intentions. It was day 4 of Gideon's Run, and I was running out of time. I couldn't stop pacing the hardwood floors of my cabin with gauze wrapped around my head. I was feeling dizzy, so I rested my head for a couple of hours. Every gunshot I heard that day seemed to put a damper on my hopes of winning the competition, as I slipped in and out of consciousness.

It was day 5 of Gideon's Run, and my head wound had ceased its throbbing. I rose out of bed, gathered up my hunting gear, and then made my way into Vilkswood. The sky was rather dreary that day, and I feared it would rain soon. If it were to rain, half the animals on the kill list would be taking refuge in burrows, dens, holes, and trees. So I built a small hut using long branches and leaves, which I situated between two thin birch trees. I then sat there in that hut waiting for hours with the end of my rifle poking out. I knew the topography of Vilkswood better than any hunter, and I knew where to camp out. I made the conscious decision to build my rudimentary hut right by *Fox Creek* (a creek that was bordered by many fox dens). I was beginning to grow impatient as the dreary day had slowly languished. My gaze was quickly averted from the fox dens when I spotted a doe lowering its head to take a drink from the creek. I took aim, but no more than a second before I could squeeze the trigger, a gunshot fired out from the east.

The doe dropped beside the bank of the creek. "Bull's-eye." I heard a hunter shout as he ran up to the fallen doe. I watched the hunter meticulously skin the deer's hide, and within fifteen minutes, he was gone with his portion. I was extremely envious of the other hunter'sportion, for I had missed my opportunity. So my gaze was once again drawn back towards the fox dens.

*****

Six hours had passed before I saw two pointed ears emerge from the den. I took aim and fired one shot, hitting the fox's right shoulder blade, sending it tumbling back a couple of feet. "Damn," I shouted in frustration at the sight of my bullet placement lodged in the fox. I wanted to bring the whole fox carcass back, but I neither hit its head, heart, nor neck. So I settled for the fox's tail instead. Something was off about my conviction during this competition. I lacked the steel-eyed accuracy that I so swiftly displayed in the past competitions. I returned to my cabin, riddled with doubt about my life as a hunter. I never felt any remorse when I kill an animal. Many hunters would say that was an inborn trait, but I had come to the revelation that that was what made me weak and unimpassioned. If I had never valued the lives of the animals I've killed, then how could I kill with purpose? I pensively stared at the boar tusks and foxtail and thought how inferior my kill portions were.

It was the sixth day of Gideon's Run when I made the trek to Vilksridge. I camped out on the summit pass for a couple of hours. I foolishly fell asleep and lost four hours of precious hunting time. I awoke to a clip-clop noise coming down the thoroughfare. I crouched down behind a rock and took aim, but I then saw something I didn't expect.

A young woman on a bronze horse was trotting towards me. I stepped out from behind the rock to meet her. She then halted her horse at the sight of me. "Excuse me, sir. Would you happen to know which way it is to Bleakton?" the young woman inquired with such a dulcet voice. She couldn't have been more than twenty years old. Her limpid sapphire eyes then widened with anticipation.

"Bleakton is about twenty miles southwest of here, but why is a woman of your fairness traveling through Vilkswood alone?" I inquired. I was immediately worried for this young woman's safety, especially during the peak of Gideon's Run. The young woman was wearing a scarlet blouse underneath a black embroidered corset, which exposed her ivory skin. She had sable hair, which was braided into a long ponytail, that streamed down the front of her chest. "I'm not by myself. I have Galahad to protect me," the young woman replied with a smile while gently stroking her horse's blond mane. She then dismounted her horse and bashfully greeted me. "I'm Heather, Heather Windemere," the young woman said as she extended her slender arm in salutation.

"I'm Vincent Belmont," I said to the young woman with an elfish smile while we shook hands. The fact that this young woman dismounted her horse and shook the hand of a mere stranger in Vilkswood simply amazed me. "Well, Ms. Windemere—"

"Oh, call me Heather. Only my students call me Ms. Windemere," the young woman interjected with a warm smile. "I ventured here from *Shors End*. It's a port city located on the northeastern coastline of the *Fray*. Word caught my ear from a traveling dignitary that there's a school/orphanage in Bleakton called the Claymore House. Teaching has always been my life's blood, and I know I can make a difference in the lives of those disregarded children. I was given directions to travel through Vilkswood, for the journey would only take me sixteen hours. If I were to go around Vilkswood, the journey would take me nearly three days," Heather said.

Heather had the purest of intentions, which was very rare in this day and age. Everything about her was beautiful, and I knew what I must do. "Your informant from Shors End obviously had no knowledge of the hunting competition known as Gideon's Run. You see, I'm a hunter by trade, and I'm competing in Gideon's Run right now. The competition will end tomorrow at dawn, and a winner will be chosen based on the three kill portions they present to the judges," I informed Heather. Heather nodded with polite discernment as I continued to explain the rules of Gideon's Run.

"That would explain all the gunshots I've been hearing. Galahad had been uneasy ever since we departed from Shors End," Heather remarked with a distressful stare.

"I'm sorry to say, but your horse will not serve as protection, especially when traveling through these woods. Please let me accompany you. I'll ensure your safe passage to Bleakton," I said to Heather. My request to be Heather's guide through Vilkswood was a proper formality. No matter what her preference was, I would not let any harm befall her from here henceforth.

"If you insist, but I don't want to sidetrack you from your competition," Heather said.

"It's no trouble at all. My cabin is about eight miles southwest of here. We'll be there before nightfall. You can rest at my cabin, as I can imagine you must be weary from your travels. Then when you're ready, we can head off to Bleakton," I informed Heather.

Heather's lucent face soon saddened after she noticed the gauze wrapped around my head. "Oh, you're hurt," Heather remarked while pointing to my head.

"Oh, this was nothing, just a minor setback," I said to Heather.

"Come on, hop on," Heather said as she mounted her horse.

"I can study the animal tracks better from down here," I said to Heather. So we made our way south down the thoroughfare. I then walked beside Heather as she slowly trotted on Galahad. Heather's trust in me, albeit innocent and naive, was a feeling I found most intriguing. What did she see in me so quickly that would constitute this trust? I pondered these feelings as we made our way down Vilksridge at 3:15 PM.

"So are all hunters like you, Vincent?" Heather inquired. I could tell by Heather's playful grin that her inquiry was rhetorical.

"What do you mean like me?" I inquired as I awaited Heather's judgment with bated breath.

"Well, every hunter that I've met displayed such gallantry and debonair," Heather remarked.

I became worried that I didn't measure up to the so-called gallant hunters whom Heather spoke so fondly of. "Well, how many hunters have you met in your life?" I inquired. I was curious to know how prevalent Heather's encounter with hunters was.

"Well, counting you, that would bring the total to…one," Heather replied with an elfin giggle. Heather's banter managed to coax a laugh out of me. She had such a lighthearted yet sophisticated air about her.

At 5:30 PM, Heather and I entered Vilkswood. I signaled for Heather to stop, as I kneeled down to examine some animal tracks. Just as I feared, the animal that left these tracks was a very formidable beast and was within a one-mile vicinity of Heather and me.

"Is something wrong, Vincent?" Heather inquired. Heather then began to look skittish as I pulled out my rifle.

"Don't be afraid. Let's keep moving," I said to Heather in a calm and stern tone. Due to springtime (mating season), most of the animals in Vilkswood displayed aggressive behavior, atypical to any other time of the year. My senses would now be on high alert for the remainder of our journey.

"About two miles till we reach my cabin," I said to Heather. I could tell that Heather's nerves were frayed from the unknown dangers of Vilkswood. "Shhhh," I said to Heather to remain still and quiet. I heard something rustling on an outcrop right near us. As the sound drew nearer, I could make out thundering footsteps quickening their pace. I stood ready with my rifle while Heather was trying to keep Galahad calm. "It's a brown bear!" I shouted, as the huge beast burst out in front of us. The bear rose on its two hind legs, standing nearly eight feet tall. Galahad then stood on its two hind legs to meet the bear. I had a clear shot of the bear when I also noticed that Heather was falling off the back end of Galahad. Heather let out a frail scream; I knew I had to make a split-second decision. So I dropped my rifle then slid on the ground, catching Heather in my arms.

"Galahad!" Heather shouted in dismay.

The bear's mighty paw had swiped Galahad in the face. This sent the horse bolting away in fear. The bear continued its assault as it stood over Heather and me. "Get behind me," I shouted as I positioned myself between Heather and the bear. Time stood still at that moment. Something felt different inside of me as I heard Heather's cries. So I took my aim at the bear as I knelt in front of Heather. I wasn't only fighting for my own life at this moment, and that selfless action had focused me in a way I've never felt before. I fired one shot, and the bear let out a ghastly roar. The bear's roar subsided to a meek grumble, as he began to fall. I grabbed Heather, and we rolled out of the way just before the bear could crush us.

"Heather…are you all right?" I inquired. I could feel Heather's heart beating through her ripped corset as she rested upon me.

"I'm all right," Heather responded in a flustered tone. I noticed Heather then began to sob as I helped her stand up. "Galahad—I had all my valuables with him. My money, books, clothes, and violin—they're all gone. Oh, Vincent, what am I going to do now?" Heather inquired and then quickly embraced me while continuing to weep over her unforeseen losses.

"I'm sorry about Galahad and all your valuables, but the sun will set in an hour, and we cannot go searching for him at night," I said to Heather in a somber tone.

"You have your portion, Vincent," Heather said while pointing to the bear. Even after all she just lost, Heather still had my interest in mind.

My bullet placement in the bear was dead flawless. One bullet was in betwixt his eyes. "I will skin this bear as fast as I can," I said to Heather.

Heather kneeled down close to me as I went to work, skinning the bear's hide. This bear would take me longer to skin than any other animal I've skinned. I wanted to have its head and claws fully intact as one piece of hide. Heather covered her mouth in disgust as I began rolling my fist deep within the bear, separating the bear's skin with as little use of a knife as possible. About thirty minutes in, I had the bear's chest, arms, and claws fully skinned. I had the most difficulty skinning the bear's head, but I managed to separate it by cutting each corner of the bear's mouth. It took me a little over an hour, but I finished skinning the bear. "That's impressive, Vincent," Heather remarked as I displayed the widespread bear pelt like a flag.

"The sun is setting. I'm sorry it took so long," I said to Heather. I wore the bear pelt around me like a cape, with the head lying on top of mine and the claws crossed over my chest.

It was 7:09 PM, and Heather and I had a little over a mile left before we reached my cabin. In this world, there were very few things that struck fear into my heart. One of those things was being in the woods at night when wolves begin hunting. It began to rain as Heather and I crossed the wooded fringe into the vale.

"Here, get underneath," I said to Heather as I stretched out the bear pelt to cover her. I could tell that Heather was reluctant to drape herself in the reeking bear pelt, but the rain made her succumb to its shelter.

We arrived at my cabin at 7:32 PM. I unlocked the door, and Heather and I both rushed inside. I began to light all the oil lamps in each room and then started a fire in the great room fireplace.

"Make yourself at home," I said to Heather as I laid the bear pelt on the floor in front of the fireplace. I then lit the wood-burning stove and started boiling water to make a pot of tea. Heather took off her black high-heeled riding boots and ripped corset and then sat down upon the sofa. I placed the teakettle and teacups down on the mahogany coffee table and then sat down next to Heather.

"Thank you," Heather remarked in a somber tone. I could see the hazy weariness in Heather's eyes as she began to slowly sip her tea. "I was looking at all the animal heads on your wall," Heather said as her eyes widened at the sight of them.

"Oh yes, most of those are my father's," I said to Heather. I went over to the mantel-piece and picked out a photo of my parents to show Heather. "That's my father, Jacob, and my mother, Elizabeth," I said to Heather while pointing at the weathered photo.

"I see the resemblance to your father," Heather remarked.

"I never knew my mother. There were fatal complications that occurred when I was born, and she died no more than five minutes after giving birth to me. All I have to remember her are these photos and what my father told me about her. My father died five years ago. He was only fifty-five years old. We were getting geared up to go hunting like any other weekend. Then I saw him lying on the floor, clutching his chest. That was the first time in my life that I've ever felt truly afraid and helpless. My father had a look of calm acceptance on his face just before he died. He not only taught me everything I know about hunting, but he also homeschooled me in this cabin. His grave is on the east side of the cabin, right next to my mother's. Whenever I feel lost, I imagine his voice in my head, and it strengthens my resolve," I said to Heather. I noticed the story of my parent's death had brought Heather to tears.

"You've lost so much, Vincent, and yet you're still so kind and gentle," Heather remarked in a somber tone while wiping the tears off her cheeks.

"I'm sorry. I know this day has been fraught with many ordeals. I shouldn't have brought up the story."

"No, Vincent, you have nothing to apologize for. We are made by our hardships and our achievements. I had the chance to teach at the most prestigious school in Shors End called the *White Crown Academy*," Heather said.

"Why didn't you take it?" I inquired. Heather then rested her legs upon my lap as she sprawled out on the sofa.

"My parents are quite wealthy, upper-class politicians in Shors End. Throughout my whole life, they've spared no expense when it comes to me. The children who enroll in White Crown Academy are so coddled and have never experienced any hardships their entire lives. Their parents' social and financial standings would get them anything they desired despite their education. I never felt beholden to my parents' wealth. When I told my parents I wanted to teach in Bleakton, they were appalled to say the least," Heather said with a sigh while she rested her head back on the armrest of the sofa.

"You're a very selfless person," I remarked.

Heather then sat up from the sofa and took my hand. "Vincent, you're the most selfless man that I've ever had the privilege of meeting. There are very few men in this world who would risk their lives for a woman the way you did for me today," Heather said as she gazed at me with such amorous eyes.

"Well, you're worth the risk," I said to Heather with a grin as she leaned in closer to me.

Heather gently placed her hand on my cheek, and her lips softly beckoned mine as we kissed. "I feel safe with you, Vincent," Heather whispered.

*****

It was 9:24 PM. Heather and I had fallen asleep on the sofa in front of the fireplace for a little while. The crackle from the fireplace woke me up. I got up from the sofa very slowly, trying not to disturb Heather, who was nestled around me. I covered Heather with a blanket and then got an ember from the great room fireplace to light the fireplace in my bedroom. I knew I had to arrive in Bleakton before dawn tomorrow, 5:42 AM, to be present at Squire's Tavern for the judging of Gideon's Run. It was a strict competition indeed. If I was absent when the judges started roll call at dawn, then I would be disqualified from the competition.

As I was lying in bed, I couldn't help but wonder what tomorrow would bring. How would I fair in the judging of Gideon's Run, and how would Heather feel in the morning? I would have never predicted this series of fateful events befalling me. I didn't realize how exhausted I was. I spent the duration of the day suppressing my weariness, so I could be a vigilant guide for Heather. Just before I drifted off, I felt a warm presence beside me; and for the first time in over five years, I no longer felt alone.

At 3:06 AM, I awoke with a groan and noticed that Heather was lying in bed with me. She had her arm draped around me, and her face pressed against the back of my neck. Heather must've gotten into bed with me just after I fell asleep. I could feel Heather's warm breath on the back of my neck as she peacefully slept. I almost didn't want to get out of bed. I wanted to hold on to that moment, lest I was dreaming. The imperative matter of Gideon's Run was at hand, so I reluctantly lifted Heather's arm as I quietly rose out of bed. Heather then let out a faint murmur as she pawed at the empty side of my bed.

So I loaded the chest assigned for carrying and concealing all the hunter's kill portions for the competition with the dried-out full bear-skin pelt, foxtail, and boar tusks. I then had a quick breakfast of coffee and smoked venison jerky. It was apparent that Heather was exhausted, and I wouldn't dare wake her. So I got geared up, and just before I departed the cabin for the eight-mile hike to Bleakton, I left a note for Heather on the pillow of my side of the bed.

> Dear Heather,
>
> I didn't want to wake you. I am heading off to Bleakton for the judging of Gideon's Run, and I will return around noon. There's coffee and smoked venison jerky in the kitchen. I hope you will still be here when I return. In the short time that I've known you, you have done nothing but strengthen my resolve as a hunter. Ever since our fortuitous encounter in Vilkswood, I was wholeheartedly beguiled by you. I am truly grateful to have met someone as beautiful as you.
>
> Sincerely,
Vincent

I left for Bleakton at 3:38 AM with my designated rifle and kill portions stored away in the chest. I could hear the hoot of a solitary owl as it resonated through the dark treetops. I'd always enjoyed making the hike across the vale compared to Vilkswood. The serene landscape was much less tiresome to traverse. The vale was eerily still this morning. I had to keep a steadfast pace if I were to reach Bleakton before dawn. The last remnants of winter made their presence known with a chilling wind that swept across the vale. I was halfway to Bleakton and was making good time. I hiked the narrow weather-beaten trail that followed the *Murk River*, which was the main river that runs through Vilkswood and Bleakton.

I arrived in Bleakton at 5:27 AM. Squire's Tavern was the only establishment that was open during that time of day. There was a crimson banner with gold trim that hung over the entrance to the tavern. The banner read, "Judging of the Ninety-First Annual Gideon's Run Competition: the Winner Will Be Announced Today." Yes, this competition only had one solitary winner who would receive all the glory as it's been for nearly a century. I stared at all the fellow hunters hugging their chests that concealed their kill portions. The panel of judges consisted of four old grizzled hunting dignitaries. Desmond Bleak, Gideon Bleak's great-grandson and the current mayor of Bleakton, was the overseer for this competition. A couple of the distinguished judges were friends with the one and only Gideon Bleak.

"So, Vincent, do you think Clayton really bagged himself a wolf's head pelt?" a hunter inquired, which made me curious to where Clayton was among the crowd.

I then spotted Clayton talking with Desmond Bleak, no doubt trying to fix his chances of winning the competition. I quickly ordered a pint of golden ale and then finished it within a minute or two. Clayton and I crossed daggers from across the tavern. We got into fistfights in this tavern before and had nearly been disqualified for it. I didn't forget the intimidation shot he made four days ago at me. Now I could only speculate what the other hunters' kill portions were.

Desmond Bleak then stepped out from behind the judging table. "Participants of Gideon's Run, I commend you all for upholding my great-grandfather's noble tradition. Gideon Bleak founded this town with a hunter's mentality. Some would say that's an archaic and barbaric way to govern a town. I say it's the greatest cornerstone of building a prosperous town. When Gideon Bleak founded Bleakton, he had one vision in mind, to preserve the oldest and noblest of professions. Now without further ado…let the judging of Gideon's Run commence," Desmond proclaimed. Desmond's commencement speech was the same every year but inspiring nonetheless. One of the judges then stepped out from behind the judging table.

"When I call your name, you will present your designated rifle and chest filled with your kill portions," the judge pronounced in a stern voice.

When my name was called, I then promptly followed the judge's commands.

"Roll call: twenty-five hunters entered Gideon's Run, and nineteen are currently present for the judging," the judge remarked. I could only speculate why the other hunters were absent from the judging of the competition. One possibility was that they were killed by various animals, most likely wolves in Vilkswood. Another possibility was that they didn't believe their kill portions would score high enough to win and absconded with their designated rifles in disgrace. When Clayton's name was called, he slammed his rifle and chest on the judging table with resounding boisterousness. By now most of the hunters were either soused or halfway there. A couple of armed constables, along with Desmond Bleak, and the panel of judges carried all the chests and rifles to a back room. This back room was where they convened as they meticulously judged every aspect of the kill portions.

So now we waited. Tensions always became frayed among all the hunters during this time. There were two armed constables guarding the entrance to the back room, and four constables spread out throughout the rest of the tavern. But the lawmen's presence wouldn't stifle the brash hubris of any of the hunters. If you got into some sort of physical altercation with another hunter when the judging was taking place, you got one warning from the constables. If you persisted with your hostile behavior, you would be taken away in handcuffs and disqualified from the competition. I wasn't the youngest hunter in this competition. There was a nineteen-year-old hunter by the name of Heinrich Finch. I could see that Heinrich was in a heated argument with Boris, a veteran hunter who was companions with Clayton. Clayton and Boris considered it a rite of passage whenever they tormented a young up-and-coming hunter.

"Give Heinrich a break, Boris, unless you're afraid about your chances of winning this competition," I said to Boris with a sneer.

Clayton was sitting alone at a table, watching the spectacle unfold.

"Mind your tone, you parentless loner," Boris said in a barking tone. I then slammed my tankard of ale on the table and sprung up from my stool to confront Boris.

"Go on, make a move," Boris said with a grin. I then figured it out. Clayton and Boris's plan was to get me disqualified from the competition. He was baiting me, but I wouldn't fall for it.

So I sat back down on the barstool. "Liquor and a hunter's hubris don't mix well," I said to Bremen. Bremen Squire was the owner of Squire's Tavern. He was usually the first man I would talk to when I visited Bleakton. He was a good man, though at times could be overbearingly lucrative, like the decision he made to serve ale at 7:24 AM.

Nevertheless, all the hunters in Squire's Tavern were drinking. I stopped drinking after my fourth pint of ale. A couple of hunters next to me were as rowdy as could be. They couldn't go more than ten seconds without laughing at each other's anecdotes. I was growing impatient by the judges' long deliberations. I kept my eyes fixed upon the door of the back room, waiting for it to open. After three and a half hours, the back room's door had finally opened. The four judges, along with Desmond Bleak, walked onto the stage and placed three chests on the table. I felt tense with anticipation as Desmond Bleak began to speak.

"Attention, participants of Gideon's Run! After much deliberation, the panel of judges has chosen a winner. Beforehand, I would like to thank all of you proud hunters, not just for competing in my great-grandfather's competition but for bringing noble publicity to the great town of Bleakton," Desmond proclaimed. Some hunters were so soused that they weren't even paying attention to the announcements. One judge stood beside Desmond Bleak and made the much-awaited announcement. "Based on Gideon Bleak's scoring system, these three hunters' kill portions had the highest scores in the competition: Heinrich Finch, Clayton Hornsborough…and Vincent Belmont."

"Fixed!" one hunter shouted in a soused tone. He then fell off the barstool that he so rakishly sat upon. A wave of laughter accompanied the hunter's drunken debacle. Two constables then escorted the besotted hunter out of the tavern.

"Would the three hunters please come up to the stage," the judge announced.

I stood on the right, next to Heinrich.

"As tradition goes, only one among you three hunters will receive the title of number 1 hunter in Bleakton, a trophy commemorating that title, and a cash prize of two thousand dollars. Now…the winner of the ninety-first annual Gideon's Run competition is… Vincent Belmont, with a score of one hundred twenty-five points," the judge pronounced triumphantly.

I felt so accomplished when I heard the judge announce me as the winner of Gideon's Run. I had finally done it; all my sacrifices and hunting methods had bestowed upon me the glory that I strived so hard to achieve. The tavern then erupted with applause. I shook the hands of Heinrich, the four judges, and Desmond Bleak. I then saw Clayton rummaging through my kill chest with a look of utter dismay on his face.

"I thought brown bears were still hibernating. How the fuck did you find a brown bear in Vilkswood?" Clayton inquired in a snarling tone and then flipped over the judges' table and stormed out of the tavern

I didn't acknowledge Clayton's tantrum. I held up my gold trophy in great prominence. Accepting defeat with grace and dignity is the true measure of a man's humility. Clayton Hornsborough lacked that humility and departed Bleakton in disgrace that day. For once, Clayton was right about something. This early into spring, it was very rare to see a brown bear awake from hibernation, but I came across another creature even rarer that day in Vilkswood. A creature that comforted me, frightened me, beguiled me, and prepared me, a creature so beautiful and compassionate, so gentle and affectionate, and a creature with snow-white skin and sapphire eyes that evoked warmth from within me. That creature's name was Heather Windemere.

CHAPTER 3

The Grim Fable

Certain fables should stay lost, lest you delve their mortal cost.

"I'm heading off to Bleakton now," I pronounced.

"Be safe, honey," Heather said as she bid me farewell with a kiss.

Audrey then embraced me around the waist before I stepped out of the cabin. Making the eight-mile hike across the vale to Bleakton was an undertaking I made roughly five times a month. This undertaking was most exhausting during the winter months. I never brought in enough money as a hunter to afford a horse for my family and me. I'd admit, owning a horse would make my travels to Bleakton much less tiresome. But I'd made these hikes since I was twelve years old, and I was very used to trudging on foot.

Bleakton always had more of a charm during the winter. I could feel the town's atmospheric allurement just as I entered through the main gates. However, I think after hiking four miles through the snow, any town would look alluring to someone. Instead of Squire's Tavern, I foremost made my way to Bleakton's town hall. I noticed that the many wooden abodes of Bleakton were adorned with wreaths and various animal antlers. The *Market Square* was bustling as usual, at any given day. There were around twenty vendors selling their provisions, oddities, fabrics, and decor in the square. The clock tower stood in the center of the square and was the tallest structure in Bleakton, standing twelve stories tall. The town of Bleakton had a population of 8,500, though its population had shown a steady increase from the past five years. Bleakton was always predominantly a hunter's town, though through the decades had become more modernized in terms of its cultural diversity, exports, and education. The Claymore House was still underfunded, and the underprivileged children were affected the most by it.

I entered the town hall and requested the necessary forms from the receptionist. One form had the information on tax levies for Bleakton residents. The other form had the information on Market Square vendors. The monthly cost for renting a vendor stand in the Market Square was one hundred dollars. There were currently nine vacant houses up for rent in the town of Bleakton. These houses had a monthly rent; the rent ranged from one hundred to four hundred dollars. The cost of living in Bleakton was more affordable than I had first estimated, though I would have to immediately start saving all my income. There was still one last issue I had to settle before I left Bleakton, so I made my way to Squire's Tavern.

Bremen had come up with a new seasonal hot-brandy cider, which he was promoting throughout the town.

"How's it going Bremen? What's the word around town?" I inquired as Bremen was routinely wiping down the bar.

"The word is that the mayor might be raising taxes soon," Bremen remarked with a sigh

"I thought Bleakton's economy was rising. Why would Bleak raise taxes now?" I inquired. This news was slightly discouraging for me, but for the time being, I just brushed it off as hearsay.

"Well, that's why Bleak is going to raise taxes. It's called supply and demand," Bremen said.

"So what'll you have? I suggest my new seasonal hot-brandy cider. The apple-cider brew is triple fermented, and then the brandy is reduced down as it simmers over a fire. I top it all off with a dash of cinnamon and nutmeg," Bremen said with a zealous tone and smirk.

"Lay one on me," I said to Bremen with a smirk.

"All right, coming right up," Bremen said.

"So how's the tavern been doing this winter?" I inquired while Bremen was preparing the hot brandy cider.

"We're treading water, but if this tax hike falls through, I might have to sell the tavern," Bremen replied as he passed me the steaming mug of cider and awaited my judgment. I blew on the brew a couple of times before I took a sip.

"It's great, the perfect winter brew," I said to Bremen with a smile.

"Maybe I'll use your testimony for the slogan," Bremen said with a grin.

"I've always considered this tavern to be the heart of Bleakton. It would be a shame if you have to sell it," I said to Bremen while shaking my head.

"We'll see what the future entails for this tavern," Bremen said.

I continued to sip my hot-brandy cider when I noticed a man out of the corner of my eye, who sat down beside me at the bar.

"What'll you have, Mordrid?" Bremen inquired.

I looked beside me and noticed the man was wearing a long black leather coat, which only further accentuated his rather macabre features. The man had long black hair, which was strewn across his face like a spider web, and a sickly pale complexion. The man's skeletal physique was hunched over the bar with his head in his hand.

"Give me a double shot of whiskey," the sullen man replied to Bremen.

"Bremen, I came here to ask you something. I'm sure you've heard many stories throughout the years in this tavern, stories from all different classes of people," I said to Bremen.

"Hell, Vincent, I could write a book from all the stories I've heard in this tavern," Bremen said with a scoff.

"Then please tell me, what do you know about white wolves?" I inquired.

The man known as Mordrid and Bremen both looked at each other in reaction to my inquiry.

"White wolf, not wolves, that subspecies of wolf was nearly hunted to extinction over forty years ago," Bremen replied.

I could tell by Bremen's furrowed brow that he had a personal connection to the story. "So there's only one white wolf left?" I inquired.

Bremen then leaned in closer to me. "The fable foretells, anyone who has caught a glimpse of this white wolf has had death befall them in some way, shape, or form," Bremen said in a near whispering tone. Suddenly Mordrid jerked his head in my direction.

"White Bane, the white wolf, you didn't see him, did you?" the sullen man inquired in such a timid yet chilling voice.

"N-no, I-I just heard the whispers around town," I replied.

"Seeing White Bane is an ill omen of grave significance," Mordrid said in a stern tone and intense stare. "Six years ago, I was camping with my younger brother in Vilkswood. One morning, he woke me up and then started raving about a white wolf. He said he saw the white wolf staring at him on a cliff right near our campsite. I humored my brother's story. Though looking back, I should've taken him more seriously."

I noticed Mordrid's hand begin to shake while he was holding his glass of whiskey.

"It happened at dawn. I awoke to find my brother absent from the campsite. Then I noticed a splattering of blood right near his tent. So I raced through Vilkswood, calling out my brother's name. I searched for what seemed like hours until I came across a most horrific sight. My brother was lying motionless near the entrance to a cave with his throat torn open.

"The blood had silhouetted his body upon the rocks from which he lain. I was far too late. My dear brother had been dead for hours. I held his bloodied body closely in mourning, and then I heard the grimmest of growls. I saw a figure standing atop the cave entrance. This figure shone with dawn's first light. I was half blinded by its radiance, but from what I could make out, its face was stained with a splash of crimson. I pulled out my rifle, but before I could take aim, the figure had vanished with the fading of dawn's light. That morning, I reclaimed my brother's corpse from White Bane. But I still live in fear for the day White Bane comes for me. To this day, I dare not tread near Vilkswood," Mordrid said.

"I'm sorry for your loss," I said to Mordrid in a somber tone.

"White Bane is merely a cautionary fable," Bremen interjected.

"Don't patronize me, Bremen. You know damn well it's true!" Mordrid shouted in an aggressive tone.

"Calm down, Mordrid. You know I don't doubt the verity of your story," Bremen said to Mordrid. I had now come to the conclusion that White Bane was a most sinister fable, a fable that remained buried in the hearts and minds of the townsfolk of Bleakton.

"Look at my eyes," Mordrid said as he leaned in close. The irises of Mordrid's eyes were palest of gray, like a dismal, cloudy autumn morning.

"How did your eyes turn achromatic?" I inquired. I'd never seen a person with eyes like Mordrid's, so I was quite astonished.

"After I laid my brother to rest beneath the earth, I looked into the mirror and saw that my once sapphire eyes had faded to gray. This is the mark that White Bane left on me, and like the loss of my brother, it will haunt me for the rest of my life," Mordrid replied and drunk the last of his whiskey and then slapped a couple of dollars upon the bar. He then stood up from the barstool with a slight stumble and proceeded to exit the tavern. On his way out, I heard Mordrid muttering something under his breath. He kept repeating the word *demon* as he left the tavern.

"After all he witnessed, Mordrid has every right to be deranged," Bremen said to me.

"What about you, Bremen? What have you witnessed?" I inquired.

Bremen then took a profound sigh just before he spoke. "When I was twelve years old, I was also on a camping trip with my sister and father in Vilkswood," Bremen said.

"I didn't know you had a sister," I remarked.

"My father was like you, Vincent, a diehard hunter through and through. Despite his countless efforts to instill his hunting prowess upon me, I was never one for the hunter's path. One brisk autumn morning, my father told me to go fetch a pail of water from the nearby creek. Just as I was filling up the pail full of water, I saw a pure-white figure prowling through the nearby birch trees. I remained frozen as I watched the figure's every movement. Due to my divided attention, the pail of water had slipped through my fingers and splashed into the shallow creek.

"Suddenly, the white figure whipped its gaze towards me, and my prior enthrallment abruptly turned to dread. I remember the white figure's deep growls and piercing eyes seemed to hinder me where I stood. I then heard my father's voice call out to me, and then the white figure dispersed like a wisp of smoke. I rubbed my eyes in shock, trying to comprehend what

I just witnessed. I then returned to my father and sister at the campsite with the pail full of water, although I didn't tell them what I had witnessed by the creek. I later on dismissed that incident as the morning light playing tricks on my overactive imagination. That same night, I shared a tent with my sister, while my father slept in a separate tent on the other side of the fire.

"My father shook me awake the next morning and asked me in a frantic tone where my sister was. I didn't hear her leave the tent, so I was also baffled by her absence. My father and I searched for her until nightfall, but even my father's masterful hunting skills couldn't track the slightest sign of her. My father wouldn't give up on finding my sister, so the next day, he gathered eight of his fellow hunting companions to scour every inch of Vilkswood, but they still couldn't find her. Days had passed and then weeks, then months before my parents and I had lost all hope of finding her. A year had passed, and my parents were inconsolable after Bleakton constables gave up their search for my sister and presumed her to be dead. 'Good night, Bremen.' Those were the last words my baby sister, Grace, spoke to me that night in Vilkswood. Some days I expect my sister to walk right into this tavern and greet me with her warm smile, but now I know that's just wishful thinking," Bremen replied in a somber tone.

Mordrid's and Bremen's stories gave me insight into the fable known as White Bane.

"Do you believe your sister is still alive, Bremen?" I inquired.

"There's a small part of me that believes she's still out there, but let's face it, it's been thirty-four years since she vanished. White Bane has been described throughout the decades as a ghost, a demon, an evil entity, and a spiteful guardian of the woods. I still have yet to discern what White Bane is, exactly, but there's one thing I know for certain. Death has followed all who have laid eyes on the enigmatic White Bane," Bremen said.

CHAPTER 4

Roses

The roses bloom despite such gloom.

"I'll keep that in mind," I said to Bremen while I sat at the bar, finishing the last of my hot-brandy cider. My visage then slowly turned pensive. The two stories of White Bane were beginning to fully sink in, and before I knew it, a rush of emotions came over me.

"Want another pint?" Bremen inquired.

"No, thanks, I should be getting back to my family," I replied as I placed a couple of dollars on the bar. "Take care, Bremen."

"You too, Vincent, don't be a stranger," Bremen said.

I left Squire's Tavern and sauntered down the main thoroughfare of Bleakton. On my way out of town, I came across a young girl who was selling roses right by the main gates. This girl appeared to be no older than twelve years old. The young girl wore a black wool jacket over a long burgundy dress. She had wavy amber hair that was tied back with a thin black ribbon.

"Show your beloved how much you care with roses," the young girl proclaimed in a lyrical tone.

The saccharine scent of the young girl's roses wafted throughout the frigid air. I walked up to the stand and surveyed the various bouquets of roses that were displayed.

"I'll take two scarlet roses," I said to the young girl. The girl then picked out two roses from a bouquet and wrapped them in black crepe paper; she lastly tied off the roses' stems with a scarlet ribbon.

"That'll be fifty cents, sir," the young girl said.

I paid the young girl and then tucked the roses in my satchel, with the tops sticking out. I departed Bleakton with a sense of unnerving doubt. I'd lived on the border of Vilkswood my entire life, yet I'd only just been informed now of the fable known as White Bane. My father must have known about White Bane but decided to keep me in the dark on the matter. I'd always known wolves to be elusive by nature, but according to Mordrid and Bremen, White Bane was no mere wolf.

The crepe paper-wrapped roses rustled with every snow-crunching footstep I took across the vale. At first, I struggled with the decision of whether or not to tell Heather and Audrey about the White Bane fable. I didn't want my family to live in fear, so I decided it would be best not to tell them. Perhaps that's why my father never told me. For some reason, I wasn't feeling as strong as I usually did on my hike across the vale. My eyes and throat were starting to feel itchy, and my bones were aching. So I rested on a rock by the banks of the Murk River, trying to diagnose my current ailment. I filled up my canteen from the river and took a long drink. Only one mile left before I reached the cabin, but I was gradually feeling more wretched with every step I took. My sudden languishment was beginning to overwhelm my body, and I found myself begin to stagger. The icy winds were increasing, and I felt them stinging my body like a barrage of needles. In concordance with my affliction, the skies began to loom with gloom, just as I arrived at the cabin I then stared back on the vale and saw a blusterous wall of white approaching.

"I'm home," I pronounced with a series of gut-wrenching coughs.

"Welcome home, Daddy," Audrey said.

"Honey…you look pale. Are you feeling all right?" Heather inquired.

"I'm fine, dear," I replied in a raspy tone. Heather walked up to me and placed her hand upon my forehead.

"You're burning up," Heather said in a distressful tone.

"I bought roses for you and Audrey," I said to Heather as I handed her the bouquet.

"That's so sweet of you," Heather remarked as she held the bouquet up to her nose.

My head was spinning, and I began to feel debilitating chills shooting throughout my body. My legs started to buckle, and I could no longer keep myself from collapsing.

"Daddy!"

"Vincent!"

I heard Heather and Audrey's' calls of dismay as I collapsed upon the hardwood floor of the great room. Just before everything faded to black, I saw the bouquet of roses fall to the floor and felt Heather cradling my head in her lap.

*****

I awoke in my bed with a cold sweat. Despite the heat from the bedroom fireplace, I was shivering uncontrollably. It was 4:38 AM, and I noticed Heather wasn't in bed with me. I would've usually gotten up to see where she was, but my strength was rather diminished. So for the time being, I remained bedridden.

*****

The rattling windowpane woke me up at 8:03 AM. It appears that the turbulent blizzard was fully upon us. I peered out the window from my bedridden state, and all I could see was a squall of white desolation enveloping the cabin. I noticed one of the roses that I bought for Heather and Audrey was placed upon the windowsill. The rose stood in a thin glass vase, half-filled with water. My stinging eyes were focused on the rose's exquisite beauty in contrast to the background of perpetual whiteness. As I intently stared at the sylphlike rose, something began to take shape on the outside of the window. A pair of fixed eyes began to materialize amidst the flurry, slowly overshadowing the sanguine rose that stood betwixt the stare. It couldn't be, could it? No, I wouldn't let that name torment my already critical condition, but the eyes continued to gaze at me with such inhumane malevolence. So I lifted my weary head upright and leaned in as close as I could to the window, without leaving the solace of my bed. Then the winds abruptly ceased their howling, and the visibility on the outside of the window became clearer, but my eyes widened as they bore witness to…

Suddenly, I heard the creak from the bedroom door and saw Heather enter the room. "You're awake," Heather remarked as she entered the room. Within those brief few seconds of Heather entering the room, the winds instantly arose with a shrieking severity, and the white desolation filled the outside of the window once more. Heather was holding what appeared to be a pail of steaming water, a sponge, a towel, and a glass thermometer. She then walked over to me and sat down at my bedside. "You frightened us half to death, Vincent. After you collapsed, Audrey and I carried you to the bedroom. Here, let me check your temperature," Heather said. I opened my mouth, and then Heather placed the thermometer underneath my tongue. "I've been very attentive at keeping the three fireplaces burning, especially during this blizzard that's upon us," Heather said. Heather then took the thermometer out of my mouth and stared at it closely. "You have a high fever. Your temperature is one hundred point nine degrees Fahrenheit," Heather said.

"I'm freezing," I whispered to Heather, not wanting to further stress my raw vocal chords.

"I know, honey, I know," Heather said in a somber tone.

"How much firewood do we have left?" I inquired. Ever since I collapsed, I'd been meaning to inquire this vital matter.

"We have about half a cord left. That's enough to keep the three fireplaces burning for another five days. Let's just hope this blizzard dies down before then," Heather replied.

Heather may have the appearance of an elegant and refined woman, but she knew as well as I did about the essentials of cabin living, especially during these most dire of circumstances. I was incapacitated for the time being, but Heather knew all the responsibilities that had befallen her. Even though I could see the distress in Heather's deep sapphire eyes, I knew beyond a shadow of a doubt that her selfless nature would perform any task for the well-being of Audrey and me.

"Can you make it to the bathroom?" Heather inquired.

"I can barely lift my head," I replied.

"Well, the bedpan is right here on the nightstand, just in case," Heather said. "May I wash you?" Heather inquired.

I then nodded my head and then removed my blanket and slowly got undressed. Heather then soaked the sponge in the steaming pail of water and wrung it out over my bare chest.

"Is it too hot?"

I shook my head, and then Heather started gently rubbing the sponge over my chest and shoulders.

"Vincent, you're such a diligent man, but you've spent so much time of your life caring for Audrey and me that you've begun to neglect your own health," Heather said.

"You and Audrey are my life, if anything ever ha—" My voice was suddenly cut short by a slew of spasmodic coughs.

"Shhhh, please promise me you won't leave this bed until your fever has gone down," Heather said.

"I promise, dear," I said to Heather in a solemn tone.

Heather then wrung out the sponge in the bedpan and resoaked it in the pail. "Turn over on your side, honey, so I can wash your back," Heather said.

The tepid water seemed to alleviate some of my chills but not fully. "How did I ever win over an angel like you?" I inquired.

Heather smiled in reaction to my inquiry and then gently padded my head with the warm sponge. "I could ask you the same question, but I believe both our answers would be the same," Heather replied.

"I must've caught this illness while I was in town," I said to Heather.

"That would explain it," Heather told me, nodding in agreement, as she washed my arms and legs. Heather then took the towel and dried me off from head to toe. "Here's an extra blanket for you. I'll have breakfast ready soon," Heather said.

Heather then picked up the pail of water and walked out of the bedroom. The thermometer was still on the nightstand. Heather must have left it there on purpose so that I could take my temperature every now and then. I noticed that Heather was barefoot and wearing her white lace nightgown. This meant that she didn't spare the time to make herself up in the morning. She first and foremost attended to my illness. I'd always preferred how Heather looks right when she wakes up in the morning though. She has such a natural glow, a beauty that complements the new morning haze. I got dressed and then tightly tucked myself underneath the two layers of blankets. I could hear the faint sounds of Heather and Audrey making breakfast in the kitchen.

"Go bring it in to him and don't drop it," Heather said to Audrey from the kitchen.

The bedroom door opened, and my little Audrey entered the room, carrying a tray of food.

"Here, Daddy, I hope you're feeling better," Audrey said. Audrey then carefully placed the tray down upon my lap.

"Princess, you shouldn't be waiting on me," I said to Audrey.

"Are you cold? I could give you my blanket," Audrey said.

"I'm not in good condition, Audrey, but you keep your blanket for yourself," I said to Audrey. Audrey then sat down in the armchair beside my bed. "Don't touch me, honey. I don't want to spread my illness onto you. I would've told your mother the same thing, but I know all too well that nothing would stop her from aiding my illness, not even me," I said to Audrey.

"Mommy was crying when you were lying on the floor yesterday evening," Audrey said with a saddened visage.

"I'm sorry, Audrey. The last thing I want to do is—" I started coughing again but instinctively turned away from Audrey.

"Maybe the tea will help your throat. It has honey in it," Audrey said.

So I took a small sip of tea and nibble of toast. I noticed that Audrey garnished my breakfast with the rose I bought for her. "Audrey, why is your rose on the tray?" I inquired.

"I want you to have it, to cheer you up," Audrey replied.

"No, no, honey, that rose is for you. You keep it in a vase filled with water in your bedroom. Besides, I have your mother's rose to look at over there on the windowsill," I said to Audrey as I pointed to the rose.

"Audrey, it's time for your lessons," Heather called Audrey while tilting her head into the doorframe.

"Yes, go take your lessons," I said to Audrey with a warm smile.

"All right, get better, Daddy, I love you."

"I love you too, princess. Here, don't forget your rose," I said to Audrey.

Audrey's way of skipping out of the bedroom with her rose in hand brought a smile to my sallow visage.

"Be careful holding that rose. Its thorns could prick you. I'll put it in the prettiest vase I can find," Heather said to Audrey.

So I spent the last four hours lying in bed, listening to Heather teach Audrey about reading, writing, history, philosophy, arithmetic, and science in the great room. Audrey always seemed to be more attentive when it came to reading. She would frequently read novels from renowned authors of yore, with her mother by the fireplace. Audrey's hazel eyes seemed to light up whenever her mother started to read those cherished novels.

My accursed illness didn't seem to subside during those four hours. When I took my temperature at 12:36 PM, the thermometer read 102.5 degrees Fahrenheit. Heather entered the bedroom, wearing a gossamer blouse underneath a long black dress. Heather's hair was braided into a long ponytail, which was her signature hairstyle.

"Vincent, how are you feeling?" Heather inquired.

"My temperature hasn't gone down a degree," I replied.

"Are you still afflicted with chills?" Heather inquired.

"The chills have lingered," I somberly replied.

"You want me to close the drapes?" Heather inquired.

"No, keep them open. I want to see how the weather is," I replied.

Heather then walked over to the window and tended to the rose. "I wish we had the proper medicine. Your illness coincided with a most unfortunate blizzard," Heather said to me.

"I know. It seems like my illness was destined to happen," I said to Heather.

"Don't talk that way," Heather said while shaking her head.

My outlook was as bleak as the ongoing blizzard, and Heather's care was my only salvation. Heather then walked over to the bedroom fireplace, kneeled down, and put another log into the dying flames.

"You're a survivor, Vincent, and I will always be by your side," Heather said.

The loyalties Heather spoke had triggered a most profound memory of my childhood. I remember when I was twelve years old, and I was afflicted with a similar illness. For days on end, my father diligently took care of me. One night, my fever had risen to a fatal level, but my father's paternal conviction held true.

*****

"Son, you're going to make it through this because you're a survivor. Remember, you're never alone. Your mother is watching over you as we speak, and I will always be by your side," my father said to me. The reassurance that my father gave me that night was as effective as any bottled medicine could be. The next day, my fever had dropped, thanks to my father's uplifting words.

*****

Now I had Heather and Audrey to uplift my spirits; their presence was all I need.

"I'll leave the door open. Call me if you need me, honey," Heather said.

The sounds of the crackling bedroom fireplace and the roaring blizzard seemed to clash in an elemental cacophony. I could gaze at either one, but my eyes were solely focused on the window. The cotton handkerchief that I held was damp from the constant flow of nasal fluid. I sipped more of the honeyed tea that Audrey brought me, in hopes of alleviating my raw throat.

When I took my temperature at 6:48 PM, the thermometer read 101 degrees Fahrenheit. This was uplifting news for me, even though I still had a fever. I reached over and grabbed a book off the nightstand. This book was part of Heather's vast collection of literature. There were hundreds of books scattered all throughout our cabin, half of them were guides and textbooks, and the other half were novels. After Heather moved into the cabin with me, she would frequently accompany me on my bartering trips to Bleakton. She would visit Bleakton's only bookstore called the *Sapient Scholar*, to replace the collection of literature that she lost on that fateful day we met in Vilkswood.

The book that I held in my hand was a novel entitled *Hearts of Yore: The Lunar Lament* by Arthur Sinclair. It was the first installment of a six-book saga. I recalled reading a few chapters of this novel when Heather first recommended it to me. From the passages I read, the story follows a knight of a prosperous kingdom who falls in love with a princess. Just before the knight gets ostracized from the kingdom by the strict and disapproving king, he forms an astrological schedule with the princess. This schedule marks specific locations where the knight and princess would rendezvous, all predetermined by the alignment of the stars and different phases of the moon. When my father homeschooled me on literature, he would just teach me the basic principles; whereas, Heather would delve more into the romance, poetry, and mystery indulgences of the literary world. I used to consider those novels as nothing more than sentimental banalities, but through time, they started to grow on me.

Heather walked into the room, holding a tray of food. "Honey, I hope you have some of your appetite back for venison stew," Heather said, as she placed the tray upon my lap.

"It smells good," I remarked.

"I love that story," Heather remarked while pointing at the hardcover copy of *Hearts of Yore: The Lunar Lament*.

"I know you do. That's why you keep it right beside you on the nightstand," I said to Heather with a smile.

"Let me take your temperature before you eat dinner," Heather said. Heather then placed the thermometer underneath my tongue and then waited a brief moment. "The rose looks beautiful, no signs of wilting yet," Heather remarked. I nodded my head in agreement. Heather took the thermometer out of my mouth and stared at it closely. Heather then breathed a sigh of relief before she spoke. "One hundred one degrees Fahrenheit, your fever has dropped over a degree," Heather said.

"Thanks to you," I said to Heather.

Heather then placed her hand on my cheek. "You see, there's nothing you can't overcome," Heather said with a warm smile.

I nearly knocked over the bowl of venison stew in the wake of more hacking coughs.

"Easy, honey," Heather told me while securing the tray from wobbling on my lap.

"It's good," I said to Heather in a raspy tone after I swallowed a spoonful of the savory stew.

"Eat as much as you can. You need your strength," Heather said.

"I want you to sleep with Audrey tonight," I said to Heather.

"Why, Vincent?" Heather inquired.

"I just don't want to keep you awake with my constant coughing," I replied.

"I have to keep feeding the three fireplaces throughout the night, so you're no disturbance," Heather said.

"You need the rest just as much as I do. Please sleep with Audrey tonight," I said to Heather.

"No, Vincent, I need to be by your side until you fully recover from this illness," Heather said.

"Don't worry, dear, just for tonight, sleep with Audrey. She needs you too," I said to Heather.

"All right, Vincent, just for tonight," Heather said.

"Besides, my chills aren't as severe as they were yesterday," I said to Heather.

"I'll go fill up a pitcher of water in case you start coughing in the middle of the night and need a drink," Heather said.

As Heather left the bedroom, I couldn't help but wonder how my illness was affecting her and Audrey. I was strong enough to sit upright in bed, and eat my stew, but my aching bones were still keeping me from walking around the cabin. Audrey entered the bedroom, holding a fuchsia-tinted glass vase, which contained her rose.

"Daddy, are you feeling better?" Audrey inquired.

"A little better," I replied.

"Since Mommy is sleeping in my bed tonight, I want my rose to keep you company," Audrey said, as she placed the vase on the nightstand.

"Audrey, have you read this book with your mother?" I inquired. I then grabbed the hardcover copy of *Hearts of Yore: The Lunar Lament* and showed it to Audrey.

"No, I don't remember Mommy reading this book with me," Audrey replied.

"Well, it's about a princess, like you, who falls in love with a knight," I said to Audrey with a smile. Heather then walked into the bedroom holding the pitcher full of water.

"Mommy, can we read this book next?" Audrey inquired and then raised the book up to Heather's face.

"We'll get to that book soon enough, Audrey. Go get ready for bed," Heather replied while stroking Audrey's auburn hair. Heather then placed the pitcher of water on the nightstand and sat down at my bedside.

"That's all I could eat," I said to Heather, as I pointed to the half full bowl of stew.

"That's all right, honey, at least you ate something," Heather said. Heather appeared exhausted, and I felt fully responsible. "Your eyes are bloodshot, try to get some sleep," Heather said.

It was imperative for at least one of us to get a good night's rest so we could take on the daily workload. I still wasn't used to being mothered by Heather. I believed that was partly due to me growing up without a mother.

"Good night, Vincent, I love you."

"I love you too," I said to Heather. Heather then extinguished the oil lamp, picked up the tray from my lap, and exited the bedroom.

It was 11:24 PM, and as expected, my illness was preventing me from falling asleep. So I took a drink of water and then rolled over on my side, so I would be facing the warmth of the fireplace. I stared at the flames, hoping they would lull me to sleep. I used to do this when I was a child, and it usually worked. As the night lingered on, I felt brief respites of drowsiness begin to overpower me, slowly giving way to the evanescence of my consciousness, and I sank deeper, and deeper until—

*****

I found myself standing over my parents' graves on the east side of the cabin. The clouds loomed ominously low with an eerie shade of gray. There were two burial mounds next to my parents' graves that were unknown to me. I then noticed two unmarked gravestones slowly emerging from the blackest mud. That's when I heard screams resonating from the cabin. I looked through the window, but all I could see was utter darkness. The cabin was engulfed by a black shroud. I now recognized the screams; they were Heather and Audrey.

I kept pounding on the door, but all my attempts of entering the cabin were thwarted by the black shroud. I looked down and saw my hands were covered in blood. Heather and Audrey's' screams grew more and more heart-wrenching by the second, and I could feel their agony swelling up inside of me. The blood on my hands began to creep up my arms and continued to spread slowly until my entire body was covered in trails of blood. So with all my might, I charged the door of the cabin and broke through the black shroud, then the screams fell silent, but then another chilling sound arose—the sound of howling.

*****

"No no…"

"Vincent!"

"No no…"

"Vincent, wake up!"

I was lying on the hardwood floor with my head leaning against the nightstand. Shards of the fuchsia vase and Audrey's rose were scattered in a puddle of water beside me. Heather was kneeling over me with bewildering eyes.

"You and Audrey, you both were screaming…crying…suffering," I said to Heather in a gasping tone.

"Shhhh, it's all right. You were having a nightmare," Heather said in a whispering tone.

"My hands were covered in blood," I said to Heather as I frantically examined my hands.

"Look at me…there's no blood on your hands," Heather said as she firmly, yet gently held both of my hands betwixt hers. Every fiber of my being was trembling at that moment. My heartbeats thundered, coursing throughout my ill-stricken limbs. "It's all right. Audrey is safe, and I'm here now. I knew I should've stayed with you tonight," Heather said while holding my head against her chest. Heather's gentle embrace failed to comfort me this time, for her screams of agony still echoed in my mind.

It was 3:56 AM. Heather helped me off the floor and then cleaned up the puddle of water and shards of broken vase. She then picked up Audrey's rose and put it in the thin glass vase that sat on the windowsill.

"I'm glad I didn't wake up Audrey," I said to Heather while she put another log into the fireplace.

"Don't worry, she's sound asleep," Heather said as she got into bed.

I lay awake in bed for the remainder of the night. I couldn't forget such a profound nightmare. Heather would rub my back in response to all my spontaneous coughing. The faint rays of dawn's light began to shine through the bedroom window. Unlike previous mornings, the light's resplendence wasn't blotted out by the desolate blizzard. I took my temperature, and the thermometer read a most dispiriting 102 degrees Fahrenheit. Twelve hours ago, I was on my way to recover from this illness, but one dreadful night with only a couple hours of sleep can make a world of difference. My mental health was disturbed, therefore exacerbating my fever. The roses that sat on the windowsill cast a shadow across the sheer linen bedsheets. The thin glass vase appeared to be an incommodious vessel for the two sanguine roses to share.

It was 7:36 AM. Heather was sleeping peacefully with her long braided ponytail softly brushing against my shoulder whenever she slept. Once again, I began to feel debilitating chills growing in my body.

"Vincent, how are you feeling?" Heather inquired.

"My temperature is one hundred two degrees Fahrenheit," I replied in a raspy tone.

"Oh dear," Heather said in a gasping tone. Heather then leaned over me and placed her hand on my burning forehead. "Your fever keeps spiking. I have to get you the proper medicine," Heather said as she frantically got dressed.

"Don't even think about traveling to Bleakton," I told Heather in a stern tone. Heather then grabbed a book off the bookshelf and started combing through the pages.

"The medical book says that all your symptoms indicate scarlet fever," Heather said.

"You cannot travel in this blizzard," I said to Heather.

"Vincent, you need antibiotics. I won't let you suffer like this," Heather said in a distressed tone.

Drastic times call for drastic measures, and Heather was about to put her life in the balance, just to ensure mine.

"It's a total of eight miles to and from Bleakton. Even in ideal weather, the hike is most tiresome," I said to Heather.

"Vincent, you expect me to just watch helplessly as you fall apart?" Heather inquired while her eyes began to well up with tears, as I pleaded for her not to venture to Bleakton amidst this harsh blizzard.

"I just need to sleep," I said to Heather in a weary tone.

Heather took a profound sigh while masking her weeping face with both her hands. I sat up from the bed and grabbed Heather's hand. Heather then turned to me and placed her other hand upon mine.

"I love you," Heather said with glossy eyes.

"I love you too, and this illness won't take me from you and Audrey," I solemnly vowed to Heather.

"I'll go wake up Audrey," Heather said.

To this day, I still couldn't bear to see Heather shed a single tear. Heather would always display her heart for the world to see. She was the living testament of how such a prominent heart can be that much more vulnerable. I had to keep my mind busy, so I grabbed a book off the nightstand entitled *The Poetry of Julia Meadows* and started skimming through the pages. From this poet's vast collection of poems, one verse in particular seemed to resonate with me.

> When two selfless mortals meet,
> With eyes that say "come hither."
> In harmony, their hearts doth beat.
> For each other, they bloom and wither.

I understood it now. *The Poetry of Julia Meadows* gave my weary mind brief respites of serenity. This verse so eloquently described Heather and I. We live and die for each other, and our selfless love can only be described as a beautiful paradox. If not for Audrey, Heather and I wouldn't hesitate to risk our lives for each other. Audrey was our trinity, and she kept our love constant and rational. Throughout the years, Heather had tamed me like a wild horse. My brash hunter's hubris was instilled into me by my father. He taught me how to survive, and after his death, surviving was my only mentality. Only until I met Heather did I truly feel like I was living.

My profound nightmare proved that mental anguish could manifest itself physically. I couldn't let those fears fester, for Heather and Audrey needed me, and I wasn't too proud to admit that I needed them as well. *So when will it end?* I kept contemplating to myself. My illness or the blizzard—I needed one to subside. I kept the promise I made to Heather, not to leave my bed until my fever drops. I'd never been bedridden for this long in my entire life. My body continued to recoil with every grating cough. I pulled the sheer white sheets over my head, and in all likelihood, my appearance surely resembled a quivering ghost. Like how the faint morning light fought to shine through squalls of white, I fought to recover from this illness.

*****

I awoke at 3:18 PM and noticed that Heather had left me breakfast on the nightstand. I took my temperature, and the thermometer read 101 degrees Fahrenheit. This was the lowest temperature my fever had read in the past three days, but I wouldn't get my hopes up so soon. I stared out the window and saw a sight I hadn't seen in four days, a sliver of cerulean sky.

"Vincent, look, the skies are clearing," Heather said as she entered the bedroom.

"That sure is a welcome sight," I remarked.

"Seeing you fully recovered is the only sight I long to see right now," Heather said as she sat down at my bedside.

Audrey quietly entered the bedroom and stared at her rose, which stood beside Heather's rose in the thin glass vase.

"I'm sorry I broke the vase that held your rose," I said to Audrey.

"That's all right. I like that my rose shares a vase with Mommy's rose," Audrey said, with a warm and forgiving visage.

"Did you get any sleep, dear?" Heather inquired while she smoothed out the sheets that covered me and then placed her hand on my forehead. "You're still a little warm, but your eyes look much clearer," Heather remarked.

"I got some sleep, and my fever dropped a little," I replied.

"You get as much rest as you can. Dinner will be ready in a couple of hours," Heather said as she left the bedroom with Audrey. So once again, I succumbed to sleep's soothing yet consuming force.

*****

I awoke at 7:04 PM. Heather entered the bedroom and carefully placed a tray of food upon my lap.

"Let me take your temperature," Heather said as she routinely placed the thermometer in my mouth. Heather then took the thermometer out of my mouth and stared at it intently. "One hundred point three degrees Fahrenheit," Heather said with an upward inflection to her voice.

"I haven't felt any chills in a while," I said to Heather.

"I also haven't heard you coughing as much. You keep it up. These are most welcome signs," Heather said with a smile.

Heather cooked venison steaks and baked potatoes for dinner. She then tucked a napkin underneath my worn shirt.

"All right, dear, I can manage from here," I said to Heather in a facetious tone.

Heather then put another log into the fireplace and left the bedroom. I felt my strength slowly returning with every bite of dinner that I took. At last, the white squalls had ceased, and the evening winds were calm. There were many tasks that I had to carry out, and I was eager to get back to my hunting regiment. Just one more restful night was all my body and mind required, and then I could finally rise from this illness that has oppressed me for the past four days.

I finished my dinner in a voracious manner and then started reading *The Poetry of Julia Meadows* for the remainder of the evening.

"It's good to see your appetite has returned," Heather said as she entered the bedroom.

"I don't feel as drained as I did yesterday," I said to Heather.

"That's because you slept soundly today," Heather said. Heather then slowly changed into her white nightgown and got into bed with me. "Audrey keeps talking about Bleakton. She's very excited about moving there in the spring," Heather said.

"We can go over the tax forms that I got from Bleakton's town hall in the morning, dear," I said to Heather.

Heather then extinguished the oil lamp and then rolled over on her side facing me. Even the evening twilight paled in comparison to the reflection of the fireplace's flickering flames in Heather's bleary eyes. In my sentiment, there was no sight more exquisite to fall asleep to.

*****

I awoke at 7:03 AM to the touch of Heather's silken braided ponytail resting on my face. As I took a deep breath, Heather's hair emitted the scent of fresh lilacs into my nose. I lifted Heather's long braided ponytail off my face and then took my temperature. I nodded my head, as the thermometer read a salubrious 99.4 degrees Fahrenheit. I quietly stood out of bed and walked over to the window.

"Vincent, you're awake," Heather remarked in a yawning yet evangelical tone.

"The roses are finally beginning to wilt," I remarked as I stared intently at the roses.

Heather then walked up behind me and wrapped her arms around my waist. "I guess all beauty withers in time," Heather said while resting her head upon my shoulder.

"Your beauty hasn't withered," I said to Heather.

"Neither has your silver tongue," Heather said and then tenderly kissed my cheek.

I felt a renewed sense of vigor as I stood betwixt Heather's warm embrace and the roses withering grace.

CHAPTER 5

Hunters' Brotherhood

Rejoice, my brothers, we've slain all the others!

Two weeks had passed since I collapsed on the floor of the great room, and now I had reestablished all my responsibilities that fell so unexpectedly upon Heather's shoulders. It was a clear winter afternoon, an ideal weather for me to get in some sharpshooting.

"I'll be hunting up in the sharpshooter's nest if anyone needs me," I pronounced while Heather was delicately braiding Audrey's hair.

The whole concept of the sharpshooter's nest came to fruition two years ago. The rustic lookout tower took me a little over a month to build. I constructed it all by myself out of oak wood, and it stands twenty-eight feet tall. Heather and Audrey were the true inspiration for the sharpshooter's nest. They would always fear for my life every time I went into Vilkswood to follow game tracks. I wanted to be around to see Audrey grow up, so I felt it would be prudent to limit my hunts into the heart of Vilkswood as much as possible. The sharpshooter's nest gave me a great vantage point for hunting pheasant and quail. In the sharpshooter's nest, I was perched at tree level among the birds, but my presence remained hidden to them. Before the construction of the sharpshooter's nest, whenever I went skulking in Vilkswood, game birds where always the first to detect me.

"How much longer are you going to be up there?" Heather shouted while looking up at me.

"As long as it takes, dear!" I shouted back to Heather.

It had been a little over an hour, and I had yet to see a bird land or take flight atop the snowcapped treetops. Vigilance is the key to becoming a great hunter. This was the mantra my father always told me. So I sat atop the sharpshooter's nest with watchful eyes, hoping to spot any signs of life from within Vilkswood. Suddenly, I spotted a fluttering of wings emerge from the chaparral.

It was a golden pheasant, a stunning opalescent game bird. I took aim with my rifle, held my breath, and then calmly squeezed the trigger. In reaction to my thunderous gunshot, a murder of crows fled from the dark pines of Vilkswood, peppering the skies in a myriad of black wings. I then watched the resplendent pheasant fall from its lofty perch. I climbed down the ladder of the sharpshooter's nest and made my way to the fallen bird. The carcass of the golden pheasant graced the snow in a manner befitting a splatter of vivid paint upon a white canvas. While holding the golden pheasant by its long cinnamon-specked tail feathers, I heard a grumbling noise coming from the nearby winterberry shrubs. So I quickly stuffed the golden pheasant in my satchel and then pulled out my rifle. The low grumble rose to a grating squeal, as I cautiously approached the shrubs. The snapping of twigs below my feet sent a boar bolting out from behind the shrubs. So I took aim with my rifle, led the target, and squeezed the trigger. My gunshot sent the fleeing boar tumbling into a mound of snow before he could take refuge deeper into Vilkswood.

I kneeled down and laid the golden pheasant beside the boar carcass.

"Thank you both for feeding my family." I spoke aloud in a solemn tone. I then immediately went to work on the fifty-pound boar, gutting him within five minutes. The boar's rotund body provided me with ten pounds of pork shoulder, ribs, and belly meat, which I stored in my satchel. "You all can have the remains." I spoke aloud to the numerous carnivores lurking in Vilkswood as I walked away from the scavenged boar carcass. I returned to the cabin at 3:27 PM with the bounty of my two kills.

"I'm back," I proclaimed as I entered the cabin.

"I heard two gunshots. What did you bring back?" Heather inquired. Heather was quite familiar with my high-caliber marksmanship skills, and she never assumed that I would return to the cabin empty-handed.

"Very astute, dear," I said to Heather as I laid my satchel down on the hardwood floor. "I killed a boar that was grazing on a winterberry shrub right near the fringe of Vilkswood. I got about ten pounds of pork shoulder, loins, and ribs from it," I replied. "Do you want to see the real prize?" I inquired with grin as I reached into the satchel and pulled out the golden pheasant.

"It's beautiful," Heather remarked with widened eyes. "Audrey, come in here and look at this," Heather said to Audrey.

"It's a rainbow bird," Audrey remarked in a zealous tone.

"It's a golden pheasant, honey. I know what you're thinking. There's no way this bird can taste as good as it looks," I said to Heather.

"I bet it tastes like a rainbow," Audrey remarked with an angelic smile.

"Now what does a rainbow taste like?" Heather inquired in a lighthearted tone while cupping her cheeks.

I'd eaten pheasants before that my father killed but never a golden pheasant. I could definitely recall my father killing a game bird as stunning as this one.

"After we eat the breast meat from this golden pheasant, I'm going to embalm it and then see how much money I can get for it in Bleakton's Market Square," I proclaimed.

"How much are they worth?" Heather inquired with a childlike intrigue as her emotive eyes magnified at the sight of the golden pheasant.

"Golden pheasants are the rarest game birds that dwell in Vilkswood. An embalmed golden pheasant can go for the sum of two hundred dollars. Of course, my embalming work must be of the highest quality if I'm to get paid the full price from a decor vendor," I replied.

"May I help you?" Heather inquired.

It surprised me to say the least, considering that Heather never wanted to assist me with skinning, tanning, hiding, or gutting my kills in the past, but it seemed that the dazzling bird had attracted her involvement.

"I was hoping you would ask me that, dear. Your delicate precision can sew up the bird after I'm done stuffing it with a framework of cotton and wires," I replied. So I studiously started skinning the golden pheasant on the kitchen table while Heather was preparing the rest of the dinner.

"It looks like there's only enough breast meat on this pheasant for two people," I remarked as I cut out the breast.

"Oh, then you and Audrey should have the pheasant for dinner. You did kill it after all," Heather said.

"No, you and Audrey should have the pheasant for dinner, and I'll have the pork ribs. Besides, I've eaten pheasants before, and the true payoff of this bird is not its meat," I pronounced. I continued to skin the rest of the bird as Heather panfried the pheasant breasts and broiled my pork ribs in the wood-burning oven. After a couple of minutes, the cabin was filled with the savory aroma of the pheasant breasts and pork ribs cooking away.

"Ten minutes left on the pheasant breasts, and thirty minutes left on the pork ribs," Heather told me in a cheerful tone.

My father's embalming tool kit helped me out a great deal with skinning the golden pheasant. The embalming kit contained needles and thread, small shears, pliers, wire, clay, wood glue, cotton, a bottle of tannic acid solution, glass eyes, and some spare varicolored feathers.

"Audrey, it's time for dinner," Heather said to Audrey.

"I'm finished. How does it look so far, dear?" I inquired, as I showed Heather the fully skinned golden pheasant.

"It looks nice, but then again, I'm no embalming expert," Heather replied with a smile while setting the table. "Do you like the pheasant, Audrey?" Heather inquired as she took my pork ribs out of the wood-burning oven.

Audrey nodded her head in satisfaction as she took the first bite of the pheasant breast.

"She's disappointed that the pheasant doesn't taste like a rainbow," Heather proclaimed in a facetious tone.

I took a short break from my embalming work to eat my half rack of pork ribs that Heather placed in front of me.

"You were right, Vincent, when you said that this bird couldn't possibly taste as good as it looks, but it's still very succulent nonetheless," Heather remarked as she took her first bite of the pheasant breast.

"The ribs are great too, dear," I said to Heather.

Heather's nine-year duration of cabin living had not unrefined her delicate table manners in the slightest; whereas, I would always eat in a manner befitting a ravenous wolf. After the sumptuous dinner, I continued my embalming work on the golden pheasant while Heather was reading a novel with Audrey by the fireplace.

I treated the inside of the golden pheasant's skin with a coat of tannic acid solution and then started bending wire to form the frame. After an hour, the tannic acid solution had leathered the skin of the golden pheasant. I left the golden pheasant skin to dry on a stand near the fireplace and then started bending wire to form the frame.

"How is it coming along?" Heather inquired from the great room.

"Three more steps, and then you can sew it up," I replied.

After I finished bending the wire into a frame, I then started wrapping cotton around the torso portion. I tried to match the original bust of the golden pheasant with the cotton wrap as close as possible. I then took some clay and started shaping it to form the head of the golden pheasant. I stuck the clay on top of the wire and then grabbed the dried-out golden pheasant skin to dress over the cotton-wrapped wire frame. I then matched up the eyehole placement and picked out a pair of white glass eyes to press into the clay head. After a little more cotton stuffing to the bust and a final examination, my portion of embalming work on the golden pheasant was finished.

"All right, it's ready, if you still want to sew it up," I said to Heather.

"Of course," Heather said in a zealous tone.

"All you have to do is sew up the torso from the tail feathers to the beak and then sew the wings to the sides so they don't spread open," I said to Heather while pointing to the lines.

"I've never sewn up a dead animal before, but I'll try my best," Heather said as she grabbed a needle and piece of scarlet thread.

"Just pretend you're sewing up a torn dress," I said to Heather with a smile. I then left Heather to her intricate needlework and sat down beside Audrey on the sofa

"What are you reading, princess?" I inquired.

"It's a book called *Whispers Through the Willows* by Eleanor Fontaine," Audrey replied. Audrey sat curled up in a contemplative disposition on the sofa with a thick, sage, hardcover book resting on her petite lap.

"I guess that's another one of your mother's novels I have yet to read," I said to Audrey.

"It's about twin sisters Sara and Maribel who live in a cabin just like me. Then one night, Maribel starts hearing faint voices coming from the nearby woods, but Sara doesn't believe her," Audrey said. Audrey's way of explaining the novel with such youthful zealousness brought a smile to my face.

"Why doesn't she believe her sister?" I inquired.

"That's as far as I read. I'm only on the third chapter," Audrey replied. "I'm sleepy," Audrey said in a yawning tone. She then closed the book and rubbed her bleary hazel eyes.

"Me too come here," I said to Audrey. Audrey then outstretched her arms and nestled up against me.

"Do you think the other animals are jealous of the golden pheasant's beautiful colors?" Audrey inquired in a dulcet tone while resting her head against my chest.

"Well, jealousy is what you call a human emotion. In many ways, wild animals are superior to us humans. Wild animals are not ruled by their emotions as much as humans are. They just live with a natural purpose," I replied.

"Well, if I were a bird, I would be jealous of the golden pheasant's beautiful colors," Audrey remarked.

"If you were a bird, you would be the most beautiful bird that ever existed, and all the other animals would be in awe whenever they gazed at you," I said to Audrey with a smile.

"Would you hunt me like the other animals?" Audrey inquired with such innocent sincerity.

"I wouldn't dare hunt you, princess," I replied as I kissed the top of Audrey's head.

After a couple of minutes, I noticed that Audrey was sound asleep in my arms.

"I'm going to take Audrey to bed," I said to Heather in a whispering tone while she was busy sewing up the golden pheasant.

"All right, dear," Heather said in a whispering tone as she briefly averted her sharp focus from the golden pheasant.

I gently scooped up Audrey's tranquil body in my arms and took her to her bedroom. Audrey's bedroom used to be my old bedroom, but soon after my father died, I started sleeping in his master bedroom whenever I felt lonely. I gently laid Audrey down on her bed and covered her with the plush quilt.

"Good night, princess," I said to Audrey in a whispering tone. I then put another log in the fireplace and extinguished the oil lamp.

"So how's it coming along?" I inquired as I watched Heather hunching over the golden pheasant.

"All I need to do is sew up the rest of the chest, and then I'll be finished," Heather replied.

"Great, I'll leave you to it then," I said to Heather. I didn't want to pressure Heather's progress seeing as how this was her first time helping me embalm one of my kills for profit. I could have sewn up the golden pheasant myself, but I knew Heather was a much more skilled seamstress. Most of the animal pelts, heads, and antlers that adorned our cabin were killed and embalmed by my father, with some minor help from me.

My crowning achievement as a hunter would undoubtedly be the brown bear I killed while guiding Heather through Vilkswood nine years ago. I embalmed that brown bear's hide into a rug, which lies prominently on the hardwood floor in front of the great room fireplace.

"Too bad we have to sell this beautiful golden pheasant. I would love to see it perched atop our cherry bureau," Heather said from the kitchen.

"I know, but think of it this way, rather than adorning the cabin with its beauty, the profit we make from selling this golden pheasant will serve us better in the long run," I said to Heather from the great room.

It was 10:43 PM. I sprawled out on the sofa, awaiting the completion of Heather's needlework.

"I'm finished, Vincent," Heather pronounced just as I was starting to fall asleep. I rubbed my bleary eyes and sprung up from the sofa to see Heather's work. "I covered up the stitches that were showing with some spare scarlet feathers. How does it look?" Heather inquired with a wide-eyed stare as I examined her needlework. "I hope it's up to your standards," Heather said in a timid tone.

"I couldn't have done it better myself, dear," I said to Heather with a smile.

"Oh, thank you. I sewed the bust extra fine. That's why it took me a little longer," Heather said while pointing at the virtually indiscernible stitches.

"I am thinking of gluing this golden pheasant to a small piece of firewood, as a stand, so it may be perched," I said to Heather. "That's a wonderful idea," Heather said while bending her slender back against the chair. "Come here," Heather said, while arching her back and outstretching her arms. Heather then grasped my face with both hands, while her upside-down visage amorously gazed up at me. Heather's puckered lips slowly drew me in as she began to tilt back in her chair. Just as we were about to kiss, Heather began to fall backward from the chair that she playfully sat upon. "Careful, dear," I told Heather, as I supported her back from falling. Heather bashfully smiled, and then promptly kissed me, as she sat with her back suspended in my arms. "Let's go to bed," Heather said.

The sound of tapping awoke me at 7:22 AM. There was a lone crow staring at me from the outside of the windowsill. Heather was already cooking breakfast; she usually wakes up before me, and does it in such a quiet manner. I walked over to the window and shooed away the pestering crow. Despite their high intelligence, I always found crows to be a nuisance at times. Prior to the construction of the sharpshooter's nest, cawing crows would always alert the rest of the animals in Vilkswood of my presence.

I picked out an ideal piece of firewood from the cord that would serve as a perch for the golden pheasant. "Come eat breakfast first," Heather said as she placed a plate of bacon and toast on the kitchen table. "I might not be back from Bleakton till tomorrow morning," I told Heather.

"I'll miss you, Daddy," Audrey said, while latching her arms around my waist.

"I'll miss you, too, princess," I told Audrey.

"Will it really take a whole day, Vincent?" Heather inquired with a sigh as she sat down at the kitchen table.

"Yes, dear, I have a lot of matters that need to be taken care of, and I'd rather not make the eight mile hike at night through a foot of snow," I replied.

I opened the embalming kit and took out the small bottle of wood glue. "I have to position it just right." I spoke aloud as I applied the glue to the bottom of the golden pheasant's feet. I then lightly pressed the golden pheasant down onto the firewood. "All right, this glue has to set for an hour to ensure a strong bond." I spoke aloud. Audrey sat beside me staring intently at the golden pheasant while nibbling on a piece of bacon.

"Audrey, it's time for your lessons," Heather said to Audrey while clearing the kitchen table. Heather then brought out a stack of books from the master bedroom and started Audrey's daily curriculum in the great room.

While waiting for the glue to dry on the golden pheasant, I took stock of the bare essentials that were running low in the cabin. One hour had passed, and the bond holding the golden pheasant to the piece of firewood was now strong enough to travel. I didn't want to store the golden pheasant inside my satchel on account of its lustrous tail feathers getting compacted. So I weaved together some rope to make a net that firmly secured the golden pheasant to the outside of my satchel, without crumpling its sylphlike body.

"Well, I'm heading off to Bleakton now," I proclaimed while adjusting the strap on my satchel. Both Heather and Audrey hurried over and embraced me as if I were a soldier departing for war. "I love you. I'll be back early tomorrow morning."

"I love you too. Be safe," Heather said while cupping my cheeks in her hands.

"You listen to your mother while I'm gone," I said to Audrey in a stern yet gentle tone. Audrey then nodded her head in response. "Don't make the pouty face, princess. You know I can't bear to see a frown on you or your mother's beautiful faces," I said to Audrey. I felt uplifted yet frightened by the pure affection that Heather and Audrey expressed towards me. My love for them was immeasurable, but a sudden fear of losing them was beginning to grow inside of me. After two farewell kisses from Heather and Audrey, I opened the front door of the cabin and stepped out into the frigid white stillness.

*****

I arrived in Bleakton at noon, and just as I was walking through the main gates, the clock tower began to chime, unwittingly heralding my arrival. The first and foremost matter at hand was buying antibiotics. So I made my way down the narrowed *South Market Street*, searching for an apothecary's shop.

I would ordinarily draw mass attention strolling through any other town with an embalmed, multicolored game bird strapped to my back, but since I was in Bleakton, the town of hunters, the townsfolk didn't look twice at my trophy kill. I remember accompanying my father to Bleakton for his weekly bartering deals when I was sixteen years old. I observed my father haggling with various vendors in the Market Square, and as I looked behind me, I saw three burly hunters carrying a massive moose through the Market Square. The fact that the three hunters had a massive moose resting across each of their broad shoulders wasn't what perplexed me. It was the fact that all the townsfolk passed them by in such a quotidian manner. At that very moment, I knew the town of Bleakton was synonymous with hunters.

I then spotted a corner shop along South Market Street called *Morvaine's Medicines*.

"Good afternoon, sir. I am Morvaine Harris. Just tell me the ailment, and I'll prescribe you the proper medicinal treatment," Morvaine said as I entered the shop. The size of the incommodious shop resembled a cubbyhole and wasn't much larger than a walk-in closet. "All my medicine is behind the counter, sir," Morvaine said in response to my curious stares.

"I need three phials of antibiotics," I said to Morvaine.

Morvaine then kneeled down from behind the tall counter and then sprung back upright within a minute, holding three amber glass phials. "Don't exceed three doses a week, or else the bacterial strain in your body will build up a resistance to the antibiotics, thus rendering them insufficient to ward off the infection," Morvaine said as he wrote down the prescription slip.

"Thank you, I'll keep that in mind," I said to Morvaine, as he placed the antibiotics in a small pouch.

"Nine dollars," Morvaine said. I then paid the costly sum for the vital antibiotics and exited the apothecary's incommodious shop.

I made my way to the Market Square to buy some provisions that were running low in the cabin. On my way to the Market Square, I crossed paths with a hunter who had a quite imposing set of buck antlers strapped to his back. The buck antlers gave the hunter a silhouette of a man with jagged wings. The jagged-winged hunter took a fleeting glance at my golden pheasant and then nodded at me in an admirable manner. The unspoken bond that all the hunters shared in Bleakton was a common occurrence that I wholeheartedly enjoyed.

The food vendors in the Market Square wafted the aroma of various meats and pastries into the frigid air. I stopped at a bakery vendor and bought three loaves of rye bread and some herbs and spices. I strolled through the Market Square and crossed the *Bovidae Bridge* into north Bleakton. There were five bridges that arched across the Murk River connecting north Bleakton to south Bleakton: the Bovidae Bridge, the *Ursa Bridge*, the *Raptor Bridge*, the *Vilks Bridge*, and the *Knights Bridge.* All the bridges of Bleakton were constructed according to their names; the Bovidae Bridge had a carving on each of its four wooden posts, depicting a buck, elk, ram, and moose.

Most of the government buildings resided in north Bleakton, such as the town hall, the post office, and the constabulary. I was on my way to the post office to check me and Heather's monthly mail. Considering that no town, city, or village would deliver mail to our sequestered cabin on the south border of Vilkswood, I bought a private mailbox in Bleakton's post office nine years ago. The outside of the post office had an iron shield hanging atop the door, depicting a wolf, bear, eagle, and buck, sectioned by two diagonally crossed rifles. The shield was the symbol of Bleakton and was displayed prominently throughout the town.

I entered the post office and walked up to the counter after waiting in line for a few minutes. "I would like to check my postbox for mail. Last name, Belmont," I said to the postal clerk.

"All right, sir, I'll need to see your identification," the postal clerk said. So I searched through my buckskin wallet and pulled out my identification to present to the postal clerk. "Follow me," the postal clerk said with my mailbox key in her hand. The postal clerk then took me to the back room and opened my mailbox 88. I reached in the mailbox and pulled out two letters and a couple of mercantile leaflets. "Will that be all, sir?" the postal clerk inquired.

"Yes, that's everything," I replied then exited the post office.

It was 6:35 PM when I made my way back to the Market Square. I crossed the Raptor Bridge that had a carving on each of its four wooden posts, depicting a crow, eagle, hawk, and owl. I then took a brief reprieve on a bench in the *Bronze Square*, which was a smaller, quiescent square of Bleakton. A ten feet tall bronze statue of Gideon Bleak stood at the center of the square. The exalted bronze statue was my first memory of Bleakton's founder, Gideon Bleak.

*****

I was eleven years old at the time when my father and I were passing through the Bronze Square. My father stopped in front of the bronze statue of Gideon Bleak and then stared intently at its glory.

"You see that man, Vincent, my boy?" my father inquired as he pointed at the bronze statue as if it were alive.

"I can't see. He's too tall," I replied.

My father then hoisted me up atop his shoulders so I could get a closer look.

"Who is he?"

"That's Gideon Bleak, the founder of Bleakton. He's the quintessential man. He wouldn't let anyone or, anything, come in between him and his vision of Bleakton. He glorified all of us hunters. Look at him, son. That man is sheer greatness," my father replied in such a reverent tone.

"I hope I grow up to be like him," I remarked in a blithesome tone.

*****

Although my admiration and respect for Gideon Bleak hadn't changed since that moment when I was eleven years old, I no longer strived to model myself after him. I knew my life wouldn't be immortalized through the founding of a town; my eleven-year-old aspiration was understandable at the time though. The love and compassion that my family showered upon me gave me a sense of grandeur befitting any king.

The evening light was starting to fade, castings rays of twilight that gleamed off the bronze statue of Gideon Bleak. I took a brief look at the two letters I received from the post office. One letter was addressed to Heather, from Shors End, and the other was addressed to me, from Bleakton's town hall. The clock tower chimed at 7:00 PM, alerting me of the couple hours I had left to sell my golden pheasant. So I tucked the letters in my coat pocket and, once more, made my way to the Market Square.

Like clockwork, the vendors began to light their lanterns and lampposts, as a result of the evening's dying light slowly welcoming the subdued night. After browsing through many vendors, I finally came across one who sells and trades decor. This vendor's stand was lavishly adorned with various rugs, animal pelts, heads, antlers, banners, oil paintings, crests, candles, clocks, tapestries, books, mirrors, maps, vases, and even miniature figurines.

"Let me know if you see anything that catches your fancy," the vendor said.

"All right, but I think I have something that you might be interested in," I said to the vendor with a grin. I then carefully detached the golden pheasant from the rope-weaved net and placed it upon the vendor's stand. "I see you're a man who has the expertise on lavish decor. Well, I present to you the rarest game bird that dwells in Vilkswood, a fully embalmed golden pheasant perched atop a piece of firewood," I said to the vendor in a boastful tone. The vendor then stood up from his fireside chair, put on a pair of spectacles with a telescopic aperture attached to one lens, and closely examined the golden pheasant.

"The tail feathers are fully intact," the vendor remarked.

"Yes, you see that I didn't ruffle a single feather on this lustrous game bird," I told the vendor as he continued his examination.

"The stitching along the breast is exquisite," the vendor remarked with a praiseful tone.

"I'll tell my wife that. She's the master seamstress who did all the needlework on the golden pheasant," I said to the vendor.

"I must say, the embalming work is nearly perfect, apart from a few minute defects on the eyes placements. I'll give you two hundred dollars for it," the vendor said.

"Two hundred dollars is the starting price for this particular multicolored game bird, and two other vendors are willing to pay that same price as we speak," I said to the intrigued vendor.

Due to the many years of observing my father, I'd grown very cunning in the art of persuasion. The first rule of haggling: keep the potential buyer hooked with other fictitious offers. The vendor sighed and then took another glance at the golden pheasant.

"Two hundred twenty-five dollars, and that's the highest I can go. Take it or leave it. I have to close up soon," the vendor said.

"You have a deal, my good man," I said to the vendor while maintaining my stoic demeanor. I then walked away from the decor vendor after the trade was made, wearing a beaming smile.

It was 8:43 PM, and all the Market Square vendors had closed up their stands and took solace in their warm houses. It was beginning to snow, so I thought I would head over to Squire's Tavern for a couple of drinks before I took up lodgings for the night. The night air was still, and each chiffon snowflake lightly floated over Bleakton in a state of suspended animation. I could already hear the joyful regalement resonating from Squire's Tavern from just across the street.

Upon entering the tavern, my cold weariness was welcomed by a copious display of townsfolk. While pressing through the bar dwellers, I found an empty barstool just over yonder.

"It's a busy night," I said to Bremen as I sat down.

"Yes, and I couldn't be happier. A band of minstrels from *Thianor* are going to perform soon," Bremen said with a smile while pointing at the minstrels who were tuning their instruments.

"I'll have a golden ale."

"Coming right up, Vincent," Bremen said with an affable head nod and smile.

"Vincent…Vincent Belmont?" A low, raspy voice inquired from the crowd. So I spun around on the barstool to see who it was. "Are you Vincent Belmont, winner of Gideon's Run?" the raspy voice from the crowd inquired.

The man who inquired of me was as burly as a brown bear. The man's shaggy mahogany beard had an imposing yet aristocratic presence. His appearance was that of a dyed-in-the-wool hunter.

"Yes, that was many years ago," I replied with a slight head nod followed by a swig of golden ale.

"I've been dying to meet you ever since I saw your name stitched in gold on the banner commemorating the winners of Gideon's Run," the man said in a folksy tone while extending his hand in salutation.

I heartily shook the man's paw of a hand, and then took another swig of golden ale. The man's appearance was common among hunters, yet there was something about the tone of his voice that resonated with me.

"I'm Gimdrick, Gimdrick—"

"Corval," I zealously interjected. "I was here the night you told everyone your harrowing encounter with the pack of wolves. I wanted to meet you then, but my wife and daughter were weary, so we took up lodgings for the night. It's an honor to meet you. Your name carries great weight throughout the town of Bleakton," I said to Gimdrick as I stood up from the barstool.

"Yes, that ordeal left me battle-scarred both physically and mentally, but I only boast about it under the right circumstances," Gimdrick said.

"What would those circumstances be?" I inquired while signaling Bremen for another pint of golden ale.

"Well, if I've been drinking far too much or the women around me are far too enticing to let be," Gimdrick replied with a grumbling laugh and then clashed his tankard of golden ale into mine. "Hell, son, what are you doing drinking at the bar like some mongrel? Come join me at my table, a man of your hunting prowess should be surrounded by his fellow companions," Gimdrick said while cheerfully patting my back.

"I should retire for the night. It's a four-mile hike back home to my cabin, and I need my rest," I said to Gimdrick.

"Just one round. It's on me. Come on, son, I won't take no for an answer," Gimdrick said in a facetious tone.

My reluctance to join Gimdrick's table diminished when the band of minstrels from Thianor began to play. "All right, I'll join you for one round," I said to Gimdrick with a smile.

Including me, ten hunters sat at Gimdrick's prominent table. Golden ale, mulled wine, mead, whiskey, and Bremen's hot-brandy cider were copiously flowing among the hunters. Despite the flamboyance and dulcet melodies that came from the band of minstrels, Gimdrick's table of hunters attracted the attention of everyone in the tavern. The smoke in the tavern was more acrid than usual, and the majority of it was emanating from Gimdrick's table.

"Everyone, this is Vincent Belmont. He's a two-time winner of Gideon's Run," Gimdrick proclaimed.

"I was wondering when you were going to join our table, Vincent. I'm Ivan. I won Gideon's Run three years ago," the hunter said and then extended his black gauntlet-covered arm in salutation.

"What kill portions did you present to the judges?" I inquired as I shook Ivan's hand.

"Two ten-point buck antlers," Ivan replied while gesturing the size of the buck antlers.

"You only won that year because the competition was feebler than your grandmother's bones," a hunter proclaimed from the far end of the table. The majority of the hunters then burst out in a unison of thunderous laughter. The hunter sitting to my right nudged me with his elbow so that I would join in on the laughter, but all I did was smirk and take a shot of whiskey.

"Shut your mead-hole, Sebastian. My grandmother's been dead for twelve years!" Ivan shouted while scornfully pointing down the table at the facetious hunter.

"So, Vincent, tell us your most esteemed kill," Gimdrick said with a mouthful of mutton. The attention of the nine brazen-faced hunters was immediately drawn towards me at that moment.

"A brown bear, eight feet tall, around five hundred pounds, as I recall," I proclaimed.

"Good kill," the hunter sitting to my right remarked in a barking tone while giving me a hearty slap on the back.

"A grand kill, indeed," Gimdrick proclaimed while raising his mug of golden ale. Following Gimdrick's toast, a praiseful rumble arose from the rest of the hunters at the table.

"Damn it, Jeremiahs, save some mutton for the rest of us!" Sebastian shouted.

"I'll feast till I'm full," the hunter sitting to my right replied in a heaving drawl.

"If anyone wants to catch a bloated boar, use some mutton as bait for your trap," Sebastian said to the townsfolk who sat at the corner table while pointing at Jeremiahs, who hunched over his plate full of mutton.

"Hold your liquor, you foolish bastard!" Jeremiahs shouted as Sebastian stumbled into the back of his chair. Jeremiahs then jabbed his elbow into Sebastian's gut, causing him to grunt and recoil. Sebastian then stumbled back to his chair at the far end of the table with a slanted simper and bleary eyes. The townsfolk who sat at the corner table looked vexatious towards Jeremiahs's and Sebastian's disports, but I, for one, felt great exaltation from these nine hunters.

"Vincent, how many shots did it take you to bring down that brown bear?" Ivan inquired from across the table and then filled up his tarnished chalice with steaming mulled wine.

"It took one shot. My first shot hit him right between the eyes," I replied while pointing at my forehead.

"Would you say you're more of a sharpshooter-based hunter?" Ivan inquired.

"Above all else, yes, but ever since I was eleven years old, my father taught me all the elements one must master to become a great hunter," I replied.

"Traps are my expertise—everything from deadfall, snare, glue, cage, foothold, steel, and spring-loaded. I build and sell them in the Market Square," Sebastian proclaimed as he sat with his arms folded and his feet resting on the corner of the table.

"The buffoon speaks the truth. Despite his antics, Sebastian's traps have a devastating rate of success," Ivan said.

"I owe a great deal to that brown bear. The kill won me my first Gideon's Run and the heart of my beloved wife, Heather," I proclaimed.

"How old are you, Vincent?" the hunter sitting to the left of Ivan inquired.

"I'm thirty-two years old," I replied.

"A virile buck in his prime already betrothed to a doe. You should take revelry in the woods and all the carnal splendors it has to offer," the hunter proclaimed with a simper and then took a puff from his black sylphlike pipe.

"Come now, Foster, don't patronize us married men with your coquettish escapades," Ivan said to the hunter sitting to his left.

"A man can only wander the woods for so long until the day comes where his heart yearns for something more," I said to Foster in a solemn tone.

"I'll tell you when that day comes for me, Vincent. Until then, a toast! To the women who beguile our hearts and loins," Foster proclaimed.

"To the women," I shouted along with the nine other hunters while raising my tankard. The debauchery of Gimdrick's table was the very heartbeat of the tavern. These nine prominent hunters of Bleakton already felt like the brothers I never had.

It was 11:06 PM, which meant I'd been breaking bread with the nine hunters for a little over two hours now.

"Can I get you more of anything, gentlemen?" a buxom, ginger-haired serving wench inquired.

"More everything," Gimdrick replied with vigor, his low, raspy voice speaking for the table.

The serving wench looked around Heather's age wearing a low-cut white sage dress, which was the designated garment for all serving wenches who worked at Squire's Tavern.

"I haven't seen her in this tavern before," I said as I leaned in towards Gimdrick.

"To my recollection, Ivy started working here about a fortnight ago," Gimdrick said.

By the time Ivy returned to the table, the majority of the hunters and I had grown into a besotted revelry. Ivy leaned over with her wispy, ginger locks hanging over each ear, and then placed a large platter of mutton in the middle of the table. She then went to the back kitchen and returned with a wooden dish filled with cheeses and loaves of bread. With each swig of golden ale, I found myself staring more fervidly at the fair-freckled, emerald-eyed visage that was Ivy. Ivy continued to bring various steaming jugs of mulled wine, mead, and hard-brandy cider from the back kitchen, adding to the abundance of the table. "Will there be anything else, big spenders?" Ivy inquired as she leaned in betwixt Ivan and Foster.

"Keep an eye on Foster. The show is about to begin," Jeremiahs whispered to me. Foster had the same fervid gaze in his eyes that I did, as Ivy's fair, ample bosom billowed with a sigh.

"That will be all, Ivy," Gimdrick proclaimed.

"Much obliged, darling," Foster said to Ivy with a simper, followed by a puff of smoke. Just as Ivy began to walk away from the table, Foster reached out and firmly smacked her backside. Ivy paused for a moment and then abruptly turned around and snatched a tankard of golden ale off the table.

"That should cool you off, darling," Ivy said to Foster while she poured the tankard full of golden ale onto his groin. This time I partook in the boisterous laughter that arose from the majority of the hunters as Foster jolted upright from his chair with a soaked lap.

"Careful, Foster, she's a fiery one!" Sebastian shouted in a mirthful tone.

"Damn it, woman!" Foster shouted while patting his lap with a handkerchief. Although I couldn't hear their conversation at the bar, Bremen's body language looked quite scornful towards the fiery Ivy.

"What a lecherous dog you are," Ivan said while shaking his head and laughing.

The band of minstrels from Thianor continued to play through all the debauchery of the nine hunters. Their dulcet melodies resonated throughout the tavern and appeared to lull some of the hunters into somnolence.

"Thianor is grateful to the hunters of Bleakton. Throughout the past ten years, their exports have bestowed a most prosperous way of life upon our town. This last song that we're about to play is a tribute to them," a minstrel proclaimed.

They toil through the snow.
They revel in the sun.
Their scars, they doth show

From journeys past won.
From journeys past won.

Companions, companions!
Through the blood and the strife
They taketh and giveth
With rifle and knife.

The band of minstrels sang harmoniously. The two young women of the band of minstrels, who appeared to be twins, played the violin and flute, while the two men played the banjo and lute. Along with the nine besotted hunters, I had positioned my chair facing the stage, as the band of minstrels played their song dedicated to us. Some of the hunters began waving their tankards back and forth as the band of minstrels got to the chorus. With somber and uplifting melodies, their song had truly captured the nobility of us hunters.

After the song had ended, I started applauding with the hunters and the rest of the townsfolk in the tavern. Gimdrick, Ivan, and Jeremiahs appeared to be tossing coins upon the stage as the band of minstrels packed up their instruments and retired for the night. The applause resonating from us hunters roared over the rest of the tavern, like prominent kings among timid peasants. In that triumphant moment in time, neither mayor nor constables existed, only us ten kings of Bleakton!

"Look, the brothers are about to arm wrestle," Jeremiahs said while pointing down the far end of the table. All the hunters immediately stood up from their chairs and gathered around the brothers. The brothers then slowly started to interlock their hands.

"I got twenty dollars on Roth to win," Sebastian proclaimed while waving the money above his head.

"I'm not betting anything on either one of these brothers. I learned my lesson the last time," Ivan proclaimed while shaking his head.

"Which one is Roth?" I inquired.

"That's Roth, and that's his younger brother Jacob," Jeremiahs replied while pointing at each brother.

"I'll take that bet," I proclaimed while pointing at Sebastian.

"You're on, Vincent," Sebastian proclaimed with a simper.

So the arm-wrestling match had begun. Jacob sat on my side of the table while his brother Roth sat across from him. The table started to rumble under the strain of the two brothers.

"Drunk too much mead, have we? Normally you would have pinned me by now," Jacob said to Roth while grimacing.

"Give it up, you whelp," Roth replied.

"Shut your gob and finish him, Roth!" Sebastian shouted. Roth's arm began to slowly incline.

"Come on, Jacob!" I shouted. The fluctuation between the two brothers was riveting to say the least. Jacob's resilience had fought back against his brother's brute force and began to gain the upper hand. "You got him," I shouted while Jacob's arm began to slowly incline. The throbbing veins and flushed visages of the brothers indicated that one would soon be victorious while the other would fall.

"Roth, I swear to God, if you lose—" Sebastian shouted. Roth's diminishing strength had fueled Jacob's vigor to the brink of victory. At this point, Roth's hand was no more than an inch above the table, and with a conclusive slam, Jacob had won the arm-wrestling match against his older brother.

"Who's the whelp now?" Jacob shouted triumphantly while his older brother lowered his head in defeat. I heartily slapped Jacob on the back while Sebastian threw his arms up in outrage.

"Roth, you fucking weakling, that's the last time I bet money on you!" Sebastian shouted.

"Pay up," I said to Sebastian with a simper.

"You fortunate bastard," Sebastian replied while slapping the twenty dollars in my hand. "I had to bet on him. Jacob was my father's name," I said to Sebastian.

"Perhaps that name is synonymous with strength, or maybe, Jacob here was wise enough to take advantage of his soused brother," Sebastian said.

"Of course, he was sloshed from the beginning," Jacob replied.

"Vincent, switch seats with me. I need to speak with the old alpha wolf," Sebastian said.

I assumed Sebastian was referring to Gimdrick when he used the name "old alpha wolf." "Sure," I said to Sebastian. So now I sat at the far end of the table facing the empty stage.

"Vincent, we haven't been properly introduced. I'm Christoph," the hunter sitting to my right said while extending his arm in salutation. The numerous pints of mead and shots of whiskey that I consumed over the course of the night were beginning to take their toll on me as I ungainly shook Christoph's hand. "I won Gideon's Run last year," Christoph said.

"What kill portions did you present to the judges?" I inquired.

"Moose antlers and two pheasants," Christoph replied.

"Pass the mutton!" I shouted while gesturing down the table for the platter.

"Well, go on, finish your story," Roth said to Christoph and then refilled his tankard with mead.

Christoph

"Right, so I'd been tracking a rather corpulent white fallow doe through the northern meadows of Vilkswood for the past three hours. I knew I had no more than an hour left to bag this doe, for nightfall would soon be upon me. The doe's tracks led me to the shores of *Willow Lake*. So I crouched down behind a weeping willow tree and waited silently as a blanket of mist began to cover the lake. Just barely visible through the mist, I saw a ripple in the water. That was when I spotted the doe carefully drinking from the partially frozen lake. I crept downwind from the doe and then took aim with my rifle. Despite the idyllic atmosphere and my best efforts of concealment, the doe immediately became aware of my presence. Her rich, sable eyes stared back at me, just as I was poised to shoot. My window of time was fleeting, so I slowly inhaled and then took the shot. The doe's legs instantly buckled as she fell upon the misty lakeshore.

"I kneeled down beside the doe and placed my hand over her pale, rotund underbelly. My shot had pierced the doe's heart, a virtually painless kill. I planned on making a coin purse and vest from the supple hide of the doe, so I took out my knife and began to skin her belly. Then I started cutting shanks from each of the doe's hindquarters. Just as I was about to cut into the doe's belly for steaks, I felt something strange. It was some sort of protuberance. I first thought it was the stomach gases expanding, which make dead bodies become bloated in size, but as I delved into the organs, I came across a most tragic sight.

"The doe wasn't corpulent. She was pregnant, and judging by the dilation of the pelvis, the baby fawn was still alive! So I carefully pierced a small hole in the uterus and then slowly stuck my hand inside. I could feel a faint heartbeat as my hand caressed over the baby fawn's wet, quivering body. I see now that my curiosity was reckless, for the next decision I made on that lakeshore brought forth such grave ramifications.

"I pulled the baby fawn out of its dead mother's womb and then cut the umbilical cord. 'What do I do now?' I despairingly inquired out loud, as the baby fawn cried in my arms. After a couple of minutes, the baby fawn had stopped crying and then stared up at me with such a pure innocence. The guilt I felt at that moment was soul-crushing. The moon had risen, as night had fallen over Willow Lake, where I stood covered in blood and afterbirth from the premature, baby fawn that rested in my arms. The night was freezing, and I knew the baby fawn wouldn't survive longer than an hour without its mother's milk to feed off. So I hastily packed up the shanks of venison and then swaddled the baby fawn in its mother's hide that I skinned earlier. Just as I was about to depart Willow Lake with the baby fawn nestled in my arms, I found myself halted by a most unforeseen and dreadful sound.

"To my uttermost dismay, I heard howling! They were coming. They always come when man is at his most vulnerable. It's almost as if they possess an innate sense that preys upon that emotion, the wolves of Vilkswood. Carrying the baby fawn through Vilkswood was decelerating my pivotal pace, a pace that couldn't linger whilst the feral hunting party pursued my bloody scent. Under such dire circumstances, my body couldn't follow my bewildered mindset, thus sending me tumbling over a tree root. The baby fawn was starving to death, and I knew the wolves drew nearer, for their dreaded howling grew more resonant in my ear. I also knew there would be no way to defend both myself and the baby fawn from the wolves' relentless bloodlust. 'I won't let you suffer,' I somberly whispered to the baby fawn as I placed it on the ground. I then pressed my knee down upon the baby fawn's neck, which brought forth cries of discomfort. So I closed my eyes and then grabbed the baby fawn's head with both hands, and with one swift, twisting motion, I ended the baby fawn's suffering."

*****

"You should have let the baby fawn to die in its mother's womb," Roth remarked. It may have come off as a bit callous, but I agreed with Roth's opinion.

"It would have been more humane for the baby fawn," Jacob said to Christoph.

"If you knew beforehand, would you have still killed the doe?" I inquired.

"If I knew the doe was pregnant…no, I wouldn't have," Christoph replied in a somber tone and then took a shot of whiskey. There was something different about Christoph. It wasn't his appearance that distinguished him from the rest of the hunters but his compassion. Despite the stoic visage he displayed, I knew he felt deep remorse for that baby fawn.

"It was a levelheaded choice. Only a compassionate fool would sacrifice their life for that of a premature, baby fawn. Pierce, what do you think about Christoph's story?" Roth inquired.

"Killing a pregnant animal would be one hell of an undertaking for me, so I would just send my winged beauties to do the job," the hunter sitting to my right replied.

"What winged beauties?" I inquired with a snicker.

"I'm a falconer, and I've been painstakingly training my four raptors for the past seven years," the hunter sitting to my right replied.

"Ah, a falconer, that explains the feathers," I remarked while pointing at the four feathers that were sown into Pierce's hat.

"This feather is from Maven, my peregrine falcon. These two feathers are from Holly and Iris, my two red-tailed hawks, and this feather is from Sheikra, my golden eagle. They're the deadliest and most disciplined raptors in the entire region," Pierce said while pointing at each feather.

"I wouldn't have the patience to train raptors to do my hunting for me. No disrespect, of course. I just rely purely on my own marksmanship skills," I said to Pierce.

"In this day and age, most hunters don't have the patience for the art of falconry. Falconry has been a part of my family's heritage since my great-grandfather, and when my son comes of age, I will train him to become a skilled falconer like me," Pierce said.

"How old is your son?" I inquired.

"He's twelve years old, but he's still a little afraid of Sheikra. It's an understandable fear. With four-inch-long razor-sharp talons and an eight-foot wingspan, Sheikra is the sovereign queen of my four female raptors," Pierce said.

"My daughter used to be afraid of the various animal heads that adorn our cabin, so scared that on many nights she would crawl into bed with her mother and me. I tried to comfort her by calling the animal heads her protectors that watch over her. Now I catch her talking to the animal heads on many occasions," I said to Pierce.

"How old is your daughter?" Pierce inquired.

"She's eight years old," I replied with a smile.

While Pierce continued to praise his four raptors, I noticed from down the table that Sebastian and Gimdrick were engaged in what appeared to be a real bull session. Gimdrick was making slashing and stabbing gestures with his dagger while Sebastian boisterously laughed and smacked the table.

"You talk more about your raptors than your wife and son," Roth said to Pierce while shaking his head.

"My four raptors provide for my family and me," Pierce said to Roth.

"I mean I could understand a hunter treating his trustworthy hounds, such as mine, as part of his bloodline, but it's a harebrained sentiment to treat raptors that way," Roth said to Pierce.

"Are you really comparing your mutts to my majestic raptors?" Pierce inquired with a scoff.

"Not this debate again," Jacob remarked with a vexatious sigh.

"My mutts, as you so ignorantly call them, are trained to track the scent of boars, rabbits, foxes, and pheasants for up to ten miles through Vilkswood. Then once the prey is within sight, I unleash my three hounds to trap and maim, therefore making my kill shot very easy," Roth replied with a scowl.

"Well, of course, your hounds have to hunt by scent. They're colorblind, and their poor eyesight inhibits them from spotting prey miles away. Now my raptors on the other hand possess keen eyesight that far surpasses even us humans. I raise all my varied species of raptors together on a large nest that I built on the balcony of my residence, which is located in *Eyrie Lofts*. When they were hatchlings, I actually managed to break them all of their siblicide behavior, which is an astonishing feat in the world of falconry. Venturing into Vilkswood with rifle in hand has become an obsolete practice for me. For an average of three days out of the week, at dawn's first light, my four-winged beauties fly in unison to Vilkswood. They're trained to hunt for any prey that they can carry back to the balcony, which includes pheasants, crows, foxes, and rabbits. Sheikra, however, is a most exceptional raptor. Every fortnight, I take her to the northern borders of Vilkswood to hunt for boar. On our previous venture, I had the pleasure of witnessing her hunt. She soared low in the air and then slowly descended towards a sizable, unwitting boar. Upon her landing, stupefied squeals resounded, as she started raking and stabbing into the boar's carotid arteries with her powerful, razor-sharp talons while rapidly flapping her massive wings. It took Sheikra twelve minutes to kill that seventy-pound boar, which later on fed my family and me for months. My radical training methods have not only revolutionized falconry but have also revolutionized the habits, longevity, and reproductive aspects of raptors as we know it," Pierce proclaimed.

"Has either of your hounds or your raptors ever killed a wolf?" I inquired.

"It would be a death wish for my hounds to hunt even a lone wolf. They know better than that," Roth replied.

"My raptors aren't trained to hunt wolves. A wolf's agile ferocity would pose a grave threat to even Sheikra, and I can't risk losing her," Pierce replied.

By this point of the night, the long bouts of drinking and feasting had rendered me numb and vertiginous. With bleary eyes, I could just barely make out Gimdrick standing up from across the far end of the table.

"Hunters…companions, I would like to make a toast." Gimdrick's low, booming voice resonated throughout the table while prominently holding his tankard at eye level. "Before I lose my wits completely, I would like to say that being in the grand company of all you hunters has brought comfort to this grizzled old bastard. The blood we have bled and shed shall leave an indelible mark on Bleakton and all across the Fray. Whether this profession was passed down to you by your forbears, mastered by your sheer will to survive, or to provide for your kin, the nobility that we hunters possess has continued to remain steadfast and true. Now I'll cease with the bullshit before I start to ramble. So rejoice, my brothers, we've slain all the others," Gimdrick proclaimed.

"Here, here!" I shouted along with the rest of the hunters and then clashed tankards with Pierce and Christoph before taking a long swig of golden ale.

"Yes, rejoice, by all means…rejoice," a gangly, dismal-looking man shouted while he staggered towards our table from a dank lit corner of the tavern. "Slain all the others, you say, what a foolish proclamation," the dismal man said to Gimdrick and then began to lurch around the table.

"Come now, Mordrid, how much have you had to drink tonight?" Ivan inquired with a snicker.

"Not enough to quell those incessant voices," the dismal man replied while pointing to his head.

It was Mordrid, but why hadn't I noticed him in the tavern until now. Uncanny gray eyes such as his didn't exactly blend in with the rest of the townsfolk.

"You all revel in the hunt, yet all you have slain is weak, predictable, squealing game," Mordrid pronounced with a sneer.

"Why don't you join us, Mordrid?" Gimdrick offered. Gimdrick's illustrious charm had fallen on deaf ears, for Mordrid snickered in response to the folksy invitation.

"Your attempts to recruit me as part of your murderous band are pathetic and futile," Mordrid replied.

If any of the hunters at the table were sober, they wouldn't hesitate to tear Mordrid to sunder, but that wasn't the case on this merriment-filled night. All the hunters were incredibly tolerant with Mordrid's scornful words. It was almost as if they pitied him.

"I still find it very curious that none of you have taken my offer. Two thousand dollars for the head of White Bane. That's the same cash reward that the winner of Gideon's Run would receive," Mordrid pronounced.

"We don't go hunting after fables," Ivan told Mordrid.

"Curious indeed. You know what I think? I think you hunters are afraid of White Bane, afraid of the calamity he ensues," Mordrid proclaimed while ungainly waving his arm at us table of hunters.

"The only thing we're afraid of is that ghostly visage of yours," Sebastian remarked with a simper.

Mordrid twitched slightly while a few of the hunters laughed at Sebastian's remark.

"Oh… I understand now. The so-called revered hunters of Bleakton are nothing more than a band of conceited beasts. Your brash facades serve as masks to hide your cowardice," Mordrid proclaimed while he crept closer towards my end of the table. Mordrid's twitching grew more spasmodic, almost as if he was being taken over by some malefic force.

"Careful, I'm not above hitting a wretch like you," Roth said to Mordrid.

"Your brutish threats don't affect me," Mordrid said to Roth while he crept past him. With a tense and fleeting glance, Mordrid's bleary gray eyes glinted at me through the pitchdark webbing that was his hair.

"He's at the end of his rope," Christoph leaned in close and whispered to me.

"What a pitiful man," I said to Christoph. I was oblivious to the level my voice rose to when I made the remark, for Mordrid's ghostly gaze fell sharply upon me.

"Ah, I remember you now...I remember you now," Mordrid said with a sneer. Mordrid's head cricked while he continued to gaze at me. "You were that shy hunter who inquired about White Bane. You claimed you never saw him, but I knew you were lying...I could see it in your eyes," Mordrid said while pointing at his ghostly eyes. I began to snicker, as did Mordrid. I poured myself another shot of whiskey while Mordrid's snickering rose to a maniacal cackle. "You have no idea what hunts you and your loved ones," Mordrid said.

"You're not fit to speak of them," I said to Mordrid while shaking my head.

"Protect your family, shy hunter," Mordrid said.

"Don't speak of them!" I shouted. At that moment, Mordrid's words ignited a rage within me, and I snapped. Within a split second, I found myself standing face-to-face with Mordrid, viciously pointing a broken whiskey bottle at his bony neck. Mordrid didn't recoil whatsoever while I stood before him fully enraged; in fact, his entire demeanor was chillingly calm. "You speak of my family once more, and I'll cut your fucking throat out," I said to Mordrid in a snarling tone.

"Did I strike a nerve?" Mordrid inquired with a sneer while eerily slanting his head.

"Stay your hand. Don't pay him any mind," Christoph said while placing his hand on my wrist. My tumultuous disturbance had drawn the eyes of the nine hunters at the table along with the majority of the townsfolk in the tavern.

"Vincent, Mordrid, what's going on here?" Bremen inquired in a stern tone.

"Oh, we were just talking," Mordrid replied.

"It's time you two retire for the night. You both have clearly drunk your fair share," Bremen proclaimed in a stern tone. With a snicker and twitch, Mordrid receded back into the shadows.

"You're right," I said to Bremen and then tossed the broken whiskey bottle on the table. I sluggishly fumbled through my wallet before taking out twenty dollars. "Here...this should cover the cost of the broken bottle and my tab," I said to Bremen while handing him the money.

"Don't fret, Vincent. You're not the first hunter to threaten Mordrid's life, and you sure as hell won't be the last," Sebastian proclaimed.

"Gimdrick...everyone, thank you for your hospitality," I proclaimed.

"So long, son. It was a pleasure, and may your future hunts sustain you and your family for many ages," Gimdrick proclaimed while raising his tankard.

"Vincent!" a hunter shouted, just as I began to staggeringly leave the table. "You wouldn't want to forget this," Pierce said while handing me my satchel.

"Oh, thank you," I said to Pierce while modestly bowing my head.

The frigid, night air cooled my flushed visage when I departed Squire's Tavern at 1:26 AM. The *Black Hearth Lodge* was my last destination for the remainder of the night. Last I recall, it was conveniently just a stone's throw away from Squire's Tavern. So I staggered down the cobblestone streets while placing my hand against some of the abodes to keep my vertiginous form from toppling over.

I shortly arrived at the Black Hearth Lodge just as the innkeeper was stoking the lobby fireplace.

"Be right with you, sir," the innkeeper said while I leaned against the front desk. Heather and Audrey accompanied me the last time I stayed the night at the Black Hearth Lodge. They found the hearty decor and accommodations comforting to their cabin lifestyle. Bear-skin rugs covered the hardwood floors of the lodge, and a grand tapestry depicting Bleakton's town symbol adorned the wall behind the front desk.

"Welcome to the Black Hearth Lodge. I'm the innkeeper, Oliver Blackwell. How may we accommodate you?" Oliver inquired while studiously writing in a ledger book.

"I-I uh…I need a room for the night," I replied.

"Very good, sir. Check in here please," Oliver said and then presented a quill, inkwell, and document upon the front desk. I could barely stand upright, let alone write my signature. So I gathered up the little dexterity that remained in me and signed my name on the document.

"Bel-Belmont, is it?" Oliver inquired while he stared closely at my slipshod signature.

"Yes," I replied in a heaving tone.

Oliver then began to skim through his ledger book. "Let's see here. Belmont… Belmont… ah, Vincent Belmont, two-time consecutive winner of Gideon's Run. You're fortunate, Mr. Belmont. In commemoration of its centenary, we're offering a 10 percent discount to all the winners of Gideon's Run," Oliver said.

"Good, what do I owe you then?" I inquired while hanging my head low.

"Six dollars," Oliver replied.

I fumbled through my wallet and then closely examined what appeared to be a twenty-dollar bill before placing it on the front desk.

"All right, fourteen dollars is your change. You will be staying in room 9," Oliver said and then selected my room key from the hooks on the back wall behind him.

"Can you make it up the stairs?" Oliver inquired.

"I can manage," I replied. I then grabbed my room key and staggeringly made my way towards the stairs. "All right, just a little help," I said to Oliver while leaning up against the wall.

"Of course, sir. Adam…Adam, get out here, son!" Oliver shouted to the back room behind the front desk. A boy who appeared to be around sixteen years old came out of the back room and attentively stood beside Oliver. "Help this intoxicated hunter to his room," Oliver said to Adam while pointing to the stairs.

"All right, sir, just put your arm on my shoulder, and I'll support you up the stairs," Adam said.

So I slumped my wavering form upon Adam's shoulders, and we slowly made our way up the first flight of stairs. Adam's boyish body buckled slightly under my weight at first but then forthwith adjusted into a sturdy brace.

"Do you work here with your father?" I inquired.

"Yes, my father and I work the evening and midnight shifts while my mother works the mornings and afternoons," Adam replied.

"You provide a noble service for the weary traveler," I said to Adam with a smirk.

"Two floors left," Adam said while pausing briefly atop the second-floor stairs.

A flickering oil lamp sat upon a nightstand at the end of the second-floor corridor. Step-by-step we lumbered up the stairs until we reached the third floor. Unless my bleary eyes deceived me, a prominent portrait of Gideon Bleak posing with his rifle hung at the end of the third-floor corridor.

"All right, last flight of stairs," Adam said with a sigh.

During our final ascension to my room, I draped myself around Adam's young, sturdy shoulders in a manner befitting an injured soldier. The fourth-floor corridor was utterly dark and silent. I caught a glimpse of our darkened, huddled reflection in an oval-shaped mirror that loomed at the end of the corridor.

"Did you see that?" I inquired with a wide-eyed stare.

"See what?" Adam replied.

"That flash of light. It came from the mirror," I replied while pointing down the corridor at the mirror.

"What flash of light? All I see is darkness," Adam said.

The mirror flashed with light once more, but this time, two eyes appeared within a dark silhouette. Those amber eyes in the mirror were neither mine nor Adam's; they were far too malevolent.

"Those eyes in the mirror—how can you not see them?" I inquired in a gasping tone.

"No offense, sir, but you drunk far too much tonight. Get some rest," Adam replied and then unlocked the door to my room.

"Thank you. I can take it from here. You don't need to tuck me in," I said to Adam with a smirk.

"Very well, sir," Adam said and then shut the door to my room.

I collapsed into a plush crimson armchair, which sat across from a black cast-iron fireplace. I could hear Adam scampering back down the three flights of stairs to his father's side while I sluggishly stripped off my outer layer of clothing. To slake my dry mouth, I took a long swig of water from the pitcher that sat atop the nightstand and then crawled under the crimson quilt of the bed. I couldn't remember the last time I partook in a night filled with such indulgences, such merriment, and such chaos, and I wonder how much of it I would remember the morning after.

CHAPTER 6

Maternal Ties

A child to cherish and mother doth perish.

My stomach was churning, and I couldn't fight back the overwhelming urge much longer. So I rolled off the bed and landed on the hardwood floor with a loud thud. I then hastily reached for the bedpan underneath the bed and vomited with such vehemence. I heaved and heaved and heaved until the contents of my stomach were all but emptied into the bedpan. That joyful poison that I consumed last night had stricken me with its aftereffects. I stood up with the crimson bed quilt draped around my shoulders and then took a swig of water from the pitcher on the nightstand. I then put a couple of logs into the faint flames of the cast-iron fireplace to chase away my quivering. Like a broken mirror, only fragments from last night remained in my memory on this chilled and hazy morning. My intense headache magnified every sound that resonated from the Black Hearth Lodge tenfold from the anxious mother trying to console her crying baby in the room next to me, to the squabbling couple in the room across the corridor. My head pounded from the morning hustle and bustle of the Black Hearth Lodge. My room was slowly warming up as I began to get dressed and gather up all my provisions for checkout.

I left the comforts of my room at 9:20 AM. I noticed an oval-shaped mirror hanging at the end of the third-floor corridor. I don't know why, but something about that mirror was unsettling to me. The door across from my room slowly creaked open, and a somberly dressed elderly couple walked out. The woman was weeping into a handkerchief she held over her nose while the man took a brooding glance at me.

"Morning," the man said in a stern tone.

"Morning," I said to the man and then walked down the stairs to the lobby.

The aroma of coffee wafted throughout the lobby of the Black Hearth Lodge. There was a large steaming copper, coffee dispenser, and various fruits and pastries that sat upon a table beside the roaring fireplace of the lobby. I got a cup of coffee and a few pastries for myself and then discreetly stuffed a few peaches, bananas, and apples into my satchel to take back to Heather and Audrey. I sat down in one of the many armchairs that faced the roaring fireplace and then began to slowly sip my coffee. I pinched the bridge of my nose and grimaced while my headache continued to pulsate.

"Are you all right, mister?" a little girl sitting in the armchair beside me inquired.

"I'm fine," I replied with a smile and then took a bite out of one of the pastries.

"You look like you're in pain," the little girl remarked while leaning in closer to me.

"It's just a headache. It will pass soon enough. In the meantime, I don't believe we've been properly introduced," I said to the little girl with a smile.

"Oh, I'm Elizabeth," the little girl said with a bashful smile and then began to dangle her petite black stocking-covered legs just above the mouth of one of the bear-skin rugs that covered the fireside floor.

"I'm Vincent. It's a pleasure to meet you," I said to Elizabeth while extending my arm in salutation. Elizabeth hesitated at first but then willingly reached out and shook my hand. "Where are your parents?" I inquired.

"My mom will be down here soon. She said I could wait in the lobby for her," Elizabeth said while combing her flaxen hair.

"You know, Elizabeth was my mother's name," I said to Elizabeth.

"That's nice. What was she like?" Elizabeth inquired with widened eyes.

I nodded my head and then took another sip of coffee. "I wish I knew her," I whispered into my coffee mug.

"What did you say?" Elizabeth inquired.

"Oh, nothing," I replied with a smile.

"Elizabeth, are you bothering this man?" a woman who I presumed to be Elizabeth's mother inquired.

"No, Mother. I was waiting for you," Elizabeth replied with a sigh.

"No bother, ma'am. She's a delight. I have a daughter myself around her age," I said to Elizabeth's mother while she quickly primped her daughter.

"Thank you, sir," the woman said with a smile.

"His name is Vincent," Elizabeth said to her mother.

"Let's go, young lady. Put your bonnet back on. You'll catch your death of cold," the mother said to Elizabeth.

"Bye, I hope your head feels better," Elizabeth said.

"It's already starting to," I said to Elizabeth with a smile.

I sipped the last of my coffee and then went over to the front desk to check out. "Checking out," I said to the woman at the front desk.

"Very well, sir. Sign here," the woman said and then presented me a quill, inkwell, and document upon the front desk. "I trust your stay at the Black Hearth Lodge was satisfactory?" the woman inquired while I wrote my signature.

"Very much so," I replied.

"Please come back anytime," the woman said.

Then with a smile and head nod, I departed the comforts of the Black Hearth Lodge.

So after the fairly lucrative overnight trip, I had at long last passed through the main gates of Bleakton at 10:04 AM, crossing over into the vale. I wondered how Heather and Audrey faired without me for the past day and how I've missed them dearly. The Murk River was almost entirely frozen over from the dead of winter's plunge. In the near distance, I spotted a murder of crows by the icy banks of the river. The crows were voraciously feeding upon an animal carcass in their huddled mass of blacken feathers. The crows then scattered into the gray gloom of the winter sky as I approached the carcass. The carcass was picked down to the gossamer bone, and all that remained was a frozen skeleton, but that was not what surprised me. Upon further examination, the frozen skeletal remains that rested on the icy banks of the river were that of a wolf's. I was no more than four miles from the cabin; for a wolf to venture out of Vilkswood this far into the vale was unheard of. This harshest of winter had drastically changed the wolves' habitat to drive them to such desperate lengths of survival.

"Even the most dominant hunters fall prey to mother nature," I whispered while kneeling over the wolf carcass. The wolf carcass was a sign, a sign of desperate times forthcoming. From here on out, I wouldn't dare make any more trips to Bleakton for the remainder of the winter. In the near distance, a most uplifting sight of rising smoke caught my eye. The cabin's chimney peeking above the hill signaled that I was home.

"I'm home," I proclaimed while entering the cabin.

"Honey, we missed you," Heather said while sveltely walking over to me from the kitchen.

"I missed you both," I proclaimed and then kissed Heather in a weary manner.

"Daddy, look what mommy and I knitted for you," Audrey said. She then cheerfully got up from the rocking chair and displayed a crimson scarf to me.

"Oh, you made this for me?" I inquired and then scooped up Audrey into my arms.

"Mommy did most of the knitting, but I helped too," Audrey replied.

"Thank you, princess. I love it, and I shall wear it from here on out whenever I brave the cold," I said to Audrey with a smile and then kissed her rosy cheek.

"Was the trip profitable?" Heather inquired.

"It was. With your help, I sold the golden pheasant for above its asking price in the Market Square, which I used to buy enough food and medicine to last us the rest of the winter," I replied. I then put down Audrey and handed Heather my satchel. "I need to talk to you…in private," I whispered to Heather while she was looking through my satchel. Heather's limpid, sapphire eyes then darted from me to Audrey in an anxious manner.

"Did you finish reading that chapter yet, young lady?" Heather inquired.

"Not yet," Audrey replied.

"Continue reading it, honey, while I talk with your father," Heather told Audrey. Heather and I then walked into the master bedroom and shut the door.

"Vincent, I can see it in your eyes…what troubles you?" Heather inquired while placing her hand on my cheek.

"I didn't want to scare Audrey with the news I'm about to tell you. On my way back from Bleakton, I came across a wolf skeleton on the banks of the Murk River four miles west of the cabin," I replied in a somber tone and then took Heather's hand and sat down on the bed.

"Why would the wolves venture so far from Vilkswood?" Heather inquired.

"Their prey must be dwindling. This harsh winter has worn Vilkswood down to the bone. The scarcity of the wolves' food source will drive them to our doorstep, and I fear attacks on humans will be more prevalent for their survival in the coming months," I replied.

Heather then sighed, lowered her head, and brushed her bangs behind her ears. "Will the wolves start hunting us now?" Heather inquired in a somber tone.

"The wolves will not harm you or Audrey, not as long as I draw breath," I proclaimed and then wrapped my arm around Heather, holding her close to my side.

"I'll start by boarding up all the windows first," I said to Heather. I then went to the storage closest and took out six one-by-four feet pieces of lumber, a jar of nails, a saw, and a hammer.

"Daddy, don't forget your scarf," Audrey said while I made my way towards the front door with the lumber and tools in hand.

"I won't," I said to Audrey with a smile and then placed the lumber and tools on the bear-skin rug, grabbed the crimson scarf off the hook on the front door, and wrapped it snugly around my neck.

"I'll get the door, dear," Heather said while walking over to me with a book in hand.

"Thank you," I said to Heather while picking up the cumbersome lumber and tools and then left the cabin. I placed the wood and tools on the workbench beside the front door.

It was freezing. The outside thermometer read fourteen degrees Fahrenheit. I started by sawing the six pieces of lumber in half and then nailed two pieces over the two front windows that looked into the great room. I then moved on to the master bedroom, lavatory, and Audrey's bedroom. Each nail that I hammered into the wood failed to bring me peace of mind, for these were dire times of survival. Throughout the years I've lived in the cabin, my father had diligently protected me from the dangers of Vilkswood while training me to combat those dangers, and now that tutelary duty would be mine to uphold. My first line of defense against the wolves was done after I finished boarding up the last window, which looked into the kitchen.

"That should do for now," I proclaimed while unraveling my scarf.

"Daddy, it's so dark in here now," Audrey remarked in a somber tone.

"Your father is just ensuring our safety, honey," Heather said to Audrey.

I stoked the great room fireplace while Heather continued to teach Audrey her daily curriculum. Audrey was right, with only thin rays of sunlight shining through the cracks of the boarded-up windows, we would have to live in near darkness from here on out. So I lit some spare oil lamps and placed them in each room throughout the cabin. "Is it bright enough to read?" I inquired while Audrey sat on Heather's slender lap, gazing into the pages of a book.

"It's bright enough," Heather replied.

I was weary, so I slumped down on the sofa and took stock of the provisions that I acquired in Bleakton. The contents of my satchel included loaves of bread, various herbs and spices, various fruits, and three amber phials of antibiotics. It was crucial for these provisions to last the remainder of the winter.

"So after nine months, the mommy gives birth to the baby?" Audrey inquired.

"Yes, very good, Audrey," Heather replied with a smile. "All right, now let's move on to penmanship," Heather said to Audrey. Heather then gently lifted Audrey off her lap and walked hand in hand with her to the kitchen table.

I continued to watch Heather teach Audrey with such benevolent tutelage from the great room sofa. *If this is what it's like to have a loving mother, then Audrey will grow up to be stronger than I could ever hope to be.* At my age, I didn't know why I'd still think of her—the mother I never knew—from time to time. My father would quickly change the subject whenever I inquired about my mother. Perhaps talking about her was too painful a wound for him to open. It was only on that dire night when I was severely ill that my father first opened up to me about my mother. My father sharpened me throughout my childhood, but whenever I watched Heather care for Audrey, I wondered what kind of man I would have turned into if I were raised with a loving mother such as Heather.

"Go practice the rest of your penmanship with your father in the great room while I start cooking dinner," Heather said to Audrey. I skimmed through the various ads and leaflets that were mixed in with the mail that I got from the post office in Bleakton until I came across something that caught my eye.

INAUGURATION OF FRANCIS BLEAK

Salutations, Bleaktonians,

On behalf of my father, Desmond Bleak, my constituents, and the town of Bleakton, I am proud to announce my inauguration into the office of the mayor, coinciding with the start of Gideon's Run.

I was born and raised in this town, and I knew that day would come when my father would graciously pass the mayoral torch unto me.

In collaboration with the hunters' council and my closest consultants, as your new mayor, I will usher in a new age of wealth and prosperity to this thriving town.

Bleakton was paved with the blood, sweat, and tears of my forebears, and I will justly uphold their noble politics during my term as mayor. Please join me, citizens. Under my management, the town of Bleakton will remain steadfast and true.

The apple didn't fall far from the tree. Francis Bleak's inauguration ad was just as flowery as his father. Throughout my many visits to Bleakton, I never noticed any civil unrest among the townsfolk. I credit this concordance to Desmond Bleak's lengthy and prosperous term as mayor. Normally Bleakton's politics had no effect on me and my family, but ever since we made that fateful decision to move there this coming spring, I would have to take into account the many laws of living in a mayoral-governed town. Heather, on the other hand, had much more experience with politicians than I did. She lived in Shors End till she was twenty years old, and last I heard, her father Henry Windemere was the chief advisor to the mayor of the metropolitan port city.

"How does my cursive look?" Audrey inquired.

"It looks far more exquisite than my penmanship, but then again, I'm not a teacher like your mother. Keep at it, princess," I replied.

"The stew will be ready soon," Heather pronounced while I walked into the kitchen. "You got a letter from your parents," I said to Heather while she was cutting up vegetables. Heather then took a brief pause from the stew preparations and glanced at the letter in my hand.

"I'll read it later," Heather said with a sigh.

So I went to the master bedroom and then placed the letter upon the nightstand beside Heather's side of the bed. It was 5:15 PM, and I was weary, for this winter had frayed my body and nerves to the near breaking point. So I sprawled out on the bed and tried to get some much-needed rest before dinner was ready—

*****

"Vincent…wake up, honey," a dulcet voice said.

I then awoke in my old bedroom to the sight of a golden light emanating from down the corridor. So I hazily got out of bed and followed the golden light. That voice that called out to me was neither Heather's nor Audrey's, but somehow, it felt warm and familiar. When I entered the kitchen, I saw a woman in a chiffon dress, facing the window. Just as the woman was turning around to face me, the radiant light that shone throughout the cabin began to quickly fade.

"You're awake," the woman said and then smiled while blood streamed from her eyes down her cheeks, just before the utter darkness fell—

*****

I jolted upright out of bed and rubbed my bleary eyes. That woman in my dream, who cried tears of blood, was my mother. Deep in my heart, I knew this to be true. One should never grew accustom to their heart rapidly beating upon awakening from sleep, but these morbid dreams that tormented my subconscious had grown more and more frequent during the past month. I knew I had to stay diligent no matter what form of torment was to befall me, foremost for Heather and Audrey.

"Dinner is ready," Heather said while peeking into the doorframe.

"Do we have any wine left?" I inquired and then slumped down into the dining table chair.

"I think we have some cabernet left. I'll go check the storage closet," Heather replied and then started attentively searching the storage closet. Heather then placed the bottle of wine on the table along with two glasses. Audrey then walked over to the kitchen table in such a blithesome manner and pushed her chair closer towards her mother's before sitting down. "Are you all right?" Heather inquired and then ladled the thick, steaming stew into my bowl.

"I'm just tired," I replied in a weary tone and then poured myself a glass of wine.

Audrey's sanguine eyes glimmered while she ate her dinner. She had the eyes of a child who was loved dearly, eyes that shone with an unsuspecting innocence of the grave dangers that surrounded the cabin, and that was how she must be kept. I consumed my bowl of stew and glass of wine within a few minutes.

"Let her eat," I said to Heather while she was primping Audrey's auburn hair. I then refilled my glass with wine and my bowl with stew. I needed to sleep tonight, and the only remedy I saw fit to treat my insomnia was the wine. So after I finished my second glass of wine, I set aside the glass and began to drink straight from the bottle. I could feel Heather's nervous glances upon me while I drunk straight from the wine bottle, but I shrugged off her refined table manners. At the dinner table, I must have come off as a beast to Heather and Audrey, who always project such grace and beauty. There was a small part of me that wished to dine in the grand company of my hunter companions in Squire's Tavern rather than here with my family. I didn't know why this guilty feeling arose in me, for my two reasons for living were sitting across the dinner table, delicately sipping their stew.

"Well, I'm done for the evening," I proclaimed and then grabbed the half-empty bottle of wine and retired to the master bedroom. I could hear Heather getting Audrey ready for bed while I sat hunched over in the fireside mahogany armchair.

"Good night, honey, I love you," Heather said to Audrey just before she closed the door to her bedroom. "Audrey said you looked sad at dinner," Heather said and then gently closed the door to the master bedroom.

"What reassuring words did you tell her?" I inquired with a smirk and then took another swig of wine.

"I told her you're just tired," Heather replied and then began to slowly unbutton her black frilled dress, baring her smooth ivory skin, which gleamed against the torrid flames of the fireplace. Heather then slipped on her sheer white nightgown and sat down on my side of the bed. "You know you can tell me anything," Heather said.

"Of course," I said to Heather while my drooping head rested in my hands.

"Please look at me," Heather said in a wistful tone.

So I raised my head to look at Heather, but when our eyes met, the morbid image of my mother crying tears of blood struck me once more. So I quickly averted my gaze from Heather's tender and entrancing visage. "Please don't fret over me. I told you before that I'm just sleep-deprived," I said to Heather and then sat down on the bed beside her. "Every creature has been drastically affected by this harsh winter," I said to Heather.

Heather then placed her hand on my cheek and gently turned my head facing her. "That's true, but together, we can overcome any hardship that befalls us," Heather said while her hand caressed my cheek. Heather then extinguished the oil lamp on the nightstand on her side of the bed and then nestled under the quilt. "Try to get some sleep, dear," Heather murmured.

Perhaps from the wine, a slow drowsiness crept upon me, lulling me to a much-needed slumber.

*****

"Mommy…Mommy," a little voice called out, waking me up from my wine-induced slumber. It was Audrey. She was standing over Heather's side of the bed, bearing a frightened visage.

"Audrey, honey…what's wrong?" Heather inquired in a murmuring tone and then sat upright in bed.

"Something's clawing at my window," Audrey replied.

"What do you mean something's clawing at your window?" Heather inquired.

"It's a scratching noise. It won't go away," Audrey replied while gesturing a clawing motion with her cherublike hands.

"It's probably just the wind, honey," Heather said to Audrey while she cupped her sullen cheeks.

"I'll check it out," I proclaimed.

Audrey's disturbance had shocked me back into my state of vigilance, so I immediately put on my boots and then took out my rifle from the wardrobe.

"Just let it be," Heather said in a distressed tone while I quickly inspected the stock, scope, and barrel of my rifle. "I won't let anything enter this cabin," I said to Heather in a stern tone.

"Then stay here. Audrey can sleep with us in our bed," Heather said while clutching my arm.

"Our bed isn't quite big enough for all three of us to sleep in," I said to Heather with a sigh.

"She's frightened. We can't let her sleep alone tonight," Heather whispered to me.

"Audrey, do you want me to sleep in your bed with you tonight?" I inquired.

"No, I want Mommy," Audrey replied.

I nodded to Heather as she permissively stared at me upon Audrey's request.

"Of course, honey," Heather said to Audrey while stroking her hair.

"Keep the door open," I said to Heather in a stern tone. Heather then gently took Audrey's hand and walked across the corridor to her room.

I kept my rifle on Heather's empty side of the bed. This wasn't the first time I chose to sleep with my rifle beside me, and it most definitely wouldn't be the last. I could see Heather nestling close with Audrey in her bed from across the corridor. Heather then reached over and extinguished the oil lamp on the nightstand.

"Shhhh, shhhh, it's all right…I'm here," Heather said to Audrey in a soothing tone.

I awoke to a melody the next morning. I sat upright in bed and noticed the source from which the melody was playing. It was my mother's music box placed upon the pillow next to my rifle. I was twelve years old the last time I recalled hearing that faint melody in my ear. It was the night I took severely ill. After my father told me my mother was watching over me during my affliction, he placed a music box upon the nightstand and opened it.

"This was your mother's music box," my father said. My father couldn't bring himself to sell any of her possessions, not even her clothes or jewelry. "Your mother's belongings are priceless, Vincent. I cherish them with all my heart, as should you. I wouldn't dare sell one single belonging of your mother's for even the heftiest sum of money," my father said in a stern tone when I once inquired the price of one of her dresses. To this day, I hold true to my father's love and devotion towards my mother's memory. So I bequeathed all my mother's possessions to Heather and Audrey, just as my father bequeathed them to me when I turned eighteen years old. So now my mother's maternal ties would remain unsevered, even in death.

"Morning, Daddy."

"Good morning, princess. Did you leave this music box on the pillow?" I inquired with a smile.

"Yes, I thought it would be a pretty song to wake up to," Audrey replied with a smile and head nod.

"Indeed, it is," I said to Audrey and then lifted her up onto my lap. "This was your Grandmother Elizabeth's music box," I said to Audrey.

"What was she like?" Audrey inquired while gazing at the porcelain figurines depicting an elegantly dressed man and woman that danced slowly together in harmony with the melody.

"Well, judging by how my father spoke of her, she shone with grace, beauty, compassion, and intelligence, much like your mother does. I wish I could tell you more about her. She would have loved you dearly," I replied and then kissed Audrey's forehead.

The cabin creaked from frigid winds that shrieked eastward from the vale on this dreary morning. I poured myself a mug of coffee and sat down at the kitchen table.

"Good morning, dear. Is that the letter from your parents?" I inquired.

Heather nodded to me while reading the letter with a pensive visage. Heather then took a profound sigh and pressed her hand against the side of her head.

"What's wrong?" I inquired.

"It's my mother…she's taken ill," Heather replied in a somber tone and then handed me the letter across the kitchen table before joining Audrey in the great room for her lessons.

Dear Heather,

This is your father writing this first passage to you. Your mother has contracted scarlet fever. For the past week, your mother's condition has been touch and go, but the doctors are worried that the infection may have late complications. Now I contracted scarlet fever when I was a boy, so I'm immune to it now. Your mother hasn't the faintest recollection of who she contracted this infection from, but I blame those filthy beggar children who linger around markets near our estate. I've always told your mother to leave all the shopping duties to our housekeeper Gretchen, but you know how particular your mother can be at times. I will be running for mayor of Shors End during this year's election, and I would love for you to be here with us, supporting our family's name during my political endeavor. Heather, I won't condemn you for the life choices you've made. I just want my beautiful and intelligent daughter back home where she belongs.

*****

Heather, this is your mother. The scarlet fever has afflicted me for the past fortnight now. My throat flared up to such painful conditions the first week to where I couldn't so much as utter a single word. The antibiotics the doctors have me on have alleviated my throat, but as your father wrote, there may be late complications. It's been nearly seven years since your father and I paid a visit to that deplorable cabin that you now reside in. That lowly man that you call your husband and father of your daughter has left your father and me with such distress these past years. All I want is to see my daughter again and hear her sweet voice for possibly one last time. Heather, a woman with your intellectual and social graces deserves nothing but the finest life has to offer, which your father and I offer to you and your daughter with open arms. Do you remember those tranquil mornings that we used to share together before you departed Shors End? Those mornings were filled with tea, music, laughter, and horseback riding along the seashore. I long for those mornings with you, with every passing day.

Love,
Henry and Cynthia Windemere

The letter from Heather's parents was filled with an array of conflicting and contradicting messages. To this day, they still despise me. They see me only as a thief who stole their precious daughter away from them. Heather's parents stood underwhelmed on the day they visited our humble cabin. I remember Henry's scornful stares and Cynthia's passive sighs while they reluctantly partook in our cabin lifestyle for a day. I showed nothing but the utmost respect for Heather's parents on that judgmental day, a respect that remains unrequited.

"Finish your porridge, honey. Then we'll start your arithmetic lessons," Heather said to Audrey.

"I'm going out on the front porch. I'll be right back," I proclaimed.

"Don't forget your scarf," Audrey said in a motherly tone while quickly glancing up from her book and pointing at the crimson scarf that Heather left neatly folded upon the mantelpiece.

I nodded with a smile before wrapping the scarf around my neck and then left the cabin. Crows were gathered in a huddled mass a couple feet away from the front porch and perched atop the roof of the cabin. It was almost as if the crows found solace and protection near the cabin. I wasn't about to fire off a shot into the air with my rifle to scare away the crows; that would be a waste of gunpowder and ammunition. So I ran towards the murder of crows gathered near the front porch and then threw an ice sickle at the crows perched atop the roof of the cabin. All the crows then fled to the sky in a frenzied panic, which left behind a peppering of blacken feathers upon the white snow.

"Those incessant crows are terribly loud," Heather remarked while I entered the cabin.

"They are a nuisance, but nothing more," I said to Heather.

"We should make a scarecrow," Audrey said.

Heather and I smiled at each other in response to Audrey's helpful idea.

"That's a great idea, but we don't quite have all the materials to make a scarecrow. We would need straw to stuff the insides with," I said to Audrey.

"Instead of straw, we could use snow, sticks, and leaves to fill the scarecrow with, and since it's so cold, the scarecrow won't melt," Audrey said while zealously gesturing the building process of the scarecrow.

"Audrey, how do you know about scarecrows?" Heather inquired with a smile.

"From *Whispers Though the Willows*," Audrey replied.

Upon Audrey's ingenious idea, I went to the storage closet and grabbed a hatchet, two burlap sacks, twine, and a piece of charcoal. I then went to the master bedroom and grabbed two long gabardine jackets and two hats out of my wardrobe. I then grabbed two pairs of worn slacks that would complete the scarecrows' ragged attire.

"I'll get the door," Heather said as I walked past her and Audrey while carrying all the tools and materials.

"I want to help," Audrey pronounced while her inquisitive hazel eyes stared at the tools and materials in my hands.

"You can help your daddy as soon as you're finished with this lesson," Heather said to Audrey while pointing at the book in front of her.

"Of course, you can help, princess, but only after you're finished with your lesson, like your mother says," I told Audrey and then exited the cabin.

The first step would be to build crosses for the scarecrows. So with hatchet in hand, I started searching for saplings along the borders of Vilkswood. The two saplings that go into the ground would be ideally seven feet in length. After briefly searching the border, I was fortunate enough to find two birch saplings betwixt two towering spruces. Although dark and indefinable, those two spruces stood like the gates to Vilkswood, but I knew no such gates could possibly exist in the wild. After I chopped down the two birch saplings, I dragged them back to the workbench. I then trimmed off the branches and sharpened the ends of the saplings with my knife. I then started tightly binding two shorter branches to the saplings, which formed the crosses. Sticking the first cross into the frozen ground proved to be a very grueling task. I forced the cross into the ground with all my might, but it wasn't in deep enough to withstand the harsh flurries.

"Daddy, I'm done with my lesson. How can I help?" Audrey inquired while exiting the cabin.

Heather dressed Audrey in several layers of clothing before letting her come outside to help me build the scarecrows. Audrey wore a gray buttoned-up wool jacket over her lapis dress. Audrey left baby fawn-sized footprints, as she trudged through the snow in her dainty black boots. Audrey's cherublike visage was all but covered up by a lapis bonnet and gray scarf.

"First, we just need to stick these two crosses deep enough into the ground. All right, just grab here with both hands and push down with all your might." I said to Audrey in a zealous tone. In unison, Audrey and I bored down on the cross, forcing it into the nearly impenetrable frozen ground. Audrey and I strained, but the frozen ground wouldn't relent.

"How's it coming along?" Heather inquired while exiting the cabin.

"Perfect timing, dear," I replied while gesturing for Heather's assistance.

"I didn't want to let you two have all the fun," Heather proclaimed with a smile.

Heather's pale visage was also all but covered up by a black bonnet and scarf. She wore a black buttoned-up, wool jacket over her garnet dress, which she lifted up to her knees, as she trudged through the snow in her slender black high-heeled riding boots.

"Help us push the cross deeper into the ground," I said to Heather. So with one hand over the other, we all grabbed the cross and pushed down. After a moment, the ground finally gave in from our collective force, and the first cross was secured deep enough into the frozen ground.

"Great job, ladies. Now for the other cross," I proclaimed and then placed the other cross roughly twenty-five feet apart from the first.

"Are you warm enough, honey?" Heather inquired and then kneeled down and attentively tucked Audrey's scarf under her jacket and pulled her bonnet down further over her sanguine ears.

"Come on, I can't do it without you two," I proclaimed with a smile and then grabbed the cross with both hands. Once more, Heather, Audrey, and I strained as we pushed the second cross down into the frozen ground.

"All right, now that both the crosses are in the ground, the fun that your mother spoke of can begin," I said to Audrey with a smile.

"Oh, dear, must you ruin your garments?" Heather inquired while I began cutting holes into the long gabardine jacket and slacks with my knife.

"If it means keeping the crows at bay, then I'm more than willing to make that sacrifice. Besides, these old garbs were my father's, and I know he would respect the manner of which we're putting them to use. We must be resourceful during this winter," I replied. I then looped twine through the slits of the long gabardine jacket and slacks and tied them together. "Go help your mother with the other scarecrow," I said to Audrey while walking over to one of the crosses. Audrey quickly joined Heather's side at the workbench while she carefully worked on replicating my cuts and ties to the other set of garbs. I started by outstretching the sleeves of the gabardine. Then I looped the twine through the holes and tied the jacket and slacks securely to the cross. I stuck a bundle of leftover sticks from the saplings into the ends of the sleeves and slacks before tying them off with the twine. I wanted the jagged sticks to jut out of the scarecrow's sleeves and slacks, thus projecting a sense of sinister ill will to the crows.

I joined Heather and Audrey while they started tying the garbs to the other cross. "You two did such precise work," I remarked with a smile while helping tie the garbs to the cross. It no longer surprised me how fast Heather always seemed to master a new skill, for she is a teacher after all. Heather could easily be an accomplished tailor if her sole passion in life wasn't teaching. I was quite certain when spring arrives and the crow's infernal noise ceases to torment us, Heather would salvage the scarecrows' garbs and turn them into lovely garments for Audrey to wear, as she had done on many previous occasions. I sometimes forgot how much of a frontier woman Heather truly was. Her upbringing of wealth and privilege was merely a facade that she wore, but never let dictate her heart's desires.

"Let's start filling these scarecrows up with snow," I proclaimed. The scarecrow I was filling with snow wore an ashen gray gabardine jacket while Heather and Audrey's' scarecrow wore a bronze gabardine jacket. "Don't pack the snow into the scarecrow, just sprinkle it in," I proclaimed.

"He's getting fat," Audrey remarked with a giggle, while plunging her little arm into the scarecrow's slacks.

"Yes, but he's still half full. Keep feeding him more snow, honey," Heather said to Audrey while reaching into the scarecrow's sleeve with a handful of snow. Just as I was sprinkling the last handful of snow around the collar of the scarecrow, a snowball suddenly hit me in the shoulder.

"Who threw that?" I inquired with a smile.

Heather shushed Audrey's sweet laughter and then continued sprinkling snow into the scarecrow with an elfin grin.

"Who was it?" I inquired while walking over to Heather and Audrey. "Was it…you?" I inquired and then ran over and scooped Audrey up into my arms.

"It was Mommy," Audrey replied in a flutter of laughter while I spun her around in the air.

"Oh really," I proclaimed with a grin and then lifted Heather up over my right shoulder. Heather and Audrey both laughed with merriment as I spun them atop my shoulders like princesses atop a rotating pedestal. Suddenly, I began to lose my balance and fell backward but with a soft crunch. Heather and Audrey's' fall was cushioned by me and the snow.

"Pile on Daddy!" Audrey shouted with a smile and then scurried upon me in a manner befitting a squirrel pawing for acorns.

"Come here!" I shouted in a playful tone as Heather began lightly tossing snow at me. So with Audrey draped around my neck, I sprung upright from the ground and pulled Heather in close to me. "Don't make me subdue you two," I proclaimed with a smile while Heather and Audrey forced me back down into the snow. Heather and Audrey then writhed with mirth as my hands fluttered across their stomachs. Audrey then quickly recoiled with elfin laughter from my frolicsome retaliation while Heather drew amorously closer to me.

"Is this how you subdue me, oh mighty hunter?" Heather inquired with a smile while her folded arms rested upon my chest and her rosy-tipped nose softly pressed against mine. "It's the only way I see fitting," I replied with a grin. Heather and I then kissed by the warmth of our beckoning breath amidst the frigid winter air.

"He's all full now," Audrey proclaimed while pointing at the scarecrow.

"That's great, honey," Heather said to Audrey.

"What Audrey must think of us, lying in the snow together?" I said to Heather with a grin.

"She'll think that her mommy and daddy are still deeply in love," Heather said with a smile, followed by another warm kiss.

"We really should get back to work," I said to Heather and then sat upright from the ground. Heather then quickly brushed the light dusting of snow off my shoulders and back and then off the fringe of her skirt. "Let's make their heads now," I proclaimed and then walked over to the workbench. "Audrey, can you draw a most frightful face on this burlap sack?" I instructed and then gave Audrey a piece of charcoal. The frightful visage I chose to draw on my burlap sack was that of Mordrid's, how that pitiful man stared at me with such an eerie smile. It wasn't Mordrid's visage that frightened me on that besotted night of revelry though; it was how much of me I saw in his ghostly eyes.

"I'm done," Audrey said while displaying the burlap sack to Heather and me.

"Let's see here," I said to Audrey.

"What is this face you drew, Audrey?" Heather inquired while we both stared at the burlap sack in discernment.

"It's a wolf. You see, there are his fangs and snout and eyes," Audrey replied while pointing at each facial feature she drew on the burlap sack. So with somber stares, Heather and I now knew Audrey's defining visage of fright. "I know I've never seen a wolf before, only pictures in books," Audrey said.

"That's fortunate, honey," Heather said to Audrey and then kneeled down and wrapped her arm around her.

"Your mother's right," I said to Audrey while I shaded in the eerie smile on my burlap sack. "We're almost finished. Now let's make the head-sized snowballs," I proclaimed while walking over to my cross with the burlap sack. I then tightly compressed a small snowball in my hands and started rolling it around in the snow. Within moments, the snowball had quadrupled to the desired size of a head. "It doesn't have to be a perfect head shape, just enough bulk to fill up the burlap sack," I pronounced. Heather and Audrey were still sculpting their head-sized snowball as if it were made out of clay. "Heather, come here!" I shouted.

"Audrey is having fun, but she and I are starting to shiver," Heather said with a smile.

"Don't worry, dear, I just wanted to show you the last step to finish building your scarecrow," I said to Heather while rubbing her folded arms.

"Well, go ahead then," Heather said while staring attentively at the headless scarecrow. So I started cutting two holes into the back of the head area of the burlap sack and then looped a piece of twine through. I then placed the head-sized snowball atop the high buttoned-up collar of the gabardine jacket and then covered the bare head with the burlap sack and fastened it to the cross.

"It's finished. You see, fastening this keeps the head from toppling over," I said to Heather while pointing at the twine that secured the scarecrow's head to the cross.

"Knife please," Heather said. So I handed Heather the knife and then proudly placed the pointed-brimmed hat atop the scarecrow's head. I kept adjusting the hat to where it rested at a rakish angle atop the scarecrow's head and then joined Heather and Audrey.

"Can I put his hat on?" Audrey inquired in a zealous tone.

"Of course, you can, honey. This was all your idea after all," Heather replied with a smile and then gave Audrey the hat.

"I can't reach," Audrey said to Heather while she repeatedly hopped upward with the hat held above her head.

"Up you go," Heather said to Audrey and then lifted her up.

"Push his hat down tightly so it doesn't blow off in the wind," Heather said to Audrey while holding her up at chest level like an oversized doll.

"Mommy, will these scarecrows scare away the wolves too?" Audrey inquired.

"Well…honey—"

"I'm afraid not, but don't worry, princess. That's my job," I interjected.

"I'll start dinner," Heather said.

"Right, thank you both for your help. Go inside and warm up. I'll be in shortly," I proclaimed. Heather then took Audrey's hand and entered the cabin.

Audrey's inquiry about the wolves brought forth a realization while I stared at the scare-crows. Wolves ate crows on occasion, but this harsh winter had drastically affected the wolves' food source to the point where they're increasingly feeding off the crows. This explained the crows' growing attraction with our cabin during the past month. The wolves' growing desperation for survival had caused a chain effect in the ecosystem of Vilkswood.

"Those scarecrows will be frozen solid by tomorrow morning," I shouted while entering the cabin. Audrey must have been in her room while Heather was in the kitchen preparing dinner. "Where's Audrey?" I inquired as I entered the kitchen.

"Oh, I think she's taking a nap in her room. Helping build those scarecrows must have tired her," Heather replied.

"I read the letter from your parents," I said to Heather while she was checking on the venison roast in the wood-burning oven.

"Can you hand me that pot please?" Heather inquired.

So I grabbed the black cast-iron pot and placed it on the stove and then rested both my hands on Heather's slender shoulders. Heather sighed faintly and then turned her head and placed her hand upon mine. Heather's silence was expected whenever I brought up the sensitive subject of her parents to whom she all but disowned. It had always been Heather's choice to remain emotionally and physically distant with her parents, yet there was still a part of me that feels responsible. This nagging guilt that Heather's parents projected upon me had lingered in my mind for the past eight years. Heather departed Shors End for Bleakton when she was twenty years old, and to this day, she hadn't looked back. I tried to sympathize with Heather, but I was born and sharpened by the death of those I hold dear. My father enlightened me about the natural order of life but kept me benighted on the sentiments of love. I learned that love follows no order or law, and its mercurial force could reign over your life when you least expect it. It's true that my childhood was sharpened by death, but now, love is what solely sharpens me.

I sat down in the fireside rocking chair and stared at the only photo of my mother on the mantelpiece. I originally found this photo of my mother tucked away in my father's wallet after he died. This photo was precious beyond words to me; it remained the only visual representation that I had of my mother. I stood up and took my mother's photo off the mantelpiece and then slowly sat back down in the rocking chair. I didn't know why my father hid this photo of my mother from me in his wallet, instead of displaying it on the mantelpiece. Over the course of fourteen years, I'd read all the thousand words that my mother's photo had to say. In the faded photo, my mother sat proper and fair, with her arms resting upon her lap, and her wavy, lucent hair streaming down her chest. She wore a dark dress with a frilled collar and a smile that exuded a quiet strength that closely resembled Heather's.

"She was very beautiful, wasn't she?" Heather remarked in a somber tone while staring at the photo. Heather then leaned in closer and rested her arm upon my shoulder.

"She was," I said to Heather in a somber tone while slightly nodding my head.

"She would be so proud of the man you grew up to be," Heather said.

"What man would that be?" I inquired.

Heather then sat upon my lap and draped her arms around me. "A man of compassion, resolve, and selflessness. Before you, I feared no such man of that nobility existed in this world," Heather replied while resting her head upon my shoulder. Then Heather and I swayed for a peaceful moment in the fireside rocking chair while staring fondly at my mother's photo.

"She was the same age as you when she died giving birth to me, yet throughout the course of my childhood, my father never once made me feel guilt over her death," I said to Heather in a somber tone.

"Your father knew your mother would want it that way. You were his precious gift, and he raised you in loving tribute to her sacrifice," Heather said and then softly kissed my cheek.

"I often felt like my father was preparing me for an approaching war, whether the war was against the wild or within me. I studiously followed his teachings," I said to Heather.

"Watch over us, Eliza," Heather whispered and then kissed her hand and gently touched my mother's photo.

Heather then went to the kitchen to check on dinner while I continued to slowly sway in the fireside rocking chair for a few moments. I then stood up and placed my mother's photo back on the mantelpiece before joining Heather in the kitchen.

"Can you set the table while I wake up Audrey?" Heather instructed. So I started placing the dishes and utensils at their respective seats at the table while Heather awoke the napping princess. "Let me do that, dear," Heather said while gesturing for the knife and fork as I started cutting pieces of the roast venison.

"No…no, sit down. Let me serve you for once," I said to Heather.

Audrey then quietly sat down at the table next to Heather and let out an elfin yawn. Heather then started compulsively primping Audrey while I filled their dishes with roast venison, potatoes, and cornbread. Heather always cherished Audrey from dawn to nightfall, and she couldn't help but keep her delicate hands off her auburn locks and cherublike visage.

"Those scarecrows should be frozen solid by tomorrow morning. That rigidity will help them withstand the shrieking winds that blow eastward from the vale," I said to Heather.

"Good, let's hope they have the desired effect on the crows," Heather said.

"We shall see, dear. I've lived among the crows my entire life and have never seen them so attracted to the cabin as they've been during the past week," I said to Heather and then bit into a hearty piece of roast venison.

"Audrey, honey, how is *Whispers Through the Willows* coming along?" Heather inquired while cutting Audrey's roast venison into morsels.

"I'm reading chapter 13 right now," Audrey replied and then rubbed her bleary hazel eyes.

"Tell us about it," Heather said to Audrey with a smile.

"Well, the sisters are having dreams about each other, and then when they wake up at night, they're both standing outside holding each other's hands," Audrey proclaimed.

"Have you read that book?" Heather inquired while carving off another piece of roast venison.

"No, I haven't," I replied.

"But don't you remember buying that novel for Audrey?" Heather said.

"Ah yes, of course, I remember now. I bought that book at the Sapient Scholar in Bleakton," I replied.

"Well, go on, Audrey. Why were the sisters sleepwalking together?" Heather inquired in a zealous tone while widening her eyes.

"I think they're being drawn towards the voices coming from the woods," Audrey replied.

"Or maybe the voices are just in their heads? Dreams have that uncanny ability that can make you lose your grip on reality," I said to Audrey in a somber tone.

"I suppose we'll have to wait for Audrey's next summary if we want to know," Heather proclaimed.

"Eat more roast venison. The protein will keep your hair and skin healthy during the winter," I said to Audrey with a mouthful of roast venison. Heather then smiled while Audrey nibbled on some more cornbread.

"Listen to your father's beauty regiments, honey. How else do you think his hair and skin remain so lustrous?" Heather said to Audrey in a facetious tone and then smiled at me.

After dinner, Heather and Audrey began quietly working with the spinning wheel in the great room while I sat down beside them on the sofa with a mug of coffee.

"You spin the wheel, honey, while I hold the distaff," Heather said to Audrey.

"What shall we make from the cotton we're spinning?" Audrey inquired while her petite foot repeatedly pressed down on the pedal.

"It will have to be small. We don't have much cotton left," Heather replied.

"I could never get that machine to work properly the way you two do," I proclaimed.

"It's simple, dear. I could teach you," Heather said while she gently guided Audrey's motions.

"No need. You're much more productive with it than I could ever be," I said to Heather.

"Can we make a handkerchief?" Audrey inquired.

"Sure we can," Heather replied with a smile.

I finished my last sip of coffee and then wrapped the crimson scarf around my neck. "I'm going to chop some firewood. Keep the door closed," I said to Heather and then left the cabin.

The days were getting shorter, and I had roughly half an hour to chop some firewood before nightfall approached. So I took the axe off the workbench and used it to brush the snow off the chopping block. I then placed a log atop the center of the chopping block, raised my axe slowly and precisely, and then split the log in one swift motion. I always found chopping firewood to be relaxing, where others would consider it arduous. I was on my tenth log when nightfall approached across the sky in a stripe of twilight. So I stacked up the firewood that I chopped and then took one last stare at the fleeting amber hues of the twilight sky before entering the cabin.

"We're done. Look, Daddy," Audrey said with a smile and then displayed a handkerchief to me.

"That was quick," I said to Audrey.

"Mommy sewed my initials into it too," Audrey said while pointing at the handkerchief.

"This is nice, Audrey," I remarked while staring at the initials *A. B.* ornately stitched in gold on the corner of the chiffon handkerchief. I then made a sneezing motion and brought the handkerchief up to my nose. "Ach-achoo, there you go, princess," I said to

Audrey facetiously with a smile as I abruptly halted my pretend sneeze and then handed her the handkerchief.

"Go get ready for bed, honey," Heather told Audrey while stroking her auburn hair. Audrey then retired to her bedroom with her handkerchief waving in her hand.

"It will be bone-chillingly cold tonight. Put a couple extra logs in Audrey's fireplace," I said to Heather and then went to the master bedroom while Heather went to Audrey's room. I put a log into the fire and then stoked the flames before I sat down in the fireside armchair. "Is Audrey warm enough?" I inquired as Heather entered the room.

"She is," Heather replied with a smile.

"Can we please talk about your parent's letter?" I suggested while Heather slowly slipped out of each frilled sleeve of her dress.

"I have nothing left to say to them," Heather replied and then rubbed her bleary sapphire eyes with a sigh.

"I'm not suggesting you make the journey to Shors End, but perhaps you could write them back this time," I said to Heather.

"My father didn't even mention you or Audrey in the letter. He only wrote to me in hopes that I would return to Shors End to help promote his self-seeking political goals," Heather said in a stern tone as her pale visage scowled.

"I know what your father thinks of me. In his eyes, I fail to measure up to the refined class of man that he saw suitable to take your hand in marriage," I said to Heather while she slid her dress down to her ankles and then stepped out one leg at a time.

"It was never his decision to make!" Heather shouted with quivering lips and then sat down across from me on the bed.

"I would've still asked him for your hand in marriage if you hadn't insisted that we elope in Bleakton," I said to Heather.

"Stop defending him. He's not here with us, nor will he ever be. He had a suitor arranged for me on the year I departed for Bleakton," Heather said while shaking her head.

"Wasn't his name Malcolm?" I inquired.

"Yes, and he was a grandiloquent fool who I detested being around, but all my father could see was his prominence as one of Shors End's most wealthy sea merchants," Heather replied while nervously stroking her long braided ponytail.

"Being a conservative politician, your father will always be attracted to wealth. That's why he despises my way of life," I said to Heather in a somber tone while she unbuttoned her corset. Heather then took my hand and placed it on her pale, silken chest.

"Do you feel that…I seek no countenance for how my heart beats or whom it beats for?" Heather said and then gently placed her hand upon my cheek.

"I shouldn't be seeking his approval after these many years. I don't know. Maybe there's a small part of me that sees him as a father figure, one that I must reconcile with," I said to Heather.

"You have a father. His name was Jacob Belmont, and he raised you with love all by himself among the perils of the wild. I know you miss your father dearly. I wish I could have met him," Heather said while caressing my cheek.

"He would adore you," I said to Heather and then kissed her hand.

"Please stop striving for my father's respect when Audrey and I respect you more than any man in the world," Heather said with a warm smile and then slipped on her white lace nightgown.

"If you want to check on your mother's condition, you can board the caravan that departs every fortnight from Bleakton to Shors End. The caravan's route will journey across the *Heslian Fields* to bypass the dangers of Vilkswood, but you needn't worry, for several armed constables will also be aboard the caravan to ensure the safe passage of its cargo and passengers," I said to Heather and then sat upright atop the quilt of the bed.

"How long will the journey take?" Heather inquired in a somber tone.

"Three days at the most," I replied.

Heather then slipped underneath the sheer linen sheets of the bed with a profound sigh and then rested her head upon my shoulder while she pensively reread her parents' letter. "My mother was always there for me as a child. I could confide in her whenever I was distraught, but now, her covetousness is equal to my father's. She told me if I ever found a man of compassion, resolve, and selflessness, that I mustn't let him slip away. Then when I found that man in you, she went back on her heartfelt words and sided with my father's courting arrangements. It was like a knife to my heart…her hypocrisy betrayed me," Heather said and then began to cry upon my shoulder.

"*Betrayed* is a strong word," I said to Heather and then wrapped my arm around her shoulder.

"It's also an appropriate word," Heather said.

"Will you renounce your mother completely?" I inquired.

"My entire childhood that I spent with my mother horseback riding along the seashore at dusk, afternoon violin lessons in the parlor room, and high tea in the rose garden was all a lie. They were merely preparations for an arranged hollow courtship. I had this foolish hope that these many years would humble her—change her—but I was wrong. Even now, she callously refers to you as that lowly man. How dare she," Heather replied in a weeping tone while pointing at the words in the letter.

"Times change, but people don't," I said to Heather in a somber tone and then rested my head against hers.

"I love you, Vincent. Please…don't ever change," Heather whispered.

"I won't…I promise," I said to Heather solemnly. Heather then kissed me deeply, and I could taste her tears as they streamed from her eyes down into the corners of her puckered lips. Upon our kiss, Heather walked over to the fireplace, wiped her tear-sodden eyes, and then cast her parents' letter into the flames. Heather's action first surprised and then relieved me, but I felt no desire to speak, for words were needless at that moment. Heather then slipped back underneath the bedsheets and embraced me for the rest of the night while her parents' letter burned to ashes.

*****

I awoke the next morning with a newfound peace of mind, for last night Heather wholeheartedly unburdened to me. I made certain not to sway Heather's decision about her parents in any way. I simply accepted her raw emotions as they poured out onto me. Those ceaseless disparagements that came in the form of letters would no longer torment us. Heather saw to that with such conviction. We could now put an end to that chapter in our lives and rise like a phoenix from the ashes of her parents' letter.

I poured myself a mug of coffee and then sat down at the kitchen table facing the great room. The cabin began to creak and rattle from the shrieking winds that blew in from the vale every morning. Suddenly, a small and dulcet sound caught my ear among the moaning winds. The small sound then slowly began to rise to a refined melody, which I could have sworn I've heard before resonating in this cabin. I stood up from the kitchen table and walked over to the great room to the sight of Heather playing her violin by the fireside while Audrey sat across from her, studiously practicing her penmanship on the coffee table.

"I remember you used to play," I said to Heather with a smile and then sat down in the rocking chair across from her with my steaming mug of coffee in hand.

"Yes, when I was pregnant with Audrey. I played the violin nearly every morning for her," Heather said with a warm smile while she delicately tuned the strings of the violin.

"Did you really, Mommy?" Audrey inquired and then drew her gaze from her penmanship to Heather.

"Yes, and you would kick my tummy whenever I played, almost as if you were dancing to the melody," Heather replied with a warm smile and then pressed the violin against her slender ivory neck. The song Heather then began to play was rather lachrymose in its pitch and tone but exquisite nonetheless.

One of Heather's most cherished possessions that she lost when Galahad bolted away from the bear attack nine years ago was her violin. I would travel every week to Bleakton hoping to come across a violin on display in the Market Square until I made a deal with a downtrodden minstrel who needed money far more than he needed his violin. One hundred dollars was a small price to pay to the minstrel for his violin, especially if it meant that it would bring a smile to Heather's face. That year I spent nearly half my $952 in prize winnings that I won from Gideon's Run in reparations for all that Heather lost on that fateful day.

"What's that song, dear?" I inquired upon Heather lowering her violin from her neck.

"It's called 'Twilight's Yearning.' It's the only song I still remember how to play over these past years, though I'm terrible now," Heather replied with a bashful smile.

"Nonsense, you play beautifully for someone who hasn't picked up a violin in nine years. This cabin could use more music," I remarked with a smile.

"That's sweet of you to say," Heather said with a smile while her hand gently caressed the part of her neck from which the violin had been pressed against.

"Mommy, what does *yearning* mean?" Audrey inquired.

"Well, honey…*yearning* is quite a powerful word. *To yearn* is 'to desire someone or something so deeply in your heart,'" Heather replied while placing her hand over her chest.

"I think of yearning as the heart overshadowing the mind," I said to Audrey.

"Eloquently put, dear," Heather said with a smile and head nod.

"Do you ever yearn, Mommy?" Audrey inquired.

"I used to, before I met your daddy," Heather replied with a warm smile while placing her violin and bow back into the dusty case from which they laid dormant for so many years.

"So Daddy saved you?" Audrey inquired.

"Yes, he did…in many ways, your daddy saved me," Heather replied with a smile and then surreptitiously wiped one of her tearful eyes while turning around to place her violin against the fireside armchair.

"We saved each other," I said to Audrey with a smile.

"Enough stalling, young lady. Let's continue your lessons," Heather said to Audrey with a smile while smoothing out the skirt of her long black dress.

"Are you all right?" I inquired as Heather walked over to me.

Heather then bent over and gently kissed my forehead. "I'm fine, dear," Heather replied with a warm smile while her hand briefly graced my cheek.

I finished my last sip of coffee and then took out four steel spring traps from the storage closet. "Well, I'll leave you two to your studies. I'm off to set some traps along the border," I proclaimed while taking the crimson scarf off the hook and wrapping it around my neck.

"Be safe," Heather and Audrey both said simultaneously.

"I will. I'll be back in an hour. Keep the door closed," I said to Heather and then exited the cabin.

Like a windswept cemetery, the morning was bleak and blustery, but I knew there was life out there in Vilkswood, and I was determined to capture it. I already had my spots marked for where I would set the traps along the border. Over the years, I studied the thoroughfares of all the four-legged creatures in Vilkswood and marked those paths of least resistance in my mind. There was a pair of fern shrubs, but betwixt them lay a thoroughfare that rabbits frequently use. This spot was where I set my first trap. There was also a fallen silver maple tree in the early stages of petrifaction, but within this hollowed vessel lay a thorough-fare that squirrels frequently use. This spot was where I set my second trap. A moss-covered outcropping was another, but beneath its overhang lay a thoroughfare that boars frequently use. This spot was where I set my third trap. A winding furrow bordered by thin birch trees was another, but within this trench lay a thoroughfare that foxes frequently use. This spot was where I set my fourth and final trap. I covered all the traps with a thin layer of snow and leaves and baited them with a mixture of venison fat scraps and blueberries that I saved from breakfast. So now I only had to wait.

"The traps are all set. I'll check them in twelve hours," I proclaimed upon entering the cabin.

Heather was sitting in the rocking chair with Audrey atop her lap. "Can you read this passage for me?" Heather requested while pointing at the page in the black leather-bound book.

"For when my head doth hang in shame and giveth into serpent's claim. For when the darkness shrouds my flame, I'll call unto her, my mother's name," Audrey replied.

"Very good, Audrey," Heather remarked with a warm smile while she nestled Audrey cheek to cheek.

"What's that book, Audrey?" I inquired while stoking the flames of the great room fireplace.

"*Always Beside Me* by Cornelius Abbott," Audrey replied.

"I don't remember buying that book," I said to Audrey while staring at the gold-printed letters on the cover.

"Well, dear, you've bought us hundreds of books over the years. I wouldn't expect you to remember every last one," Heather said.

"Three hundred eighty-six books," Audrey proclaimed.

"I still have yet to read a fraction of them," I said to Heather in a somber tone.

"I remember studying Cornelius Abbott in school. He was a praised author from across the sea. His words are beautiful," Heather said. I slowly sat down in the fireside armchair with a sigh while Heather and Audrey continued reading.

To me, writers seemed to live lonely lives fraught with pain and loss, or at least the most renowned ones did. I suppose if you possess such a brilliant, poetic mind, then the pain of loss could only inspire your writings, enriching them like a plot of land that's been swidden in order to cultivate more bountiful crops. I pondered these trials of a poet's life while I took out my knife and started sharpening it with the whetstone I kept on the fireplace mantle. Under Heather's caring tutelage, there was no doubt in my mind that Audrey would grow into a compassionate and intelligent woman. When Heather gave birth to Audrey, I regret there was a small part of me that wanted a son. Now I couldn't be more grateful to be the father of such a princess like Audrey. I sometimes wondered if Heather shared the same fate as my mother while giving birth. Would I have been prepared to raise Audrey by myself, like my father raised me? Now I understood that the mother's role in a child's life far surpasses the father's. I believed you could tell if someone was loved by the look in their eyes, and I saw that glimmer of love in Audrey's hazel eyes every time she read with her mother.

"You see, honey, whenever Cornelius fell into darkness, his mother's love was always there to bring him back into the light. Just as I will always be there for you," Heather said to Audrey and then kissed her cheek.

"His mommy died that winter," Audrey said to Heather in a somber tone. Audrey's rosy, cherublike visage then began to sadden.

"Yes…but even in death, the memories he had of his mother comforted him. Her very spirit continued to live on right here in his heart," Heather said to Audrey while placing her hand on Audrey's petite chest.

It was just as I presumed. Cornelius Abbott's life was indeed fraught by the pain of loss. The death of his mother shaped him thus shaping his poetry. Though heartfelt Heather's words to Audrey were, they did not come from experience. Heather's mother was living her life in Shors End, but in Heather's heart, she died a long time ago. I felt no need to speak on the matter of my mother's death to Audrey, for whenever I tried, I found myself a loss for words, just like my father.

*****

The bleak and blustery morning gave way to frigid stillness as the evening hour approached.

"I'm going to check the traps now. Keep the door closed," I proclaimed.

"All right, dear, be safe," Heather said while she quietly prepared dinner in the kitchen with Audrey by her side, in hopes that my traps would prove successful. I then wrapped the crimson scarf around my neck, lit a lantern, and left the cabin.

I set four traps along the border, which meant I had a very high capture rate. I shone the lantern over the first trap set betwixt the two fern shrubs but then shook my head in dismay from the dispiriting sight. The trap was sprung, but all that remained betwixt the steel jaws were scraps of blood-soaked fur, perhaps from a rabbit or gopher. Then upon closer examination, I noticed tracks in the snow that lead to and away from my trap. There was no mistaking it; a wolf had gotten to my trap and ripped my capture right from the steel jaws. The second trap inside the hollowed silver maple tree was sprung, but more scraps of blood-soaked fur, perhaps from a squirrel, were all that remained betwixt the steel jaws, and more wolf tracks in the snow leading to and away from the trap. The third trap beneath the moss-covered outcropping was sprung, but all that remained was the hind leg of a substantial beast, a boar, roughly fifty pounds, upon closer examination. The boar's hind leg was picked clean down to the bone. The wolf couldn't tear free the entire boar from the trap this time, so he simply devoured around the steel jaws until nothing but a bare and bloodied leg bone was left. This boar could have fed Heather and Audrey for a fortnight at the least. So now, all my hopes of capture rested on the fourth and final trap set in the furrow bordered by birch trees. Enraged at the sight of yet again more blood-soaked fur scraps, perhaps from a fox, and wolf tracks in the snow around the fourth sprung trap, I shouted abruptly into the darkness of Vilkswood and kicked the fourth trap a couple of feet into a birch tree. On this evening, the wolves' ravenous instincts had thwarted me. So I then collected all the traps and returned to the cabin with failure resting heavily on my shoulders.

I entered the cabin and walked straight to the storage closet without speaking a word to Heather or Audrey.

"What did you catch, Vincent?" Heather inquired with a smile as she walked over to me from the kitchen. Heather then stared curiously at my right arm, which threaded the four steel traps.

"Nothing, I'm afraid," I replied in a somber tone and then hung the lantern on a hook above the storage closet doorframe.

"What's that blood from?" Heather inquired while pointing to one of the traps.

"It was the wolves," I replied in a somber tone while opening the door to the storage closet.

"I don't understand," Heather said.

"All my traps were successful, but the wolves had gotten to them before I could…they devoured everything," I replied in a vexed tone.

"Oh…well, at least you're not hurt," Heather said while she gently grabbed my arm. Audrey then walked over from the kitchen and stood quietly beside Heather.

"I practically fed those vicious beasts on a silver fucking platter!" I shouted and then threw all the traps into the storage closet and kicked the door shut.

"You're scaring Audrey," Heather said in a distressful tone while Audrey clung to her skirt half hidden from me.

The rage from all the failure that I felt had overwhelmed me at that moment. "I'm sorry…it's my fault. I should have checked the traps before nightfall," I said to Heather in a somber tone while shaking my head.

"We still have plenty of venison left in the ice cellar," Heather said.

"No…I'll get it," I said to Heather while gently grabbing her arm before she could leave the cabin to take out venison from the ice cellar. So I grabbed the hatchet beside the great room fireplace and exited the cabin. I then unlocked the ice cellar door and started hacking off a couple of shanks. I then heard a faint howl on the still frigid air, just as I was about to open the cabin door.

"Could you get one more shank, please?" Heather said upon me tossing the frozen meat on the kitchen table.

"No need. I won't be eating dinner," I said to Heather in a somber tone.

"Don't do this to yourself," Heather said while cupping my cheeks with her hands.

"I'm fine. You and Audrey eat," I said to Heather while grabbing her wrists and lowering them from my cheeks. I then sat down in the rocking chair with my hands clenched together in frustration while Heather and Audrey continued cooking dinner.

*****

"Audrey, honey, how is *Whispers Though the Willows* coming along? " Heather inquired.

"Well…in the chapter I'm reading, the sister Maribel starts seeing Tobias in the woods," Audrey replied.

"Who's Tobias?" Heather inquired.

"He's the boy she used to play with when she was my age," Audrey replied.

"So…Tobias hasn't aged since Maribel last played with him as a child. How can that be?" Heather inquired.

"I know. I think he's a ghost," Audrey replied.

"Then let's hope all ends well for Maribel," Heather told Audrey.

Even my two princesses' dulcet dinner table discussion on literature weren't enough to calm my torrid temperament as I listened in from the great room. I thought I had the wolves' hunting patterns all figured out, but they'd continued to surprise me this winter. Now the wolves had adapted to an uncharacteristic hunting behavior, hunting like monsters or, worse, like men. The ravenous wolves of Vilkswood and the harsh winter that provokes them were testing me now as a hunter more than I'd ever been tested in the past, and I was failing.

"Go get ready for bed, honey. I'll be there soon to tuck you in," Heather said to Audrey.

"Don't be sad, Daddy," Audrey said while wrapping her cherub arms around my drooping head.

"I could never be sad with a princess like you to keep me company," I said to Audrey with a warm smile.

"I hope you're getting ready for bed, young lady," Heather said to Audrey.

"All right, Mommy," Audrey said to Heather.

"Good night, princess," I said to Audrey with a warm smile.

"Good night, Daddy," Audrey said with a smile and then scampered off to her bedroom.

I then tossed another log into the great room fireplace, stoked the flames, and retired to the master bedroom for the night. I went to the cherry bureau and took out one of the ashen gray wolf pelts from the bottom drawer. I believed time had a way of gradually purging one's weaknesses or thus exacerbating them. Was it a stroke of luck that I managed to kill those two wolves twelve years ago, or had my hunting skills faded into a mere shadow of my youthful prowess? I pondered these questions as I stared pensively at the wolf pelt that I displayed in front of me with outstretched arms. I then quickly put the wolf pelt back into the drawer just before Heather entered the master bedroom.

"Audrey insists on finishing the chapter she's currently on in *Whispers Through the Willows*, but I told her princesses need their beauty sleep," Heather said with a warm smile and then sat down on the bed with a faint sigh.

"She'll always be beautiful, come rain or shine, rested or weary," I said to Heather with a smile.

"I just want her to be well rested for her lessons every morning," Heather said while slipping out of her black dress.

"She reads much more fluently than I did at her age. I'm no teacher, but I believe her reading has improved greatly these past couple of months," I said to Heather.

"Oh, it has, dear. She's always had a passion for literature," Heather said while she slipped into her sheer white nightgown.

"Well, she does take after her mother. Pretty soon she'll be teaching you," I said to Heather with a smile.

"She's already starting to," Heather said with an elfin laugh and then leaned over and kissed me.

"You're a far greater teacher than my father ever was," I said to Heather.

"Don't fault him, dear. I'm sure he tried his best," Heather told me.

"Hunting always came first in my mind. So my father would reward me with hunting as an incentive whenever I excelled in my lessons," I said to Heather.

"That was wise of him," Heather said while sveltely slipping under the covers of the quilt.

"I used to love setting traps with my father in Vilkswood after I was finished with my lessons. He sure would know how to combat the wolves."

*****

"Dad, can we hunt now?" I inquired in a zealous tone while my father took a profound sigh.

"Not until you write a proper, grammatically structured essay about your passion for hunting," my father replied in a stern tone.

"These lessons don't matter in the wild. A wolf doesn't care if you're well-read and have proper penmanship. It will still tear you limb from limb," I said to my father.

"If you write a proper essay, then we can set a couple of traps in Vilkswood," my father said while pointing at the blank sheet of paper on the table.

"It's almost noon. If we wait any longer, we'll miss our chance to catch fawn grazing on the sage thickets," I said to my father in a sulking tone.

"Enough, son. Look at me…I promised your mother I would teach you, and I'm not one to ever break a promise," my father said with a steely-eyed stare and stern tone.

I then studiously started writing my essay upon my father's solemn behest.

*****

"Vincent…Vincent, anybody home in there?" Heather inquired with a smile while gently tapping my forehead.

"Oh, sorry, I was just thinking about something my father told me when I was a stripling boy," I replied.

"More words of wisdom?" Heather inquired in a weary tone and then rested her head upon my shoulder.

"I'm not sure. What he said back then is cryptic to me now," I replied.

"What did he say?" Heather inquired.

"He said he promised my mother that he would teach me," I replied.

"Maybe that was your mother's dying wish," Heather said in a somber tone.

"That would explain why he always acted so duty-bound, but why would my mother wish that of my father just before she died?" I inquired. At that moment, I was distressfully trying to get into my mother's mindset just before she died, in hopes of finding some closure about the promise my father made to her.

"Perhaps your mother was a teacher," Heather replied.

CHAPTER 7

Don't Be Afraid

Crimson-wrapped sorrows and the heart-wrenching tomorrows.

I awoke to tepid rays of sunlight shining on my face through the window. The last words Heather spoke to me before she fell asleep last night were revelational. Heather was right about everything. My mother was a teacher. I didn't know why I failed to realize it before, but it all made sense now. My father was a hunter first and foremost, not a teacher, but he wouldn't break the solemn promise he made to my mother. So he must have taught himself my mother's curriculum first in order to then teach me when I was old enough.

I noticed a pair of goldfinches perched upon the outside of the windowsill while I rubbed my bleary eyes and sat upright in bed. The goldfinches were chirping merrily, almost as if they forgot the dead of winter was still upon them. Morning sunlight seemed to have that effect on all creatures. I learned over the past winters not to take a fleeting moment of morning sunlight like this for granted. Before I met Heather, it was moments like this that uplifted my spirits. No matter the array of hardships I endured, discovering those fleeting moments of tranquil beauty wherever they may be would always outshine my dismal drudgery.

"Thank you," I said to Heather while pouring myself a mug of coffee.

"Thank you for what, dear?" Heather inquired with a warm smile while stroking her long braided ponytail.

"For giving me closure," I said to Heather with a smile.

Heather then placed her hand on my cheek and kissed me softly. "Your beard is getting long," Heather remarked with a smile while gently caressing my cheek.

"Too long, should I shave it?" I inquired while scratching my beard.

"If you want to, dear, but if you grow it any longer, you'll start to resemble a bear," Heather replied with an elfin laugh.

"A bear you want to tame," I said to Heather with a smirk and then grabbed her waist with both hands and pulled her in close.

"Go check on Audrey," Heather said while playfully pushing me away.

"What are you drawing there, princess?" I inquired as I sat down in the rocking chair. At first glance, Audrey appeared to be drawing a fox cub with a small piece of charcoal.

"It's a baby wolf…see," Audrey replied in a zealous tone while displaying the drawing to me.

Even though I nodded my head and smiled, Audrey's drawing worried me, for her interest in the wolves was growing.

"Daddy, you're the only one that's seen a wolf. Can you please tell me what they look like, so I can draw them better?" Audrey inquired.

"I've never seen a wolf cub before. Why don't you draw something else?" I replied.

"No, Mommy said I can draw any animal I want to," Audrey said while continuing to studiously sketch another wolf cub on the paper.

"I know, I know, but this morning, I spotted a pair of goldfinches perched upon the windowsill. They're gold-colored birds that sing merrily to greet the morning sunlight. Now wouldn't you rather draw them instead?" I inquired.

"Daddy, it's all right if you're scared of the wolves," Audrey said.

At that moment, I cricked my neck to try to suppress a sudden anger I felt awaken within me. "That's enough. Now draw something else," I said to Audrey in a stern tone and then crumpled up her wolf-cub drawing and threw it into the fireplace.

Audrey then started to whimper while her tearful, hazel eyes looked upon me in dismay.

"Audrey, honey, what's wrong?" Heather inquired in a distressful tone and then hurried over to Audrey's side and wrapped her arms around her.

"Daddy threw my picture into the fire," Audrey replied in a whimpering tone while pointing to the great room fireplace.

"Vincent, how could you?" Heather inquired in a gasping tone and with the same look of dismay in her sapphire eyes while holding Audrey's tear-sodden visage closely against her chest.

What have I done? I was breathing nervously while my eyes darted from Heather and Audrey to the fireplace and then down to my trembling, clenched fists. Then without speaking a word, I stood up from the rocking chair and stormed out of the cabin, leaving behind the crimson scarf.

"Oh my god," I whispered as I gazed upon a most catastrophic sight. There must have been hundreds of dead crows peppering the snow in front of the cabin like blots of ink upon a white sheet of paper. Many questions began to race through my mind as I walked among the crow carcasses. I would normally pay no attention to a couple of dead crows, but a near genocide of a species such as this was bound to drastically affect the ecosystem of Vilkswood. Upon examining roughly a dozen crow carcasses, an unnerving suspicion started to grow within me. The crow carcasses were fully intact, not torn apart by any predator, almost as if their hearts suddenly stopped beating in midflight. This evidence brought me to the conclusion that the crows' mass death wasn't natural; it couldn't be. Many people would consider a mass death of crows upon their doorstep a grave omen that should be feared at all costs, but my father always told me, from death comes opportunity.

The way I see it, I had two options. Either I simply let the hundreds of dead crows rot while flies and worms feast upon them as they decompose into the earth, or I could use them to bait the wolves. So I forthwith chose the latter, to use the dead crows as bait for the wolves. Nevertheless, the wolves were cunning, more cunning than I remembered, perhaps even more cunning than me, but I wouldn't stand defeated to the likes of them.

I entered the cabin and went straight to my gun wardrobe in the master bedroom without speaking a word to Heather or Audrey. Out of my six guns, I chose my father's air rifle with the gold butt plate, walnut stock, hair trigger, and steel swing swivels. This masterfully crafted rifle would serve me well in hunting the wolves as it had served my father in the past to a successful rate. Three bullets were all I needed, for I wouldn't waste any more ammunition on those beasts.

"Keep the door closed," I proclaimed in a stern tone while loading my father's rifle.

"Daddy, don't forget to—" Audrey shouted just before I left the cabin with my father's rifle strapped across my back.

I then immediately started eviscerating crow upon crow, spilling their blood and entrails upon the snow with my knife. I managed to eviscerate thirty-two crows within the span of an hour, but would that be enough to lure a wolf in for a kill shot? I then climbed the ladder to the top of the sharpshooter's nest and perched myself upon the wooden stool. Now I had to wait for the wind to blow west to carry the scent of blood to the wolves being downwind in Vilkswood. The wolves' incredible sense of smell was one of their innate abilities that make them such formidable hunters, but in this case, it could prove to be their downfall. This hunting method of mine wasn't foolproof, but I wasn't about to set more traps or venture into Vilkswood to hunt the wolves. An hour had passed, and the only animals attracted to the eviscerated crows were more crows and one cautious fox that barely nipped at one crow carcass for a brief moment before scurrying back into Vilkswood.

I had to stay vigilant, but I was freezing, so I slung my father's rifle over my shoulder and then quickly climbed down the sharpshooter's nest while staring intently at the border of Vilkswood for any signs of movement.

I entered the cabin and went straight to the kitchen. I then grabbed a black cast-iron pot, which I filled with several pieces of firewood and burning embers from the great room fireplace. I then quickly wrapped the crimson scarf around my neck. "I'll need this," I said in a stern tone while grabbing the oil lamp from the coffee table. The pot was already starting to catch fire, so I had to hurry back up the sharpshooter's nest.

"I can barely see now," Heather said.

"Don't worry. You'll manage," I said to Heather and then left the cabin.

I carried the oil lamp in my mouth by the handle betwixt my teeth while I climbed the ladder to the top of the sharpshooter's nest in a hurried manner lest I burn my hand. I placed the flaming pot and oil lamp down beside the stool as I reached the top of the sharpshooter's nest. I was never one to wear gloves while sharpshooting for hours on end, for I needed a feel for the trigger of the rifle to shoot with the most deadly accuracy. Another hour had passed as I kept repeatedly warming up my hands over the flaming pot beside me. Was I underestimating the wolves, playing them for simple bloodthirsty fools? Time would tell on this day if my vigilance could hold true. A few of my bones cracked like twigs under foot as I took a brief pause from holding the rifle to stretch my stiff body. The wolves might already be aware of my presence in the sharpshooter's nest, but would that suppress their most primal instinct to feed upon the dead crows? I think not, for hunger had a way of turning even the soundest mind into nothing but a ravenous beast, and the wolves were no different. I then heard the cabin door slowly creak open, immediately breaking the frigid silence and my focus on the border of Vilkswood.

It was 12:30 PM. Heather walked out from the porch and fell silent for a moment. She simply stared at the mass of dead crows laid before her in a peppering of black and crimson upon the snow with her hand over her mouth and awestruck eyes.

"Vincent, what happened?" Heather inquired.

"I told you before not to disturb me when I'm up here," I replied in a stern tone while keeping my gaze drawn upon the border of Vilkswood.

"Are you all right?" Heather inquired.

"I'm fine. Go back inside and tend to Audrey. I'm handling this," I replied with a sharp, scornful stare and snarling tone.

Heather gasped and slowly walked backward into the cabin. Heather had gotten into the habit lately of immediately inquiring my current condition upon seeing blood, almost as if she was losing faith in my hunting skills. I found Heather's diminished faith in me as a hunter to be quite vexing, for I was still the same hunter who saved her from the bear attack nine years ago. If I were to bleed during a hunt, then I would make sure my prey bleeds with me. My body may not be riddled with scars that tell stories, but I'd experienced just as much death as any other hunter, if not more. I saw nothing but crows feasting upon the entrails of their own kind, but the three bullets I had were for wolves only. I knew there would be another chance of encountering a desperate, lone wolf scavenging far beyond its territory when I came across the skeletal remains of that one wolf on the banks of the Murk River. It was beginning to dawn on me that the wolves were no longer afraid of my presence. The hunter in me found this enticing while the husband and father in me found it frightening. The wolves crossed their boundaries in order to survive the constant loom of death from this harsh winter; whereas, I must stay within mine in order to live.

At 3:45 PM, the visibility was low due to a light snowfall, but such a minor hindrance wouldn't deter me from hunting. I was tempted to set up camp in Vilkswood to hunt the wolves, but I had to stay within close proximity to the cabin to protect Heather and Audrey. Those bold days of me venturing into the dark heart of Vilkswood to hunt were over. Those very woods that brought Heather to me could very well take me from her. This haunting irony was a prime example of how mercurial the wild can truly be.

The flaming pot was dying down. So I opened up the oil lamp and dripped a couple of drops of oil into the weak flames. The flames of the potted fire instantly grew as the drops of oil fed them. I then took a bite of some smoked, venison jerky, which I kept stored in a pouch on the left-hand side of my coat. I then took a sip of water from my canteen and reverted back to my stiff position atop the wooden stool with my father's rifle poised and ready.

At 5:38 PM, the winds started howling as if to herald the arrival of the wolves, which was what my wishful thinking presumed at that moment. The temperature was dropping, and I was freezing despite the heat from the flaming pot, which I dripped a couple more drops of oil into. Soon the wolves would have all the hunting advantages, and I would be nothing but a shivering mass perched atop a watchtower shooting in the dark. So I reluctantly put on my black leather gloves and then rewrapped the crimson scarf tightly around my entire head, covering all but my eyes. If the wolves could suffer day in and day out to venture far beyond their boundaries to hunt and to feed upon the prey caught in my traps, then I could suffer this dark and frigid night in order to hunt them. Even if it meant devouring one of their own, the wolves would do so with no hesitation. They didn't suffer from vulnerability. They instinctively preyed upon it, but the wolves wouldn't find such a weakness within me on this night.

At 7:13 PM, the twilight hour was upon me, and slivers of amber began to slowly cut through the gloomy veil of the winter sky.

"I know you're out there," I whispered while staring intently at the dark and ominous borders of Vilkswood. The howling winds then suddenly subsided, and an eerie calm fell over the borders. The only sound I heard at that moment was the beating of my heart. My aim and heartbeat held steady amidst the chilling silence until I spotted movement. "There you are," I whispered as something slowly emerged from the borders. It was a dark figure, southeast, roughly twenty-five yards away. At first, the darkness and size of the figure led me to believe it was a boar until the beast became more visible to my transfixed eyes. No, the shape of the beast was too long and slender; whereas, boars were short and rotund. I was torn with a decision to make at that moment as the beast sniffed at a crow carcass. Whether the beast was a wolf or boar, this was my last chance, and I had to take the shot. So I took aim, held my breath, and just as I was squeezing the trigger, the beast's eyes glinted at me. The shot of the rifle abruptly ended the chilling silence while a sharp yelp and faint whimpers followed. Judging by its limp, I shot the beast in the leg, missing my kill shot to the head or chest. "No," I whispered as the beast began to slowly limp back towards the darkness of Vilkswood. I didn't have enough time to reload my rifle for another shot before the beast would vanish into the darkness of Vilkswood. No matter what the circumstance was, I wouldn't venture into Vilkswood at night. So I then made a most desperate and drastic decision.

With the oil lamp in hand, I clutched the rails with my feet and then hastily slid down the ladder. In my careless descent, I immediately lost my grip on the rails and plummeted to the ground with my right foot landing askew. Upon hitting the ground, I let out a hissing groan as a sharp twinge shot through my right ankle, but there was no time to let pain overwhelm me at that moment, for the beast continued limping closer and closer to Vilkswood. So I stood up with the oil lamp in hand and then started hastily limping towards the retreating beast. My breathing and heartbeat were frantic as I closed the distance between the beast and me at a fast rate. I reached the border and was close enough to where the light from the oil lamp revealed the beast's true identity. It was a wolf, with grim black fur and piercing sapphire eyes. So there we stood, both desperate and injured on the border. With teeth unsheathed, ears pointed back, and eyes fixed upon me in a ferocious gaze, the wolf was ready to fight for its life. I wouldn't recoil from this fight, not a single step back lest the wolf detects weakness from me. The wolf's sinister snarling shook me on the inside, but my body didn't project any such cowardice. I had to catch the wolf off guard, and nothing surprises an alpha predator more than being suddenly attacked. So without hesitation, I took out my knife, dropped the oil lamp, and undauntedly dove atop the wolf with a malicious shout.

The wolf then instantly collapsed under my weight but was in no way willing to submit to my sudden attack. A vicious writhing of claws and teeth were then beset upon me as I tightly wrapped both my arms around the wolf's neck. Then in a few frenzy-filled moments, the wolf's sheer ferocity managed to break free from my grasp and retaliate. The neck—I had to cover my neck at all cost lest the wolf's teeth go in for the kill. My crimson scarf was already betwixt the wolf's jaws before I could even raise my forearm to shield my neck. Amidst that desperate struggle with the wolf, I saw a fleeting chance to take control of the fight, and I took it without hesitation. I hastily unraveled the crimson scarf from around my neck and then tightly wrapped it around the wolf's snarling mouth. The wolf's vicious growls were then muffled by the crimson scarf, which held strong and didn't rip under the tension of the wolf's thrashing combined with my pulling. I then rolled over back atop the wolf, but the thrashing still had yet to cease despite my attempts at restraining it. The fight with the wolf was lasting too long and was far too loud. I had to end it now lest other wolves became attracted to our desperate struggle. Then with cold conviction, I swiftly stabbed the wolf in the neck. The wolf let out a faint yelp from the first stab but continued to thrash underneath me. So I continued to stab repeatedly while the wolf's warm blood splattered upon my cold, grimaced face. The thrashing lessened with each stab until the wolf finally fell silent and motionless upon the bloodstained snow. I then let out a profound sigh while wiping the wolf's blood off my face with the crimson scarf. I found it deeply unnerving that the wolf's piercing sapphire eyes were still open as I gazed intently into them. So as I reached in to shut the wolf's eyelids, a sudden outburst of life filled them once more. I then shouted out in pain and dismay as my left hand became clenched betwixt the wolf's jaws. "Die!" I shouted as I stabbed right between the wolf's sapphire eyes, which were lifeless just a moment ago. Then with a twist of my knife, the wolf's eyes shut and jaws loosened. "Remarkable," I whispered in a heaving tone while my bloody hand trembled in pain. I then slung the wolf over my shoulders and started limping back to the cabin.

At 7:40 PM, the resiliency of the black wolf was far beyond anything that I could have prepared for. I feared that if I hadn't shot the wolf in the leg from atop the sharpshooter's nest, then the outcome of the fight would have been fatal for me. I knew my father would be proud of me as a hunter on this cold and still night fraught with death, for my sheer will prevailed in the end.

"Heather…Heather!" I shouted as I entered the cabin.

Heather then hurried over to me from Audrey's bedroom. "Oh my god!" Heather remarked in a gasping tone while placing her hand upon her chest.

"Quick, get a blanket from the storage closet and lay it down in front of me," I said to Heather in a stern tone while the wolf continued to bleed out upon my shoulders.

"You were gone so long I was beginning to worry," Heather said in a distressed tone.

"The blanket, now!" I shouted.

Heather then hurried over to the storage closet, took out a worn, beige blanket, and then laid it down on the hardwood floor in front of me. I then flipped the black wolf off my bloodstained shoulders onto the beige blanket. Heather then recoiled with a faint gasp as the black wolf landed upon the beige blanket with a heavy thud.

"Don't bother trying to clean this coat. It's too saturated with wolf's blood. The scent will linger with it forever…it's ruined," I said to Heather as I took off my coat and threw it into the great room fireplace. Heather remained speechless as I took off my tan vest and black undershirt and then tossed them on the coffee table. "Audrey, come here!" I shouted.

"She's getting ready for bed. She was showing me all her charcoal drawings just before you came in," Heather said. Audrey then slowly walked out of her bedroom wearing a white nightgown while rubbing her bleary hazel eyes.

"What is that, Daddy?" Audrey inquired while pointing down at the bloodied black wolf.

"It's a wolf, princess. Remember, you asked me what a real wolf looks like, so you can take a more accurate charcoal rendering of them? Well, here you go," I said to Audrey with a smirk and then grabbed the black wolf by the scruff of its neck and raised it up closer towards Audrey. Audrey then cringed with both hands over her mouth as she stood face-to-face with the black wolf.

"Come now. It's time to go to bed, honey," Heather said to Audrey as she quickly stood up from the hardwood floor. Heather then took Audrey's hand and hurried her back to her bedroom.

While Heather was tucking Audrey into bed, I went to the kitchen and filled a small pan with water from our reservoir. I then heated up the water over the wood-burning stove for five minutes. I then took a rag and started washing all the blood off my face and neck. The tepid water from the pan soon turned crimson from all the blood being repeatedly wrung out from the rag. I then dried myself off and began to skin the black wolf.

"Vincent, how could you show Audrey such a grim sight right before she goes to bed? Do you want her to have nightmares?" Heather reprimanded in a distressed tone.

"She's seen dead animals before," I replied as I made a long cut down the chest of the wolf.

"We're not all as impervious to death as you are, Vincent," Heather remarked as I started rolling my fist underneath the wolf's skin.

"Well, maybe you both should be. I mean look around you. We're set upon by death," I said to Heather in a stern tone while aggressively waving my knife back and forth.

"Your hand," Heather remarked in a gasping tone.

I took a profound sigh as Heather quickly stood up and went to the storage closet. "Get the tannic acid while you're in there, please," I said to Heather just as I finished skinning the wolf's fur.

Heather then returned from the storage closet with two bottles and a roll of gauze in hand. Heather then pulled her braided ponytail back and sat down beside me. "Give me your hand," Heather said as I began cutting off ribs and thighs from the wolf.

"It's fine. I don't want you to get blood on your nightgown," I said to Heather.

Heather then gently grabbed my bitten hand and pulled it in close to her. "How did this happen?" Heather inquired as her fingers caressed the bite marks on my hand.

"The wolf refused to die without leaving a mark on me," I replied while shaking my head.

"I have to treat it…this may sting a little," Heather said and then started dabbing the bite marks on my hand with a piece of cotton soaked in gin.

"You should go to bed. You don't have to stay awake on my behalf," I said to Heather as her healing touch negated the sharp stinging from the gin.

"Please don't be a martyr. You don't have to suffer for anyone or anything in this world," Heather said and then began wrapping my hand up with the gauze.

"I would suffer a pack of wolves in order to protect you and Audrey," I said to Heather in a solemn tone while she tied off the gauze firmly wrapped around my hand.

"He was beautiful," Heather remarked in a somber tone while staring at the skinned and butchered carcass of the black wolf.

"She…she was beautiful indeed," I said to Heather. "Did you know that the aboriginal tribes that used to live in Vilkswood would eat the wolf's heart and brain in order to attain their strength and cunning?" I inquired while cutting a scrap off from the black wolf's brain and heart.

"What an archaic ritual," Heather replied and then placed her hand over her mouth in disgust as I ate the scraps of brain and heart from the black wolf. Both still warm and bloody, the scraps of heart and brain were difficult to stomach at first, but I fought back the urge to vomit and swallowed them both down.

"Now she is a part of me," I said to Heather.

"I think I'm going to be sick," Heather said as her visage grimaced in dismay. I then soaked some of the gauze in the tannic acid and started applying it to the wolf skin. "What are you going to wear now that you burned your coat?" Heather inquired with a sigh.

"Don't worry. I can wear my father's old hunting jacket. Sure, it's not as thick as my coat was, but I have an idea that will improve upon it," I replied.

"Vincent…why did you throw Audrey's drawing into the fireplace this morning?" Heather inquired.

"She's far too fascinated with creatures that could very well bring our downfall," I replied in a stern tone.

"Didn't you share that same fascination with wolves when you were her age?" Heather inquired while staring at me with her head tilted downward as I continued applying the tannic acid to the skin of the wolf.

"That's different. Audrey's fascination with the wolves comes from an innocent curiosity, whereas mine was born from fear and respect, which my father instilled in me as a hunter.

"I love Audrey with all my heart, and I dare not see her in a state of perpetual fear," Heather said in a distressed tone.

"Sometimes fear is necessary. It keeps you alive," I said to Heather in a somber tone.

"To live in fear is to live a life unfulfilled and oppressed. It's merely survival," Heather said.

"That's how I lived after my father died, but I learned to use that fear to sharpen my will."

Heather then stood up from the hardwood floor with a faint sigh. "Audrey isn't like you. She's a rose among a grove of hemlock, and I will nurture and protect her from the poison. Good night," Heather said while gently placing her hand on my bare shoulder. Heather then retired to the master bedroom for the night, leaving me alone with the black wolf carcass splayed before me.

After I finished applying the tannic acid, I gathered up all the remnants of the black wolf and stored them in a large burlap sack. I then grabbed an oil lamp and cautiously opened the door to the cabin. The frigid night winds cut through my bare chest as I quickly unlocked the ice cellar door and placed the wolf's remains atop the mounds of frozen venison. Something then caught my eye as I stood up with the oil lamp in hand. There where wolf tracks in the snow right near the porch. I then quickly entered the cabin and slammed the door shut. My fight with the black wolf had indeed attracted other wolves, and they traced the scent of blood back to the cabin. I must have been too weary to hear them prowling around the cabin's doorstep while I was skinning one of their own. The wolves' stealthy night maneuvers were enough to send a chill up my spine, such an unnerving feeling knowing alpha predators are stalking you. I didn't want to worry Heather or Audrey. So I quietly crept into the master bedroom and opened my gun wardrobe. I then grabbed one of my prized Gideon's Run rifles and put another log into the fireplace.

"Vincent…what are you doing?" Heather inquired in a faint murmur while she rolled over in bed.

"Shhhh…go back to sleep," I replied, and then grabbed the rifle and left the master bedroom. Heather was right, Audrey wasn't like me, and I am grateful for that. If I truly felt that raising Audrey with the fundamentals of hunting was vital, then I would have already begun teaching her despite Heather's disapproval. I didn't doubt Audrey could become an adept hunter under my tutelage, for she already possesses all those ambitious traits that I did at her age. My father taught me that the act of killing is inborn and you cannot teach someone to take a life. Whenever I gazed into my princess's hazel eyes, I saw a life glimmering with a purpose far greater than skinning and gutting boar; that responsibility fell on my weathered shoulders.

It was 2:30 AM, and I couldn't sleep. I sat leaning against the back of the sofa loosely holding my rifle with my left hand still twinging from the wolf bite. The night was eerily silent, even the cabin failed to speak with its familiar creeks and shudders. One would think these conditions are conducive to sleep but not to a hunter's mind such as mine. I came to learn that utter silence in the wild is a most certain foreshadowing of death, like a withheld breath just before you squeeze the trigger. Perhaps that's why sleep had eluded me this past month. I couldn't help but feel death loom over me during placid times such as this. My father was the same way. I often remembered waking up in the dead of night and peering around the corner of the great room to see my father slowly rocking in the chair with his rifle on his lap, a bottle of whiskey betwixt his legs, and a glazed look in his eyes. There was a part of me that wanted to confront my father during those quiet and unnerving times, but I was too afraid of what his reaction might be. So I always crept back to my bedroom and continued to listen to the creak of him rocking back and forth in the chair. I didn't fully understand why I feared my father during those times, for he never once laid a hand on me in anger, but I was now beginning to understand what my father felt during those times as I sat here on the sofa drearily staring at the front door with my rifle in wolf-bitten hand.

*****

"Don't be afraid," a faint voice said.

I then jolted awake to the sight of Audrey standing beside me. "What did you just say?" I inquired in a breathless tone as I clenched my rifle.

"I said look what we made," Audrey replied with a smile as she presented me with a doll.

"Oh, very nice craftsmanship," I remarked with a smile as I examined the doll.

"Mommy and I used many different materials to make her," Audrey said and then sat down beside me on the sofa.

"I see, I see," I said to Audrey as I gently held the doll by its slender waist.

"Isn't she pretty?" Audrey remarked with a smile while kicking her legs out from the sofa.

I nodded my head in agreement as I continued to closely examine the doll's ornate craftsmanship. "What's her name?" I inquired.

"Angela, but I'll call her Angie," Audrey replied.

"That's a beautiful name," I remarked and then kissed the top of her head.

"Mommy thinks so too," Audrey said with a smile.

The doll that Heather and Audrey made while I was sleeping was exquisite. The body of Angie was roughly a little over a foot long and made from white wool filled with cotton and stitched finely around the contours. She wore a white satin dress adorned with a lace pattern around the bottom of the skirt. Around her slender waist Angie wore a thin crimson ribbon, which caught the eye with its vibrant contrast against her ivory dress and skin. The shoes Angie wore were made from white leather adorned with white ribbons, which were wrapped in a crisscross pattern halfway up her legs. Angie's hair was dark sable and braided into a long ponytail that reached her backside and was tied with another white ribbon. Angie's hair uncannily resembled Heather's hair right down to the scent of lilac and lavender, which it gave off. Angie's face consisted of an elfin mouth stitched with crimson thread; a slender, fine-pointed nose; and teardrop-sized topaz gems for the eyes. Angie was a true testament of Heather and Audrey's' resourcefulness. How they could create such beauty from the simplest materials was a joy to behold and lifted my spirits to start the day.

"Take good care of her, princess," I said to Audrey with a smile as I handed her Angie.

I then stood up from the sofa with my rifle in hand and went to the master bedroom to put on a shirt and my father's gray hunting jacket. "Heather, did you cut your hair to make Audrey's doll?" I inquired as I entered the kitchen.

"Yes, Audrey wanted her doll's hair to look exactly like mine, and I felt yarn was much too plain of a material to fulfill her wish," Heather said.

"How much of your hair did you cut off?" I inquired as I stared at Heather's braided ponytail.

"Don't worry, dear. I have plenty of hair to spare," Heather replied with a smile and then started filling a bowl with porridge that she had been stirring in a copper pot on the stove.

"You cut your nightgown too," I remarked as I stared down at a cutout section of Heather's nightgown, which exposed her slender right calf.

"Yes, Audrey expressed before how much she likes the lace pattern on the bottom," Heather said while lifting her nightgown up to her knees.

"Seems like a heavy price to pay—cutting your hair and nightgown just to make a doll," I said to Heather and then poured myself a mug of coffee.

"No such thing. No price is too great if it will bring my Audrey such joy—that's immeasurable," Heather said with a smile.

"You should have woke me up then. I could've helped with the doll," I said to Heather.

"No, no, you went through a grave ordeal last night. You needed your rest," Heather said as she placed her hand on my cheek just before taking the bowl of porridge to Audrey in the great room.

I suppose I shouldn't have been surprised over Heather's acts of selflessness, especially when it involves Audrey, to whom she would sacrifice it all for.

"Vincent, why are you limping?" Heather inquired as I entered the great room.

"It's nothing serious, dear," I said to Heather as I sat down in the rocking chair with a profound sigh.

"Is it from last night?" Heather inquired.

"I was careless. It's just a sprained ankle," I replied in a somber tone as I lifted my right leg up and rested it upon the ottoman.

"I can make you a splint," Heather said as she stood up from the sofa.

"A splint won't be necessary, dear. I didn't break any bones," I said to Heather while waving my hand in disagreement.

"You let me know right away if you need any help moving around the cabin," Heather said.

"I think I can manage," I said to Heather with a smile.

"I'm going to get dressed. Start reading chapter 7 when you've finished eating," Heather said to Audrey and then went to the master bedroom.

"All right, Mommy," Audrey said to Heather while holding Angie closely against her chest with one hand and a spoonful of porridge in the other.

I stood up from the rocking chair with a twinge and grabbed my knife and whetstone from the mantel above the fireplace. I then noticed Audrey quickly drop her spoonful of porridge into the bowl and cringe away from the coffee table as I was sharpening my knife.

"What's wrong, Audrey?" I inquired.

"There's a spider. Look," Audrey replied while pointing at the coffee table.

So I stood up from the rocking chair with a twinge and sat down on the sofa next to Audrey. "Oh, he's a big one," I said to Audrey as the black spider crawled across the coffee table. The spider then crawled upon the blade of my knife as I blocked its path.

"Why don't you kill it, Daddy?" Audrey inquired as I went to the front door of the cabin with the spider crawling upon my knife.

"He poses no threat to us unless you want to eat spider for dinner," I replied.

"Ah no," Audrey said as her cherub visage scrunched up with a grimace of disgust.

"Then it's settled then," I said to Audrey. I then opened the front door of the cabin just a crack, kneeled down with a twinge, and let the spider slowly crawl off my knife onto the porch. I then shut the front door and sat down on the sofa next to Audrey.

"You should have killed it. Some spider bites can give you a fever," Audrey said.

"Where did you learn that, princess?" I inquired with a smile as I gently patted Audrey's tiny nose with one finger.

"I read it in a book called *The Entomology Guide*," Audrey replied.

"I read that guidebook too," I said to Audrey with a smile.

"But you kill all the other animals," Audrey said with her mouth full of porridge.

"I only kill to protect and provide for you and your mother. Only wealthy aristocrats kill for sport. They don't know what it means to be a true hunter," I said to Audrey.

"You're the greatest hunter, Daddy. You won two trophies," Audrey remarked just as Heather entered the great room wearing a white frilled blouse underneath a black dress.

"You know, you and your mother were the soul inspiration for me winning those trophies," I said to Audrey with a smile.

"All right, young lady, enough feeding your daddy's pride and start reading," Heather said to Audrey in a facetious tone while pointing at the opened book on the coffee table.

Heather and I then shared in a snicker as she went to the kitchen while primping her shortened braided ponytail. I then decided to check on the condition of the black wolf fur that I treated with tannic acid last night and left splayed out on the hardwood floor in front of the fireplace to dry out. So I kneeled down and closely examined the wolf skin by running my hands across it. The tannic acid had done its job, for the wolf skin's texture was dried and leathered but still pliable enough for my intended purpose.

I stood up from the hardwood floor and draped the black wolf fur around my gray jacket like a cape. I wanted the black wolf fur to cover my shoulders, chest, and upper arms of the gray jacket. I then went to the master bedroom and stared at myself in the ornate mahogany cheval mirror. I was very pleased with how the black wolf fur adorned my gray jacket in such a majestic fashion.

"How do I look, Audrey?" I inquired as I entered the great room wearing the black wolf fur and a lordly smirk.

"You look like a bear, Daddy," Audrey replied with a snicker.

"Did you know that the bear is the only other alpha predator in Vilkswood that the wolf dare not challenge?" I said to Audrey.

"It's because bears are gigantic," Audrey said in a zealous tone while raising her arms up in the air like a bear standing on its hind legs.

"That's right, but bears are solitary hunters," I said to Audrey and then sat down beside her on the sofa.

"What does *solitary* mean?" Audrey inquired as she stared at me with a curious glimmer in her hazel eyes.

"*Solitary* means 'to be alone,'" I replied.

"Oh, does the bear ever get lonely?" Audrey inquired.

"I'm sure the bear does. You see, that's where the wolf reigns superior over the bear. No matter how vicious, a lone wolf will feel just as vulnerable as any other creature, but within its pack, the wolf is fearless. I used to be like the bear before I met your mother. Now I'm like the wolf, and you and your mother are my pack," I said to Audrey with a smile. I then snickered while draping my arm across Audrey's petite shoulders as she howled in a dulcet tone.

"Heather, could you sew this wolf fur onto my jacket?" I inquired as I entered the kitchen.

Heather then turned around from the stove to face me with a sigh and elfin smile. "Oh, of course, I can, dear," Heather replied.

"I just want the fur sewn onto the shoulders, chest, and upper arms of the jacket," I said to Heather while pointing to the areas on my jacket.

Heather then slowly circled me with her hands on her hips as she stared intently at the wolf fur draped upon my jacket. "Wait one moment," Heather said as she left the kitchen and grabbed something off the spinning wheel in the great room. Heather then returned holding a tailor measuring tape outstretched between both her hands. "I just need to take some measurements. Arms out, please," Heather said with a smile. Heather then proceeded to measure my shoulders, chest, and upper arms in a gentle and studious manner. After Heather was finished taking my measurements, she then started writing them down with a sliver of charcoal onto a small scrap of paper, both of which she had stored in a pocket on her dress. "All right, I have all your measurements. You should go lie down. You don't want to aggravate your ankle by putting too much weight upon it," Heather said while taking off my jacket.

"Thanks, dear," I said to Heather and then went to the master bedroom.

I felt sharp twinges whenever I put even the slight bit of weight upon my ankle, but I couldn't let Heather see my painful grimace, for she would most likely overreact and devote too much of her precious time caring for my minor sprain. I was far from incapacitated but, for the time being, I felt that I needed rest, just as Heather advised. I then took out my mother's music box from the nightstand drawer and winded it up. The dulcet melody that the music box played was almost enough to lull me to sleep, if I were a child. There was a time when all I needed to fall asleep was Heather's warm embrace in bed beside me, but now even her nightly presence couldn't calm the maelstrom in my weary mind. Maybe that's why my father drunk late at night, but I wasn't about to succumb to that crutch in order to fall asleep. The only liquor left in the cabin was a small half-full flask of gin, but it was strictly for treating wounds. So I breathed a heavy sigh while rubbing my bleary eyes and then slipped underneath the quilt of the bed. I then reached over and rewound my mom's music box on the nightstand, turned onto my side, and then gazed into the flames of the fireplace. Hours had passed by before I finally closed my mom's music box and sat upright in bed. Hours of gazing into flames while a dulcet melody plays was yet another method that failed to lull me to sleep. My sprained ankle and bitten hand would heal in due time, but my insomnia had spread like a plague throughout my mind, and the respites of sleep that I did manage to get were awoken abruptly by such vivid nightmares.

To keep my restless mind occupied, I grabbed a random book off the shelf above the black oak headboard of the bed. The book was entitled *The Brubaker Clan* by Killian Reaver. I remember my father ordered me to read this novel when I was a stripling boy. The story tells of a band of five brothers who were also quite skilled and vicious hunters. On one grim and fateful day, their industrialist father dies, and the brothers are informed upon reading their father's will that he bequeathed unto them an entire inheritance. A hefty sum of two hundred thousand dollars was to be divided among the five brothers, but the last part of their father's will bewildered the brothers. Each of the brothers where then given a key to a strongbox that stored the inheritance, for their father had the foresight to hide the strongbox in an undisclosed location in the woods by his manor before he died. So the only way the brothers would find the location of the strongbox is by working together to solve the cryptic messages in their father's will.

The ending of this story wasn't for the faint of heart, but my father expressed a great significance towards its morals. In fact, this was the first novel I ever read that left me feeling truly astounded by the time I closed its crimson hardcover. So I intriguingly flipped to the last few pages and began to read the conclusion of *The Brubaker Clan.*

*****

"This is the spot. It has to be. Beneath the tree where ravens crow lies your mother six feet below. In life, she set my world aglow. In death, your treasure, she shall bestow," Nathaniel read aloud in a bewildering tone to his younger brothers who surrounded him with somber visages.

"Wait, I thought mother was cremated," Quentin said to Nathaniel.

"So did I, or perhaps that's what the old bastard wanted us to believe," Nathaniel proclaimed.

"So that gold urn in father's bedroom was just a fucking ruse!" Anton shouted as rain began to fall from the sullen sky.

"The sooner we dig her up, the sooner we get our inheritance," Lucius proclaimed as he picked up the two shovels off the ground.

"I don't want any part of this," David said to Lucius while shaking his head in contempt as Lucius offered him the shovel.

"Aw, don't tell me that little David still harbors fond feelings for Mommy who died when he was four years old? How infantile of you," Lucius proclaimed with a sneer.

"Let's get on with it!" Nathaniel shouted and then grabbed a shovel from Lucius.

"Tell me, David. Is Mother's worm-infested skeletal remains really worth more than forty thousand dollars?" Lucius inquired in a stern tone as David began to walk away from his brothers.

Enraged by his brother's horrid remarks, David then swiftly drew a knife from his gauntlet and threw it at Lucius's head with deadly accuracy. A loud ting then resonated throughout the downpour of rain as Lucius quickly raised the shovel in front of his face, deflecting the lethally aimed knife that his tempestuous younger brother threw.

'You'll have to do better than that, David. I've killed shrews who have put up more of a fight than you," Lucius remarked with a sneer and then picked up his brother's knife off the muddy ground and tucked it away in the breast pocket of his jacket.

"You may not respect the dead, but I do!" David shouted as Lucius and Nathaniel began digging up their mother's unmarked grave in a nervous manner.

"David, if you walk away from this now, then your share of the inheritance will be forfeited and divided among us!" Nathaniel shouted.

"That's fifty thousand dollars for the rest of us," Lucius said to Nathaniel with a snicker as he continued to dig.

"Besides, Father unearthed Mother's grave first in order to hide the inheritance. So spare us the fucking saint facade when we all know how vicious you can be," Anton said to David as lightning flashed and thunder roared.

David then halted his departure and reluctantly rejoined his brothers with a spiteful grimace. David then sat idly by on a rock beside the crimson king maple tree, which loomed over his mother's grave in a canopy of fuchsia leaves while staring intently at his brothers. Ravens then began to perch in the tree while crowing incessantly at the brothers beneath them.

"That's an omen. Just as Father's will foretold," Quentin proclaimed while pointing up at the ravens.

"Dig faster. I'm sodden to the bone," Lucius said to Nathaniel.

"Quit whelping, you fool. We're halfway there," Nathaniel said to Lucius. Both brothers then stepped down into the waist-deep hole and continued digging.

Meanwhile, Anton quietly takes Quentin aside from the rest of the brothers. "I heard Lucius whisper to Nathaniel that the inheritance is all theirs, for they're the ones to unearth it. Then Nathaniel whispered back, not to worry, for he has enough bullets to take care of us," Anton whispered.

"Nathaniel wouldn't dare betray us. He knows all too well what we're capable of," Quentin whispered as he took a quick glance at his older brother.

"Oh, but he would. He never failed to boast about how Father respected and favored him above the rest of us…I know you remember. Now he means to take the inheritance all for himself. I don't doubt that he will put a bullet in each of our heads, for he has been waiting for this moment," Anton whispered while staring spitefully at Nathaniel.

"So it has come to this," Quentin whispered while also staring spitefully at Nathaniel from the corner of his eye.

The brothers' loyalty to one another was nowhere near ironclad. In fact, it had deteriorated over the past twenty years to the point where it now hung by a thread. Anton saw the paranoia in his brothers' darting eyes and knew how persuadable they were. Among the five brothers, he was the serpent, the true snake in the grass waiting for that opportune moment in which to strike. So with a few devious remarks, the seeds of mistrust were sown, but who among the five brothers would reap the harvest?

Quentin then began slowly pacing back and forth in front of the now shoulder-deep hole that his two older brothers had been digging for an hour.

"Waiting is such sweet agony, isn't it," Lucius proclaimed with a heavy sigh and then took a quick nip of bourbon from his silver flask.

"Did you hear that?" Nathaniel inquired zealously while staring at Lucius with widened eyes, just after his shovel struck the earth with a clunk. Nathaniel and Lucius then tossed their shovels out of the hole and began pawing away at the mud beneath them like a couple of ravenous wolves, until…

"At last," Lucius said to Nathaniel in a heaving tone.

"We found it!" Nathaniel shouted triumphantly.

Nathaniel's shout had alerted the other three brothers like wolves to the scent of blood. "Mother's coffin," David remarked in a somber tone. The three brothers then took quick darting glances at one another, just waiting for the other to make that first and possibly deadly move as Nathaniel and Lucius slowly opened the black lid to their mother's coffin.

"Do you see the inheritance?" Anton inquired as he slowly kneeled down and grabbed a shovel off the mound of mud.

Nathaniel and Lucius gazed at their once beautiful mother Abigail's skeletal remains dressed in a sheer black veil and crimson frock. Lucius then took out his knife and cut open his mother's frock, revealing a black strongbox protruding out of her brittle ribcage.

"It's in her chest," Lucius replied.

"What was that, Lucius?" Anton inquired.

"I said—" Lucius's shout was then abruptly silenced with a swift blow to the head from a shovel swung by Anton as he stood up atop his mother's coffin.

With no hesitation, the snake had struck first, leaving his older brother unconscious and bleeding profusely from the head. There was no turning back now, for Anton's vicious act had set in motion the very fate of the five brothers. Blood was now no longer thicker than water, for the downpour of rain washed it away into the cold black mud.

"Hands up, Nathaniel…now!" Anton shouted while pointing his pistol down at his older brother.

"You're making a grave mistake," Nathaniel said to Anton while gritting his teeth.

"This is where it all ends. I have lived under your shadow for far too long," Anton said to Nathaniel in a snarling tone as he seethed with rage.

"So end it then, little brother," Nathaniel said to Anton as he slowly turned around with a sneer.

"As you wish," Anton said to Nathaniel and then pulled the trigger, but the pistol misfired.

Nathaniel then swiftly drew both his pistols from each holster and pulled the triggers, but Nathaniel's pistols fired instantly, hitting both Quentin and Anton in their shoulders. "That's what happens when you let your powder get wet!" Nathaniel shouted and then climbed out of the hole and stared contemptuously at both his brothers whom he laid grimacing in pain.

Nathaniel then began to walk slowly towards Anton with his knife in hand but was halted by a piercing pain, which collapsed him instantaneously to the ground right betwixt his two younger brothers. Nathaniel then cried out in agony while Quentin rolled over and cackled fiendishly.

"Always mind where you tread," Quentin said to Nathaniel with a sneer while clutching the bullet wound on his shoulder.

One after another, the brothers fell to each other's skills. Unbeknownst to Nathaniel, Quentin had a steel spring-loaded trap strapped to his back, which had been concealed by his jacket. Quentin then seized that small window of opportunity when Anton and Nathaniel where quarreling to clandestinely set the trap beneath the mud and cripple his older brother indefinitely. Four brothers now lay bleeding while the fifth and youngest brother lurked nearby in the shadows, unscathed by the brutality that unfolded.

"You conniving rats!" Nathaniel shouted as he tried to free his ankle from betwixt the steel jaws of the trap.

"Don't bother struggling. You know all too well how those traps are made, and nobody here is about to help you," Quentin said to Nathaniel as he stood up. "Come on, get up," Quentin told Anton as he grabbed his hand and pulled him upright off the ground.

"Stay down!" Anton shouted as Nathaniel kept repeatedly collapsing to the ground like a newborn fawn learning how to walk for the first time.

"You better sleep with one eye open for the rest of your lives. You will rue this—" Nathaniel's menacing threat was abruptly silenced with a swift kick to the head by Anton. So Nathaniel was laid unconscious like his brother Lucius before him, all by the hand of his deceitful younger brother Anton.

"Take his key to the strongbox while I get Lucius's," Quentin said to Anton. Quentin then took out a syringe from a pouch on his jacket while Anton was frantically searching Nathaniel for the key.

"I got the key!" Anton shouted.

"Good," Quentin said to Anton with a sneer as he stood behind him with the syringe in hand. Quentin then swiftly stuck the syringe into Anton's neck just as he began to turn around. Anton then drew his knife and slashed Quentin across the cheek in retaliation.

"What did you inject me with?" Anton inquired while gritting his teeth and clutching his neck. Anton then collapsed to the ground and began threshing like a wounded boar.

Quentin then stepped on Anton's arm, pinning it to the ground, and pried the knife out of his hand.

"Oh, you mean this?" Quentin replied with a snicker as he took out a small phial of liquid from his jacket.

"What is that?" Anton inquired with a painful grimace as Quentin loomed over him. Quentin then kneeled down and clutched Anton by the hair to direct his visage closely towards his own.

"Look at me…did you honestly believe that you could manipulate me like that whore you laid with last night back in town? While you, Lucius, Nathaniel, and David were all sleeping this morning from last night's drunken debauchery, I was in these woods hunting a very deadly snake called the peridot phantom, which I managed to successfully catch after several trap and bait modifications. Before I skinned the snake for my belt, I milked all of its venom into this phial. Oh, right, I should get straight to the point seeing is how you only have one minute left to live. The pain must be excruciating. You've always spat venom in your words, brother. So I simply gave you a dose of your own medicine," Quentin replied as his younger brother writhed in agony.

"Curse you, Quentin! You…fucking…bastard," Anton remarked in a heaving tone just before falling silent and motionless.

Quentin then took both strongbox keys from his lifeless younger brother and began to walk slowly towards the hole. Suddenly, within a flash of lightning, Lucius emerged from the hole like a rabbit popping its head out of a burrow. Lucius then swiftly drew his pistol from the holster and fired in unison with the following roar of thunder, hitting his younger brother in the stomach and collapsing him to the ground.

"You were never quick on the draw, Quentin," Lucius remarked as he climbed out of the hole and staggered towards his younger brother. "I thank you for taking care of Anton and Nathaniel for me. It saves me a lot of trouble," Lucius said to Quentin while gritting his teeth and clutching his head wound.

"I thought your neck was broken," Quentin said to Lucius with a bewildering stare as he clutched his gut, which bled out profusely upon the black mud.

"Here I thought you were the most intelligent among us, Quentin. Father was an old fool for praising your intellect," Lucius remarked as he loomed over his younger brother with shovel in hand. Quentin then slowly took out the half full syringe of peridot phantom venom from the pouch on his jacket as his older brother stared scornfully down at him.

"Father was right about you, Lucius—how you can be such an insolent mongrel," Quentin remarked in a heaving tone while gritting his teeth. Lightning then struck at that fateful moment as did Lucius and Quentin. Quentin thrusted his syringe of venom towards Lucius's leg, but Lucius knocked it out of his hand with a swift swing from the shovel before it could inject him with the deadly venom. Lucius then reigned down upon Quentin's head over and over again with the shovel until his younger brother's bloody caved-in skull laid unrecognizable.

Two brothers lie dead while three remain alive to a certain extent. While Quentin's intellect proved superior over his younger brother's deception, it fell swiftly to his older brother's stark brutality. The brothers showed no remorse for their siblicide, for the only tears they shed were ones of uttermost bodily pain inflicted by each other. The remaining brothers' masterful skills in tracking prevented them from fleeing the site of the inheritance, for it bound them together in blood. The wounded beast Lucius knew all too well the threats his remaining brothers posed to the inheritance and was hellbent on silencing them both just as he so brutally did with Quentin.

Lucius then tossed the bloodied shovel aside and took a long swig of bourbon from his silver flask as he loomed over his younger brothers' corpses. "What did Father ever see in you?" Lucius whispered with a scornful stare as he took the three strongbox keys from Quentin. "Ah, still alive, I see," Lucius remarked as Nathaniel rolled over onto his back. "It appears Quentin didn't quite finish you off," Lucius said to Nathaniel and then picked up the bloodied shovel and slowly staggered towards his older brother.

"Help me with this fucking trap," Nathaniel shouted with a painful grimace.

"Still barking orders are we, brother?" Lucius said to Nathaniel.

"Just push down on one of the springs," Nathaniel said to Lucius.

"You sound just like Father. He would always go off hunting with you right after he ordered me to do his grunt work," Lucius said to Nathaniel with a scornful stare.

"I protected you from Father's hand. Whenever you neglected your work, it was I who took the beatings that you should've received," Nathaniel told Lucius while gritting his teeth. "You did indeed…but nobody will protect you from me," Lucius said to Nathaniel and then raised the shovel above his head…

David then burst out from the shadows like a charging boar and tackled Lucius to the ground just before he could make the first strike upon Nathaniel. "You choose now to show yourself?" Lucius said to David in a heaving tone.

"Enough!" David shouted as he clutched the collar of Lucius's jacket with both hands. Lucius then hastily grabbed a rock from beside him and struck David in the head, sending his younger brother tumbling off him.

"You fucking whelp, I'm going to enjoy killing you the most," Lucius said to David as he crawled towards Quentin.

"You reach for that pistol…and I'll kill you," David said to Lucius while gripping his holstered pistol.

"You don't have the conviction," Lucius said to David with a sneer as he halted his reach for Quentin's holstered pistol.

"Look what you've been reduced to!" David shouted.

"David, when will you learn that this world is devoid of all humanity?" Lucius inquired in a somber tone and then lunged for Quentin's holstered pistol. David then swiftly drew his pistol and fired, shooting Lucius square in the forehead.

"Thank you for teaching me, brother," David replied in a somber tone and then collapsed to his knees.

Three brothers lay dead while two remain alive. All the suppressed resentment and envy that Lucius felt towards his brothers throughout their childhood was culminated. Despite David's efforts, Lucius wouldn't appeal to reason, and his madness forced his younger brother's hand to take his life. The two remaining brothers would now be tested more than they have ever been in their lives. Nathaniel knew he had to cast aside his pride and plea with his younger brother in order to free himself from the trap; whereas, David knew the consequence in showing his older brother compassion.

The storm had finally ended as the sullen clouds diminished, giving way to a twilit sky.

"David, what transpired here was a horrific disgrace to the Brubaker name, and I understand completely if you take the inheritance and leave me here," Nathaniel said to his younger brother in a somber tone and painful grimace.

David then took the last loaded pistol from Quentin and walked slowly towards Nathaniel. "Rest your foot flat," David said to Nathaniel and then stepped down on both springs of the trap and pried the jaws open, freeing his older brother.

"Thank you," Nathaniel told David while gritting his teeth and clenching his ankle. David then holstered Quentin's pistol and extended his hand to his older brother. "That trap pierced my tendons," Nathaniel said to David as he took his hand. Nathaniel then draped his arm across David's shoulders as they walked slowly towards the hole. "Father always told me to take care of you…and that's what I must do now," Nathaniel said to David in a somber tone and then drew the pistol from his younger brother's holster and fired, hitting David in the stomach and collapsing him to the ground.

Nathaniel then kneeled atop his younger brother whom he laid, grimacing in pain.

"Hundred thousand dollars wasn't enough for you," David said to Nathaniel as he clenched his gut in agony. "Father's inheritance was never about the money. It was about determining who his strongest son was," Nathaniel said to David while waving the pistol aggressively in the air.

"You're…you're not my brother," David said to Nathaniel with a scornful stare.

"I'm sorry, David," Nathaniel said to his younger brother in a somber tone as he bled out profusely.

"Enough lies," David said to Nathaniel and then coughed up blood.

"When you see Father, tell him he gave me in death what he failed to give me in life—peace of mind," Nathaniel said to David in a somber tone. "What was that?" Nathaniel inquired while leaning in closely as David muttered in a gut-wrenching heave.

"Tell him yourself," David said to Nathaniel with a scornful stare and then swiftly drew a knife from his gauntlet and stabbed his older brother in the neck. David's eyes then locked with Nathaniel's in a tempestuous stare.

"I knew you had it in you," Nathaniel said to David with a sneer and choking heave as blood spurted out of his neck. Nathaniel then collapsed beside his younger brother while blood continued to pour out of his neck. David heaved and bled along with Nathaniel for a few agonizing moments until one of them finally fell silent.

David then slowly crawled towards the hole in agony as his bullet wound dragged across the ground. With one last pull upon the edge of the hole, David then fell heavily upon the skeletal remains of his mother with a hissing groan. A murder of ravens then began to gather around the edge of the hole as David pulled out the black iron strongbox from his mother's brittle ribcage. The murder of ravens then began to crow in unison like a choir shrouded in black robes as David took out his key and inserted it into the lock of the strongbox. David then slowly turned the key to the right, and with a definitive click, the lid to the strongbox opened. David then froze with widened eyes as he stared in dismay at the sight of nothing but a single folded-up letter stored inside.

"No…no…no," David whispered while shaking his head in bewilderment. David was at death's door, but wouldn't enter until he found closure in life. So he began to read the letter as he lay bleeding atop his mother's skeletal remains.

Dear Sons,

Do you remember that day we all went hunting in Pyre Ridge? You were all stripling boys back then, but I saw your collective strength when that brown bear attacked us. Instead of firing your rifles, you boys instinctively climbed atop one another's shoulders and faced the bear with all your might. You boys intimidated that seven-foot brown bear enough to make him retreat back into the woods. This was the single most courageous act I have ever witnessed in my life, which brings me to the matter of your inheritance.

Your mother always praised you boys for setting your own paths in life instead of going into the family business. I know I've treated you boys harshly, but that was all based in the rejection that I felt from you boys choosing to be hunters. This is why I stored the strongbox in your mother's chest and furthermore why it contains no money. I hope you boys don't fret over my last will, and if you do, remember these words spoken by your mother "Cherish your brotherhood, for together, you five boys can accomplish anything."

Love,
Victor and Abigail

Upon reading the letter, David coughed up splotches of blood onto the white paper and then began to snicker. David's snickering then rose to a delirious cackle, which then slowly languished into an irrepressible deluge of lamentation. The murder of ravens that loomed above David fell abruptly silent as he stared up at them with sorrowful eyes. Sheer coldness began to engulf David at that moment, leaving him utterly petrified. Just before David breathed his last breath, his darkening sight bored witness to the murder of ravens' mordant stares ushering him to his death.

So ends the tale of the Brubaker clan.

*****

I closed the cover of the book with a profound sigh and then stared pensively for a few moments. I understood why my father urged me to read this book when I was just a stripling boy, for it was a grave cautionary tale of greed, deceit, and brutality within a family. It made me wonder how my life would have been if I had any brothers.

"Daddy, Mommy said she's finished working on your jacket," Audrey said, as she entered the master bedroom with Angie in hand.

"Ah, good. Your mother is always so quick and efficient with her tailoring," I remarked.

"What are you reading?" Audrey inquired in a zealous tone and then sat beside me upon the bed.

"This is a book my father urged me to read when I was a little older than you," I replied.

"Can I read it…I mean, may I read it?" Audrey inquired while curiously staring at the cover.

"I don't think so, princess," I replied and then placed the book inside the nightstand drawer.

"Why not?" Audrey inquired in a sulking tone.

"You're not quite old enough. Besides, you should follow your mother's curriculum," I replied.

"Your jacket is hanging on the door, dear," Heather said as I entered the kitchen. I then walked over to the door, grabbed my jacket off the hook, and displayed it in front of me with both hands. "There is enough wolf fur to cover the shoulders, uppers arms, and chest. Do you like it?" Heather inquired as she walked over from the kitchen and then stood behind me while pointing at the additions she made to the jacket.

"Masterful tailoring as always. This jacket will now be the covetous item for any hunter in the entire Fray," I replied with a smile.

"I'm glad. Well, try it on," Heather said with a warm smile. I then tried on the improved jacket while Heather stared back at me, closely examining the work she had done. Audrey and I then kissed with a snicker while she ran her pale, slender fingers through the thick, black wolf fur upon my chest.

"I have to get my rifle. I left it atop the sharpshooter's nest last night in my hasty pursuit of the black wolf," I said to Heather.

"I'll get it, dear. I don't want you to aggravate your ankle any further," Heather said as she walked towards the door.

"I told you before I'm not incapacitated," I said to Heather in a stern tone.

"All right, be careful. Dinner will be ready soon," Heather said with a sigh just before I exited the cabin.

The remaining crow carcasses where blanketed by the light snowfall from last night. My ankle twinged with each slow but steady step up the ladder of the sharpshooter's nest until I finally reached the top.

"Why were you spared?" I inquired with a smirk as a lone crow stood perched atop the fence. I then sat down on the stool with a sigh and examined the condition of my rifle. The lone crow stared at me like a curious baby with cold black eyes, not uttering a single noise. "You shouldn't be up here. Next time I see you, I can't promise I'll be so merciful," I said to the silent crow with a smirk and then tossed the ember-filled pot off the sharpshooter's nes, and slung the rifle around my back. The silent crow then took flight towards Vilkswood as I made my slow descent down the ladder of the sharpshooter's nest.

I then grabbed the axe from the workbench on the porch and began chopping firewood. I was just about to chop my seventh log when I noticed something that lingered my hand.

There was a set of tracks in the snow around the porch, but my eyes widened once I kneeled down and identified what animals had left them. The tracks were left by three wolves, which encircled the cabin. The unnerving restlessness that I felt in the dead silence of last night was justified, for wolves had been prowling around the cabin at night.

I entered the cabin to the savory aroma of Heather cooking dinner while Audrey slept curled up on the rocking chair with Angie in her arms. So I took off my jacket and hung it on the door and then quietly sat down on the sofa. My mind struggled with the decision of whether or not to tell Heather and Audrey that wolves were now prowling around the cabin at night. Like Heather, I didn't want Audrey to live in a constant state of perpetual fear, but I also didn't want her to be oblivious to the infringing threats that surround the cabin. Seeing their beautiful eyes transfixed with fear was a sight I couldn't bear. So I decided not to tell Heather and Audrey about the wolves.

"Dinner is ready," Heather proclaimed as she peeked her head out from the kitchen.

"Wake up, princess. Dinner is ready," I said to Audrey while gently shaking her shoulders.

"Honey, leave Angie on the rocking chair. You wouldn't want to stain her dress," Heather said to Audrey with a warm smile. Audrey then gently left Angie sitting upright on the rocking chair and sat down at the kitchen table with a yawn.

"What is this?" I inquired and then sat down across from Audrey at the kitchen table with a sigh.

"My variation on cottage pie. I substituted lamb with a mixture of venison and wolf rib meat. Hope you like it," Heather replied.

"My father used to make this," I said to Heather and then took a bite of the steaming cottage pie.

"How is it?" Heather inquired.

"Yours is much better than his," I remarked with a snicker.

"I'm sure he tried his best, dear," Heather said with a smile and then sat down next to Audrey.

"Audrey, honey, how is *Whispers Through the Willows* coming along?" Heather inquired and then took a steaming bite of cottage pie.

"I don't know," Audrey replied.

"I thought that was your favorite novel," Heather said to Audrey.

"I haven't read any further," Audrey said to Heather.

"Eat your dinner, princess," I said to Audrey as she picked away at the cottage pie on her plate.

"Do you need any help with certain words?" Heather inquired.

"No, I'm just afraid," Audrey replied in a somber tone. I then stared pensively at Audrey as she continued to pick away at the cottage pie.

"Why are you afraid, honey?" Heather inquired while caressing Audrey's hair.

"Maribel wants to follow Tobias into the woods, but what if something bad happens to her?" Audrey replied.

"I see, but don't you want to know how the story ends? Or else you will never know what happens to Maribel. That's called having closure, honey," Heather said to Audrey with a warm smile as she embraced her sulking shoulders.

"I'm done. Make sure she eats," I said to Heather in a stern tone while pointing at Audrey's full plate of cottage pie.

"All right, dear," Heather said as I stood up with a twinge. I then went to the great room, grabbed the whetstone off the mantle, and then sat down in the rocking chair with a sigh. Audrey then skipped into the great room and grabbed my tattered crimson scarf off the door hook.

"What are you up to, princess?" I inquired as I began to sharpen my knife against the whetstone.

"I'm going to sew up all the tears in your scarf that the wolf made," Audrey replied and then began searching through the cherry sewing box on the floor underneath the spinning wheel for a needle and thread. Audrey then sat down on the floor and neatly arranged her sewing supplies upon the coffee table. I then found myself sinking lower into the rocking chair with each stroke I made with the knife against the whetstone until somnolence slowly but surely overwhelmed me—

*****

I found myself bare-chested in the woods during a harsh blizzard, and all I could see amidst the white desolation was a trail of blood beginning at my feet. So I hastily followed the crimson trail in the snow while my bare skin began to freeze. I then spotted a dark jagged spire over yonder where the crimson trail had led me to. The dark jagged spire appeared to be a burned pine tree, but something was hanging eerily from one of its branches. My eyes widened in appeasement at the sight of my wolf fur jacket hanging from the blackened branch of the pine tree. I then snatched the jacket from the tree and hastily put it on. The blizzard then suddenly ceased its fury, and I felt warmth return to me, but the trail of blood appeared to be following me now. So I took off the jacket and displayed it in front of me with outstretched arms. My eyes then widened in dismay at the sound of vicious snarling and the sight of blood dripping from the bottom of the jacket. A black wolf's head suddenly burst out of the jacket and clenched my neck betwixt its jaws before I could even scream—

I jolted awake with a gasp, recoiling back into the rocking chair, while thrusting my knife forward.

"Vincent, what's wrong? Did you have another nightmare?" Heather inquired as she stared at me with distressful eyes.

"I need a drink of water," I replied in a raspy tone as I grasped my neck.

"All right, dear," Heather said in a distressed tone and then scampered to the kitchen.

"How long was I asleep for?" I inquired while rubbing my bleary eyes as Heather handed me a tankard of water.

"Around an hour, I didn't want to wake you though. You looked so peaceful," Heather said.

"Maybe you should have," I said to Heather in a somber tone and then took a long swig of water.

"Audrey sewed up all the tears in your scarf, see?" Heather said while displaying the scarf with outstretched arms.

I said nothing to Heather as I passed her by with a slight limp on my way to the master bedroom while taking a pensive glance at my jacket hanging on the door.

I wearily got undressed and then slipped beneath the quilt of the bed while Heather was tucking Audrey in.

"How is she?" I inquired as Heather entered the master bedroom.

"She asked me if she could read the novel you were reading this evening," Heather replied and then slowly slipped her black dress down to her ankles.

"That book is too brutal for her. I told her she's not old enough to read it," I said to Heather in a yawning tone as I sat upright in bed.

"I trust your judgment, but you know how inquisitive our Audrey can be," Heather said with a warm smile and then slipped on her cut-up white lace nightgown.

"Yes, I love and hate that about her," I said to Heather as she slipped beneath the quilt of the bed.

"Can you please tell me about the nightmare you just had?" Heather inquired.

"I don't know what you're talking about," I replied in a stern tone.

"I know something's troubling you. Nobody awakens from a sound sleep in the manner which you did unless something horrible is eating away at their subconscious," Heather said.

"I see now where Audrey gets her inquisitive nature from," I said to Heather.

"We used to confide our deepest thoughts to each other, but now I feel like you're drifting away from me. Please…let me in," Heather said in a somber tone as she gently placed her hand on my cheek and directed my pensive visage towards her gaze.

Whenever I locked eyes with Heather in times of distress, her sapphire gaze would never cease to beguile me. Heather had that effect on me ever since our fortuitous encounter in Vilkswood nine years ago. Her gaze would pierce through my armor and evoke a warm vulnerability within me, like wisteria vines growing throughout the cracks of a stone wall. All I wanted to do at that moment was unburden to Heather, but I couldn't. My damnable pride wouldn't let me.

"Good night," I said to Heather in a somber tone as I averted my gaze from hers and then extinguished the oil lamp on the nightstand. I then felt Heather's soft breath on the back of my neck as she embraced me closely.

"I love you," Heather whispered and then gently kissed the back of my neck with a faint whimper.

My heart could never bear that sound. So after a few moments, I slowly turned over to face Heather, but she had already fallen asleep with tear-stained cheeks. "I love you too…I wish I had your strength," I whispered as I gazed into Heather's still visage, hoping to find peace of mind.

*****

I awoke the next morning to a tapping on the windowpane. I then sat upright in bed and rubbed my bleary eyes to the sight of a crow perched upon the windowsill. I then went to the windowsill and stared closely at the crow through the frosted glass. It was the same crow—the silent crow—that I encountered yesterday atop the sharpshooter's nest.

"Oh, you again. Didn't I warn you to stay away from here?" I said to the silent crow with a smirk. The silent crow was a paradox to me, just like a gentle wolf. I thought it was impossible for one to exist in the wild. The only logical explanation that I could think of for the crow's silence was that it suffered an injury to its vocal cords. "What is it you want?" I inquired.

"Who are you talking to, dear?" Heather inquired as she entered the master bedroom wearing a frilled white chiffon dress.

"This crow on the windowsill. It seems to be following me," I replied while pointing at the windowsill.

"What crow?" Heather inquired as she stared at the windowsill.

I then averted my gaze from Heather back to the windowsill to see no crow. "Oh, it must have flown away," I replied.

"Why would a crow be following you?" Heather inquired with a snicker.

"Forget it," I replied with a sigh.

"Maybe you're a 'charmcrow,' and your allure contravenes both scarecrows in front of the cabin," Heather said in a facetious tone. An elfish smile then slowly grew on Heather's visage as I stared at her.

"How is Audrey doing?" I inquired in a yawning tone and then put on my black leather vest.

"She's begun reading *Whispers Through the Willows* again," Heather replied.

"That's good to hear," I said to Heather while buttoning up my vest.

"Breakfast is ready," Heather said, and then exited the master bedroom with a sigh. I then took a brief glance at the windowsill before following Heather into the kitchen.

"How does your ankle feel today, Daddy?" Audrey inquired.

"Better, it still twinges a little though," I replied and then sat down at the kitchen table across from Audrey.

"How is your hand healing, dear?" Heather inquired while pouring me a mug of coffee.

"It stings. It will most likely leave a scar," I replied while flexing my wolf-bitten right hand.

"That's a shame," Heather remarked as she gently caressed my right hand.

"Scars build character whether they're physical or emotional. I should really feel grateful she didn't bite my whole hand off," I said to Heather and then took a bite of toast.

"You have plenty of character, regardless of the scars," Heather said.

"All right, I'll leave you two to your lessons. I'll be in the sharpshooter's nest if anyone needs me," I proclaimed and then took my last sip of coffee.

"Be safe, dear," Heather said as I left the kitchen.

I then grabbed my wolf fur jacket from the door hook, shook it twice, and then put it on, along with the sewn-up crimson scarf. I then went to the master bedroom and took out one of my prized Gideon's Run rifles from my gun wardrobe, loaded it, and then exited the cabin.

*****

The silent gloom of the frigid morning was a dispiriting atmosphere that I was accustom to. A shrieking wind then suddenly blew in from the east as I began to slowly climb up the ladder of the sharpshooter's nest. The shrieking winds continued to blow sporadically as I sat down on the wooden stool atop the sharpshooter's nest and meticulously inspected the scope and barrel of my rifle. I then heard an unmistakable sound—the cacophonous cawing of crows—which hadn't caught my ear in a fortnight. A murder of crows suddenly flew in from the west like swift smoke upon the shrieking winds and floutingly perched atop each of the scarecrows in front of the cabin. I stared down pensively at the murder of six crows perched upon each point of the crosses that the scarecrows were attached to while they incessantly caw back up at me. "Away with you!" I shouted and then broke off an ice sickle from the roof of the sharpshooter's nest and threw it down at the murder of crows.

The murder of crows then frantically dispersed into the gray gloom of the morning sky and flew eastward back to Vilkswood. It was apparent now that the crows no longer feared the two scarecrows in front of the cabin, rendering them nothing more than a pair of rustically made macabre decorations. I then wanted to dismantle the scarecrows and salvage the garments that were used to make them, but it would most likely sadden Audrey to see her idea torn down. So for Audrey's sake, I proudly left the scarecrows where they stood in front of the cabin. I then began to feel an unnerving suspicion that all the animals of Vilkswood no longer feared the cabin. It was only a matter of time before it came to this. All the animals had now shifted their hunting patterns to survive the harshness of this winter. In their desperate attempts for survival, the crows had brought the wolves to the cabin. An unnerving silence fell again, just as it did two nights ago when the wolves were prowling around the cabin. Rays of sunlight then began to shine through the gloom of the morning sky, but with no such pleasant amber hues. The sky appeared to be bleeding, as slivers of crimson light cut through the gloom, like deep wounds upon skin.

"Vincent...Vincent," a voice called out to me upon the still winds.

"What is it, dear?" I inquired and then averted my gaze from the border of Vilkswood down to the porch of the cabin, but neither Heather nor Audrey where there. So I slung my rifle around my back and began to climb down the ladder of the sharpshooter's nest as the sky continued to slowly bleed in an ominous crimson hue.

"What is it? What do you need?" I inquired as I entered the cabin to the sight of Heather writing down lessons on the small chalkboard while Audrey studiously took heed.

"We don't need anything, dear," Heather replied without averting her gaze from the chalkboard to me.

"Then why did you call for me?" I inquired.

Heather then quickly turned away from the chalkboard to face me. "Nobody called for you. We're in the middle of a history lesson at the moment," Heather replied with a distressful stare while shaking her head. I then stared leerily at Heather as she began to timidly walk towards me.

"All right then," I proclaimed and then left the cabin just as Heather began to slowly reach out her hand towards me.

*****

Dead silence fell upon the border of Vilkswood once more. In all my thirty-two years living on the border of Vilkswood, I'd never seen the sky look so foreboding as it does now.

"Vincent...Vincent," the mysterious voice called out to me once more.

"Who's there?" I shouted and then aimed my rifle towards the border of Vilkswood. At that moment, I ignored the vow I made to Heather and Audrey to never set foot in Vilkswood ever again as I slowly walked towards the voice. I knew now this voice calling out to me was neither Heather nor Audrey being facetious. Was I losing my mind, or was there someone or something calling out to me from Vilkswood?

"Where are you?" I shouted as my hands began to shake, not from the cold but from the eerie atmosphere of Vilkswood encompassing me.

"Vincent, you will…" the voice called out to me once more in a low raspy tone and then drifted off.

I then heard bone-chilling screams slicing through the silence, like a knife across my skin. The screams were resonating from the west. These screams were unmistakable to my ears, for I've heard them once before from Heather and Audrey in my nightmare. I then began to run back to the cabin. The beating of my heart matched the pace of my footsteps as I ran the fifty yards back to the cabin. My sprained right ankle then twinged sharply, causing me to fall and hit my head on a snow-concealed log.

"No…no!" I shouted in a gasping tone as I jolted up onto my feet and continued running towards the cabin. The screams then fell silent, and to my dismay, I could now see the front door of the cabin was opened. "Heather… Audrey!" I shouted in a frightened tone.

I then burst through the front door of the cabin, and then time stood still again, just as it did nine years ago when Heather and I encountered the brown bear in Vilkswood. There are many sights in this cruel world that no man should ever witness, but none of them compare to the sheer horror that I laid eyes upon at that moment I entered the cabin.

My eyes widened, and I couldn't breathe at the sight of Heather and Audrey lying on the floor with three wolves atop their still bodies. "No!" I shouted in such a frightened tone as my heart wrenched. I then swiftly drew my two pistols from their holsters as the wolves abruptly stared at me with crimson-stained fangs. I then pulled the trigger of both my pistols, shooting two of the ashen gray wolfs square betwixt the eyes before they could evade my fire. I then pulled my rifle out on the third white wolf. Just as I was about to fire, the white wolf leaped towards me, passing through my body, and I clenched my chest as a frigid sensation froze me to the core. I fell to the floor gasping as I stared out the front door at the white wolf staring back at me with such malevolent amber eyes.

"Those eyes…I've seen you before…White Bane!" I shouted in a gasping tone. To my utter dismay, the fabled white wolf then vanished upon the wind in a flurry of snow. I then slammed the front door of the cabin shut and dropped to my knees in front of Heather and Audrey.

Heather and Audrey were covered in blood, their white lace dresses stained in crimson from severe neck wounds. I hastily unraveled my crimson scarf from my neck and cut it in half with my knife. I then firmly wrapped one half of the scarf around Heather's neck. Heather then raised her bloodied hand and pointed at Audrey.

"Princess, open your eyes ... please," I said to Audrey, as I wrapped the scarf firmly around her slender neck and held her tightly against my trembling chest. I then kissed Audrey's forehead as tears began to stream down my visage. I then gently rested Audrey's motionless body down on the floor beside Heather.

Heather then slowly reached out and took Audrey's hand. "I'm sorry...I shouldn't... have opened...the door," Heather said as her neck wounds gushed blood out her mouth, choking her every word.

"Shhhh, don't speak, honey," I said to Heather in a somber tone.

"I...love...you," Heather said with a warm smile as she placed her bloodied hand upon my cheek.

"Please don't leave me. I can't live without you," I said to Heather in a trembling tone as tears continued to stream down my visage onto her bloodied hand.

"Vincent, don't...be...afraid," Heather whispered.

I then kissed Heather's bloodied lips just before the light in her vibrant sapphire eyes extinguished.

CHAPTER 8

A Dark Path

When left alone to mourn, a fervid vengeance is born.

At 11:06 AM, the ground was frozen as I began to dig Heather and Audrey's' graves. All the ways I'd failed as a husband and father then struck my mind as I struck the ground with the shovel.

"This can't be happening." I spoke aloud in an incredulous tone as I finished digging both Heather and Audrey's' graves. I then dropped to my knees in front of the empty graves as tears streamed down my visage. "Wake up…wake up!" I shouted as I began to slap my tear-sodden cheeks repeatedly, hoping I was having another one of my vivid nightmares. I continued to slap myself for five minutes before I realized there would be no awakening from this nightmare.

I entered the cabin and lifted Audrey up into my arms off the bloodstained hardwood floor of the great room. I carried Audrey in a gentle manner to her grave as if she were sleeping in my arms. I then carried Heather in the same gentle manner to her grave. I wanted so desperately for Heather's arms to suddenly reach out and wrap around my neck as I carried her, but they just hung motionless, like a marionette whose strings have been cut.

I dropped down into each grave and then gently laid Heather and Audrey down upon the cold black earth. I then climbed out of the grave and stared down at Heather and Audrey with eyes frozen in disbelief yet pouring with sorrow. My only two reasons for living were now gone, taken from me by a monster not of this world. I dared not revert back to who I was before Heather and Audrey graced my life and gave purpose to my lowly existence. If I could no longer be with them in this world, then this world was no place for me anymore. It was settled then. After I'd given Heather and Audrey's' eulogy, I would end my suffering.

Tossing each shovelful of earth over Heather and Audrey was the most unbearably heart-wrenching task that I ever performed in my life. Knowing that with each shovelful of earth that I tossed over them, the less of them I would see until they would ultimately disappear. All the warmth left me at that moment, and I was now merely a shell of a man. My father and Heather both stared back at me with a warm smile just before they died. They both showed such grace and courage in life and in death. No man should ever have to bury a family member. My father had buried one; I now had buried three. I then took out the handkerchief that Heather and Audrey made for me to wipe the tears that continued to pour from my eyes, cleared my throat, and began to give Heather and Audrey's' eulogy. I began with my little princess Audrey first.

"My precious Audrey, even in the darkest of times, you never ceased to warm my heart and bring a smile to my face. You taught me an invaluable lesson when you were born—how to be a father. You had all the beautiful traits that I failed to possess at your age. My distress always seemed to disappear whenever I cradled you in my arms. Not a single moment had passed where I didn't feel eternally grateful that you were my daughter. Your ambition and intelligence were going to take you places in this world that I could only dream of. I wish more than anything that I could have watched you grow into a young woman and meet a man one day who only treats you like the princess that you truly are…I love you.

"My beloved Heather, you taught me how to love when all I knew was how to kill. Your gentle strength and compassion are what kept me sane during the most chaotic of times. I knew from the first moment I saw you on horseback in Vilkswood nine years ago that you would change my life forever. Your nurturing heart made me look forward to waking up every morning. You truly understood me better than anyone else could. You shattered the armor that was my stoic pride and replaced it with something far stronger. You weren't just my wife…you were also my best friend. My father never showed any vulnerability around me, but you taught me that being vulnerable is how we grow and become stronger. Whenever I felt unworthy of your love, you would always reassure me with such a beautiful stare. You gave me purpose in life far greater than myself when you gave birth to Audrey. No man could ask for a more loving wife and mother than you, my dear. You saved me in every possible way…I love you.

"I'm so sorry I've failed you both miserably. I don't deserve to walk this earth while you both rest beneath it. I truly am cursed to survive while everyone I've ever loved in this world dies before me. No more…no more misery… no more surviving." I spoke aloud in a somber tone and then wiped the tears from my eyes with the handkerchief once more.

I then entered the cabin and picked up my rifle off the bloodstained hardwood floor of the great room. I quickly but thoroughly inspected my rifle to make sure it wouldn't misfire when I pulled the trigger. I then took the black iron fire poker from the fireplace and sat down on the sofa. My hands were trembling uncontrollably as I braced the butt of the rifle against the armrest on the far end of the sofa. So then I stared despondently into the black void that was the barrel of the rifle. The heavy beating of my heart was all I could hear at that moment as I touched the trigger of the rifle with the hook end of the fire poker. I could see out of the corner of my eye one of the dead wolves staring back at me. Even in death, the wolves tormented me. *Do all the wolves die with their eyes open?* I then spotted Audrey's doll, Angie, underneath the coffee table. Not a drop of crimson was on the pristine white doll.

"No…no!" I spoke aloud in a stern tone and pained grimace while I fervidly locked eyes with the dead wolf. I then tossed the rifle aside and took a profound sigh with my head in my trembling, bloodstained hands. There was something I needed to do before I could end my misery. I then left the cabin and walked out to the border of Vilkswood. "I know you're out there…you're always out there. You were there when I was bedridden, leering at me through the window. You were there in the corridor mirror of the Black Hearth Lodge, leering at me once more. You were even there in my nightmare. You fucking monster, you've taken everything from me! Mark my words…I will not rest until I have your head mounted on my wall. I will not rest until your blood stains my hands. I will not rest until I hear your sweet cries of agony resonate in my ear. I will not rest until you lie eternally still…and I will not rest until I watch the light extinguish from your amber eyes!" I shouted in a venomous tone while tears continued to pour from my eyes.

*****

One week had passed since I buried Heather and Audrey. I finished chiseling each of their inscriptions upon stone tablets, which served as the headstones for their graves, just as I did with my father. I also managed to skin and tan the hide of the two ashen-gray wolves that killed Heather and Audrey. I had three wolf furs in my possession now. It wouldn't even take a hunter to know how very valuable wolf fur is throughout the Fray, yet I would trade it all in a heartbeat for just one more moment with Heather and Audrey.

I spent what seemed like hours this evening scrubbing the area on the hardwood floor where Heather and Audrey died. Tried as I may, but the blood stained the hardwood floor too deeply and was now a permanent, grim reminder. So I reluctantly placed one of the ashen-gray wolf furs down upon the bloodstained hardwood floor. Every evening, I would sit down in the fireside rocking chair pensively sharpening my knife as I ominously stared at that wolf rug that was covering up the bloodstains on the hardwood floor where Heather and Audrey died. One of the fucking wolves that were responsible for killing Heather and Audrey was now covering up their bloodstains on my hardwood floor! I should have thrown the two wolf furs into the fireplace, but it killed me to stare at that bloodstain on the hardwood floor every day. I could also sell the two wolf furs to a number of vendors in Bleakton's Market Square for a hefty sum of money.

I saved the heads of the two wolves that killed Heather and Audrey and then masked each of them over each of the scarecrow's heads in front of the cabin. This was my way of sending a clear and grim warning to the wolves; albeit, my warnings to the wolves were what led to Heather and Audrey's' untimely death, but now I had nothing left to lose anymore. I now knew that the wolves feared me about as much as they feared a rabbit. They attacked Heather and Audrey in the morning, which was unheard of for wolves. Judging by their struggle, Heather and Audrey tried to run to the storage closet just as I instructed them to, but the wolves swiftly cut them off. For such beautiful and delicate creatures as Heather and Audrey to die in such a brutal manner pained my heart beyond measure.

At 7:05 AM, I awoke with a cough, and I sat upright in bed. The sweet, lilac scent of Heather's hair still lingered on her side of the bed. I then noticed something quite perplexing as I was getting dressed in front of the cheval mirror in the master bedroom. Some beard and the sides of my hair had started to turn white! I recalled that wretch in Bleakton who goes by the name of Mordrid had similar marks appear on him, just a couple of days after encountering White Bane. The cabin had never felt so empty to me now. Every morning I woke up without Heather's braided ponytail gracing my visage was a morning I couldn't find joy in. Every morning I walked into the kitchen without Audrey giving me a tight waist-high embrace was a morning that felt dark and surreal. It was almost as if the happiness I lived with Heather and Audrey was just a dream that I now had awakened from. There wasn't a single crow to be heard on this bleak and frigid morning as I sipped my coffee at the kitchen table. Perhaps the wolf's heads masked over the scarecrows in front of the cabin were really proving effective. I took a profound sigh as I rubbed my bleary eyes.

"I should've buried you with Audrey…I guess you're stuck with me now." I spoke aloud in a somber tone while holding Angie. I really should be grateful for Heather's and Audrey's remnants, for I need them now more than ever. In no more than a month, we were going to move to Bleakton to begin our new lives. "It's not fair," I whispered while tightly clenching Angie. Tears then began to stream down my pain-grimaced visage. I then finished drinking my coffee, tucked Angie into the breast pocket of my jacket, and then left the cabin.

The front porch thermometer read twenty-two degrees Fahrenheit. I brought my leather satchel full of provisions and my two loaded pistols with me for my reconnaissance in Vilkswood. The wolves had flanked me on that morning they killed Heather and Audrey. I was too blind to notice it. So I meticulously searched around the cabin for wolf tracks in the snow, and lo and behold, I found them! Judging by the wolves' footprints, they were waiting for a signal. They then simultaneously bolted through the front door and attacked Heather and Audrey. There was no third set of wolf footprints made in the snow. "White Bane," I whispered. When he attacked me that morning, he phased through me, like the most frigid winter winds. I could feel the very core of my body instantly freezing as it passed through me. With these supernatural powers he possesses, it was no wonder why he left no tracks in the snow.

"I may not be able to track you directly, but I can sure as hell track your betas, and they will lead me to you." I spoke aloud with a sneer.

At 10:25 AM, the clouds shone in a silvery hue but nonetheless bleak as I continued to track the footprints of the two beta wolves that would ultimately lead me to White Bane. To my discouragement, it began to snow. This meant that the wolf tracks would be covered up soon by a blanket of new fallen snow. I had to track the wolves' footprints as far as I could before that happened lest the trail would go cold and I'm left by their will. The wolves' footprints were becoming more and more difficult to track as they weaved their way through pine groves, ravines, and furrows. I was freezing though and had to warm up for ten minutes lest I get frostbite. My extremities were already beginning to sharply tingle. So I found a spot beside a giant boulder and then proceeded to start a fire with the provision in my satchel.

I took a bite of venison jerky, which I stored in the pocket of my jacket while the fire began to warm me up. The sheer face of the giant boulder that was directly behind me reflected the heat from the fire quite effectively, just as I hoped it would, and I became warm in a few short moments. Suddenly, a crow landed on a log just beside me while I was boiling water in a small pot to make tea.

"Go away!" I shouted while waving my hand aggressively at the crow, but the crow did not fly away or even caw. "Oh, it's you again. You know you shouldn't follow me. Wolves eat crows," I said to the silent crow in a stern tone while my tea steeped. The silent crow then stared back at me with curious, mordant eyes while I slowly sipped my tea. "What a strange bird you are," I remarked and then tossed a piece of venison jerky at the silent crow's feet. The silent crow stared at the venison jerky but quickly averted its crooked gaze back to me. "You don't like that?" I inquired in an incredulous tone. I then went searching through my satchel for food that the silent crow would eat, but as I turned back around, the silent crow was gone. I then examined the snow-covered log beside me that the silent crow was standing on for footprints, but there were none! "Strange indeed." I spoke aloud.

Now wasn't the time to get sidetracked by the transient, silent crow, for I had to track the wolves' footprints to their source before the snowfall covered them up completely. So I built up my fire with three pieces of firewood from my satchel instead of putting it out and then continued to track the wolves' footprints. The wolves' footprints were gradually diminishing as I tracked them through crag and creek. It was a dead end. I searched the perimeter of the last visible wolf footprints to see if they picked up, but they didn't continue on any further. The trail was cold. Thus the wolves' point of origin, perhaps White Bane's point of origin, was undiscoverable even to an experienced hunter such as me. I then saw it just over yonder, just as dark and foreboding as I remembered it to be twenty years ago.

*****

"Not there. We don't ever hunt there," my father said in a stern tone.

"Why not?" I inquired in a sulking tone while I aimed my rifle towards the large black mouth of the cave.

"Get over here now!" my father shouted. I then walked over to my father with my head hung low. "Vincent, you do as I say, understood?" my father reprimanded in a stern tone while placing his hand on my shoulder.

"Yes, Dad," I replied in a timid tone. "Dad, there's no beast in Vilkswood that can defeat the two of us hunters together," I proclaimed.

"Don't be foolhardy, son. Foolhardy people have spurs of bravery, which lead to a quick demise," my father said while we slowly walked through the pine groves.

"If a bear lives in that cave, then you aim for the heart, and I can aim for the head," I said to my father in a zealous tone.

"No, son. What dwells in that cave is more dangerous—far, far more dangerous—than any bear or even wolf, and you must respect it," my father said in a stern tone.

*****

"*Crimson Cave*," I whispered with widened eyes while crouching down and grabbing both my pistols. Of course, I must have been subconsciously avoiding this foreboding cave all these many years because of the fear my father instilled in me on that day we were hunting. According to my father, Crimson Cave got its name from the abundance of garnet found in the rocks of the cave, which resemble crimson veins. Word caught ear of the cave's riches by a group of miners and was soon excavated by their sledgehammers, pickaxes, and shovels. The miner's excavation for garnet was a horrible failure though, for eight miners entered Crimson Cave that day, but only three made it out alive, or so my father told me.

So I sat and waited, patiently biding my time in the frigid cold with my eyes fixed upon the mouth of Crimson Cave. An hour had passed, yet I still didn't see any wolves emerge or enter the ominous cave. My extremities were beginning to go numb again, but I couldn't very well build a fire within this close proximity to the cave lest the wolves detect my presence. *Is Crimson Cave just a wolves' den, or is it the lair of White Bane, which my father warned me of twenty years ago, or perhaps even both?* All of these thoughts raced through my mind as the mouth of Crimson Cave beckoned me with such a foreboding allure. I was ill-prepared. If

I were to die this afternoon, then I highly doubt I would be able to take White Bane with me. My father was right about what he said to me on that day about foolhardy men. My foolhardiness was what led to Heather's and Audrey's deaths after all. I went off chasing a voice in Vilkswood that may have well been in my head when I should have been in the cabin protecting Heather and Audrey. So I followed the rising smoke back to my campsite beside the giant boulder to warm up before I went back to the cabin. I used to take solace when returning back to the cabin from a hunt or reconnaissance mission. Just knowing that Heather and Audrey were there waiting for me would instantly warm my heart. My misery followed me everywhere, but the cabin didn't feel like home to me anymore, not in the absence of Heather and Audrey. Such a devastating realization then clenched at my heart, just as I was about to enter the cabin. I had nothing and nobody to return to.

At 1:06 PM, I entered the cabin with a profound sigh. No sound but the crackle from the three fireplaces resonated throughout the cabin. No joy or love or laughter was to ever be heard again in this cabin. I took Angie out of the breast pocket of my jacket and then sat her down on the sofa in the great room. I then took the ice cellar key off the hook on the front door and left the cabin. I opened the ice cellar and then started chopping off a venison shank from the mass of frozen meat with my axe. I then entered the cabin and proceeded to cook what I have cooked hundreds of times, a simple but hearty hunter's stew. I filled the black cast-iron pot halfway up with water from the reservoir and then grabbed what vegetables that were left and that weren't molded. I hung the pot of water over the great room fireplace to boil, which was where I used to cook most of my meals before I met Heather. I then began chopping up the venison shank into bite-sized chunks with a cleaver. I couldn't take the silence of the cabin as I prepared the stew. I needed loving eyes watching me even if they weren't real. So I grabbed Angie from the sofa and placed her facing me on the kitchen counter while I prepared the stew. I had sparse variety of vegetables consisting of potatoes, carrots, celery, and wild onion to make the stew, but those ingredients were more than I had had in the past, so I was grateful nonetheless. The water in the pot was beginning to boil while I was nearly finished chopping up all the vegetables. I then seasoned the meat and vegetables with salt and pepper and then poured it all into the boiling pot above the great room fireplace. I moved the pot away from the center of the flames of the fire so the stew would simmer. This would give me time to contemplate my next move regarding White Bane.

At 3:24 PM, I made a pot of coffee while the stew continued to slowly simmer. I poured roughly a cup of flour into the pot to thicken the stew and then stirred it. I then sat down at the kitchen table with a mug full of bitter, strong coffee in one hand and Angie in the other. I knew what I witnessed on that day Heather and Audrey died. The powers that White Bane possesses were beyond man. *How can I possibly kill such a beast?* On that day that I defended Heather from the brown bear, I was frightened but fully aware and prepared for the danger that stood before me. White Bane, however, invoked such a confounding dread within me, the likes of which I'd never felt before in my life. I knew many would tell me that hunting the fabled beast that had instilled fear in the hearts of men all throughout the Fray is a suicidal undertaking. That may very well be the outcome, but I swore to avenge Heather and Audrey if it were the last thing I do.

All the ingredients of the stew had melded together quite nicely. So I lifted up the pot from the great room fireplace and then placed it on the kitchen table. I then seasoned the stew with a handful of chopped wild onions before ladling the thick, steaming stew into a bowl. I ate ravenously, and within a few moments, I was already ladling a second bowl of stew. All I could think about while I ate the stew was how much more savory and heartwarming it would have been if Heather cooked it. I then ripped off a piece of honey wheat bread from the loaf in the pantry and took a quick bite out of it. With the void of Heather and Audrey at the kitchen table, I would have to settle for Angie. That doll that I propped upright so she would be sitting down at the table staring at me was in a way the incarnation of Heather and Audrey. Heather spared a good portion of her braided ponytail and white lace nightgown in order to create the doll Angie, which I now stare longingly at from across the kitchen table. I used to find solace in silence before I met Heather, but now every moment that passes without hearing her dulcet voice was slowly driving me mad. I finished eating my third bowl of stew and then placed the lid over the top of the pot. I then grabbed Angie from the kitchen table and began to pace back and forth in front of the great room fireplace. The creaking of the hardwood floor echoed in my mind as my pacing nervously quickened. I will discover White Bane's weakness. Everyone has a weakness, and I refuse to believe that White Bane is unassailable. It's only a matter of delving into the mind of your enemy and seeing life from their perspective. My father always told me that the mind is the deadliest weapon a hunter can possess, though I fear now that my mind had begun to fray.

I stored the remainder of the stew in the ice cellar so that it would freeze, thus preserving it. I had roughly about ten pounds of venison and five pounds of pork left in the ice cellar. I wouldn't need to hunt for food for at least another fortnight. I stoked the flames of the fireplace in Audrey's room. Even though this room would be vacant forevermore, I still kept the fire burning. The glow of the fireplace made me believe Audrey could still be in here, just sleeping peacefully in her bed. I would now cling to any shred of solace I could find, whether it be from a doll or a fire's warm glow. I then sat down in the fireside rocking chair of the great room and began to sharpen my knife with the whetstone.

The first thaw of spring would arrive in no longer than a month. I could then hunt White Bane more comprehensively, without the frigid cold repressing the full range of my abilities. Mordrid was right when he told me I had no idea what hunts me, but why did Heather and Audrey have to suffer such brutal deaths while my life was spared? If White

Bane was hunting me, as I was hunting him, then he knew exactly where to find me. I, on the other hand, was still uncertain where White Bane resides. This gave White Bane a distinct advantage over me, but what hunter would be bold enough to attack his prey on their home territory?

My father had me to keep him company in the wake of my mother's death. It must have been so difficult for him to raise me all by himself without a mother around. The only responsibility I was left with now was the vow I made to Heather and Audrey. I sat down on Audrey's bed and then picked up a book from her nightstand. The book was *Whispers Through the Willows.*

"She never got to finish it." I spoke aloud in a somber tone. Judging by the black ribbon bookmark, Audrey had only twelve pages left of *Whispers Through the Willows*. I would miss her talking about this book when we were all eating dinner at the kitchen table. The way her amber eyes lit up and the tone of her voice filled with zealous joy never ceased to uplift my spirits. All those memories of happiness were now haunting me.

At 7:52 PM, I knew in dark times such as these, the bottle was the last place a man should ever turn to, yet I still craved a drink so desperately. The only liquor that was left in the cabin was a small amber bottle of gin used to treat wounds from becoming infected. I couldn't resist the urge any longer, so I opened the door to the storage closet and then grabbed the medical kit off the dusty top shelf. I then sat down in the fireside armchair of the master bedroom with the bottle of gin in one hand and Angie in the other. The bottle of gin was half empty, but that was more than enough to numb my senses from this heart-wrenching pain. My visage grimaced in disgust immediately after taking a sip from the bottle of gin. The gin meant for treating wounds must have been nearly twenty years old by this point, and it sure tasted like it. Each sip I took of the extremely potent gin felt like a blow to the head and a tepid fire all at once. Now I understood how my father coped with the death of my mother. All those many nights I witnessed him in the great room with a bottle of whiskey betwixt his legs were his moments of grieving. I'd never felt as alone in my entire life as I did right now. I began to drink more frequently as those happy memories of Heather and Audrey raced through my fragile mind. I was bereft of happiness; that emotion seemed so unattainable to me now. I finished drinking the gin with one last swig and then vehemently threw the empty amber bottle into the fireplace. The flames of the fireplace then intensified in a short burst as the bottle shattered into pieces. I then collapsed upon the bed of the master bedroom with Angie in hand, just before everything faded to darkness.

*****

At 6:15 AM, I awoke with a heaving cough to a sharp thudding noise, which seemed to resonate from just outside the cabin. So I entered the kitchen in a weary daze to get a drink of water. After I slaked my besotted thirst, I then quickly examined my pistol. I then put on my jacket and exited the cabin to investigate the thudding noise, which continued at a slow pace. There was no mistaking that noise now; somebody was digging. My eyes then widened with rage at the sight of a gangly man digging up one of the graves of my family.

"Drop the shovel and slowly turn around, or I'll put a bullet in the back of your head… now!" I said to the grave robber in a venomous tone while slowly walking towards him. The grave robber complied with my demands and dropped the shovel and slowly turned around to face me. The grave robber had a dismal visage with a jagged scar running down his neck. "Hands up!" I shouted. I then noticed that the grave that the grave robber was digging up was Heather's grave. The grave robber just eerily stared back at me while my pistol-wielding hand began to shake nervously. "I fucking despise grave robbers. So what was your reasoning for choosing my wife's grave among the others?" I inquired.

"Women are buried with jewelry in this day and age. It's as simple as that," the grave robber replied in a contemptuous tone and smirk. Such a fervid rage was swelling up within me at that moment, but I had to stay focused.

The left side of my face then began to twitch with rage as I stared daggers at the grave robber. I wanted to inflict so much pain upon him for desecrating Heather's grave.

"Vincent," a voice suddenly called out to me.

"That voice—" I spoke aloud in dismay while quickly turning my gaze from the grave robber to Vilkswood. I made a grave mistake at that moment, for then I could see out of the corner of my left eye the grave robber drawing his pistol. I then instinctively dove sideways as the grave robber and I fired our pistols simultaneously. I hit him, and he hit me as we both recoiled. The bullet had grazed my right shoulder. I then stood up with a hissing groan while clenching my right shoulder with a painful grimace. I then grabbed the shovel off the ground and stood over the grave robber. I had shot him in the left ribcage, about one inch from his heart, judging by how he was clenching his chest in agony.

"Did you come here alone? Who else knows you're here?" I inquired in a distressed tone as I kneeled down and grabbed the grave robber by the collar of his weathered black jacket. The grave robber only responded back to me in sporadic blood-laden coughs for a few moments and then fell silent. I'd killed many different animals in my life, but on this dreary morning was the first time I ever killed a man.

I found nothing as I frantically searched the pockets of the grave robber's jacket and pants, nothing that would identify him or inform me where he's from. It was almost as if the grave robber's only purpose on earth was to die by my hand. In all honesty, I felt more remorse from killing a rabbit than I did from killing the grave robber. The grave robber did have that distinguishing jagged scar running down his neck, so he could be identified easily if questions arose. I had to dispose of the grave robber's body lest any of his family or constables end up at my doorstep. So I holstered the grave robber's pistol and then started dragging his body by the collar. I dragged the grave robber's body roughly a hundred feet into Vilkswood before stopping. I then sat down on a rock beside the grave robber's body with a profound sigh. I then took out the grave robber's pistol and placed it in his limp hand.

"The wolves will devour any trace of you—that I'm sure of." I spoke aloud in a venomous tone and then followed the grave robber's trail of crimson back to the cabin. I took nothing but the shovel from the grave robber. Even though the act of robbing the dead body of a grave robber seemed just, it was still far beneath me. Besides, I had to make it look like the grave robber was killed by wolves while hunting in Vilkswood. I knew my father would have acted the same way I did towards the grave robber, only with no hesitation.

My right shoulder was burning with pain, as I reburied Heather's half-excavated grave with a couple shovelfuls of dirt. I entered the cabin and then immediately went to the storage closet and grabbed the medical kit off the dusty top shelf. "Of course," I remarked with a sigh while shaking my head at the sight of the empty compartment in the first-aid kit where the bottle of potent gin would have been. I now had two options left to treat my shoulder gash, but both of them would be very painful. It would be difficult, long, and painful with one hand, but I could stitch up the gash on my shoulder. I remember once stitching up a wound on my father's shoulder when I was a stripling boy. Or I could perform the quick but excruciating method of treating my shoulder gash by cauterization.

Seeing as how I only had one hand to work with, I chose to cauterize the gash on my shoulder, but with great reluctance. So I took off my shirt, grabbed the black iron fire poker from beside the great room fireplace, and then stuck it into the flames. My shoulder gash was dripping blood all over the bear skin rug, as the tip of the black fire poker began to glow rose. This would be a morning of terrible firsts for me—the first time I killed a man and the first time I had to cauterize my wound. I took a piece of thick leather out of the cloth box beside the spinning wheel, rolled it up, and then stuck it in my mouth for me to bite down on for the excruciating pain that was imminent. The pace of my breathing then began to quicken nervously as I held the glowing fire poker closer to the gash on my shoulder. No longer than five seconds would I have to hold the glowing fire poker against the gash on my shoulder, but those five seconds felt like a lifetime. I couldn't stall any longer, for the fire poker was cooling off. So in one motion, I pressed the glowing poker against the bleeding gash on my shoulder. *One thousand one,* I let out a muffled scream and bit down hard on the leather in my mouth from the searing pain. *One thousand two,* sizzling and smoke began to emanate from the gash on my shoulder, as the glowing poker burned my flesh. *One thousand three,* I continued screaming for the likes of which I'd never screamed from physical pain, as tears streamed down my pain-grimaced visage. *One thousand four,* my entire right arm was now beginning to feel numb as I clenched the edge of the coffee table. *One thousand five,* I removed the glowing fire poker from against my shoulder and then aggressively threw it into the kitchen just before everything faded to darkness.

*****

I awoke on the bear skin rug. The excruciating pain from the cauterization had caused me to faint. Hissing groans were all I could muster as I sat upright with some strands of bear fur sticking to my cauterized shoulder. Even the slightest motion from my right arm would exacerbate the pain. I stood up from the floor and then grabbed a sponge from the counter in the kitchen. I then soaked the sponge in the water reservoir and began to gently wash away all the dried blood from the perimeter of my cauterized gash. After padding my shoulder dry, I then went to the medical kit on the coffee table in the great room and took out a roll of gauze. I had performed the cauterization well, for the gash on my shoulder was black and burned to a seal. I then began wrapping the gauze around my shoulder, which was now throbbing in pain. I thought about Heather as I was dressing my cauterized shoulder gash. If Heather were here now, she would dress my wound in such a gentle way that I would feel no pain for a brief moment. Heather would always stare at me with those soothing sapphire eyes and smile warmly no matter how severe my wound was. *How I long for her healer's touch, for now I'm left with nothing but my own rough and scarred hands to treat me.* I tied off the gauze around my shoulder and then sat down on the sofa next to Angie.

"Where do we go from here, Angie?" I inquired in a somber tone while staring down at the doll. "We can't live here anymore…I can't live here anymore." I spoke aloud while holding Angie. The cabin was no longer a home for me. Although I was positive the wolves would devour the grave robber's corpse, I still risk being arrested by constables or being killed by a vengeful relative of the grave robber with every passing moment I reside here in the cabin. "I can't allow anyone to imprison or kill me before I kill White Bane," I solemnly vowed. It was finally time to embark from here, for nothing and no one held me to this cabin any longer.

Where would I go? Of course, Bleakton was the first town that came to mind, the town where Heather wanted to live come the first thaw of spring, but I wanted to remain anonymous, and too many hunters and townsfolk know of me in that town. "Thianor… yes, Thianor." I spoke aloud as I stood up from the sofa with Angie in hand. I'd only visited Thianor once when I was a stripling boy. I was with my father, and we were selling furs to an upscale boutique. That must have been nearly fifteen years ago. I couldn't imagine how that bard's town must have changed since then. "How about it, Angie? Shall we go to Thianor?" I inquired with a smirk as I stared at Angie. "I'll take your silence as a yes. Thianor it is then." I spoke aloud in a stern tone.

The hike to Thianor would take four days, ten hours if I cut through Vilkswood, which would be the path I take. So I began to load my satchel with the essential provisions first. I stored one loaf of honey wheat bread, a hatchet, two pounds of venison jerky, a coffeepot, twenty-five feet of rope, a whetstone, two phials of antibiotics, a small pot, a small lantern, a tin of coffee, a box of matches, all the money left in the strongbox (which was $1,608), two ashen-gray wolf furs, and three changes of clothes into the satchel, which was now nearly bursting at the seams. I then opened my gun wardrobe and stared contemplatively. After a few moments, I decided to take my father's rifle, one of my prized Gideon's Run rifles, my two pistols, and all the gunpowder and ammunition for each respective gun along with me. I then randomly grabbed a book from the shelf of books above the bed. The title of the black leather-bound book read *A Dark Path* by Valmont Lesieur, in crimson letters. "How appropriate." I spoke aloud in a somber tone and then stored the novel in my satchel with the rest of the provisions. I then went to the great room and put on my wolf fur jacket. "I can't forget you now, can I?" I spoke aloud and then grabbed Angie and tucked her into the breast pocket of my jacket with only her head peeking out. I then draped the two wolf furs and slung the two rifles over my back. I'd lived in this cabin my entire life, and now I didn't know when or if I'd even return. So I took one last pensive gaze into every memory-laden room. "Farwell." I spoke aloud in a somber tone and then exited the cabin with a profound sigh.

At 9:55 AM, I had reached the spot where I left the grave robber's body, but nothing but bloodstained snow remained. The wolves had already devoured him, just as I predicted. I was already beginning to breathe heavily from carrying the thirty pounds of provisions on my back, so I slowed down my pace. My jacket and the two wolf furs draped over my back were keeping me very warm despite the frigid winds blowing in from the west. It was unfortunate for me that the thoroughfare known as *Barden Pass* only went from Thianor to Shors End. I would soon be passing by the ominous Crimson Cave, so I had to remain vigilant.

The shrieking winds emanating from the mouth of Crimson Cave beckoned me once again, but I continued to walk until the cave was out of sight but not out of mind. I couldn't get sidetracked now on my hike to Thianor, or I would have to camp overnight in Vilkswood. There were forces of man, nature, and the supernatural that could very well be hunting me at this very moment, which was why I must make haste to Thianor. I took a scrap of venison jerky out of my satchel and quickly bit into it. I'd need my strength if I were to traverse the crags. Each snow-covered rock I cautiously stepped on was a potential ankle breaker, and my right ankle still slightly twinged from when I sprained it falling down the sharpshooter's nest a month ago. I then spotted a dead standing birch tree while I was crossing a frozen creek that flowed into the Murk River. This was fortuitous for birch bark makes for great tinder, because of all the oils within it. I then began scraping strips of bark from off the birch tree with my knife and then stored them in my satchel. I could afford to take my first rest now, so I set down my satchel and guns against a log and then began collecting wood to build a much-desired fire.

At 12:45 PM, the birch bark had proved to be very efficient, for I couldn't recall the last time I started a fire so quickly. I then took out the coffeepot from my satchel and began to brew a quick cup of coffee. I spotted a red-tailed hawk perched on a branch just over yonder. A murder of crows kept persistently dive-bombing upon the hawk. It was common knowledge throughout the Fray that wolves hold dominion over Vilkswood, but I often considered crows to be the true rulers. Crows' minds were so deceptively intelligent in a way which I hadn't witnessed from any other animal. I was making good time, but I could only afford to stop and rest just once more before I would arrive at Thianor. I poured the quick-brewed coffee into a tin cup and then cut a slice of bread. There was a time when I used to love Vilkswood. Back when I was a stripling boy, everything about the woods beguiled me. Now Vilkswood just loomed over me like a shadow. There was no wonderment left, only survival mentality. I remember my father told me that the true measure of a man could be tested the most during times of great loneliness. Only in those times of great loneliness did I feel truly broken both body and mind. I then took one last bite of bread and sip of bitter coffee, before I put out the fire, loaded my satchel, and continued on my hike east to Thianor.

My cauterized shoulder was throbbing in pain, and by this moment, I was most likely bleeding through the gauze my shoulder was wrapped in. I then noticed something most perplexing as I took a long swig of water from my canteen. My heart raced and eyes widened at the sight of a crimson handprint upon a white birch tree.

"It can't be," I whispered and then kneeled down to search for footprints in the snow, but there were none. I watched him die; there was no way the grave robber could still be alive and crawling throughout Vilkswood! I was then able to confirm upon closer examination that the bloody handprint was actually a paw print left by a wolf. I felt like I was beginning to go mad, for my mind was laden with paranoia. My right ankle twinged as I climbed down an outcropping of boulders into the gorge that lay betwixt Vilksridge. This gorge was very dangerous to traverse in the winter even for the most experienced hunter. I treaded slow but steady over each rock that was scattered before me, like a fawn learning how to walk. Despite the six layers of clothing I wore, I could feel my extremities beginning to go numb. I needed to take a rest and start a fire soon, lest I succumb to frostbite. I then heard a soft rustling coming from a thicket just over yonder. A fox then suddenly burst out of the thicket and swiftly ran past me. I then quickly drew my pistol and took aim at the fox. "No need." I spoke aloud and then holstered my pistol. I had plenty of food for the trip to Thianor, and I dared not draw attention to myself by firing any of my guns.

The jagged gorge then finally began to diminish gradually into a flat patch of dense spruce trees. Hiking over this level terrain was pleasant compared to the perils of the gorge but also brought about different dangers. These were ideal grounds for predators. Nevertheless, among these spruce trees was where I would stop to take my final rest.

At 5:57 PM, the twilight hour was upon me as I sat fireside holding my tin cup of bitter coffee. I had to reach Thianor before nightfall, lest I freeze to death, but my body was in no such haste to depart from the comfort and warmth of the fire. A new life awaited me in Thianor, if I could even call it a life. I took out Angie from the breast pocket of my jacket and touched my nose against the top of her head. Angie's hair still smelled of lilacs; she was created from Heather's hair after all. This scent brought me back to lying in bed with Heather. It was incredible how just a mere scent could evoke so many memories and emotions within me. I then tucked Angie back into my jacket with a somber visage. I put some more wood onto the fire and then took a bite of bread as amber hues tinted the sullen sky. I couldn't rest fireside any longer, for it was already getting dark. Due to nightfall's impendence, I took out the small lantern from my satchel. I then lit the lantern, put out the fire, and continued on my hike east to Thianor.

I was nearly there, only about two more miles before I would arrive at Thianor. I kept periodically checking my compass to make sure I was still hiking east, for nightfall was now fully upon me, and I didn't want to be hiking in circles in the dark. I was already feeling the frigid cold no more than a few minutes from departing the fire. So I took one of the wolf furs, which was draped over my back, and wrapped it around my face. The wolf fur resembled a lengthy gray beard as it covered my cold, grimaced face and ended at my knees. Audrey would probably laugh in such a sweet tone if she saw what I looked like now. I wondered if the townsfolk of Thianor would be as kind to me as I remembered them to be, but that was over a decade ago. The bards of Thianor have always had a harmonious; some would say even mutualistic relationship with the hunters of Bleakton—a relationship I hoped has been preserved over the years.

At 7:50 PM, I was freezing, and I needed shelter, but I could sense how close I was to Thianor. I continued steadily on my hike, which now took me uphill through a patch of undergrove. I then halted my pace as two glowing lights in the distance became clear to my bleary eyes. "I made it." I spoke aloud with a smile and weary tone. I was sure of it now as I crossed the eastern border of Vilkswood. I had finally arrived at Thianor! I now stood before the ornate main gates, which greeted me with two lit lampposts and a sign reading, "Welcome to the Town of Thianor," in elegant bronze lettering. My new life was now underway.

CHAPTER 9

Wolf Among Doves

Immersed in art, in a town apart.

"Excuse me, sir. Where in this town could I find lodgings for the night?" I inquired while removing the wolf fur from around my face and draping it over my back.

"Follow the main thoroughfare straight until you see the *Rosewood Inn*. There's a large sign of a white dove holding a rose hanging above the entrance," the constable replied while pointing in the direction of the inn.

"Thank you," I said to the constable and then continued to walk down the main thoroughfare. Mellifluous melodies of a violin being played and saccharine scents of roses awoke my weary senses as I passed by various stores. There were baskets of roses outside of nearly every storefront window along with bands of minstrels performing on the corner of the streets. Even the horse-drawn carriages were adorned with roses. Thianor was already a sight to behold for me. Its elegantly adorned streets displayed a stark comparison to the rough and raw streets of Bleakton. I was beguiled to say the least. The charm of Thianor was abundant everywhere I laid my eyes. I then noticed a rather large structure arching over the center of town. I wondered what the purpose of that prominent structure was as I slowly walked down the main thoroughfare. I then spotted the sign of the Rosewood Inn that the constable told me about, just over yonder.

I entered the inn to the sound of bells ringing from atop the doorframe. There was a dule of white doves quietly perching in a large cage, which hung behind the front desk of the inn.

"Welcome to the Rosewood Inn. My name is Roselyn Merchant. How may we accommodate you on this beautiful night?" the raven-haired innkeeper inquired with a warm smile.

"I need a room for…for two nights," I replied in a weary tone.

"Splendid. That will be fifteen dollars. If you would be so kind to sign here, sir," Roselyn said and then began filling up a small bowl with seeds and placed it in the cage of doves with a smile.

I then took out fifteen dollars from my satchel and placed it on the front desk.

"Where do you hail from?" Roselyn inquired as I signed my name with the crimson quill on the front desk.

I wanted to remain anonymous and keep a low profile lest the constables of Thianor were already on the lookout for a hunter. "Bleakton," I replied as Roselyn gently petted a dove with a smile.

"I adore Bleakton, and if I may say, you embody that town perfectly, sir," Roselyn remarked with a smile.

"Yes, I feel somewhat out of place here," I said to Roselyn with a grin.

"Nonsense! Even though hunters are not as common in Thianor as they used to be, we still welcome you all with open arms," Roselyn said with a smile.

"Thank you," I replied with a grin and sigh.

"Oh, you will be staying in room 16. My sister will show you."

"Good evening. My name is Sara. May I carry that for you, sir?" a stripling girl inquired while reaching out her slender arms towards my satchel.

"No need. I carried it all this way. A few more steps won't kill me," I replied with a grin.

"All right, then right this way," Sara said and then began walking up the first flight of stairs with me in tow.

"Those are beautiful doves at the front desk," I remarked.

"Oh yes, doves are the symbol of Thianor and my sister's pride and joy," Sara said as we reached the top of the second flight of stairs, which was adorned with wreaths of roses hanging from the wall.

"I don't think I've ever seen so many roses in my life," I remarked.

"They're one of Thianor's main exports. We grow them in the field south of town. They will soon bloom again come first thaw of spring," Sara said and then stopped at room 16 and unlocked the door with the room key.

"Thank you," I said to Sara as I entered my room and tossed my rifles and satchel on the fuchsia bed quilt with a sigh.

"If you don't mind me asking, is that genuine wolf fur you're wearing?" Sara inquired in a zealous tone.

"Yes, it is. I killed, skinned, and tanned them myself," I replied.

"Incredible. You must be such a revered hunter," Sara remarked with a smile and widened eyes as she ran her fingers through the wolf fur draped over my chest.

"Those hollow titles hold no significance to me anymore," I said to Sara in a somber tone.

"These wolf furs can fetch you a pretty penny in Thianor's various boutiques and haberdasheries," Sara said.

"I'll keep that in mind," I said to Sara as I draped the wolf furs on the fireside armchair.

"I hope your stay in our town is a most pleasant one, sir," Sara said and then placed my room key on the nightstand.

"Thank you. It already has been and call me Vincent," I said to Sara with a grin. Sara then bashfully smiled and bowed her head before leaving my room.

At 9:02 PM, I was exhausted from my hike. So I put another log into the fireplace, got undressed, and then sprawled out on the bed with a profound sigh. I could hear the melody of a violin being played nearby. The sound was faint, but dulcet nonetheless to soothe my weary ears. I then couldn't help but think of Heather and how she used to play the violin so beautifully. I doubt there's a single aspect of this world that won't remind me of her.

*****

At 7:45 AM, I awoke to a gentle knock on the door.

"Good morning, sir. Oh, I mean, Vincent," the maid Sara said in a timid tone and elfish smile as she placed an ornate silver tray of pastries and a steaming pot of coffee down upon the nightstand.

"Good morning…what are these?" I inquired in a raspy tone while rubbing my bleary eyes.

"These are called rose blossoms. They're made from thinly sliced apples splayed out in a fan shape, wrapped in dough, drizzled with honey, and then sprinkled with sugar. My sister and I bake them up fresh every morning," Sara said with a smile as I picked up one of the pastries and took a bite.

"Very good," I remarked as I quickly ate one of the pastries in two ravenous bites.

"If there's anything else you need, feel free to let me know," Sara said to me with a smile and slight bow before exiting the room. I stood up with a sigh and stared out the frosted window while holding a mug full of coffee. I wanted to experience Thianor and all it has to offer. I could hopefully create new memories in this town, memories that fill me with comfort, instead of leaving me a hollow shell. After finishing my breakfast, I walked downstairs to the front desk and tapped the bronze bell three times.

"I'm in room 16. Can I trust that all my provisions will be well kept?" I inquired as Roselyn averted her attention from her cage of doves to me.

"Absolutely, sir! My sisters and I will see to it personally," Roselyn replied.

"Good. I can see why this inn gets good business when you bake such delicious pastries every morning," I said to Roselyn with a smirk.

"You must be talking about our rose blossoms. We only bake those on the weekends," Roselyn said with a smile while feeding her doves.

Curious, today is Tuesday. Then why did Sara serve me those rose blossoms in such an obsequious manner this morning?

The frigid, rose-scented air caressed my warm face as I departed the Rosewood Inn and stepped out onto the streets of Thianor. I took one of my pistols with me, although I doubt I would ever use it in this town full of such grace and civility. All the townsfolk of Thianor looked courtly yet affable, but looks can be ever so deceiving in the eyes of a distant traveler such as me. I continued to saunter down the street until a group of minstrels befell me. Two pairs of men and women dressed in dark garments were singing a jubilant song, which was foreign to my ears but dulcet nonetheless. I didn't know where I was going in this town, for I only had my instincts to guide me.

"Step right up and take your shot. You, sir…you look like a man who's hunted his fair share," a man wearing a tall top hat and crimson jacket shouted while pointing a cane at me.

"What gave that away?" I inquired with a smirk.

"Your demeanor, your posture, but most of all, that striking wolf fur on your jacket," the man replied.

"What's the price to play?" I inquired while slowly walking towards the shooting gallery game.

"Only twenty-five cents," the game operator replied.

"All right I'll play," I said to the game operator and then tossed a coin upon the stand. "Very good, sir. Just shoot the wolf among doves and win a prize, you get one shot," the game operator said while handing me a toy version of a rifle. The game operator then began to quickly turn a crank, which moved a peg-and-gear system for the game. I took a deep breath and then took aim. Several embalmed doves were moving back and forth, but every few moments, a portrait of a snarling wolf appeared. My heart began to race at the mere sight of the wolf portrait. My shoulder wound suddenly flared up in pain as I pulled the trigger.

"Damn it!" I spoke aloud in a stern tone as I shot an embalmed dove square in the breast.

"Care to try again, sir?" the game operator inquired with a smile.

"No, I've had enough," I replied in a stern tone and then walked away from the game.

"I spent three dollars trying to shoot that wolf. Rather vexing, isn't it?" a dapperly dressed man sitting on a stone bench said as I walked past him with a flout.

"Excuse me, where's the local tavern located?" I inquired as an elderly man wearing a striped tailcoat befell me.

"That would be the *Wishing Well.* Head east down this street until you reach the center of town. The Wishing Well is right across the street from the *Thespian Pavilion,*" the man replied and then coughed sporadically into a handkerchief.

I paid no heed that it was still morning, for I desperately needed a drink. The elegant streets of Thianor were a stark comparison to the seedy streets of Bleakton. I didn't know how long I would have to live in this town. There was no statute of limitation for murder, even if I was morally just in killing that grave robber. I would remain in this town indefinitely, and as for White Bane, Heather and Audrey would be avenged with his blood.

I reached the center of town to the sight of a pair of harlequin-dressed men performing for a group of townsfolk. One harlequin was dressed in a vibrant array of gold and violet while the other harlequin was dressed in sharp black and silver. The harlequins wore masks covering their eyes and hats with each of their respective colors. The harlequins were performing dazzling acrobatic feats around a central stone fire pit. The harlequins then each lit three torches in the fire pit and began to juggle with each other! I clapped along with the townsfolk, as the harlequins skillfully juggled the flaming torches. I could tell these two men had practiced this amazing display of hand-to-eye coordination fraught with danger for many years. The harlequins then tossed all but one torch into the fire pit. The harlequins then drunk from a flask that was tucked away in their outfits while mutterings of suspense resonated throughout the growing group of townsfolk quietly beholding the spectacle. The harlequins then stood about ten feet apart from each other and quickly spat out the liquid from their mouths on to their torches. The silver-and-black-dressed harlequin turned the flames of his torch sapphire with the liquid he spat out while the gold-and-violet-dressed harlequin turned the flames of his torch garnet. The harlequins then spat in unison, combining each of their flames to make a remarkable violet flame! Cheers and thunderous applause resonated among the townsfolk as the harlequins then extinguished their torches and bowed in unison with a smile. I, along with most of the townsfolk, then tossed coins into a large basket that the harlequins stood beside.

"Thank you, thank you. I'm Dante, and this is my brother, Corpulas. This display was but a mere taste of what's to come this Saturday night when we perform in *Jesters of the Court* at the Thespian Pavilion," the gold-and-violet-dressed harlequin pronounced while pointing to the Thespian Pavilion just over yonder.

"There it is." I spoke aloud as I spotted the Wishing Well tavern across from the Thespian Pavilion.

That same song that was foreign to my ears and that the minstrels were singing earlier now greeted me upon my entry into the Wishing Well. That song was being played by three women in the nook of the tavern. The trio of female musicians appeared young and fair with wavy, flaxen hair. One woman played the violin; one woman played the lute; and one woman played the flute. I then slowly walked past the trio of female musicians before I sat down on a stool at the bar.

"What can I get you?" the female barkeep inquired while my head rested solemnly in my hands upon the bar.

"Anything hot and strong," I replied in a stern tone.

She was beautiful. In fact, she was the most beautiful barkeep I'd ever laid eyes on! She had vibrant sapphire eyes; lustrous auburn hair, which cascaded down her ample bosom; and an ivory visage, hued with a rosy glow.

"We have a seasonal mulled wine, which is served hot," the barkeep said to me.

"Stronger," I said to the barkeep in a stern tone.

"Our honeyed bourbon is quite popular. It's strong but sweet, just like all the women of Thianor," the barkeep said with a smile.

"Good. I'll take a double," I said to the barkeep.

"Double honeyed bourbon, coming right up," the barkeep said and then began making my drink.

My weary body began to feel warm and numb with each sip of the honeyed bourbon. "Excuse me…what's that song they're playing?" I inquired while pointing at the trio of female musicians in the nook of the tavern.

"Oh, you must not be from around here. That's the 'Bard's Ballad.' It's the official anthem of Thianor," the barkeep replied with a smile while quickly washing a mug.

"It's a soothing melody," I said to the barkeep.

"Indeed, traveler. All *Thianorians* know that song by heart. They're quite good. I believe they're called *the Sister Sages*," the barkeep said and then waved to the trio of female musicians.

"I'll have another," I said to the barkeep after finishing the rest of my double honeyed bourbon in one gulp.

"Carmella, I can take it from here," a slender man with sable hair said to the barkeep.

"All right, double honeyed bourbon for this gentleman," Carmella said to the man while pointing at me. The beautiful barkeep known as Carmella then retired to the back room of the tavern. Even though the new barkeep made my drink twice as fast as Carmella did, I still scornfully stared at him, for I needed a beautiful woman to gaze at while I was numbing my senses. I then sighed and took another slow sip of the sweet and numbing concoction.

The tavern was becoming more crowded during eventide, as two men sat beside me at the bar. The two men who sat beside me appeared to be dignitaries, but then again, so did most of the townsfolk of Thianor. Heather would've loved it here in Thianor, the culture and all the vibrant people, but her heart was set for Bleakton because teaching those impoverished children at the Claymore House was her life's calling, a calling that was viciously stolen from her. I now see Heather in the eyes of every woman I encounter. She encapsulated all of them, and the pain I felt from losing her was insurmountable to the point where I often have trouble drawing breath. I'd never felt so alone in a crowded tavern in my entire life.

"Another one," I said to the barkeep in a somber tone while sliding my empty glass towards the inside of the bar.

"Young man, where did you acquire such beautiful wolf fur?" an elderly man wearing an eye patch inquired as he sat down beside me at the bar.

"I acquired it from the wolf I killed," I replied in a scornful tone while slowly turning towards the eye-patched man sitting beside me.

"That's most brilliant. You must be an accomplished hunter," the eye-patched man remarked and then took a puff from an ivory sylphlike pipe.

"I get by—come on," I said to the eye-patched man as my impatience began to swell up. I then began aggressively smacking the bar in anticipation of my drink being served.

"Oscar von Luc, pleased to make your acquaintance," the eye-patched man said while extending his hand in salutations.

I then quickly disregarded Oscar's hand as I reached for my drink, which the barkeep had just finished making. "So what's your story?" I inquired while pointing at Oscar's eye patch.

"Yes, of course, my right eye. It's, by all means, a story of stupidity over bravery. You see, I'm a zoologist, and about five years ago, I was studying the effects of peridot phantom venom. The properties in that deadly snake's venom are used to concoct many lifesaving medicines. I let my ambition blind me quite literally though. One night in my lab, I was milking the venom from a particularly aggressive phantom when the snake then slipped through my tight grasp and sunk its fangs into my right eye. There were two options at that moment—die in one minute from the venom instantly reaching my brain or cut out my right eye and bleed out the venom. I chose the latter. So now I see the world half in darkness, all because of my obstinance. Pray that you never suffer such a tragic fate as I have, hunter." Oscar said in a somber tone.

I finished my fifth double honeyed bourbon in a large gulp and then scoffed while sneering at Oscar. "Tragic fate, you say. Tell me, do you have any family, Oscar?" I inquired.

"Yes, a wife and son. We've resided here in Thianor for about ten years now," Oscar replied.

I then began to scoff, which then quickly intensified into a wild cackle. "You…old… fool. You have no fucking idea what a tragic fate is until you've come home to witness a pack of wolves hunched over your wife and daughter. Until you've held them in your arms while they cough up blood. Until you've watched the light from their eyes extinguish and their bodies lie motionless. Until you've dug their graves and given their eulogies. Only then can you speak to me about tragic fate. I would give my right eye, my left eye, and any other part of my fucking body if that would bring them back to me. You have a family. There's nothing tragic about your life!" I shouted as tears began to well up in my bleary eyes.

At that moment, the entire Wishing Well was silent and fixed upon me with a bewildered stare.

"I didn't mean to upset you," Oscar said in a timid tone and then took his leave from the bar.

"What—don't tell me I disrupted all your merriment. Keep playing, keep laughing, keep drinking!" I shouted as I grabbed my empty glass of bourbon and threw it down upon the ground. Gasps then resonated among the Wishing Well as the glass shattered.

"All right, I think you've had enough, sir," the barkeep said to me in a stern tone as he grabbed my arm.

"Marcus, what's wrong?" Carmella inquired in a distressed tone as she ran to the barkeep from the back room of the tavern.

"Everything's fine, Carmella dear. This man has just had one too many," Marcus replied.

"Let me help," Carmella said to Marcus as she draped my other arm over her shoulder. "Where are your lodgings for the night, traveler?" Carmella inquired as she and Marcus escorted me out of the Wishing Well.

"Rosewood Inn," I replied as I clung to Carmella in the manner of a drowning man clinging to the banks of a river.

"All right, let's get you a carriage," Carmella said while waving her hand.

We three then waited for a few moments on the street until a carriage arrived.

"Take this man to the Rosewood Inn," Marcus said to the coachmen as he opened the door of the carriage.

Marcus and Carmella then carefully assisted me into the carriage.

"Good night, traveler. Get well soon," Carmella said with distressed eyes and a farewell wave before closing the door to the carriage.

"Hello," a stripling boy said in a faint tone.

"Oh, I didn't see you there," I said to the stripling boy as I sat upright in the carriage.

"I'm glad you see us now," the stripling boy said with a bantam grin. Despite my current state of immense intoxication, the eeriness in which the stripling boy who sat across from me evoked was quite unnerving. The boy wore a black suit and string tie, which matched his hair that resembled a cast-iron pot. The boy vacantly stared at me with a cold detachment that exuded from his dark eyes. He also had a small crow, which was perched quietly upon his shoulder.

"Is that your pet crow?" I inquired while pointing at the crow.

"No, we may appear different, but we're of the same origin," the boy replied as he slowly turned his head towards the crow and nodded.

"What...what are you talking about, boy?" I inquired while rubbing my bleary eyes.

"We're all creations of another creation," the boy replied while staring intently into the crow's abysmal black eyes.

"That crow is very quiet. I know of a crow just like him," I said to the boy.

"He's worried about you, as am I," the stripling boy said.

"Don't fret over me," I said to the boy with a snicker.

The carriage then began to slow down before it came to a complete halt.

"Well, this is my stop," I said to the boy as I opened the carriage door and stumbled out onto the street.

"What will you do now?" the boy inquired.

"Sleep...and hope nightmares fail to find me. Good night then," I replied in a somber tone.

"Good night, Vincent," the boy said, just before I closed the door to the carriage.

"What—who are you?" I shouted in bewilderment as the carriage took off. I then reached for the carriage door but slipped on a patch of ice and fell heavily upon the cobblestone street. I stood up from the street slowly with a hissing groan and then stumbled my way to the entrance of the Rosewood Inn.

"Good evening, sir," the innkeeper said from behind the front desk while twirling her wavy amber hair around her finger.

"Good evening," I said to the innkeeper in a raspy tone.

"Do you need help to your room?" the innkeeper inquired as she walked towards me.

"No, no, I'm fine," I replied with a dismissive wave.

"All right, I offered...don't blame me if you tumble down the stairs!" the innkeeper shouted as I slowly walked up the first flight of stairs.

The stairs were dimly lit, which made it more difficult for me, as I staggered up them one heavy step at a time. I used the crimson-and-lavender-striped runners, which adorned the stairs, as a trail for me to follow. I then made it to my room on the third floor as I clutched the banister. After a few frustrating moments of searching through my pockets for the room key, I took it out and proceeded to unlock the door.

"Open, damn it!" I spoke aloud while I frantically shook and turned the doorknob.

"Let me help you with that, sir," a young maid said. So I handed her the key, and within an instant, she had unlocked and opened the door to my room.

My pocket watch read 11:25 PM. This meant I spent twelve hours drinking at the Wishing Well.

"Did you have a rough night?" the young maid inquired as she placed my key upon the nightstand.

"Yes, I believe I'm cursed," I replied in a somber tone as I sat down in bed and slowly took off my jacket and boots.

The young maid then sat down beside me with somber eyes. "Why would you say such a thing?" the young maid inquired in a timid tone while making fleeting glances at me.

"Death follows me like a close friend," I replied in a somber tone as I fell back in bed.

"Then all you need are better friends," the young maid said with a warm smile and then reached out and grabbed my hand gently.

"I wish life were that simple," I said to the young maid with a yawn.

"Well, if you need anything else, just let me know. Good night," the young maid said as she stood up and exited my room.

"Good night, Audrey." I spoke aloud, just before my weary, bloodshot eyes succumbed to a bittersweet darkness.

*****

At 8:30 AM, I awoke to a knock on the door. "Come in!" I shouted as I sat upright in bed.

"Good morning, Vincent," Sara said with a smile as she entered the room holding a pot of coffee and silver tray full of rose blossoms. "You were the worse for wear last night. How are you feeling?" Sara inquired and then sat down beside me on the bed.

"My head still feels like a maelstrom," I replied with a series of sporadic coughs. I then poured a glass of water and quickly drank it to slake my besotted thirst.

"What do you recall from last night?" Sara inquired as I took a bite of a rose blossom.

"Well, I remember the innkeeper yelling at me as I walked up the stairs to my room," I replied and then took a sip of coffee.

"Oh, that was just my sister, Francesca. She works the night shift with me. I know she may seem harsh and impatient with people at first, but she's really a caring person," Sara said with a giggle.

"It's all right. I understand," I said to Sara as I got dressed.

"Is that all you recall from last night?" Sara inquired in a timid tone.

"All the events that transpired last night are rather hazy to me now," I replied while examining my pistol.

"You called me Audrey as I left the room," Sara said and then brushed a strand of wavy flaxen hair behind her ear.

"Oh, did I?" I inquired as I sat down on the bed beside Sara.

"Was she your wife?" Sara inquired as she placed her hand on my knee and leaned in towards me.

"No, my daughter," I replied in a somber tone.

"My heart weeps for your loss, but as long as—"

"That will be all," I said to Sara in a stern tone while my visage quivered in sorrow. I then put on my satchel and stormed out of my room, leaving Sara sitting there quietly upon my bed.

A mellifluous melody resonated as I walked down the stairs to the front desk of the Rosewood Inn. I then noticed a woman elegantly playing a harp in the lobby as I rang the bell upon the front desk.

"Oh, it's you. This just arrived in the post for you," Francesca said to me as she handed me a letter.

Dear Wishing Well patron,

Enclosed is a bill for the services that the Wishing Well has provided for you.

Five double honeyed bourbon	=	$6.25
Carriage service	=	$2.00
Tumbler	=	25¢
Total	=	$8.50

Best regards,
Marcus and Carmella Sandoval.

"This is a bill." I spoke aloud in a vexatious tone.

"You should feel lucky, Mr. Belmont. Marcus and Carmella could've easily chosen to ban you from their establishment," Francesca said with a smirk.

"I suppose so," I said to Francesca while she blissfully twirled her hair and studiously wrote in the ledger book upon the front desk.

"If I were you, I would pay that total right now so you may retain the services of the Wishing Well," Francesca said while pointing to the front door of the Rosewood Inn.

"I'll see to that right away. Thank you," I said to Francesca.

"Don't forget your checkout is at twelve thirty. Should you fail to depart your room before then, we will take all your possessions and lock them up in the chest behind the front desk for you to pick up," Francesca said.

"Once again, thank you," I said to Francesca and then exited the Rosewood Inn.

My head was spinning, and my stomach was raw from last night's debauchery. So instead of struggling to walk the entire distance to the Wishing Well, I managed to hail a carriage. "To the Wishing Well tavern," I said to the coachman before entering the carriage.

"Good morning," an elderly man said while reading the newspaper.

"Good morning," I said to the elderly man with a sporadic cough.

The elderly man who sat across from me was reading the newspaper aloud, a habit I found most vexing. *How long could I reside in this lavish town before I expend all my recourses?* This question was gnawing away at the back of my mind. Thianor was beautiful, indeed. It was so much more vibrant than I recall when I was a stripling boy. I couldn't continue with my tumultuous behavior in the Wishing Well. I learned how polar opposite the taverns of Bleakton and Thianor truly are. If I wanted to be welcomed in the Wishing Well, then I would have to change my attitude or at least suppress it for the time being. Far be it from me to arouse attention in this town. I must lay low as best as I can lest word catches ear of a hunter on the run for murder. The carriage then began to slow down before it came to a complete halt. A panel then opened inside of the carriage where the coachman stared at me through.

"Your fare is two dollars, sir," the coachman said. A small brass compartment then opened up beside my head.

"Oh, of course," I said to the coachman. I then took two dollars out of my wallet and placed it in the brass compartment.

"Farewell, sir," the coachman said. The brass compartment then quickly closed followed by the ringing of a bell. I then exited the carriage with the Wishing Well's bill in hand.

Upon my entry into the Wishing Well, I noticed that Marcus was working behind the bar.

"Here, it's all paid in full," I said to Marcus while handing him the bill.

Marcus then opened the envelope and quickly counted the money. "Good. Remember, traveler, we welcome all kinds of people to this establishment with open arms, unless they're disturbers of the peace," Marcus said.

"I understand. Tell Carmella I'm sorry for last night," I said to Marcus. I then exited the Wishing Well with shame weighing heavy on my shoulders.

I had two hours left to form a plan of long-term residency in Thianor. I then spotted a clothing shop just across the street called *Ophelia's Boutique*. So I hastily ran across the street, nearly getting hit by a horse and then entered the boutique.

"Good afternoon, sir. Can I help you find anything in particular?" an elderly woman wearing a black dress and ostentatious hat inquired in a raspy tone from behind the counter. The elderly woman's frail and weathered body was covered in jewelry, like a gilded saddle placed atop a moribund horse.

"I'm just browsing," I replied. I then began meticulously searching every article of clothing in the boutique for wolf's fur. After a few moments of searching, I came to the conclusion that there was no wolf fur anywhere in the boutique. This could mean great or terrible news for me.

"Good morning, ma'am. If you're in the business, then I have in my possession a most valuable material that is coveted all throughout the Fray that you might be interested in," I said to the elderly woman with a smirk.

"I'm always in the business, young man," the elderly woman said and then took a puff from a sylphlike black pipe.

"Then I present to you...genuine wolf fur," I said to the elderly woman as I took the wolf fur out of my satchel and laid it down upon the counter.

"Heavens me," the elderly woman remarked while placing her hand over her chest. The elderly woman then began to closely examine every inch of the wolf fur. "The tanning work is shoddy to adequate at best. The size is ordinary...and the luster of the fur is somewhat faded. I will pay you five hundred dollars for this wolf fur," the elderly woman said.

I knew the game this clever boutique owner was playing, but her first reaction when I presented her the wolf fur told me all I needed to know.

"Five hundred dollars? In Bleakton, the set price for wolf fur is one thousand dollars," I said to the elderly woman.

"Young man, you're not in Bleakton. Here in Thianor, we have much higher standards when it comes to the quality of garments, fabrics, and materials," the elderly woman told me with a scoff.

"Very well, ma'am, then I'll just take my business to Bleakton, where they respect hunters," I said to the elderly woman as I grabbed the wolf fur and began stuffing it back into my satchel.

"Wait...I'll pay nine hundred for the wolf fur, but that's as high as I can go," the elderly woman said while reaching out her skeletal hand.

"You have a deal," I said to the elderly woman, with a smile, as I laid the wolf fur back down upon the counter.

"Forgive me if I was callous with you, young man. My grandfather was a hunter, and I had the utmost love and respect for him and his trade," the elderly woman said while she counted out my money.

"I would've liked to meet him," I said to the elderly woman, with a smirk.

"You two would've been thick as thieves," the elderly woman said with a wheezing laugh as she handed me the money.

I then exited the boutique one wolf fur lighter and nine hundred dollars heavier.

"Sir, a rose for your beloved?" a little girl inquired as she walked up to me in a timid manner. The little girl appeared to be Audrey's age, wearing a black dress and bonnet while holding a large bouquet of roses with both hands.

"If I had a beloved, I would," I replied. The little girl then began to walk away. "Wait... how much for all the roses you're carrying?" I inquired while kneeling down in front of the little girl.

"Well, each rose is fifteen cents so—"

"So that would be two dollars and seventy cents." I said to the little girl. I then paid the little girl, and she then handed me the large bouquet of roses in return. "Here...take them," I said to the little girl, with a smile, as I handed her back the large bouquet of roses.

"Really, all for me?" the little girl inquired in a zealous tone and widened eyes.

"Absolutely," I replied, with a smile.

"Thank you, sir," the little girl said. The little girl's somber demeanor was instantly uplifted at that moment, which brought a very brief feeling of happiness to my life.

Thianor was an expensive town to live in. I expected nothing less from a town that lives and breathes art in all its forms. I could rent out a flat, but I'd read many newspaper headlines of people being murdered in their flat. No, I needed to reside in a place that was in a constant transient state, so I would be more difficult to locate by anybody. I needed to stay indefinitely at the Rosewood Inn.

It was 12:02 PM. Carriage rides where an expensive but convenient mode of transportation in this day and age, but I feared my health was worsening, so I needed all the help I could get. Besides, there was little time left before all my possessions would be taken out of my room, so I needed to get to the *Rosewood In* as soon as possible.

"Rosewood Inn," I said to the coachman and then hastily entered the carriage. I had the carriage all to myself, which had me breathing a sigh of relief. I didn't know why Bleakton hadn't adopted carriages as a means of transportation throughout the town. I supposed it was because Bleakton is a town founded by hunters who are not attracted to such luxurious conveyances. "I know, two dollars," I said to the coachman as the brass compartment opened. I then paid my fare and exited the carriage.

Upon my entering the Rosewood Inn, I noticed that Roselyn was working at the front desk. "About my checkout...I was wondering if I could stay here indefinitely?" I inquired. Roselyn then stared at me intently with a smirk before combing through the ledger book.

"Sir, we need your room for other people traveling to Thianor. Besides, the only ones living here are my sisters and I," Roselyn said.

"I understand that, but I'm willing to pay you a down payment of nine hundred dollars," I said to Roselyn as I placed the pile of money upon the front desk.

"We do need more help around here. Please give Vincent a chance," Sara said to Roselyn in a timid tone, as she quietly emerged from the back room.

"Sara's right. We have been shorthanded lately. I'll tell you what…as long as you're willing to work hard for us as a maid, you may stay here free of charge. Now understand that we can only afford to pay you very little," Roselyn said in a stern tone.

"Thank you very much, ma'am, but room and board is all I need. Don't pay me a dime of your hard-earned money," I said to Roselyn with a smile.

"Thank you so much, Roselyn," Sara said to Roselyn, with a smile, as she embraced her older sister tightly.

"All right, all right, there's work to be done. Now you go with Sara. She will teach you everything," Roselyn said while pointing to Sara.

"Of course, right this way, Vincent," Sara said with a smile and then walked to the back room.

"My younger sister is quite fond of you, Mr. Belmont. You better treat her with the utmost respect and kindness while you're living here," Roselyn said to me with a smirk.

"You have my word, ma'am," I said to Roselyn with a smile as we shook hands in agreement.

CHAPTER 10

Ms. Luna LaGrange

Newfound beauty evokes as creeping sickness chokes.

A fortnight had passed since I began working for the Merchant sisters at the Rosewood Inn. I was settling in comfortably with my daily rounds of cleaning all the sheets, quilts, and bed-pans, and also procuring a surplus amount of firewood for every room. Spring was beginning to bloom, along with the town of Thianor. There would be a greater demand for the export of roses now that the weather permits their growth outside, but that wasn't my business. Most men would scoff at the idea of taking orders from a woman half their age, but I was truly grateful for all the kindness that Sara and her sisters had shown me.

"Vincent, come help me load all this produce into the wagon," Beatrice said.

"Yes, ma'am," I said to Beatrice as I scampered over to her side. Beatrice was the middle Merchant sister who I would regularly accompany on trips to the market, florist, and even boutiques. I found Beatrice to be the most candid of the four Merchant sisters. She would often act facetious with me in the manner that an old friend would. Yes, Beatrice was a real salt of the earth woman whom I felt comfortable with.

"Thank God spring has arrived. I don't know about you, Vincent, but I feel like the frigid weather is slowly turning me into my grandmother," Beatrice said with a sigh while she fed a carrot to Sigmund, the Rosewood Inn's resident black stallion.

"I never knew my grandmother, so I couldn't say. Please tell me though if I begin acting like an elderly woman," I said to Beatrice with a smirk as we both sat down in the wagon with Beatrice holding the reins. Beatrice then laughed as she began to drive us back to the Rosewood Inn.

"Isn't it great to have a strong man working for us now?" Beatrice pronounced as we entered the Rosewood Inn carrying crates of produce.

"You mean I'm not strong enough for you, Beatrice?" Francesca inquired with a scoff from behind the front desk.

"You're strong-tempered, but when it comes to heavy lifting, like carrying firewood for instance, you're always too tired for such strenuous labor," Beatrice replied with a giggle.

"Oh, shut up! Vincent can finish unloading the rest of the produce. You go help Sara make up rooms twelve through fifteen," Francesca said to Beatrice while she twirled her hair and pointed up the stairs. I then continued loading the remainder of produce into the kitchen.

"Vincent, when you're finished unloading all the produce, stoke the fireplace in the lobby and then brew a pot coffee," Francesca said.

"Yes, ma'am!" I shouted. There was always work to be done at the Rosewood Inn, honest and noble work that accommodated others but, most importantly, work that I respected. The Merchant sisters were a rare breed of kindness in this day and age, a kindness that I hadn't felt since Heather and Audrey died. I would graciously serve them to the best of my abilities for the time being.

"Vincent, go feed Roselyn's doves while I do inventory," Francesca said as I just finished brewing a pot of coffee in the lobby.

"Yes, ma'am!" I shouted as I scampered over to the front desk. I then poured seeds from the large glass jar underneath the front desk into a bowl and placed it into the cage of doves. I worked as a maid alongside Beatrice, who was twenty years old, and Sara, who was sixteen years old, while Roselyn, who was twenty-six years old, and Francesca, who was twenty-four years old working at the front desk and managing all the finances and room bookings. My work shift would alternate every other day between Beatrice and Sara. They were competent young women whom I trusted wholeheartedly. Each of the Merchant sisters reminded me of a different part of Heather's personality, and if I close my eyes, I could almost imagine her here with me.

"Francesca, my shift is over now. May I take Sigmund for a stroll?" I inquired.

"Very well, just don't forget to tie him up, or else we'll have to ride you for transportation," Francesca replied in a facetious tone.

I then exited the Rosewood Inn to the back alley where Sigmund was tied up and grazing on a bale of hay. I then untied Sigmund's reins and carefully mounted him.

It was a clear and brisk evening as I rode Sigmund down the main thoroughfare of Thianor. I noticed a mass gathering of people departing the Thespian Pavilion as I reached the center of town. "It must be a play." I spoke aloud. I then dismounted Sigmund and tied him firmly to a lamppost in front of the Wishing Well.

Upon my entry, I noticed the Wishing Well was packed with a vast array of flamboyantly dressed people. "Carmella, one pint of ginger ale!" I shouted as I waved and pointed to myself.

"One moment," Carmella said with a profound sigh as she studiously served everyone at the bar in a frenetic pace. Every seat at the bar was taken, so I waited patiently, ready to pounce on the first seat that opens up. After a few moments, I managed to get a seat at the corner end of the bar. This was the most crowded I'd ever seen the Wishing Well. All the patrons were packed shoulder to shoulder in a mass of chaotic merriment. Everyone who attended the play a few moments ago, including the thespians, must be in this tavern now. I could spot out all the thespians in the tavern, for they were dressed in such vibrant costumes.

I then noticed a woman sitting at the other end of the bar. Judging by her attire, she was most definitely a thespian. She wore a sleeveless, chartreuse dress gilded in gold, and a crown of what appeared to be white dahlias atop her wavy flaxen hair. The woman shone with an ethereal and willowy radiance. Her visage seemed to bend all the light in the tavern towards her. I stared at the woman intently as she playfully pushed the man sitting beside her with an elfish smile. She then took a sip of wine and brushed a strand of flaxen hair behind her ear. Even surrounded by her fellow thespians, the woman was a captivating sight to behold. I then noticed the flaxen-haired woman was gone as I finished my pint of ginger ale. I wouldn't linger in this tavern the entire night, for the Merchant sisters always needed my help. So I tossed a couple of coins upon the bar towards Carmella and then exited the Wishing Well.

The night air was refreshing as I walked over to Sigmund, who was chomping at the bit.

"Don't touch me!" a woman's voice shouted from the back alley beside the Wishing Well.

"Hold on," I said to Sigmund with a pat to his head and then slowly walked towards the back alley with my hand on my pistol.

"You were so seductive with me in the tavern," a man remarked as he pressed himself against the woman, pinning her to the wall.

"You're soused to high hell, Otto," the woman said to the man who continued to rapaciously fondle her. It was her, the same flaxen-haired woman in the tavern who wore a crown of white dahlias.

"Just give me what I want," Otto said to the woman, as he pulled out a small knife.

"The woman said stop. I suggest you take heed," I said to Otto in a stern tone while pointing my pistol at him.

"Shove off, you fucking lout. W-we're busy here!" Otto shouted as he averted his gaze towards me.

The woman then saw her opportunity and took it with no hesitation as she swiftly kicked Otto in the groin. I then smiled as the woman quickly primped her flaxen hair. Otto then instantly dropped to his knees while crying out in pain. "You shrewd whore!" Otto shouted in a contemptuous tone. The woman then swiftly kicked Otto again, this time, square in the head, which made him drop his knife and lie motionless upon the ground. The woman then scampered over to me while holding her dress above her slender ankles.

"I thank you, sir. You think you know somebody until they begin drinking," the woman said with a profound sigh. Even in the dimly lit street, the woman's visage was stunningly beautiful. She stared at me with peridot eyes and a sprinkling of freckles, which adorned her cherub nose and cheeks, like snowflakes upon a statue.

"Looks like you had the situation under control," I said to the woman as I holstered my pistol.

"Not as well as you might think. He was my ride home," the woman said while she adjusted her dress.

"I can give you a ride home, Ms.—"

"Luna LaGrange, and I graciously accept your offer," the woman said with a smile. Ms. Luna LaGrange was a vibrant twenty-seven-year-old woman who shone with such a light. I felt both exalted and inferior by her close presence, very much like the moment I first encountered Heather in Vilkswood.

"I'm Vincent Belmont. I work at the Rosewood Inn," I said to Luna.

"Oh, that inn is resplendent," Luna remarked as she took off her chartreuse heels.

I then untied and mounted Sigmund as Luna stored her shoes in Sigmund's saddlebag. "Hop on," I said to Luna while outstretching my hand down towards her. Luna then grabbed my hand and mounted Sigmund, with her arms gently wrapped around my waist.

"So where do you live?" I inquired as we rode past the Thespian Pavilion.

"Just go six blocks down this street. My flat is the one on the left with ivy vines growing up the side of the facade," Luna replied.

"You're a thespian, right?" I inquired as we entered the White Stone district of Thianor.

"Yes, I performed in the play 'Gwendolyn the Faint' this evening. Although my reception from the audience was rather dismal," Luna replied.

"I'm sure you were brilliant. Sorry I missed it. When is your next performance?" I inquired.

"In a fortnight from today. My troupe and I have been rehearsing around the clock," Luna replied in a zealous tone.

"You're very brave to bare your soul to an entire audience of strangers," I said to Luna.

"It's in my blood to perform for people. What about you? You look more like a hunter with all this beautiful wolf fur on your jacket than a man who works at an inn," Luna remarked.

I could then feel Luna's fingers running through the wolf fur on the shoulder of my jacket. "That's because I am a hunter. I work for the Merchant sisters for free, and in return, they offer me free room and board at the inn."

"That's wonderful. If everyone in this town had half the heart that the Merchant sisters have, then there would be no pain or suffering," Luna said.

"I don't know about that. Thianor has been very hospitable to me," I said to Luna.

"Only on the outside does every town appear as a diamond, Vincent," Luna said in a somber tone.

"This must be your flat," I said to Luna as we stopped at the front entrance.

"It was lovely to meet you, Vincent, despite such vile circumstances," Luna said as she dismounted Sigmund.

"I feel the same way. Oh, don't forget your shoes," I said to Luna as she began to walk away.

"Oh, of course, good night," Luna said, with an elfin giggle, as she reached in Sigmund's saddlebag and took out her pair of chartreuse heels. We both then waved farewell to each other as Luna entered her flat and I galloped down the street left with a heartwarming sense that only two weary souls on a cool spring night could evoke within each other. Ms. Luna LaGrange—I hope to meet her again soon.

"Francesca, any work for me?" I inquired as I entered the Rosewood Inn.

"Surprisingly no, Vincent. Everything is in order at the moment," Francesca replied.

"Then would you care to have a drink with me?" I inquired as I grabbed a bottle of chardonnay from underneath the front desk and two wine glasses.

"Not now, Vincent, and you'll have to pay for that wine," Francesca said while studiously writing in the ledger book.

So I put back one wine glass, paid Francesca, and then retired to an armchair in the lobby. I then poured myself a glass of chardonnay with a sigh and pensively stared at the lobby fireplace. I could almost feel at home at the Rosewood Inn, but would I allow myself to feel such solace? It was peaceful in the lobby of the Rosewood Inn at this time of night despite Francesca's vexing glances at me. I took out Angie from the breast pocket of my jacket and then poured my third glass of chardonnay. Angie was always a solemn reminder of the vow I made to avenge Heather and Audrey. A sharp pain in my chest suddenly erupted in a series of sporadic coughs. To my dismay, Angie's once white, immaculate fabric was now splattered in blood. So I quickly took out my handkerchief and wiped my mouth. My white monogram handkerchief was now stained in blood too.

"Good night," I said to Francesca as I hastily scampered up the stairs to my room, with the chardonnay bottle in hand.

I was just tired. I'd been working unabated for a fortnight, and it must be taking its toll on my body. I entered my room and then immediately fell upon my bed. It would pass; this sudden affliction would diminish with rest. After all, I couldn't yield to any sickness, for I had too many people who depended on me, and feeling needed gave my life purpose for the time being.

*****

At 7:05 AM, I awoke to Sara's wake-up knock on my door. There was much work to be done, so I quickly gathered myself and then exited my room.

"Good morning," Beatrice said in a cheerful tone as I walked past her down the stairs.

"Mail for you, Vincent," Roselyn said as she handed me the gold envelope.

"I'll read this later when my shift is over," I said to Roselyn as I tucked the envelope in the breast pocket of my jacket next to Angie.

"Go help Sara make up rooms 1 through 4," Roselyn said.

"Yes, ma'am," I said to Roselyn and then began on room 1 where Sara was already gathering all the sheets and quilts to be washed.

"You got in late last night," Sara said in a timid tone as we began gathering all the sheets and quilts in room 1 to be washed.

"Yes, sorry if I woke you," I said to Sara in a raspy tone.

"It's all right. I was already awake in bed knitting," Sara said.

I then restocked the fireplace with more firewood and stoked the flames. Sara and I then moved on to room 2, which was left in disarray.

"Did a bear stay in this room?" I inquired.

"I've seen worse. So where did you go last night?" Sara inquired as we finished making up room 2 and then moved on to room 3.

"The Wishing Well—the tavern was bursting at the seams with all the attendees and thespians from the play that had just ended," I replied.

"I haven't attended a play at the Thespian Pavilion in so long. Beatrice and I used to attend plays there every week," Sara said.

We then moved on to room 4. After Sara and I finished making up room 4, we then went downstairs to the laundry room and began to wash all the sheets, quilts, and bedpans that we collected from all four of the rooms. It was strenuous work cranking the washing mills for one hour, but Sara and I were used to it. Sara would often use this time to talk to me about her older sisters and how she's either happy or upset with them at the moment.

"Beatrice and I once dressed up as thespians so we could drink for free at the Wishing Well," Sara said with a giggle.

"Did it work?" I inquired with a smile.

"Yes, but now the tavern proprietors request thespian identification in order to drink for free," Sara replied with an elfin smile. Sara and I then took all the sheets and quilt out of the washing mills and ran them through the wringers a couple of times before we hung them out on the clothesline in the back alley to air-dry.

"Tell Roselyn I'll be back in five minutes," I said to Sara. I then walked down the back alley to the main thoroughfare of Thianor. I then took out Angie and stared at the bloodstains upon her snow-white fabric with distressed eyes. A savory aroma then suddenly enticed my nose as it emanated from the west. After a few moments, I managed to track the aroma to its source, which was at the corner of the street.

"Grilled mutton chops with mint jam!" a vendor shouted through a bullhorn from behind a large rack of sizzling meats.

"I'll take five" I pronounced as I walked up to the vendor.

"That will be two dollars and fifty cents," the vendor replied. So I paid the vendor, and in return, he served me five sizzling mutton chops dolloped with mint jam in a small wicker basket. I then walked back to the Rosewood Inn with the mutton chops in hand.

"Here, Roselyn, take one," I said to Roselyn as I offered her a mutton chop.

"Oh, thank you, Vincent," Roselyn said as she grabbed a mutton chop.

"Oh, does Vincent have food?" Beatrice inquired as she walked up to me.

"Yes, have a mutton chop," I replied as Beatrice quickly grabbed a mutton chop before I offered her one.

"Give this to Francesca," I said to Roselyn as I handed her a mutton chop. "Here, Sara, are you hungry?" I inquired as I walked over to Sara, who was sitting on the sofa in the lobby quietly knitting.

"I'm famished. Thank you, Vincent," Sara replied as she grabbed a mutton chop.

I then sat down in an armchair in the lobby and began to read my mail while eating a mutton chop.

Dear Vincent Belmont,

Present this letter at the entrance to the Thespian Pavilion for any play that I'm performing in, and you will be granted free admission. I'm grateful for our serendipitous encounter last night. You're a good man, and it would warm my heart if you would attend my next play entitled *Madam of the Crimson Manor* on Friday, April 12 at 7:00 PM.

Best regards,
Luna LaGrange of the LaGrange troupe

"I'll be there." I spoke aloud with a smile as I finished eating my mutton chop in one ravenous bite. I had a feeling that watching Luna perform in her play would be a most captivating experience for me. This would be the first play I attend in my life. I didn't know what to expect, but I was sure it would be a welcome reprieve of entertainment from my mundane life. I was already excited just by reading Luna's letter, which pales in comparison to staring into her peridot eyes. For once, I now had something to look forward to in my life.

It was 6:23 PM. Tonight was the night I would attend *Madam of the Crimson Manor*, the play Luna told me that she and her troupe have been rehearsing around the clock for. Beatrice and I finished making up rooms 8 through 10 in an efficient and meticulous manner. I then entered my room and stared at myself in the bureau mirror. Judging by the attendees from the last play at the Thespian Pavilion, I should probably dress in formal attire for the play. Then again, Luna did express adoration for my wolf fur jacket. So I decided to wear an ashen-gray collared shirt underneath a black leather vest. I then put on my wolf fur jacket and tucked a single rose in the pocket.

"Francesca, may I take Sigmund for a ride?" I inquired.

"No, Beatrice and I need Sigmund now to run a few errands," Francesca replied.

"Very well, I'll just take a carriage," I said to Francesca. I then exited the Rosewood Inn and eagerly waited for a carriage.

"To the Thespian Pavilion," I said to the coachman as I entered the carriage.

"Are you attending the play as well, sir?" an ornately dressed woman sitting across from me inquired with a smile.

"Yes, I have an invitation from a thespian performing in the play," I replied with a smirk as I quickly flashed her Luna's letter.

It was a clear and calm spring night, ideal conditions to attend a play. There was no doubt I was out of my element when it comes to the arts, but this town had taught me to be open-minded to new experiences. I wondered how warmly the attendees would receive Luna's performance. Thespians were exalted in Thianor, just as hunters were exalted in Bleakton. Two classes of people who couldn't be more different, yet tons of people treated them as thanes. I think thespians and hunters were valued as thanes because of their dedication and service to the people, whether it be providing entertainment for our weary minds or nourishment for our hungry stomachs. The carriage then came to a halt, and the couple sitting across from me and I promptly paid the coachman's fare and exited the carriage.

The entrance to the Thespian Pavilion was vastly crowded with an array of finely dressed people eagerly waiting in line. I noticed from the entrance that the Thespian Pavilion was extravagantly decorated with banners, ribbons, flags, roses, and bonfires.

"Tickets are now being accepted for all attendees of the play. Present your tickets at the main gates for admission!" a man shouted through a bullhorn. I then presented Luna's invitation letter to a man at the main gates. The man read the letter quickly and then stared closely at the ornate stamp design at the bottom of the letter. "You must be held in high esteem from Ms. LaGrange for her to send you a personal invitation like this…row *a*, seat 5," the man said and then waved me through the main gates.

I then grabbed a slip of paper that a man was handing out to all attendees entering the Thespian Pavilion. The slip of paper had the cast list for the play. I was flattered by how exceptional my seat location was in the Thespian Pavilion. I sat front row center to the stage, and at that moment, I felt lordly, like a mayor or king, as I read the cast list on the slip of paper.

Madam of the Crimson Manor
Harriett Le Fae

Madam Clarice Constantine—Luna LaGrange
Lord Fredrick Constantine—Horace Williams
Gabrielle Constantine—Emily Morton
Samuel Ashford—Edmund Stalworth
Morgan Winsted—Felicia Lansden
Barbara Ashford—Helena Credence

Luna was cast as the lead role in this intimate play. There must have been around two thousand attendees seated in the Thespian Pavilion right now. I didn't know why, but I was nervous for Luna, and I could only imagine how she is feeling right now, just moments before the play begins.

"Attention, ladies and gentlemen, we do ask that you show our thespians the utmost respect during the play. Now without further ado, *Madam of the Crimson Manor*," a man pronounced and then quickly exited the stage. The crimson and gold curtains then slowly rose, and light flooded the stage from the many torches and bonfires being reflected through angled glass lenses. I applauded along with the rest of the attendees, as I could see Luna standing there, or should I say Clarice. She wore a wig of gleaming straight black hair and a dress to match. Clarice held a glass of wine in one hand and a sylphlike pipe in the other. She stood quietly and stared longingly at a portrait of a man, which hung on the luxurious manor backdrop of the stage. A dreary yet beautiful melody then resonated from a piano being played.

*****

"Fredrick, where have you been?" Clarice inquired in a distressed tone as a man entered the manor.

"I was helping the widow Winsted with some legal matters," Fredrick replied as he scampered over to the bar to fix himself a drink.

"That poor creature has not a soul on this earth anymore. Don't forget about Gabrielle and me, dear," Clarice said to Fredrick and then took a puff from her sylphlike pipe. "Gabrielle longs for your embrace, as do I," Clarice said to Fredrick as she placed her hands on his broad shoulders.

"Damn it, I cannot be with you and Gabrielle every waking moment," Fredrick said to Clarice in a stern tone as he shrugged off her gentle embrace.

"Every waking moment—we hardly see you at all anymore. You've become a ghost in this house," Clarice said to Fredrick in a distressed tone.

"It's late. I'm going to sleep. We'll talk about this in the morning," Fredrick said to Clarice with a profound sigh and then finished his drink in one gulp.

"Morning, after morning, after morning, you treat me like a child!" Clarice shouted.

"Calm down, you're being hysterical," Fredrick said to Clarice and then exited the stage.

Clarice then screamed in contempt as she threw her wine glass against the door, shattering it into pieces. "All I've ever done was love you." Clarice spoke aloud in a somber tone as she fell to her knees and began to weep.

The curtains then fell as I and the rest of the attendees applauded. It was only the first scene, and I was already awestruck by Luna's performance as Clarice.

After a few moments, the curtain rose to begin scene 2. I applauded along with the rest of the attendees to the sight of Clarice and a little girl in a winsomely decorated bedroom.

"Gabrielle, come here, honey," Clarice said to the little girl who wore a frilled sapphire dress while Clarice wore a sleeveless white gown. Gabrielle then hopped on her mother's lap as they both sat down in an armchair.

"Mommy, why do I have to go to Grandmother's house?" Gabrielle inquired in a sulking tone.

"It's only for a couple of days, darling, and then you'll be back in my arms before you know it," Clarice replied as she brushed Gabrielle's flaxen hair with a warm smile.

"Is Daddy mad at me?" Gabrielle inquired in a somber tone.

"Nonsense, don't ever think such terrible thoughts, my angel," Clarice replied and then firmly embraced Gabrielle.

"There's my darling," an elderly woman pronounced as she entered the bedroom.

"Sweetheart, go play in the parlor for a moment. I have to talk to your grandmother," Clarice said to Gabrielle.

"Bye, Mommy. I love you. Kiss Daddy for me," Gabrielle said to Clarice as her dainty arms wrapped around her.

"I love you, too, my darling," Clarice said to Gabrielle in a somber tone. Gabrielle then exited the stage, and the play returned to a somber atmosphere. "He's been away for two days. I feel my heart and mind fraying in his absence," Clarice said to her mother with a distressed visage as she paced back and forth.

"Fredrick was always a wanderer. Give him time, dear," Barbara said to Clarice.

"Time doesn't solve everything, Mother. I am spurned. Fredrick won't even touch me," Clarice said to Barbara in a distressed tone, as tears began to well up in her eyes.

"Dear, you need to get out of this house. Go shopping. Do anything that takes your mind off such toxic thoughts," Barbara said to Clarice.

"Fredrick was never a toxic thought in my mind up until now," Clarice said to Barbara.

"Gabrielle and I have to go now. Please take my advice, dear," Barbara said to Clarice as she warmly embraced her. Barbara then exited the scene, and the curtain fell upon Clarice. I then applauded along with the rest of the attendees. Luna's performance was utterly captivating. She fully immersed herself into the role of Clarice to the extent where she became her. If it weren't for Luna's piercing peridot eyes, she would be unrecognizable to me. So I sat zealously waiting for the curtain to rise on scene 3.

After a few moments, the curtain rose to begin scene 3. I applauded along with the rest of the attendees to the sight of Fredrick and another woman dressed in an emerald gown, which was pulled down below her chest, exposing her bra. Fredrick and the half-dressed woman were in the throes of passion upon a bed in a luxuriously decorated bedroom backdrop.

"Morgan, we mustn't. Clarice could be home at any moment," Fredrick said to Morgan in a distressed tone as she lay atop him.

"Don't tell me your heart still harbors love for her when I can feel all your love for me at this moment," Morgan said to Fredrick with a smile as her hands traced over Fredrick's chest. Fredrick then rapaciously turned Morgan over so that she lay beneath him and began fervidly kissing her neck while Morgan's legs wrapped around Fredrick, like silken vines. A sharp and suspenseful note then resonated from a violin being played.

"Fredrick, are you home?" a voice inquired as the bedroom door opened. There stood Clarice in dismay at the sight of Fredrick and Morgan in the throes of passion. Fredrick then jolted off Morgan and frantically began to gather himself.

"How could you…how could you betray Gabrielle and me!" Clarice shouted as tears began to well up in her eyes.

"What about my needs and desires, Clarice? Did you ever stop to think about that!" Fredrick shouted.

"I understand…what you desire I cannot give you. So you indulge in this harlot!" Clarice shouted while aggressively pointing at Morgan.

"I didn't want you to find out this way, Clarice. Just accept that Fredrick's heart no longer beats for you," Morgan said to Clarice in a distressed tone as she pulled her emerald dress above her chest.

"You lost your husband, so now you covet mine. Get out…get out of this house, and may God forgive you, for you shall never receive such mercy from me!" Clarice shouted in contempt.

Morgan then exited the stage in a scamper, leaving Clarice and Fredrick alone in the bedroom.

"We're all human, Clarice. Your heart is no more special than anyone else's," Fredrick said to Clarice as she wept with her back turned to him.

"All I've ever done was love you," Clarice said to Fredrick. Clarice then grabbed a knife from the corner bar of the bedroom and swiftly stabbed Fredrick in the chest.

All the attendees in the Thespian Pavilion then gasped at that climactic moment as Fredrick fell to the floor, and blood splattered upon Clarice's white gown.

"Gabrielle told me to give you this," Clarice said to Fredrick, who lay motionless, and then kissed his bloodied lips.

The curtains then fell as the rest of the attendees vigorously applauded, but I sat silently stupefied and awestruck by what I just witnessed.

*****

"Attention, ladies and gentlemen, there will now be a ten-minute intermission so that the thespians may gather themselves," the same man from the beginning of the play pronounced and then quickly exited the stage.

Luna was a true talent of the thespian world. I wondered if she'd noticed me seated in the front row. I wouldn't be surprised if she hadn't. She was too great of a thespian to be distracted by any attendee. The elderly woman seated next to me was using a handkerchief to wipe tears away from her eyes. That was how evocative Luna's performance was. I see now why Luna and her troupe were rehearsing around the clock for this play. This bold and daring play, which Luna was an integral part of, shone a light on many topics that are stigmatized in this day and age. The tones and themes of this dark play were a pleasant departure from what I was expecting, and my eyes were fixed upon the curtain, waiting for it to rise.

"Attention ladies and gentlemen, I present to you act 2 of *Madam of the Crimson Manor*," the man pronounced and then quickly exited the stage.

The curtain then rose to begin scene 4. I applauded along with the rest of the attendees to the sight of Clarice still wearing her bloodstained white gown and holding a shovel in a garden backdrop behind the manor while Fredrick lay in a sack on the ground beside Clarice.

"I trusted you with all my heart." Clarice spoke aloud as tears streamed down her sorrowful visage. Clarice then began to dig Fredrick a grave, one slow and agonizing shovelful at a time, an experience which I was painfully familiar with. This scene was incredibly difficult for me to watch. My heart pounded heavily with each shovelful of earth that Clarice tossed atop Fredrick's body. "Forgive me." Clarice spoke aloud as she patted the topsoil of Fredrick's grave with the shovel. The curtain then fell as I sighed in distress and grief from having to relive the most painful moment of my life, as a form of entertainment.

The curtain then rose to begin scene 5. I applauded along with the rest of the attendees to the sight of Clarice wearing a sleeveless crimson gown with Gabrielle and Barbara in a parlor backdrop.

"I take it Fredrick still hasn't returned, dear?" Barbara inquired as she poured herself a glass of wine and then sat down on the sofa beside Clarice.

"No, I haven't seen him in four days," Clarice replied in a weeping tone.

"I miss Daddy," Gabrielle said to Clarice as she played with a doll.

"Me too, sweetheart, but we'll always have each other. I will never leave you like Daddy did," Clarice said to Gabrielle as she embraced her firmly.

"I have to go now. You keep your mother company," Barbara said to Gabrielle with a warm embrace and then exited the stage.

"Gabrielle, stay in the parlor while I attend to the garden," Clarice said to Gabrielle and then exited the stage, leaving Gabrielle alone, quietly playing with her doll. You could then see Clarice in the garden through the parlor window. She was on her knees professing her despair over Fredrick's grave. Gabrielle then slowly walked over to the window and stared intently at Clarice in the garden.

"Uncle Sam!" Gabrielle shouted as a man dressed in a tailcoat entered the parlor and scooped up Gabrielle in his arms with a smile.

"I have some business matters to discuss with your father, princess. Has he returned yet?" Samuel inquired.

"Mommy is talking to him in the garden," Gabrielle replied as she pointed to the parlor window.

"Sweetheart, your father isn't out there," Samuel said to Gabrielle with a bewildered visage as he stared at Clarice through the parlor window. "Oh my god!" Samuel spoke aloud in dismay.

"What's wrong, Uncle Sam?" Gabrielle inquired as Samuel put her down.

"Listen to me…your mother isn't well. I need you to go to your bedroom and not come out till I say," Samuel replied in a distressed tone as he placed his hands on Gabrielle's dainty shoulders.

"All right," Gabrielle said to Samuel and then exited the stage with her doll in hand.

Clarice then entered the parlor and immediately poured herself a drink. Clarice then finished her drink in one large gulp as her hand quivered while holding the glass.

"Constable, open up!" a stern voice shouted from behind the door.

A shrieking note from a violin being played suddenly resonated as all the attendees of the Thespian Pavilion gasped.

Clarice then slowly opened the door, and two constables stormed in.

"Explain this intrusion upon my home," Clarice demanded in a distressed tone.

"We have reason to believe that you're responsible for the death of Lord Fredrick Constantine," a constable said to Clarice in a stern tone as he guarded the door.

"Death? My husband is away on business," Clarice said to the constable in a distressed tone.

"Dig there," Samuel said to the two constables, who then began to frantically dig right where Clarice had buried Fredrick's body.

"Stop! I just planted those roses…Samuel, what are you doing?" Clarice inquired as tears poured from her eyes, but Samuel didn't respond. He just stood in silence, watching the two constables dig. After a few suspenseful moments, the constables unearthed Fredrick's body and then entered the parlor.

"Clarice Constantine, you're under arrest for the murder of Fredrick Constantine," one constable pronounced in a stern tone as he and another constable handcuffed and restrained Clarice.

"What have you done, Clarice?" Samuel inquired in dismay and with a grief-stricken visage.

"No…no…all I've ever done was love him. Gabrielle…Gabrielle!" Clarice shouted as tears poured down her sorrowful visage.

The two constables then dragged Clarice out the door as she continued to cry for Gabrielle. The curtain then fell, and I stood up before any attendee in the Thespian Pavilion and began vigorously applauding. The rest of the attendees then quickly followed and applauded the heartbreaking end of *Madam of the Crimson Manor*. The standing ovation continued for several minutes before the curtain rose to the sight of the entire cast lined up on stage.

I took the rose from the pocket of my jacket and tossed it upon the stage right in front of Luna's feet. The entire cast then bowed in unison as the rest of the attendees of the Thespian Pavilion also threw flowers upon the stage. Luna then stared down at me with a smile and gestured for me to meet her backstage. The attendees began pouring out of the Thespian Pavilion, but I patiently waited for Luna backstage. I then saw Luna kissing and embracing her fellow troupe members warmly before she made her way to me.

"You came," Luna said with a smile.

"Of course, you were remarkable," I said to Luna with a smile.

"Thank you. This was the greatest reception my troupe and I ever received," Luna remarked in a zealous tone. "I'm going to go change really quick. Don't go anywhere, Vincent," Luna said as she took off the long and gleaming black wig of Clarice from atop her head.

"I'll be right here," I said to Luna with a smile. Luna then scampered into one of the backstage dressing rooms while lifting her crimson gown above her ankles.

After a few moments, Luna exited the backstage dressing room wearing a black gown fringed with a garnet trim along the sleeves and skirt and a silver shawl wrapped loosely around her shoulders.

"That's better. That crimson gown was beautiful, but the fabric was awfully itchy," Luna remarked.

"Do you want to go to the Wishing Well to celebrate?" I inquired.

"Oh, that tavern is far too boisterous right now. I have a much quieter place in mind," Luna said, with an elfin smile, and then grabbed a large bottle of wine from a table beside the dressing rooms.

"Lead the way," I said to Luna with a smile.

Many people were shouting praises to Luna for her performance in *Madam of the Crimson Manor* as we waited on the street for a carriage.

"White Stone district, flat *A*-2," Luna said to the coachman as we entered the carriage. "It's such a calm night," Luna remarked with a sigh as she primped her flaxen hair, which lay lightly upon her chest.

I felt somewhat nervous riding in a carriage with such a prominent woman like Luna. She seemed to effortlessly exude grace and loveliness wherever she went, and I stood in the shadows of her radiance.

"Are you always this quiet, Vincent?" Luna inquired with a smile as she leaned in close.

"No, I'm just stunned by your incredible performance tonight. That was the first play I've ever attended," I replied.

"Thank you. I'm honored. I saw you in the front row," Luna said with a smile as the carriage halted.

"No charge, Ms. LaGrange. You were superb tonight," the coachmen said to Luna.

"Thank you, dear. This gentleman is with me," Luna said to the coachman.

I then exited the carriage and opened the door for Luna as she took my hand. I then followed Luna through a black gate into a small courtyard beside her flat, which was lit by several candles and lanterns.

"Please sit down. Oh, I forgot glasses. Oh well, we can just share this bottle one sip at a time," Luna said with a smile as I sat down on a white stone bench with Luna sitting across from me.

"This is a nice area," I remarked.

"Indeed, it's quite peaceful. I often come here to rehearse for plays or just to have a serene moment alone with my thoughts," Luna said as she uncorked the bottle of wine and then took a small sip. The white stone table betwixt Luna and I had a carving of two doves holding a single rose on it and a candle upon it, which casted light on Luna's visage in such a warm and delicate manner.

"The crickets are quite loud tonight," Luna remarked.

"I always found their chirping to be a soothing sound," I said to Luna and then took a swig of merlot.

"You're not from Thianor, are you, Vincent?" Luna said with a smile as she walked around the courtyard with the merlot bottle in hand.

"No, I'm not. I lived in a cabin on the western boarder of Vilkswood most of my life," I said to Luna as she handed me the bottle of merlot.

"That must have been a tiresome life. I've heard stories of how dangerous those woods are," Luna said as she sat back down on the white stone bench with a sigh.

"It's the only life I knew. That little girl who played your daughter in the play was wonderful," I said to Luna and then took a swig of merlot.

"Oh, Emily Morton. She is such a rare gem. I'm sure she will have a leading role very soon," Luna said.

"All the cast performed their roles well, but your performance upstaged them all. The prominence of your raw emotions enticed me like a moth to the flame," I said to Luna in a zealous tone.

"I'm so flattered you enjoyed my performance. I must say, Vincent…you don't speak like a hunter. You speak with the passion and eloquence of a thespian," Luna said with a smile and then took a swig of merlot.

"Not all of us hunters have the brains of the pheasants we hunt. My father homeschooled me. He wouldn't allow me to hunt unless I finished my curriculum for the day. This gave me incentive," I said to Luna.

"He sounds like a wise man. When did he die?" Luna inquired in a somber tone as her peridot eyes glimmered amidst the candlelight.

"I never told you he died. How did you know?" I inquired.

"The tone of your voice when you speak of him—it's laden with grief," Luna replied in a somber tone.

"He died when I was eighteen years old," I replied and then took a swig of merlot.

"I'm sorry. There isn't a shadow of a doubt that he's responsible for the man you became," Luna said as she reached out and gently placed her hand upon mine on the white stone table.

The night carried on as Luna and I continued to talk and drink wine in her courtyard, and with each passing moment, we confided more and more with each other.

"That scene where you kissed you husband, just after killing him, was chillingly brilliant," I said to Luna.

"Oh, that was my idea to improvise that scene. It wasn't in the original play by Harriet Le Fae," Luna said as she slowly spun around the courtyard in besotted joy with the wine bottle in hand.

"Your parents must be so proud of you," I said to Luna as I gestured to her for the merlot.

Luna then halted her merriment and sat back down on the white stone bench. "My father and younger sister call me the greatest thespian this world has ever seen," Luna said with an elfin smile.

"How does your mother feel?" I inquired and then took a swig of merlot.

"I never knew her. She died giving birth to me. I would like to imagine that she would be proud of me if she were alive. That's what my father tells me," Luna replied as she grabbed the wine bottle.

"I'm sorry. My mother died giving birth to me as well," I said to Luna in a somber tone, followed by a sporadic cough.

"I'm grateful we found each other," Luna said as she reached out from across the white stone table and gently took my hand.

"It's like you said…even though we never knew our mothers, we still owe our lives to them," I said to Luna in a somber tone as I took a swig from the bottle of wine, which was now half empty.

"I find you very interesting, Vincent. You appear as a hunter, but you speak like a thespian," Luna said with an elfin smile as her head rested in her hand upon the white stone table.

"You've never met a hunter before?" I inquired.

"I've met many hunters, but none like you," Luna replied.

I then stared at Luna with a bashful smile as she took a swig from the bottle of wine. "I've noticed that thespians get all the benefits in this town," I said to Luna.

"No, no, only during the day of our performances. Every other day, we're treated the same as any other townsfolk," Luna said to me as she adjusted her dress.

"How are you able to cry so easily during your performances?" I inquired and then took a swig from the bottle of wine.

"It's a thespian technique, which takes a lot of practice. During a scene that requires tears, I immediately evoke the most painful moments in my life in my mind, and then the tears flow," Luna said.

"My father once told me that thespians were an eccentric class of people from a different world in which hunters could never relate to. I see now that he was wrong," I said to Luna.

"Have you any other family, Vincent?" Luna inquired.

I then took a profound sigh and rubbed my bleary eyes. "I had a wife and daughter to whom I loved more than anything on this earth, but they were taken from me by a wolf, a monster," I said to Luna in a somber tone and then took a long swig from the bottle of wine. Luna then reached out again from across the white stone table and took my hand betwixt both her soft hands.

"There's a darkness over you, Vincent, but it doesn't have to rule your life. That love you felt for your wife, mother, father, and daughter is a most beautiful and pure light that can repel all darkness, but only if you let it," Luna said in a somber tone as her visage turned to sorrow in reaction to mine.

"It's why I'm in Thianor. To gather recourses and information on White Bane," I said to Luna as I stood up from the white stone bench and slowly walked around the courtyard.

"I've heard stories of that infamous wolf of Vilkswood. Is that the sole reason you're here, Vincent?" Luna inquired as she sat atop the white stone table and took off her black heeled boots.

"He killed my wife and daughter, and yet he still draws breath. You've heard stories of White Bane. Well, I've seen him with my own two eyes and his white fur stained with Heather's and Audrey's blood. I will avenge my wife and daughter by killing White Bane… if it's the last thing I do," I replied in a stern tone as I paced back and forth in front of Luna.

"Vincent, if you truly believe that's what your wife and daughter would want for your life now, then you hunt this White Bane to the fullest extent of your heart," Luna said in a somber tone and then took a swig from the bottle of wine.

I continued to pace in front of Luna as she sat atop the white stone table with her legs crossed. Luna then took out a silver hairbrush from her emerald reticule and began to slowly brush her wavy flaxen hair.

"Vincent, please sit down. Let's make a promise. Whenever either of us feels heartbroken and despondent, we come here to this courtyard. This place can be our private sanctuary," Luna said in a solemn tone as I sat down beside her on the white stone table.

"All right, deal. But you do live all the way across town," I said to Luna with a grin. Luna and I then shook hands in agreement.

"I'm serious, Vincent. Come here to this courtyard whenever you feel lost. Though I may not always be home to join you out here, know that my heart is always here," Luna said.

"I will. I promise," I said to Luna. Luna then placed her hand upon mine as she leaned in close and kissed me on the cheek.

At 12:45 AM, Luna then playfully grabbed the wine bottle from me with a giggle just as I was about to take a swig.

"Daisy and I will have to clean this courtyard more often now. We should plant a row of roses over here," Luna said as she pointed to the back side of the courtyard.

"You don't have to decorate this place just for me," I said to Luna and then took a swig from the bottle of wine.

"It's not just for you. Being enveloped by beauty inspires me when I'm rehearsing for an upcoming play," Luna said and then took a swig from the bottle of wine. "All gone," Luna said with a smile as she shook the empty wine bottle and then placed it back upon the white stone table. Luna then sighed with a smile as she lay back upon the white stone table with her bare feet playfully kicking.

"It's late," I said to Luna with a sporadic cough.

"Oh, I must tend to my father and tell him and Daisy how well my play was received," Luna said as she jolted upright from the white stone table and put on her black heeled boots.

"Is he all right?" I inquired.

"My father—he has been ill for months now. Daisy and I take care of him. Hopefully the news of my performance tonight will uplift his spirits," Luna replied in a somber tone.

"What afflicts him?" I inquired in a somber tone.

"The doctors are calling it the white plague. They say there's no cure," Luna said as a single tear streamed down her freckled cheek.

I then draped my arm around Luna's shoulders as she softly wept. "What are his symptoms?" I inquired.

"He's turned pale, and his vigor has left him. But what pains me the most is how he's begun to cough up blood," Luna said in a weeping tone.

"I'm sorry. I must go now," I said with a bewildered visage. My heart then shook in sooth as I removed my arm from atop Luna's shoulders.

CHAPTER 11

The White Plague

The crusade to resist death, with every crimson breath.

"Mail for you, Vincent," Roselyn said as she handed me the gold envelope. It'd been two days since Luna and I shared that bottle of wine in her courtyard. If I were afflicted with the white plague, then I couldn't risk spreading it to Luna. I needed to find a doctor in town with haste, lest the Merchant sisters discover, and they might evict me from the Rosewood Inn. So for the time being, I must keep my possible affliction a secret to all. Luna told me there was no cure for the white plague. This news would be devastating to a man with something to lose, which he values far greater than his own life, but I was no such man. I could tell from the gold envelope that the letter was from Luna. So I sat down on the sofa in the lobby and began to read Luna's letter.

Dear Vincent,

I hope all is well with you. I was worried since you left with such haste. I haven't connected with another man in the beautiful manner that I did with you that night. We may be different classes of people, but our hearts beat in unison. Even as I write you this letter, I can still feel your gentle presence beside me. For the first time in a week, my father stood up out of bed and warmly embraced me after I told him how greatly my performance of *Madam of the Crimson Manor* was received. My sister caught a glimpse of you from our balcony that night, and she thought you appeared tenebrous. I told her not to judge a book by its cover and

> that she was terribly mistaken, for you have such a beautiful heart. Daisy and I will be adorning the courtyard with roses, ribbons, and banners tomorrow, to keep our sanctuary beautiful. I hope to see you there soon, Vincent.
>
> Sincerely,
> Luna

Luna's sentiments written so eloquently in her letter echoed mine. I felt so grateful that such a beautiful and coveted woman of Thianor showed interest in a lowly hunter like me. I wanted to be with Luna. I felt solace in her presence—a solace I haven't felt in such a long time, a solace I no longer believed was possible after Heather's and Audrey's death. Death did follow me wherever I go in this world, and now it'd taken a new form. I couldn't risk infecting such a beautiful creature such as Luna with my possible affliction.

"Vincent, come to the florist with me," Beatrice said.

"Yes, ma'am," I said to Beatrice as I jolted upright from the lobby sofa.

"Vincent, you have to stop calling me ma'am. It makes me feel ancient," Beatrice said as we attached the wagon to Sigmund in the back alley.

"Very well, Beatrice. I would never want to make a woman feel old," I said to Beatrice with a smirk, as we boarded the wagon with Beatrice holding Sigmund's reins.

"It's horrible that the white plague has spread to Thianor," Beatrice said in a somber tone.

"No town is safe from the infinite reach of death," I said to Beatrice in a somber tone, as we drove south into the Black Marble district of Thianor.

I noticed warnings of the white plague posted on the facades of shops and flats. The posters read, "BEWARE THE WHITE PLAGUE. AVOID HUMAN CONTACT," in prominent print.

"Avoid human contact. Now how on earth are we supposed to do that?" Beatrice inquired in a vexed tone.

"It must be contagious then," I remarked. I then put on my black leather gloves to heed the poster's warning.

"We're here," Beatrice said. Beatrice and I then tied up Sigmund to a streetlight and then entered the florist shop called *Sanguine Solarium*.

My nose was instantly filled with the sweet fragrance of roses as I entered the florist. I noticed the solarium through the back room of the florist, where all the roses were grown.

"Beatrice, how many roses do we need?" I inquired as Beatrice and I walked up to the front counter of the florist.

"Roselyn told me we needed twelve dozen. She should be here with us right now. Roses aren't exactly my expertise," Beatrice replied with a sigh as she placed her hand upon her forehead.

"Welcome to Sanguine Solarium, the crown distributor of roses in Thianor. How may I help you?" a woman inquired with a smile as she walked up to the front counter from the solarium.

"Good afternoon, we need twelve dozen roses," Beatrice replied.

"Wonderful. Will that be long—or short-stemmed roses?" the woman inquired. Beatrice then stared at me for advice on the matter, and I stared back at her with uncertainty. "Long stems please," Beatrice replied.

"All right, ma'am, we'll have your twelve bouquets of long-stemmed roses wrapped and ready for you momentarily." the woman said to Beatrice and then exited the shop to the solarium with two other women.

"This florist must be very profitable," I remarked as I stared at the rose ornaments made out of crystal and porcelain underneath the glass of the front counter.

"Very profitable, indeed, perhaps the most profitable business in the entire Fray," Beatrice said.

"Only during warm season do roses grow. How does this business remain so profitable all year round?" I inquired.

"Not only roses, jewelry ornaments and garments, all centered on the theme of roses. Roses always uplift people's spirits, and you can't put a price tag on that," Beatrice replied.

"That will be eighteen dollars," the woman said to Beatrice as she and another woman pushed two carts filled with the twelve dozen long-stemmed roses wrapped in black paper to Beatrice's side.

"Looks like you can put a price tag on happiness," I remarked with a smirk.

Beatrice then playfully shoved me with a smile and then paid for the roses. Beatrice and I then carried six dozen roses each and loaded them onto the wagon.

"Beatrice, there's a personal matter I must attend to now. Will you be all right unloading the roses?" I inquired.

"All right, don't take too long," Beatrice replied and then drove off down the street. "Take me to the nearest hospital," I said to the coachman as I hailed a carriage. I knew not what my possible affliction entailed, but I needed closure from a doctor on this dire disease known as the white plague. Through the window of the carriage, I noticed a distraught man carrying a young boy in his arms. The young boy appeared pale as a ghost and motionless, as he lay in the man's arms. What was happening to this town? It was just as Luna told me; only on the outside did every town appear as a diamond. The rose curtain of Thianor had been torn down, and I now saw death and suffering just as I would anywhere else in the Fray.

Man is an arrogant creature; we all like to think that we're above death. We delude ourselves day by day, but no matter what your status is on this earth, death will always find you.

The carriage then halted in front of a large white stone building. I then paid my fare and exited the carriage.

"Excuse me," a man with a somber visage said as he hastily pushed a pale elderly woman in a wheelchair passed me as I stood at the main gates of the *Thianor Infirmary*. The white-plague warnings were posted all over the white-stone facade of the hospital. The atmosphere as I entered the hospital could be described as suppressed chaos. There were dozens of men, women, and children bedridden in the hospital with only a few doctors and nurses trying their best to take heed their wretched pleas.

"I need a diagnosis please. I must know if I've contracted the white plague," I said to a nurse as she took a patient's temperature.

"Wait in the clinic, and a doctor will be with you as soon as they can," the nurse said as she pointed towards the clinic down the corridor.

"Thank you," I said to the nurse and then walked to the clinic as cries of agony echoed throughout the hospital.

The clinic ward of the hospital wasn't as crowded as the main entrance. So I sat down and pensively stared at a portrait of a doctor that hung prominently on the white wall of the clinic. There were six other people eagerly waiting in the clinic for a doctor just as I was. I surreptitiously stared at each of the six people waiting in the clinic, wondering what brought them here and how afraid they were at this moment.

"Next," a nurse pronounced as she opened the door of the clinic. An elderly couple then stood up at the nurse's behest and followed her to the doctor. I could also get the doctor to examine the bullet wound on my right shoulder and check whether it's healing properly.

"Next," the nurse pronounced as another couple followed her to the doctor.

"Who will take care of me if you perish?" an elderly woman sitting beside a man with a handkerchief over his mouth inquired in dismay.

"Banish those thoughts from your mind, Mother," the man replied in a stern tone, followed by a sporadic cough.

Everyone waiting in the clinic had either a loved one or a family member with them for emotional support for the potentially devastating news except for me. Perhaps this was why they appeared so petrified for what the ramifications of their death would have on the ones they leave behind.

"Next," the nurse pronounced as the elderly mother and son followed her to the doctor. I was next in line to be called for a diagnosis, and I sat alone with a grave anticipation.

"Next," the nurse pronounced.

I then stood up and followed the nurse down the narrow white corridor to a burgundy door that read, "Pathology Lab."

"Good afternoon. I'm Dr. Mathias Hadden of the pathology department," Dr. Hadden said.

I recognized this doctor; there was a prominent portrait of him in the clinic. He had a gray beard and wore gloves and a mask over his mouth and nose, which covered most of his grizzled visage.

"I'm Vincent. Doctor, I must know if I've contracted the white plague," I said to Dr. Hadden as I sat down on the lab table.

"Yes, of course. Let me first ask you some important questions. Have you experienced any chest pain, fever, chills, fatigue, or weight loss in the past month?" Dr. Hadden inquired as he listened to my heartbeat.

"Perhaps I have lost some weight, but that's all," I replied.

"I see, and how often do you consume alcohol, weekly?" Dr. Hadden inquired.

"Every day, but a week ago, I coughed up blood after drinking wine," I replied.

Dr. Hadden continued to examine my condition with a stoic and meticulous nerve. "The white plague has claimed the lives of six people in Thianor. This disease has swiftly begun to ravage mankind, but my calling is to heal the sick, no matter what obstacle befall me. I will remain steadfast in my research to develop a cure for the White Plague. Did you know that the origins of my name translate to gift of God?" Dr. Hadden said.

"With a name such as yours, you have a great deal to live up to, doctor," I said.

"Unfortunately science seems to be one step behind this emerging disease. Have you coughed up blood since?" Dr. Hadden inquired as he took my temperature. I then shook my head no, with the thermometer in my mouth. "Ninety-nine point two, a low-grade fever, and your heartbeat is regular," Dr. Hadden remarked.

"This is actually the first time I've ever been examined by a doctor. When I was a stripling boy, I was deathly sick, but I survived that affliction, and a couple of months ago, I survived scarlet fever as well," I said to Dr. Hadden.

"I see. Well, I wish the white plague was as simple to treat as scarlet fever, but I'm afraid that's not the case. Your condition is stable for now, Vincent, but I'm afraid that you have contracted the white plague, but in its latent form. This means that the chances of it progressing are very low, but each year, the disease will progress if gone untreated. First and foremost, you must limit your alcohol consumption. My studies have concluded that alcohol exacerbates the progression of this latent disease," Dr. Hadden said.

"My friend told me there's no cure for the white plague. Please tell me she's wrong," I said to Dr. Hadden in a somber tone.

"I'm afraid she's right. I'm sorry. This is the worst part of my line of work of being a pathologist," Dr. Hadden said in a somber tone.

"I have two phials of antibiotics. Surely they could help treat this disease?" I inquired.

"I've already conducted trials using antibiotics to fight the strain of this disease, and all cases have proved to be ineffective," Dr. Hadden said with a profound sigh.

"Doctor, what are the chances of me infecting others with this disease?" I inquired in a distressed tone.

"Very low. As I said before, you have a latent form of this disease," Dr. Hadden replied as he took off his mask.

"Oh, is my shoulder wound healing properly?" I inquired. I then took off my jacket and unbuttoned my shirt to reveal my wound to Dr. Hadden.

"Cauterization, very resourceful…the epidermis appears to be healing properly with no signs of infection," Dr. Hadden remarked as he closely examined my shoulder.

"Good. I'll take any silver lining I can," I said to Dr. Hadden as I put on my shirt and jacket.

"Young man, please don't leave this hospital in despair, for your prognosis is far more hopeful than many others I've seen," Dr. Hadden said.

"You have my thanks," I said to Dr. Hadden in a somber tone and then exited the pathology lab.

I exited the main gates of Thianor Infirmary with an array of mixed emotions weighing heavy on my mind. My days were numbered indeed, but I still had many more to live, though only with my own consent. I wasn't expecting words of solace from Dr. Hadden, just closure, which was what I received. Man was unequipped to fight this disease known as the white plague, and because of that, death and suffering had ensued. I now knew what I must do in order to prolong my existence, but not drinking would prove to be incredibly difficult for me during these times. Each drink would only fuel the fire of disease that burns within me now.

"To the Rosewood Inn," I said to the coachman as I entered the carriage. For now, I could still work for the Merchant sisters at the Rosewood Inn. I just had to resist the urge to drink at all costs, and as for Luna, I must be honest with her. We'd already confided a great deal in each other. I needed to remain focused on the task at hand. The white plague was just another obstacle in my life that I must endure. My father always told me I was a survivor; he told me I would endure all forms of death because of his teachings. I had no desire to live a long life; all I desired was to see the light from White Bane's eyes extinguish by my hand. I wondered if any of the Merchant sisters had contracted the white plague. They did come into contact with many possessions that could be possibly infected by white-plague carriers at the Rosewood Inn. If this was the case, then there would be no running from this disease.

I was sure the townsfolk of Bleakton and Shors End are also infected with the white plague. Would I have still contracted the white plague if I remained in my cabin and not ventured to Thianor? This question now weighs heavy on my mind, but I was easy prey in that cabin, and I could no longer live in such a place that was filled with memories of Heather and Audrey; it was far too painful. I then paid my fare to the coachman as the carriage halted in front of the Rosewood Inn.

"Roses…roses!" a little girl shouted as she stood at the entrance of the Rosewood Inn holding a large basket full of roses in her dainty arms. That little girl selling roses was the same little girl whom I bought all those roses for a fortnight ago.

"We'll take six roses," a man said to the little girl as he stood with a finely dressed woman by his side.

The little girl then began to cough sporadically just as she was handing the man the roses.

"Oh my god, Richard, she has the white plague!" the woman remarked in a gasping tone as she quickly covered her mouth with a black handkerchief.

"No, please!" the little girl shouted in dismay as the man and woman ran away from her. The little girl then gathered up the roses from off the ground and walked down the street with tears welling up in her eyes. Such a cruel stigma was beginning to take shape in the town of Thianor. Those who were now infected with the white plague were seen as monsters by those who were not, and thus a divisive rift had been drawn in the hearts of man.

"What work do you have for me, Roselyn?" I inquired as I entered the Rosewood Inn and walked up to the front desk.

"Vincent, where have you been?" Roselyn inquired in a distressed tone.

"I'm sorry. There was a personal matter I had to take care of," I replied.

"Vincent, respect our time, and we will respect yours. Remember, we always need your help around here," Roselyn said.

"I do, and I will, ma'am," I said to Roselyn in a timid tone.

"All right then, go help Francesca, Beatrice, and Sara decorate all the stairs and corridors of the inn with roses," Roselyn said as she pointed towards the stairs.

"Yes, ma'am," I told Roselyn with a sigh, and then walked up the stairs to find the other Merchant sisters.

"Look who decided to show up," Francesca pronounced as I entered the third-floor corridor.

"Sorry, how can I help?" I inquired.

"All right, you can begin by placing four roses in each vase that hangs on the walls beside doors," Sara replied.

I then took a basket of roses and began carrying out the task of decorating the Rosewood Inn.

"No, more uniform…like this," Beatrice said to Francesca as she displayed a small bouquet of roses to her.

"I've done this countless times," Francesca said to Beatrice with a scoff.

"Well, it's never too late to do it right," Beatrice said to Francesca with a smirk.

"Do you think the white plague can spread to roses?" Sara inquired.

"If that were true, then all of us would be coughing up blood right now," Beatrice replied.

"That's not how the disease works, Beatrice. Remember what the doctor told us? Come now, let's decorate the third floor," Francesca said to Beatrice as they both grabbed a basket of roses and walked up the stairs to the third floor of the Rosewood Inn.

"Vincent, help me decorate this mirror with a border of roses. Just weave the stem of the rose through this wicker frame like this," Sara said with a quick demonstration.

"All right," I said to Sara and then began to weave each rose stem one by one into the wicker frame.

"You seem quiet, Vincent. Is something wrong?" Sara inquired.

"I'm just tired. I could use more rest," I replied.

"We all could. I often find myself drifting off in the evening," Sara said with a sigh.

"How does that look?" I inquired as I pointed at the side of the rose border I had finished working on.

"That's good, Vincent," Sara remarked with a warm smile as she placed her hand upon my shoulder. Audrey would have loved the Merchant sisters; their maternal warmth and kindness had a way of instantly comforting a weary soul. Perhaps that's why they chose to run an inn together. Sara and I then gently attached the rose wreath around the border of the oval mirror, which hung at the end of the second-floor corridor.

"All right, on to the first floor," Sara said. Sara and I then each grabbed a basket of roses and walked down the stairs to the first floor. "I'll bet we can finish decorating our share of the inn before Francesca and Beatrice do," Sara said with an elfin smile.

"We don't have to compete," I said to Sara as we began placing four roses in each of the vases that hung on the walls beside the doors.

"You're such a fast learner though. I feel like you could easily master any task," Sara said.

"Thank you, but I didn't possess half your work ethic when I was your age. I can however gut and skin a boar in under a minute," I said to Sara with a smirk.

Sara then giggled as we gently attached another rose wreath around the border of the oval mirror, which hung at the end of the first-floor corridor. "All right, on to the lobby," Sara said.

"Do we have enough roses left?" I inquired as Sara and I decorated the lobby with small bouquets of roses.

"Yes, we just have one last thing to decorate," Sara said as she pointed to the large gilded mirror, which hung above the fireplace.

"We're finished," Francesca pronounced as she and Beatrice entered the lobby carrying two empty baskets.

"Wonderful. Now you two please make up rooms 10 through 13," Roselyn pronounced as she pointed up the stairs.

"We have names, Roselyn," Beatrice remarked with a smirk as she and Francesca walked up the stairs.

"Vincent, can you reach the mirror?" Sara inquired as she stood on the tips of her toes.
"I can't quite reach the top," I replied.

"May I sit atop your shoulders then, so I can attach the wreath to the mirror?" Sara inquired.

"All right, hop on," I replied with a smirk and then kneeled down in front of Sara. Sara then slowly sat atop my shoulders and then grabbed the large oblong rose wreath.

"Be careful, you two!" Roselyn shouted from the front desk as Sara cautiously attached the rose wreath around the border of the large gilded mirror.

"All right, finished," Sara said. I then slowly kneeled down as Sara dismounted my shoulders. "Roselyn, how does the lobby look?" Sara inquired.

"It looks beautiful, Sara," Roselyn replied with a smile.

"I'll be in my room if anyone needs me," I proclaimed.

"Will you join us tonight, Vincent?" Roselyn inquired.

"What's happening tonight?" I inquired.

"We're all having dinner to celebrate the ten-year anniversary of the inn," Roselyn replied.

"Sounds like a family affair. I wouldn't want to impose," I said to Roselyn.

"No, we want you to celebrate with us," Roselyn said.

"Vincent, please join us tonight," Sara said with a wide-eyed stare.

"All right, I'll be there," I said to Sara and then walked up the stairs to my room.

At 3:58 PM, I was already weary; whether it was from the white plague or just over exertion, I needed to rest. So I took a long swig of water and then sat down in the fireside armchair. The Merchant sisters saw me as part of their family. This was a heartwarming sentiment, which I didn't expect considering the short duration of time I'd spent living in the Rosewood Inn. To be part of a family again already seemed foreign to me now, and I didn't know if I could let myself feel that comfort knowing that a new death looms over everyone in this town.

I took off my jacket and boots and then sat upright in bed. I held Angie in one hand and my knife in the other. Angie's hair still gave of the sweet scent of lavender and lilacs as I held her against my nose. If the scent of Angie's hair was the only semblance of comfort in my life, then I was in desperate need of something more. My bleary eyes began to feel heavy as I stared pensively at Angie and my knife before my eyes closed—

*****

I found myself crawling on my hands and knees in the streets of Thianor, but all the townsfolk were frozen in place. Try as I may, I couldn't rise to my feet, so I continued to crawl past all the petrified townsfolk. Upon closer examination, the townsfolk appeared as stone statues. I then noticed a flickering of light that shone in the distance. I knew not what the source of this light was, but it felt warm and comforting as it shone upon me, so I crawled with haste towards it. The light then began to shine brighter as I crawled closer and closer towards it. Suddenly all the frozen townsfolk crumbled into pieces, like stone statues of yore, but the light remained. The light that shone upon me became more identifiable now, for it took the form of a person standing over me. It was Luna to which the warm light emanated from! She wore a white dress and a crown of daisies upon her head, and she smiled with such warmth down upon me. I then found the strength to rise to my feet in the presence of Luna's warmth.

"Vincent, here," Luna said with a smile as she offered me a single rose. I then took the rose from Luna's hand, and a warm light began to shine from within me as well—

*****

"Vincent, someone's here to see you," Sara said from behind the door, as I jolted upright in bed.

"Come in!" I shouted in a raspy tone while rubbing my bleary eyes.

"It's good to see you again. You left the courtyard so quick I was worried," Luna said as she entered the room. Luna wore a teal gown adorned with embroidered roses.

"Luna, I'm glad you're here. Please sit down. I have to tell you something, and I hope you don't think less of me after you hear this news," I said in a somber tone.

"Please tell me," Luna said as she placed her hand upon mine.

"Today I went to the infirmary, and the doctor diagnosed me with the white plague, but I'm latent, which means that the chances of me infecting you are very low," I said to Luna in a somber tone.

"Thank you for telling me. My sister and I have been taking care of my father for months now, and we haven't been infected. I call that a miracle," Luna said with a smile.

"I just don't want to infect—"

"Stop, you don't have to be a martyr for me," Luna said in a stern tone.

"It's in my nature. I can't help it," I said to Luna in a somber tone.

"Oh, what a beautiful doll," Luna remarked as she grabbed Angie.

"That's Angie. She was my daughter's doll," I said to Luna as she ran her fingers down Angie's hair with a warm smile.

"She's beautiful. Vincent, I don't look upon anyone with downcast eyes. We found each other, and no disease will change the way I feel about you," Luna said with a wide-eyed stare. Luna then made a kissing sound as she pressed Angie against my cheek, which evoked an elfin smile from me.

"Vincent, dinner is almost ready," Sara said, as she peeked into the doorframe.

"I'll be right down," I said to Sara.

"She is just darling," Luna remarked.

"Oh, Sara? Yes, she is indeed. Won't you join us for dinner?" I inquired as I put on my beige deer hide vest over my black collared undershirt.

"It does smell delightful, but I wouldn't want to impose," Luna said with a smile while shaking her head.

"No, I'm sure the Merchants would love to have you. This is an inn after all. Hospitality is their business," I said to Luna.

At 7:03 PM, Luna and I then walked down the stairs and entered the lobby together to the sight of a table decorated with a prominent centerpiece made from roses and crimson tablecloth.

"May Luna join us for dinner?" I inquired as Roselyn carried a large roasted pheasant on a silver platter to the table.

"Of course, Vincent. I was just going to ask her to stay," Roselyn replied with a smile as she placed the roasted pheasant down in the center of the oval table.

"Thank you all for having me. This all looks delicious," Luna proclaimed with a smile as I brought an armchair over from the lobby for her to sit down.

"You ladies have outdone yourselves," I proclaimed and then sat down in the chair beside Luna.

Francesca, Beatrice, and Sara then walked over to the table and placed sides of herb-roasted potatoes, gravy, corn, rose blossoms, and rolls down upon the table, which encircled the roasted pheasant.

"Let me take care of that," I said to Roselyn as I reached for the knife and fork she was about to use to carve the pheasant.

"We have merlot, chardonnay, and if anyone is feeling adventurous...absinthe," Beatrice proclaimed with a smile as she placed the three bottles down upon the table.

"I'm not drinking tonight. Is there any cider left?" I inquired and then began to carve the pheasant piece by piece.

"Oh yes, we do. I'll go get it," Sara replied and then stood up from her chair and scampered over to the kitchen.

"Your dress is beautiful, Ms. LaGrange," Beatrice remarked with a smile.

"Thank you. Call me Luna," Luna said to Beatrice with a smile, as she poured herself a glass of merlot.

"I'm Beatrice. This is Roselyn, Sara, and Francesca," Beatrice said to Luna while pointing to each of her sisters at the table.

"Here's your cider," Sara said as she placed the jug of cider upon the table. I then finished carving and serving two large slices of pheasant to everyone at the table.

Roselyn then stood up while holding her glass of merlot. "I would like to make a toast. Thank you all for being here. This inn wouldn't be in business if it wasn't for the love and dedication of my sisters—Francesca, Beatrice, and Sara. I would also like to thank Vincent for helping us these past couple of months. I'm sure our mother, Gloria, is looking down upon us right now and smiling. May God rest her soul," Roselyn proclaimed with a smile and then took a sip of merlot.

"This pheasant is cooked perfectly, Roselyn," I proclaimed with a mouthful of succulent pheasant.

"Francesca and I basted it every thirty minutes," Roselyn said.

"Luna, I read the review of *Madam of the Crimson Manor* in the *Daily Rosette.* Everyone says you're a remarkable talent among thespians," Sara said to Luna and then took a bite of pheasant.

"Oh, thank you, dear," Luna said to Sara with a warm smile and then took a small bite of pheasant.

"Luna, pray tell, why I haven't heard of your remarkable talent up until now?" Francesca inquired and then took a sip of chardonnay.

"Don't be rude," Beatrice said to Francesca.

"It's quite all right. Thespians aren't as prominent in Thianor as they once were, and now the white plague is keeping townsfolk in their homes," Luna replied.

"I've noticed that too. The inn's revenue for the month of April has fallen compared to the past months," Roselyn remarked.

"People are afraid. The townsfolk of Thianor no longer feel comfortable partaking in such festivities," I proclaimed and then took a swig of cider.

"I have faith that the people of Thianor will prevail from the white plague," Luna proclaimed and then placed her hand upon mine.

"Luna, have you tried a rose blossom?" Sara inquired while pointing at the plate of pastries.

"I don't believe I have…they're wonderful," Luna remarked with a mouthful of rose blossoms. I knew that Luna and the Merchant sisters would become instant friends, and there was no place else I would rather be in the world than at this table with the five of them. I felt at home, like I was no longer being hunted or doing the hunting. I just felt safe among these five women.

"Did you hear Mayor Crane is proposing a strict vetting process to all travelers who come to Thianor?" Beatrice proclaimed.

"What on earth would that accomplish?" Francesca inquired as she poured herself a shot of absinthe.

"Perhaps Mayor Crane believes that travelers brought the white plague to Thianor," Roselyn said to Francesca and then took a bite of a rose blossom.

"That would be a terrible mistake on the mayor's part. Thianor needs diversity. It's how our art flourishes," Luna proclaimed.

"Luna's right. He cannot close off the gates to Thianor and grant passage for only those he deems worthy," Beatrice proclaimed.

"He's the mayor. I suppose he can do what he believes is in the best interest of Thianor," I proclaimed.

"Vincent, do you know the story of Thia Lynsetta?" Beatrice inquired.

"I don't believe so," I replied while shaking my head.

Luna then gasped with excitement as her peridot eyes widened at Beatrice's inquiry. "Oh, let me tell him the story please," Luna said to Beatrice in a zealous tone.

"Oh, all right, but only because you're a thespian who could probably tell the story better than I could," Beatrice said to Luna.

"I would say most definitely," Francesca remarked with a giggle.

"Oh, be quiet," Beatrice said to Francesca as she playfully shoved her.

"Thia Lynsetta was a most beautiful and talented thespian who lived during the golden age of the performing arts. What made Thia so beautiful though was her grand benevolence. All the money that she and her troupe made from traveling and performing in each town was all donated to various hospices throughout the Fray. Thia's benevolence soon caught the ear of a doctor named Bartholomew Crane, who was the great-grandfather of the current mayor, Salvatore Crane. Throughout their travels together, Thia and Bartholomew soon fell in love and courted in the spring, but tragedy soon struck the benevolent couple. One night, Thia took ill from a mysterious affliction, which confounded Bartholomew. Henceforth,

Bartholomew dedicated his entire life to treating his beloved wife, Thia, but all his medical knowledge wasn't enough. On Thia's deathbed, Bartholomew vowed to Thia that he would erect a statue of her so that all may remember her beauty and benevolence. The white stone statue of Thia Lynsetta soon began to draw gatherings of people throughout the Fray. A hamlet was then built around Thia's statue, which then grew into a village, which then grew into the town of Thianor, named after the beautiful and benevolent thespian Thia Lynsetta. Thia's statue still proudly stands to this day at the entrance of town hall. I aspire to be more like Thia with every breath I take, and every day I ask myself what would Thia do? That's the story of Thia Lynsetta, the patron saint of Thianor," Luna said in a zealous tone.

"I told you she would tell the story better," Francesca remarked with a smile.

I felt like Luna was performing a private play for me, as she told me the story of Thia Lynsetta. Luna's expressive peridot eyes and tone of voice could enthrall me no matter what the story was.

"It's a great story. You could be Thia's reincarnation," I said to Luna with a smile.

"That's the highest praise I could ever receive, but I'm not half the woman Thia was," Luna said with an elfin smile while shaking her head.

"To Thia Lynsetta, may your beauty and benevolence guide us like a beacon in our times of need," Roselyn proclaimed with a smile as she proudly raised her wine glass. I and everyone else then echoed Roselyn's sentiment in joyous unison.

The dinner had carried on into the night, and Luna and the Merchant sisters shared stories of Thianor's history, art, music, and fashion. I learned very quickly that when you're sitting at a table full of women that it's best to just listen.

"Oh, what a beautiful harp! Is it yours?" Luna inquired as she pointed at the ebony harp sitting in the corner of the lobby.

"It's the inn's harp. We rent it out to bands who wish to perform here on occasion."

"Do you mind if I play?" Luna inquired as she stood up from her chair and walked over to the harp in a svelte manner.

"By all means," Roselyn replied with a smile and then took a sip of merlot.

Luna then sat down on the padded stool and began to play the harp. Watching Luna play the harp so beautifully harkened back memories of Heather playing the violin. If I closed my eyes, I could almost imagine that it was Heather playing the harp, but I had no desire to.

"Is that the 'Bards Ballad'?" I inquired.

Luna then nodded her head with a smile as she continued to play the mellifluous anthem of Thianor.

"Does anyone want coffee?" Sara inquired.

"I'd love some right now," Roselyn replied with a sigh.

I then echoed Roselyn's request and then took a large bite of a rose blossom. Sara then stood up from her chair and began to make a pot of coffee in the lobby fireplace.

"Let me help you all with the dishes," I proclaimed as Roselyn, Francesca, and Beatrice began clearing the table.

Luna was still playing the harp as I took the dishes to the kitchen behind the front desk. "Careful, Francesca, absinthe is deceptively strong," I remarked as Francesca took another shot of the peridot liqueur with a cringe.

"Oh hush, Vincent. I'm not a child. I could probably drink you under the table," Francesca said with a smirk.

At that moment, my hunter's pride wanted to drink with Francesca so much, but I knew that would only fuel the white plague within me. So I poured myself a mug of coffee and then sat down on the sofa in the lobby as Luna continued to fill the Rosewood Inn with dulcet melodies from her harp playing. I then began to clap while smiling as Luna stopped playing the harp and joined me on the sofa with a glass of merlot in hand.

"You play beautifully," I said to Luna.

"Thank you. I first learned to play the harp when I was eight years old. That's such a sanguine age where anything seems possible," Luna said with a sigh.

"When I was that age, I constantly begged my father if we could go hunting, and his reply was always the same, 'Only if you finish your lessons,' he said in a stern voice," I said to Luna.

"I think you could learn to play the harp," Luna said with a warm smile.

"No these scarred hands are not meant to play such an elegant instrument," I said to Luna while displaying my scarred right hand.

Luna then took my hand betwixt both her hands and gently traced my scars with her fingers. "We all have scars, Vincent. They're not there to condemn us but remind us of what we've overcome in our lives," Luna said.

"All I know is that the pain is always there," I said to Luna as she continued to gently examine my scarred right hand.

"How did you get these scars?" Luna inquired in a somber tone.

"From a wolf that nearly took my whole hand off in its jaws, but I prevailed, and now I wear its black fur upon my jacket," I replied.

"My sister, Daisy, once trapped a rat in our flat. I wanted her to set the rat free outside, but she told me the rat would just keep returning, so she had to kill it," Luna said.

"She was right. Rats are very resilient animals," I said to Luna.

"It was a lovely dinner, Vincent. I'm glad I stayed," Luna said with a smile.

"We're glad to have you. You're welcome here anytime," I said to Luna.

"I wish my sister could be here, but one of us must be at home to take care of Father," Luna said and then took a sip of merlot.

"How's your father doing?" I inquired in a somber tone.

"His condition hasn't changed, but he continues with a facade of bravery just for the sake of my sister and me," Luna replied in a somber tone.

"I would like to meet him someday. We have a lot to talk about," I said to Luna and then took a sip of coffee.

"My father hasn't been fond of most of the men I've brought home, and they were all thespians and dignitaries," Luna said.

"Be that as it may, I would still like to meet him, only if he feels strong enough, of course," I said to Luna.

"How does tomorrow around noon sound?" Luna inquired.

"All right I'll be there," I replied.

"Just meet me in the courtyard first. I can't wait for you to see how Daisy and I have decorated it," Luna said with a smile.

"Really, how does it look now?" I inquired.

"No, no, I want it to be a surprise," Luna replied with a smile.

"I want to…tell you something, but I don't know what it will signify if I do," I said to Luna. I wanted to tell Luna about the dream I had, but I knew from past sorrows how prophetic my dreams were. Luna then turned towards me on the sofa with a pensive gaze. The light from the lobby fireplace glimmered in Luna's peridot eyes. If I were to bear my soul to Luna, now was the perfect time.

"Please…you can tell me anything, Vincent," Luna said as she held my scarred right hand gently betwixt her two soft hands.

"I…I dreamed of you," I said to Luna in a timid tone.

"I dreamt of you, too," Luna said in a gasping tone as her peridot eyes widened. "Tell me your dream first," Luna said in a zealous tone and warm smile as she bounced up and down on the sofa with excitement.

"All I remember was that I was crawling on my hands and knees, and there you were, standing above me, glowing so radiantly. I then rose to my feet to greet you. You were smiling, then you offered me a rose, and as I took the rose from your hand, I then began to glow with the same warm and radiant light," I said to Luna.

"That's beautiful…this is so remarkable. In my dream, you offered me a rose amidst an ashen world, and as I took the rose from your hand, the world then became vibrant with life and color," Luna said with a smile and zealous tone as she placed her hand over her chest.

"What do you think our dreams mean?" I inquired.

"It means we need each other now more than ever," Luna said.

"They're just dreams," I remarked.

"No, I believe dreams are a form of guidance that we all possess. Dreams are visions born from the innermost desires of our hearts and minds," Luna said in a zealous tone.

"Do you believe in prophetic dreams?" I inquired with a pensive stare.

"I do, with all my heart. Two years ago, I performed in a play called *Illumination,* which was based on a true story. I played Maria, a woman who kept having vivid dreams of her husband dying every week. Maria's husband continued to disregard her until one tragic day. Maria warned her husband to stay at home, for something terrible would happen to him if he went to work that day. Surely enough, there was a cave in at the mines where Maria's husband was working that morning, and he and two other men died," Luna said.

"I had a dream—a nightmare—of my wife and daughter. They were screaming for me, but by the time I reached the cabin, their screams swiftly fell silent…and then I heard the howling," I said to Luna in a somber tone.

"It's not your fault, Vincent," Luna said as she leaned in close.

"If I only possessed more vigilance—"

"Stop…this guilt you feel is false, Vincent, and it will consume you," Luna said.

"The dream I had of you was the only good dream I could remember in a very long time," I said to Luna with a smile.

"Then you should keep that dream sacred as I will keep my dream of you," Luna said with a warm smile.

"I will," I said to Luna with an elfin smile.

"I should be getting back home now," Luna said with a sigh.

"I'll walk you to a carriage," I said to Luna as we both stood up from the lobby sofa and walked to the front desk.

"It was a lovely dinner. Thank you for having me," Luna said to Roselyn as she fed her doves.

"You and your beautiful harp playing are welcome back anytime," Roselyn said to Luna with a smile.

"Tell your sisters I said good night," Luna said to Roselyn with a smile and wave.

Luna and I then exited the Rosewood Inn and waited for a carriage as we stood under the glow of a streetlight.

"I'll write to you as soon as I can," Luna told me with a smile as a carriage stopped in front of us.

"I look forward to reading your letters," I said to Luna.

"Good night," Luna said and then leaned in and softly kissed me on the lips.

"Good night," I said to Luna with a smile as I opened the carriage door for her. Luna then sveltely sat down in the carriage and waved goodbye to me as I closed the door. "Any work for me, Roselyn?" I inquired with a smile as I entered the Rosewood Inn.

"All is well at the moment. I'll call you if I need you. Oh, Vincent, Luna is wonderful. I'm very happy for you," Roselyn replied with a smile.

"Thank you," I said to Roselyn as I walked up the stairs to my room. I entered my room and then put another log into the fireplace. I then got undressed and slipped beneath the quilt of the bed. For the first time in months, I actually looked forward to going to sleep at night and waking up in the morning. Just knowing that Luna is in this world gave me another purpose, a purpose that didn't involve hunting a monster. Ever since Heather's and Audrey's death, I never thought that I could feel at home anywhere in this world, but tonight gave me hope. Luna was a beautiful person, and the path that led me to her was paved with tribulations, but I felt so grateful to have walked that dark path. There was no White Bane, no white plague, and no memories of Heather and Audrey. Luna was the only one to whom I thought of, just as my bleary eyes began to close.

*****

At 7:02 AM, I awoke to Sara's wake-up knock on the door and then quickly rose out of bed. The sun's rays shone brightly and illuminated my entire room as I began to get dressed. Everything and everyone felt new, as if a flame awakened within me and cast away the dark veil to which my eyes had been covered by. If I could only live in this moment forever, but there was work to be done and people who depended on me.

"Help Beatrice make up rooms 10 through 12," Francesca said as I walked up to the front desk.

"Good morning to you too, Francesca," I said to Francesca with a smile.

"Not so loud. My head is still pounding from that absinthe," Francesca said with a hissing moan as she massaged her temple.

"Francesca is still feeling the effects of that absinthe from last night," I said to Beatrice with a smirk as I began helping her with room 10.

"She'll never learn. Once, Francesca and I went to the Wishing Well for a nightcap, and it quickly turned into a drinking competition between her and me," Beatrice said as we gathered the sheets and quilts from the bed.

"So who won?" I inquired with a smirk as I put a log into the fireplace and stoked the flames.

"She did but just barely. We were so soused that night that we left our shoes in the tavern and didn't even notice till the morning after. Thank heavens for Carmella. She kept our shoes in the lost and found, and then we picked them up the morning after," Beatrice said with a lilting laugh as we moved on to room 11.

"She did seem more relaxed last night," I remarked as I put another log into the fireplace and stoked the flames.

"Who? Oh, Francesca? Yeah, she's always been that way, but I love both sides of her equally," Beatrice said as we gathered the sheets and quilts from the bed.

"Hold on…look," I said to Beatrice as I pointed at a coin-sized bloodstain upon the white sheet.

"Oh, that's blood, isn't it?" Beatrice inquired with a sigh.

"Should we burn the sheet because of the white plague?" I inquired.

"No, we can't afford to do that. Could you just cut out that bloodstain with a knife?" Beatrice inquired.

"I can do that," I replied. I then took out my knife and quickly cut out the bloodstained patch from the sheet and threw it into the fireplace. Beatrice and I then moved on to room 12.

"How do you feel about people who are infected with the white plague?" I inquired.

"It's a tragic fate to be dealt, but they all should be helped and never condemned," Beatrice replied in a somber tone as we gathered the sheets and quilts after inspecting them for bloodstains this time.

"I believe Luna is right. This town and its people will prevail from the white plague," I said to Beatrice as I put a log into the fireplace and stoked the flames.

"I can tell she's already brightened your outlook on life," Beatrice said with a grin.

Beatrice and I then took all the sheets and quilts from rooms 10 through 12 down to the laundry room and began to wash them in the washing mills. Beatrice and I then began the arduous process of cranking the washing mills for one hour. I felt tempted to tell Beatrice that I was infected with the white plague as we washed the laundry, but I ultimately decided to stay silent about the matter.

"Vincent, if you don't mind me asking, how were you like when you were my age?" Beatrice inquired.

"Well, I was basically the same as I am now, only I had much more vigor back then," I replied with a smirk.

An hour had passed, and Beatrice and I had finished washing the laundry, so we then hung the sheets and quilts out on the clothesline in the alley behind the Rosewood Inn to dry. It was almost noon, which was the time that Luna told me to meet her in the courtyard next to her flat. I was excited to see Luna and meet her father for the first time. I hoped I'd make a good impression towards the man.

"Francesca, may I take Sigmund out for a little while?" I inquired as I walked up to the front desk.

"Very well, Vincent...as soon as you finish watering all the roses in the inn," Francesca replied and then took out a small silver watering can and a bucket of water and placed them upon the front desk.

"Yes, ma'am," I said to Francesca as I grabbed the watering can and bucket of water.

I then began to water the roses in the lobby first. These roses were the showcase roses, the ones that everyone sees first when they enter the inn, so they needed to be well taken care of.

"Oh, the mighty hunter, you've killed three wolves and a brown bear, and now you're watering roses for a living." I spoke aloud with a smile. I then walked up the stairs to the second floor and began watering all the roses in each vase that hung on the wall beside each door and the rose wreaths that were attached to the mirror at the end of the corridor.

I then walked up the stairs to the third floor and began to water the last of the roses in the inn. I then noticed something strange as I was watering the four roses in the vase that hung on the wall outside of my room. One of the roses was dead, not wilted, but dead, as if that one rose was exposed to the harshest of conditions. I watered 144 roses in the inn, and none of them even showed any signs of wilting. I couldn't dwell on such trivial matter. I finished my task, and now it was time to go meet Luna in the courtyard.

"I'm finished," I said to Francesca as I placed the bucket and watering can upon the front desk.

"All right, you may take Sigmund," Francesca said while twirling her hair and pointing towards the back entrance of the Rosewood Inn.

"Thank you. Oh, drink plenty of water to relieve your headache," I said to Francesca with a grin and then exited out the back of the Rosewood Inn.

It was 12:17 PM. It was a clear and crisp spring afternoon as I rode Sigmund down the main thoroughfare of Thianor. Bands of minstrels were still singing joyously despite the white plague. I weaved in between a congestion of carriages as I rode Sigmund into the White Stone district. It appeared that the townsfolk of Thianor no longer wanted to be out on the streets. Perhaps this was because of the white plague, but didn't they know they're far more likely to become infected sharing an enclosed carriage than walking out on the streets?

This quiet fear, which the townsfolk of Thianor were displaying was inconsequential to me now, for I already carried the white plague. I had finally arrived to the familiar sight of Luna's flat with vines growing up the side of the facade. I then fed Sigmund a couple of carrots from the saddlebag and tied him to the streetlight. The courtyard was now a sight to behold, and I entered through the gate and stared in wonderment. There were three ornate fuchsia banners hanging from each of the three facades of the wall of the courtyard. Rows of roses also bordered the three walls of the courtyard in a vibrant scarlet fringe. Two small glass birdfeeders hung from hooks on the walls with a small white stone birdbath in the shape of a cherub holding a large seashell. The center white stone table and benches were adorned with a crimson tablecloth fringed with gold trim and ornate bronze candelabra. It was quite apparent how much time and effort Luna and her sister put into decorating the courtyard.

I sat down on the white stone bench and eagerly waited for Luna. Various songbirds fed from the two glass birdfeeders and drunk from the stone cherub birdbath as I waited for Luna.

"Do you like the courtyard?" a voice shouted from above.

I then looked up to see Luna sticking her head out the second-story window and waving with a smile. "It looks so regal!" I shouted with a smile.

"I'll be right down!" Luna shouted and then closed the window.

Luna then entered the courtyard through the back door of her flat carrying a bowl of fruit, a bottle of wine, and two glasses. Luna wore a lacy lavender dress with two doves embroidered on the bust.

"Oh, let me help you," I said to Luna as I scampered over to her to help her carry the wine bottle and glasses.

"You were quite accurate when you called the courtyard regal. Daisy and I decorated the courtyard specifically in the style of a courtyard from the kings of yore," Luna said with a smile as she placed the bowl of fruit down upon the stone table.

"Oh, I'm not drinking. Dr. Hadden told me that alcohol fuels the effects of the white plague," I said to Luna as I sat down on the stone bench with a sigh.

"Oh, heavens me, I'm sorry. I should've known," Luna said in a distressed tone as she sat down upon the stone bench.

"No, no, please by all means. I don't want to inhibit you in any way," I said to Luna while gesturing to the wine bottle.

"You're so sweet, Vincent," Luna said with a smile as she poured herself a glass of merlot.

"Now what on earth is this contraption?" I inquired as I stood up from the stone bench and walked over to the left corner of the courtyard.

There was a large interwoven scarlet rope with two wooden rods splaying out the rope on each end, which hung from two hooks on the corner of the wall.

"Isn't it lovely? It's called a hammock. My father had it stored away in a chest for years. He purchased it during his travels in Shors End. It's a form of leisure invented by the sailors," Luna said in a zealous tone as she walked over to the hammock.

"What do you do with it?" I inquired in an incredulous tone with a mouthful of grapes.

"You lie down on it, silly," Luna said with a giggle.

The hammock then slightly swayed as Luna carefully sat down upon it. Luna then outstretched her entire slender form upon the hammock, kicked off her shoes, and then hung one of her slender legs over the side of the hammock with a smile.

"It's more comfortable than it looks. Come try it," Luna said as she stood up from the hammock.

"All right," I said to Luna with a grin and then lay upon the hammock, but my balance was quickly thrown askew, and I fell out of the hammock upon the stone floor.

"Oh, are you all right?" Luna inquired with a giggle.

My own clumsiness then evoked an elfin laugh, which echoed Luna's angelic giggle. Luna then kissed me on the cheek as she helped me to my feet.

"Those sailors must have great balance," I remarked with a grin as I sat back down upon the stone bench.

"All right, maybe the hammock isn't for everyone, but I find it delightful," Luna remarked with a smile and then took a sip of merlot.

"How are you feeling?" Luna inquired.

"Better…my wrenching coughing has subsided a great deal, and it's been a fortnight since I've coughed up any blood," I replied and then took a swig of water from my canteen.

"That's great to hear. Perhaps if my father changed his detrimental habits like you have, then his current condition wouldn't be so bleak," Luna said in a somber tone.

"May I meet your father now?" I inquired.

"Let me go see if he's ready for a visitor," Luna replied. Luna then entered her flat through the back door, leaving me to wait once more in the lavishly decorated courtyard. If Luna's father was anything like her, then there was no doubt that we would get along. Heather's parents always harbored such contempt for me since the day I met them. I hoped Luna's father is different.

"Come in. We're ready for you," Luna said as she opened the back door of the flat. I then stood up from the stone bench and scampered over to Luna. An amber cat quickly passed by me as I entered Luna's flat. "Oh, don't mind her. She comes and goes as she pleases," Luna said as I followed her up the stairs. "Well, here we are *9-B*," Luna said as she unlocked the door to her flat and gestured me to enter with a smile.

"It's great to finally meet you, Vincent," a slender woman with short flaxen hair wearing a black frock and white apron told me with a warm smile as I entered Luna's flat.

"You must be Daisy. It's great to meet you as well," I remarked with a grin. I then sat down on the plush emerald sofa beside Luna and waited for her father to join us. "Your flat is very nice," I remarked as I stared at the black marble fireplace, portraits, and various antiquities that adorned the flat.

"Luna tells me you're an accomplished hunter, Vincent," Daisy said as she sat down on the sofa beside me.

"I am—well, as accomplished as a hunter can be in this day and age," I said to Daisy.

"You see that hanging on the wall just over yonder?" Daisy inquired while pointing towards the dining room.

"Oh, bison horns," I remarked.

"Yes, our great-grandfather was a hunter who supposedly killed that bison with one shot," Luna said in an incredulous tone while rolling her peridot eyes.

"Luna doesn't believe our great-grandfather Cyrus killed that bison with one shot. She thinks it's a tall tale made up by our father," Daisy said.

"I wouldn't doubt your great-grandfather it's definitely possible if your aim is true. The bison of the Heslian Fields are gigantic beasts, but any beast can be killed with a bullet right betwixt the eyes," I said to Luna, as I pointed betwixt my eyes.

"You see, Luna, Vincent and I are already getting along splendidly," Daisy said to Luna with a smile.

"You must be Vincent. I'm Jonathan, Luna's father," an elderly man said in a raspy tone as he slowly entered the great room in a wheeled chair.

"It's great to meet you, sir. Luna has told me all about you," I said to Jonathan as I quickly stood up from the sofa.

"I know what you're thinking. Luna's beauty definitely wasn't passed down from me," Jonathan said with a wheezing laugh.

"Oh, Father," Luna remarked with a giggle as she stood up from the sofa.

"I would advise against that," Jonathan said as I extended my hand in salutation towards him.

"Vincent has the white plague as well, Father," Luna said to Jonathan as we both sat back down upon the sofa.

"Is this true, Vincent?" Jonathan inquired in a somber tone.

"I'm afraid so, but I'm innate, which means I won't infect anybody," I replied.

"Luna, Daisy, honey, could you make us coffee?" Jonathan requested.

"Of course," Luna and Daisy replied in unison as they walked into the kitchen.

"It's tragic, isn't it, how such a deathly disease can swiftly befell Thianor. I don't know how much longer I have before this disease claims my life, but before I go, I must know exactly what measure of a man you are, Vincent. Only a man of pure nobility is worthy of Luna's heart," Jonathan said in a stern tone, followed by a series of sporadic coughs.

"I understand wholeheartedly, sir, and to be honest, I don't consider myself to be worthy of Luna's heart. She's a beautiful person who's given me a newfound purpose," I said to Jonathan as we stared intently into each other's eyes.

"What was your purpose before you met Luna?" Jonathan inquired.

"I hope you two are behaving yourselves," Luna proclaimed in a facetious tone as she entered the great room with Daisy.

Luna and Daisy then placed a large silver pot of steaming coffee, four porcelain cups, and a silver platter of full of various pastries upon the ornately engraved ebony coffee table. Daisy then draped a crimson quilt over Jonathan's lap before sitting down on the sofa beside me.

"So, Vincent, I understand you attended Luna's play *Madam of the Crimson Manor*," Jonathan said.

"I did, and Luna was captivating," I remarked with a smile as I took Luna's hand. "Did she emote to the audience with the fullest reserves of her heart?" Jonathan inquired in a zealous tone.

"Absolutely! She stole the play," I replied with a smile.

"My father used to manage my troupe," Luna said as she poured coffee for herself and the rest of us.

"Yes, that was before this disease drained my vitality, but now my darling Luna manages the troupe herself and is doing a wonderful job," Jonathan remarked with a smile followed by a series of sporadic coughs.

"Thank you," Luna said to Jonathan with a smile.

"I wish I could've been there to see you perform," Jonathan said to Luna in a somber tone.

"Me too. I've heard and read nothing but praise on your performance," Daisy said to Luna with a smile.

"You both were there with me," Luna proclaimed with a warm smile as she placed her hand upon her chest.

"That's an impressive trophy," I remarked as I pointed at the golden trophy, which sat prominently upon the fireplace mantel. The trophy depicted two golden masks. One mask was smiling while the other mask was frowning.

"Oh yes, this was my first Thialite I won when I was right around Luna's age," Jonathan said to me as he wheeled himself over to the fireplace.

"They give out trophies to thespians?" I inquired.

"Oh yes, it's my dream to win a Thialite," Luna replied.

"You will very soon, dear," Jonathan said to Luna as he wheeled back to the sofa with a sigh.

"Of course, she will. It's in her blood to perform," I said to Jonathan.

"What about you, Vincent? What accolades do you value above all else?" Jonathan inquired, followed by a heaving cough.

"I'll go get you some water," Daisy said to Jonathan as she scampered into the kitchen.

"Well, I've got two trophies for winning first place in Gideon's Run for two consecutive years," I replied and then took a sip of coffee.

"Here, Father," Daisy said to Jonathan as she handed him a glass of water and then sat back on the sofa beside me.

"I've heard of this Gideon's Run from a hunter in the market. It's a hunting competition," Jonathan said and then took a long swig of water.

"Yes, it's a hunting competition that came to fruition by the founder of Bleakton, Gideon Bleak. Each hunter is assigned the same rifle to hunt with, and each animal is worth a certain amount of points. You're allowed three kill portions to store in your chest, which then are graded by a panel of veteran hunters, and then whoever has the highest score wins the first-place trophy and the assigned rifle," I said to Jonathan.

"You never told me about that, Vincent," Luna said.

"You must be quite the hunter to win such coveted trophies," Jonathan remarked in a raspy tone.

"Those trophies hold no value to me now. To answer your question about my accolades, I present this to you," I said to Jonathan as I reached into the breast pocket of my jacket and took out Angie.

"Oh, a doll. Let me see her," Daisy proclaimed as she reached out her hands towards Angie with a smile.

"This is Angie. She was my daughter's doll," I pronounced.

"How did your daughter die?" Jonathan inquired in a somber tone.

"Father, how could you be so callous?" Luna inquired in a vexed tone.

"You're right. I'm sorry. When you're as close to the end as I am, you have no inhibitions when it comes to talking about the grim subject," Jonathan proclaimed.

"Don't talk that way," Luna said to Jonathan in a distressed tone.

"She's made very well," Daisy remarked with a smile as she handed me back Angie.

"Well, it was a pleasure to me you, Vincent, but I'm afraid I must retire now," Jonathan said.

"It was a pleasure to meet you as well, sir," I said to Jonathan.

"I'll take you to your room," Daisy said to Jonathan as she wheeled him out of the great room.

"I'm sorry if my father offended you. I never told him or Daisy about the death of your daughter," Luna said in a somber tone.

"It's all right. Now I see where you got all your thespian traits from. Your father must have found out from the tone in my voice," I said to Luna.

"What did my father say to you when I was in the kitchen?" Luna inquired.

"Those words are between him and me," I replied.

"All right, you two have your secrets," Luna said with a smile.

"I should be getting back to the inn now. There's work to be done," I said to Luna as I stood up from the sofa.

"When can I see you again?" Luna inquired with a wide-eyed stare.

"Soon. In the meantime, you can keep your eye out for me in the courtyard," I replied with a grin.

"I miss you already. I'll write you as soon as I can," Luna said with a warm smile and then gave me a quick kiss just before I exited her flat.

"Oh, it's you again." I spoke aloud as I walked past the same amber cat that crossed my path when I first entered the flat. I then exited the courtyard with one last stare back at the second-floor window, hoping to see Luna waving goodbye to me, but she wasn't there. Jonathan was sickly indeed, but he continued to carry himself with an unabashed dignity despite his illness. If I were to become a frail and pale man gasping for breath, then I would live my life to the fullest right now. Unlike my father-in-law, Jonathan LaGrange was a noble and kind man who was stricken with a grim fate. I could see the sorrow in Luna's eyes every time Jonathan wretched in pain from the white plague, and it hurt me to see her in such a state of helpless despair. The white plague was a death sentence, though I may not be dying at the alarming rate as Jonathan is. I would in the distant future depending on my habits.

My carriage ride back to the Rosewood Inn was dismal. Spring was in full bloom, but the townsfolk of Thianor didn't reflect it. When I first arrived in Thianor, I was overwhelmed by the vast abundance of art and merriment in all its forms, but now the town had lost its luster. The once vibrant streets bustling with an array of townsfolk had now fallen silent due to the white plague. Only a few townsfolk still remained on the streets of Thianor; they were the ones who either cast their fear of the white plague aside or had no choice but to be in public. Still it saddened me to see the very spirit of the Thianorians break when faced with a deathly and incurable disease. I hoped Luna's sentiment was true when she said she has faith that the townsfolk of Thianor will prevail from the white plague. Luna was my only light, my only thought of happiness, and I already began to fear what I would revert back to if I didn't have her in my life.

After I paid my fare to the coachman, I exited the carriage to the sight of a new banner that hung above the door of the Rosewood Inn. The banner read, "White-Plague Infected Are Welcome," in bold letters. I didn't know which of the Merchant sisters ordered this message or what it truly meant exactly, but I was about to find out.

It was 5:20 PM. "Good evening, Roselyn. Did you hang that banner outside the front door of the inn?" I inquired as I entered the Rosewood Inn and walked up to the front desk.

"Yes, I did. I've heard that shops and establishments around town are now shunning those infected by the white plague, and I want every townsfolk infected to know that the Rosewood Inn will never harbor such prejudice against them," Roselyn replied in a stern tone.

"Isn't that what hospitals are for? Aren't you worried you could become infected?" I inquired.

"Vincent, my parents first opened this inn with the vision of providing solace to all the weary, and I intend to uphold that vision," Roselyn replied in a stern tone.

"You're right. Any work for me?" I inquired.

"The lobby and kitchen need to be swept," Roselyn replied while writing in the ledger book and then pointed to the broom leaning against the kitchen doorframe.

I then grabbed the broom and copper dustpan and began to sweep the lobby. I noticed a man sitting at the corner table of the lobby holding a handkerchief over his mouth and nose as he read the newspaper while I swept up the ash from around the fireplace and sofa.

"How are you, Vincent?" Sara inquired as she sat down on the sofa in the lobby.

"I'm doing fine," I replied. I then swept underneath the dining table as the man covering his mouth and nose with the handkerchief stared condemnably at Roselyn just before he exited the Rosewood Inn. I then noticed Sara quietly sobbing while holding a letter in her hands. "Sara, are you all right?" I inquired in a somber tone as I sat down beside her on the sofa.

"My friend has the white plague," Sara replied as tears poured from her eyes. Sara then handed me the letter and scampered over to Roselyn at the front desk. Sara continued to weep as Roselyn embraced her in consolation. I then averted my stare away from Sara and Roselyn to the source of the sorrow and began to read the letter.

> Dearest Sara,
>
> It pains me to write you this letter, and it pains me even worse knowing how it will affect you. One week ago, I received a devastating piece of news from a doctor at the infirmary. The doctor diagnosed me with the white plague in its most aggressive stage. My heart instantly sank when I heard those words, knowing that my days are now numbered. I've been coughing up blood every day since then, and I lack the energy that I once had. I remember when I first saw you working at the inn and how kind and beautiful you were. I will never forget you, Sara, but you must forget me now. Please don't visit me, for I couldn't bear infecting you.

> So I write you this letter in farewell, and know that my life was a little brighter with you in it.
>
> Love,
> Isaac

My heart wept for Sara and Isaac; young love such as theirs should never be torn apart in such an abrupt manner. The boy was playing the martyr role as I did with Luna, but judging by his condition described in the letter, I believed he made the right choice. Sara would most definitely become infected by Isaac if she came into contact with him.

"I'm truly sorry," I said to Sara in a somber tone as I walked past her and entered the kitchen.

The kitchen smelled of sage and cinnamon as I swept underneath the oven, center counter, and pantry. Now was the right time to unburden myself to the Merchant sisters about being infected with the white plague. Roselyn was so welcoming to the infected, and my condition was still innate.

"All right, I'm finished. Roselyn, could you gather Beatrice and Francesca?" I inquired.
"What's wrong, Vincent?" Roselyn inquired with a sigh.

"I just need to make an announcement to everyone," I replied.

"Sara, go get Francesca and Beatrice, please," Roselyn said to Sara. Sara then scampered upstairs with a sorrowful visage.

"Please sit down," I said to Roselyn as I walked over to the dining table in the lobby and sat down with a sigh.

"Make this quick, Vincent. There's much work to be done," Roselyn said as she sat down in the chair.

"All right, Vincent, what is it? I hope you're not asking for a raise," Francesca said as she sat down in the chair.

"Yes, because I'm next in line for a raise," Beatrice remarked with a grin as she sat down in the chair.

"You four have done so much for me. You all deserve the truth," I pronounced.

The four Merchant sisters then stared at me with widened eyes as I stared back at them with reluctance.

"You can tell us, Vincent," Sara said in a weeping tone.

"All right, I have the white plague," I pronounced.

"First, Isaac, now you," Sara remarked as she stood up from her chair and began to scamper away in tears.

"Sara, wait. The doctor said I'm innate, which means I won't infect anybody," I pronounced.

Sara then slowly sat back down in the chair and dried her tear-laden visage with a black handkerchief.

"How long have you known, Vincent?" Roselyn inquired in a somber tone.

"For a week," I replied.

"Why didn't you tell us sooner, Vincent?" Beatrice inquired in a distressed tone.

"I was afraid you wouldn't allow someone who was infected with the white plague to work for you at the inn," I replied in a timid tone.

"That's absurd. Did you not see the banner hanging outside the entrance to the inn? We would never shun you, Vincent," Roselyn said.

"Yes, without you, who would carry all the heavy firewood?" Francesca said.

"Oh, far be it from you to break a nail," Beatrice said to Francesca.

"Please don't leave us, Vincent," Sara said in a weeping tone.

"Sara, I'm not leaving. I was just afraid. The white plague has divided the townsfolk of Thianor," I proclaimed.

"You won't find such division with us. You're part of our family, Vincent, for better or worse," Roselyn said with a warm smile as she reached out and placed her hand upon mine.

"All right, everyone, back to work, chop, chop," Roselyn pronounced.

Beatrice, Sara, and Francesca then scampered upstairs while Roselyn remained seated at the lobby dining table.

"Now I know why Sara is so fond of you, Vincent," Roselyn said.

"Why is that?" I inquired.

"You remind me so much of our father, Charles," Roselyn replied with a warm smile as she stood up from her chair and walked back to the front desk.

I now wholeheartedly trusted the Merchant sisters. Despite my infection, they've embraced me as part of their family. Poor Sara, I now felt a responsibility to console her whenever she may be distraught. Perhaps now I looked upon Sara in the manner in which I looked upon Audrey if she were still alive. Although I never knew the Merchant sister's father, Charles, I felt honored to emulate his fond memory.

"Excuse me, but is the banner outside of your inn true? I mean, do you really welcome those infected with the white plague?" a woman dressed in tattered gray rags inquired as she slowly walked up to the front desk.

"Absolutely, ma'am," Roselyn replied with a warm smile.

"I…I need a room for a couple of nights. My landlord evicted me because I'm infected with the white plague," the woman said to Roselyn in a somber tone, followed by a series of sporadic coughs.

"What a travesty! That's against the law," Roselyn remarked in a stern tone.

I then stood up from my chair and walked over to the front desk. "How long do you need to stay here?" I inquired.

"A fortnight, but I have very little money," the woman replied in a somber tone.

"Here, take this. You need it more than I do," I said to the woman as I opened my wallet and handed her forty dollars.

"Oh, bless you, bless you, sir. You're an angel," the woman said in a weeping tone and quivering smile.

Roselyn then stared at me with a warm smile as I walked up the stairs to my room.

"Sara, what are you doing in here?" I inquired as I entered my room to the sight of Sara sobbing quietly as she sat in the fireside armchair.

"Oh, sorry. I just didn't want everyone to see me crying still," Sara replied in a weeping tone.

"It's all right. You may stay here as long as you need," I said to Sara as I sat down on the bed with a sigh.

Sara then immediately stood up from the chair and sat down beside me on the bed. "Why do bad things happen to such good people?" Sara inquired with a flushed, tear-laden visage.

"I wish I had the answer," I replied as I draped my arm over Sara's quivering shoulders.

"I loved Isaac so much. I was ready to fully give myself to him," Sara said as she rested her head upon my shoulder.

"Judging by his letter, he loved you very much as well. That's why he didn't want to risk infecting you. No matter how much it hurt him, he placed you above his own well-being," I said to Sara in a somber tone.

"It's not fair. It's cruel what this world has become," Sara remarked in a weeping tone.

"I know…believe me, I know," I said to Sara in a somber tone while tears continued to pour from her eyes onto my shoulder.

"Francesca calls me a baby all the time. She's always so cold with me whenever I need her," Sara said.

"Perhaps that's her way of coping with grief, to bury it deep down. Not everyone is so brave to bear their despair for the world to see," I said to Sara.

"You think I'm brave for crying?" Sara inquired in an incredulous tone.

"I do. I learned the hard way not to bury my sorrows because they will always rise to the surface one way or another," I replied.

"Knowing I'll never see Isaac again hurts so much," Sara said as her sobbing intensified.

"Roselyn told me that I remind her so much of your father," I said to Sara.

"You do indeed…so much," Sara said as she lifted her head off my shoulder and stared intently into my eyes.

"If you don't mind me asking, what kind of man was your father?" I inquired.

"He was good…and gentle. He died when I was twelve years old, so my sisters knew him longer than I did. He never once raised his voice at me like he did with my sisters. He would call me his princess," Sara said.

"I used to call my daughter princess too," I said to Sara in a somber tone.

"What was she like?" Sara inquired and then blew her nose in the black handkerchief.

"Audrey—she was my princess. She was smarter and more competent than I could ever dream of being at her age. She had an inner light that shone every time her sweet voice spoke to me," I replied in a somber tone and quivering smile.

"Vincent, could you call me your princess, please?" Sara inquired with widened eyes.

"Sara, please…it won't—"

"Please, Vincent, just this once. I need to hear those words so badly," Sara told me in a distressed tone.

"All right…it's going to be all right, princess," I said to Sara in a somber tone.

I continued to console Sara for another hour before she finally composed herself and went back to work. I had to be careful henceforth how I treated Sara. She lost her father, and I lost my daughter, but Sara and I were friends, and that's how our relationship must remain. Although Sara saw me as a father figure, I was afraid I couldn't be there for her in such a way that her sisters could, yet she still came to me for support.

I wanted to drink. Every fiber of my being was begging for that warm and numbing effect that a glass of bourbon could achieve, but I couldn't, for each sip of alcohol would only fuel the white plague within me. So now my life felt slower and quieter in the wake of the white plague. I could no longer live with a reckless hunter's hubris. I had to now take into account every action I made and how it would help sustain or shorten my life. I was grateful to have the Merchant sisters and Luna in my life, but I still felt like there was an imperceptible part of me that was missing.

*****

"Was Sara in here earlier?" Beatrice inquired with a sigh as she entered my room.

"Yes, she was distraught," I replied as I took off my jacket and boots with a weary groan.

"I met Isaac once. He was a good and noble boy. It's so terrible what's befallen him. Let Sara know that she can always come to me whenever she's in despair," Beatrice told me.

"I will. I'm going to go to bed early. I feel fatigued," I said to Beatrice.

"Do you think it's because of the white plague?" Beatrice inquired.

"Maybe, but I've sworn off drinking, so I have much more energy now than if I wasn't sober. Alcohol fuels the effects of the white plague," I replied.

"That's good. You do what you must to ensure your health. Good night," Beatrice said as she closed the door.

That heartfelt moment of consoling Sara made me feel like a father again, and it felt great, but I couldn't make it a regular occurrence. If Sara were in despair and she came to me first instead of one of her sisters, then that habit would grow until I'd inadvertently divide the Merchant sisters.

The faint sound of sobbing then resonated throughout the third floor of the Rosewood Inn. Perhaps it was from Sara or that woman infected with the white plague to whom I gave forty dollars to. Whoever was crying, I knew that the white plague must be the cause of it. *How does one remain cheerful when death surrounds them at every turn? How does one find solace in the arms of another when those same arms could infect them? How does one find purpose in life when death has clouded all their perceptions?* I was certain I wasn't the only person in Thianor who was contemplating these questions as they lie awake in bed at night, just as I did now. It was just as I told Sara. I wish I had the answer, but I was fighting my own battle just as everyone else is. It still felt good to be needed by Sara as she wept upon my shoulder.

"Don't worry, ma'am. We'll accommodate to your every need," a voice just outside my room remarked.

I recognized that voice. It was Sara, and she must be trying to console that infected woman who's now checked in to the Rosewood Inn. What would've happened to that woman if I hadn't given her forty dollars? Perhaps she would've perished out on the streets, but at least now, she would have a fighting chance, and that was all anybody really needs in life. I then soon succumbed to my overpowering fatigue as my eyes closed to the dulcet sound of a woman singing.

*****

A week had passed since I unburdened myself to the Merchant sisters about me being infected with the white plague, but I still possessed enough strength to complete my daily tasks at the Rosewood Inn. There was a cause for celebration, for I hadn't coughed up blood in a month.

"Mail for you, Vincent," Roselyn said as she handed me the letter. The gold envelope was an indication that the letter was from Luna. So I immediately sat down on the sofa in the lobby and then began to read the letter in a zealous manner.

Dear Vincent,

I hope that you're doing well, for I need you now more than ever. Two days ago, my sister found our father lying cold and motionless in bed one afternoon. Daisy tried to awaken him, but he was gone. Daisy and I have spent the last couple of nights crying ourselves to sleep. Although Daisy and I have been preparing for this moment for months, it's still the most devastating pain we've ever had to experience. We miss him so much. His voice, his warmth, and his guidance still echo in our hearts and minds.

I'm glad you got to meet my father before he died, and he was glad to meet you, Vincent. He told me that you were not what he expected and that he saw fear but also love in your eyes. He told me that you and I have his blessing. He used the word *noble* three times when he spoke of you, and that is such high praise. I only wish that you and my father could've had more time to get to know each other. I don't know where Daisy and I will go from here. We feel so afraid and lost without his presence. Being the elder sister, Daisy looks to me for strength, but I can't help but find myself weakened by the death of my father, like all the strength he instilled in me has now vanished with his passing. My father's wake will be held April 28 at 10:00 AM at the Thespian Pavilion. My troupe, along with many other thespians from across the Fray, will be there to pay their respects to my father. My father will then be buried beside my mother in the *Mourning Dove Cemetery*.

I will be taking a fortnight in bereavement from performing in any upcoming plays. I don't know how I could even bring myself to perform any longer, knowing that my greatest teacher will no longer be there to critique me. I need you, Vincent. I would ask you to live with me and Daisy in our flat, but I know that you have responsibilities to the Rosewood Inn and the lovely Merchant sisters, and I wouldn't want to ever infringe upon those responsibilities. I sent invitations to my father's funeral to each of the Merchant sisters, and it would mean so much to me if one of them joined you in attendance.

Love,
Luna

PS: Please bring a rose to place upon my father's coffin.

CHAPTER 12

Call to Arms

For the ones you knew, may your shot be true.

"He was a great man, and I will be attending his funeral tomorrow morning. Now I know you've all received the same invitation to Jonathan LaGrange's funeral, but which one of you would care to join me?" I inquired in a somber tone as I stared solemnly at each of the Merchant sisters standing before me.

"I'll go," Sara and Beatrice replied in unison.

"Vincent, you may choose who you want to join you," Roselyn said.

"Please, Vincent, I want to express my condolences to Luna," Sara said with widened eyes.

"I do too," Beatrice said.

"I wish I could take you both," I proclaimed as I stared at Sara and Beatrice.

"Why don't you flip a coin?" Francesca said while she twirled her hair with her finger.

"No, leaving this to chance is unfair," Sara remarked in a distressed tone.

"Flipping a coin is unbiased though," I remarked as I took out a coin from my pocket.

"May I call it?" Sara inquired.

"All right, Sara, you may call it," I replied and then flipped the coin in the air.

"Heads," Sara proclaimed.

"Heads it is," I pronounced as I stared at the coin in my hand. "All right, Sara, you do what you must to be ready tomorrow morning for the funeral," I told Sara.

All the Merchant sisters were fond of Luna, but only Sara would be joining me to attend her father's funeral. Sara needed to spend some time out of the inn. Even though attending a funeral wasn't exactly a respite from the doldrums of life, she still needed time away to focus on someone else other than Isaac.

"What was he like, Luna's father?" Beatrice inquired as we made up room 6.

"He was noble, kindhearted, but most of all, fearless in the face of his impending death," I replied as I put a log into the fireplace and stoked the flames.

"So the white plague claims another good person in this town," Beatrice said with a sigh as she gathered the quilts and sheets.

"Yes, disease has no prejudices. It doesn't matter what kind of person you are when it infects you," I said to Beatrice in a somber tone.

"I'm glad Sara is going with you. I know it's a funeral and not a ball, but it will still do her good to be there for Luna," Beatrice said.

"You're a good sister," I said to Beatrice with a warm smile.

"Thank you. I try my best to be there for Sara, even in times when she pushes me away. One time, Sara and I were trying on our mother's dresses in her bedroom when Sara accidentally stepped on the skirt and tore a big hole in the dress. Later that day, Mother called us both into her bedroom and asked us how her dress got torn. So I immediately spoke up and took the blame for Sara's accident," Beatrice said.

"Were you punished?" I inquired.

"Yes, I was, severely. Mother made me scrub all the bedpans in the inn with a tiny brush, but now that's my job," Beatrice replied with a grin.

"I never knew that feeling of having a sibling always there to look out for your well-being. I grew up with just my father," I said to Beatrice as we walked to the laundry room.

"Was your father kind or very strict?" Beatrice inquired as we loaded the laundry into the washing mills.

"Well, I would say both. Those times that he felt the need to discipline me he did so without hesitation, but he also had a way of uplifting me," I replied as Beatrice and I began to crank the washing mills.

"How did he do that?" Beatrice inquired.

"Well, whenever I would go on hunts with my father, he would make me feel strong by telling me that I will grow up to be a far greater hunter than he was," I replied.

"Do you think he was right in telling you that?" Beatrice inquired.

"Honestly…no. I know many people compare themselves to their parents, but I harbor no such insecurities like that towards my father. After all, he taught me all I know, and his dying visage smiled at me, as if to say, that he was proud of me and that he had faith that I was strong enough to carry on without him," I replied.

*****

"Very good, gentlemen. You will be in rooms 13 and 14. Here are your keys, and Sara will show you to your rooms," Roselyn said to the two rather brutish-looking men who stood with a cold disposition at the front desk.

Throughout my life, I'd grown very familiar with fellow hunters. I would know a hunter when I see one, and those two men at the front desk were definitely hunters. One man had a robust, copper beard with a jagged scar running down his forehead, and he wore a tan buck-hide jacket. The other man had long sable hair and a cold, vacant stare, and he wore a black leather jacket and gloves.

"Good evening, brother," the copper-bearded man said as he and the sable-haired man walked past me up the stairs to their rooms.

"Roselyn, who were those two men?" I inquired.

"Oh, they're probably here because of the article the mayor posted in the *Daily Rosette*."
"What article?" I inquired.

"Right here," Roselyn replied as she placed the newspaper on the front desk and pointed at the article. I then sat down on the lobby's sofa with the newspaper in hand and began to read the article.

The Scarlet Hunt

> Salutations, Thianorians and visitors to Thianor! I, Salvatore Crane, am issuing a proposition to all skillful hunters, which will take place at the south eastern boarder of Vilkswood on April 30 to May 3. This is an offer of a lifetime, so if you believe that your hunting skills are adept enough, then please sign up at town hall. I cannot disclose what the winner of my competition will receive, but know that it will greatly improve your well-being in life. I know you're all wondering why I'm suddenly interested in the services of hunters. Well, it's quite simple; hunters were the first to build a settlement around the statue of our saint Thia Lynsetta. Hunters and thespians are two sides of the same coin, and I believe we share a synergy in this world that has encouraged growth and prosperity. I'm aware that the legendary hunting competition of Bleakton known as Gideon's Run will begin one week after my competition, and I'm in no way mimicking that honorable tradition. Only ten hunters will be allowed to compete in my competition, so make haste and sign up now! I would also like to address the devastation in which the white plague has ensued upon Thianor. My heart weeps for all those who have perished from this disease. I've received reports

from Bleakton and Shors End, and both towns have also been stricken by the white plague with death counts in the dozens. It's true that man is defenseless against the white plague, but I believe we Thianorians will prevail, for we shine with a lustrous light that no disease can blot out. Henceforth, I will be putting into motion a meticulous vetting process to all travelers entering Thianor to ensure the safety and security of our precious town. I now bid you all adieu. Carry on, Thianorians, with steadfast resolve and illuminative mirth in your hearts!

Mayor Salvatore Crane

*****

"You should enter, Vincent," Roselyn said with a smile as she petted one of her doves.

"I don't know why the mayor is keeping the prize of this competition a secret. It all sounds rather deceitful to me," I remarked.

"It's just his way. Mayor Crane just wants to create a sense of mystery and allure, which will attract hunters to enter his competition," Roselyn said.

"Are you going to enter, Vincent?" Beatrice inquired in a zealous tone as she scampered over to me and pointed at the article in the newspaper.

"I'll think about it. Right now, I have more important matters to address," I replied to Beatrice and then wearily walked up the stairs to my room.

What were the mayor's true motives for holding this hunting competition? Could they be personal or beneficial for all of Thianor? It had been over two months since I fired a gun, and I knew that my once steely-eyed aim isn't what it once was when I was competing in Gideon's Run ten years ago. I contemplated the mayor's article as I entered my room and stoked the flames of the fireplace. Despite such fierce competition, I won Gideon's Run for two consecutive years, but all the rules and details to that competition were posted upfront and forthright. If I were to enter the Scarlet Hunt, I would need to undergo vigorous training to sharpen my aim, for I fear it has grown dull over the past three months, but I only have two days to train before the competition begins. I then took my pistol in hand and aimed at my reflection in the bureau mirror. My left arm still twinged a bit from the gunshot wound whenever I flexed it, and that slight twinge was all it would take to compromise my aim. I would once again have to overcome these adversities, which I'm plagued with in order to claim a prize unbeknownst to all but the mayor. Boisterous laughter then resonated throughout the third floor of the inn, just before my bleary eyes closed.

*****

At 8:00 AM, I awoke with my pistol resting upon my chest. I then rubbed my bleary eyes and began getting dressed for Jonathan LaGrange's funeral. I wore my black leather vest over my black collared shirt. The only vibrancy that adorned my somber attire was the single rose that I would toss atop Jonathan's coffin.

"I'm almost ready. I just have to do my hair," Sara said as she entered my room wearing a lacy black gown and matching black pearls around her neck. Sara then stared at her reflection in the bureau mirror and began brushing her hair.

"Nice necklace," I remarked as I stood beside Sara and stared at my reflection in the mirror.

"Thank you. It was my mother's," Sara said as she tied her hair up and then pulled down two thin strands from each side of her visage. "I could give you a shave if you like," Sara said in a timid tone.

"I don't know. I suppose my beard has grown rather scruffy. What do you think?" I inquired as I stroked my beard.

"It's your decision," Sara replied.

"All right, then have at me," I said to Sara with a grin.

"All right just sit down in this chair. I'll be right back," Sara said as she moved the armchair in front of the bureau mirror and then exited the room.

Sara then entered the room moments later with a bowl full of soap, a towel, a bucket of water, a straight razor, a brush, and a paddle strop.

"I used to shave my father every once in a while whenever he needed to look his best. Sure, my mother could've shaven him more efficiently, but she insisted I do it," Sara said as she applied the soap to my face with a brush. The soap paste smelled of oranges and lavender as Sara applied it onto my beard.

"I'm sure your mother just wanted you to bond more with your father. That's why she insisted you shave him," I said to Sara.

"She's was right. Letting someone else shave you is a huge sign of trust," Sara said. Sara then began to hone the straight razor on the paddle strop.

"I've always groomed myself. I've never even been to a barber. I always thought that those kinds of luxuries were for dignitaries," I said to Sara as she began to shave my beard.

"I'm honored to be your first barber," Sara said with a warm smile. Sara's shaving technique was gentle and meticulous to the point where I felt completely comfortable in her delicate hands. "Look up," Sara said and then shaved underneath my jawline. "I actually nicked my father a couple times, but he continued to let me shave him," Sara said.

"You're doing a great job so far," I remarked.

"All right, just one last pass, and you're all done," Sara said.

"Nice…more smooth now than I'm used to," I remarked as I touched my bare cheeks.

"How many people do you think will be attending the funeral?" Sara inquired.

"Well, we're about to find out. Jonathan LaGrange was a well-renowned man in the world of thespians, so I would expect his reception to be grand," I replied.

"My father's funeral was nice. I can still remember every word of my mother's beautiful eulogy," Sara said.

"Is he buried in Thianor?" I inquired as I poured myself a mug of coffee.

"Yes, in Mourning Dove Cemetery beside my mother," Sara said in a somber tone.

"Let's go sit in the lobby, shall we?" I told Sara.

"You two look nice. Tell Luna I'm sorry for her loss and that she's welcome here anytime," Roselyn proclaimed as Sara and I walked up to the front desk.

"I echo Roselyn's sentiment," Beatrice proclaimed and then walked up the stairs. Sara and I then both sat down on the lobby sofa with a sigh.

"Vincent, are you going to enter the Scarlet Hunt?" Sara inquired and then took a bite of a rose blossom.

"Your sisters have already asked me that same question, and I told them I would think about it," I replied and then took a sip of coffee.

"It's your calling, and I'm sure you would be more comfortable in your own element than here," Sara said.

"I'm very comfortable here. Are you trying to get rid of me?" I inquired with a grin.

"No, never. I just thought it would make you happy to be hunting again," Sara said in a distressed tone.

"We'll see, Sara, we'll see," I said to Sara with a sigh and then took a sip of coffee.

"All right, time to go. We can take a carriage since your sisters might need Sigmund to run errands," I said to Sara. Sara then took a rose from the bouquet on the front desk just before we exited the Rosewood Inn. Sara and I then waited on the street for a few moments before a carriage arrived.

"To the Thespian Pavilion," I said to the coachman as I opened the door of the carriage for Sara.

"The sky is so sullen, but I suppose that's fitting for a day such as this," Sara said as she stared out the window of the carriage.

"This will be the first funeral I've attended for someone outside of my family," I said to Sara.

"Me too. I want Luna to know that I share her loss of a father," Sara said in a somber tone.

"As do I. The most important thing we can do is be there for her and her sister," I said to Sara as the carriage halted in front of the Thespian Pavilion.

I then paid my fare to the coachman, and Sara and I exited the carriage.

"What a grand reception! Luna's father must have been loved by many," Sara remarked as we stood at the main gates of the Thespian Pavilion to the sight of droves of finely dressed dignitaries and thespians.

"Looks like the wake is about to begin. Let's find Luna," I said to Sara.

"My funeral won't attract even half as many people as this," Sara said.

"You're too young to be thinking about that," I said to Sara as we walked through the main gates of the Thespian Pavilion.

"Not when the white plague continues to ravage Thianor," Sara said.

The Thespian Pavilion was adorned with roses and banners as if a play was taking place there. People were already seated, and I scanned the congregation for Luna.

"There's Luna," Sara said as she pointed at the stage.

Luna and Daisy stood in a greeting line alongside her fellow thespians beside Jonathan's coffin and a prominent, gilded-framed portrait of him. Luna wore a lapis gown embroidered in a black rose pattern along the skirt and bust and black lace gloves. Daisy wore a stark-black gown with a matching black veiled hat, which covered her eyes like a fixed shadow. Luna's smile and eyes resembled a wilted rose, displaying beauty and sorrow at once, as everyone in line expressed their deepest condolences to her and Daisy, who wiped tears from her cheeks with a black handkerchief. Poor Daisy—she was the first one to find her father lying cold and motionless in bed. I knew intimately the devastating effects that could have on someone.

"What a beautiful coffin," Sara remarked at the sight of Jonathan LaGrange's ebony coffin with silver handles adorned with a large bouquet of roses.

Dulcet music then began to play from a band dressed in black, which formed beside Jonathan's coffin, as people began to take their seats.

"Vincent, you shaved your beard," Luna remarked.

"Oh, you noticed," I said to Luna.

"Indeed, you look younger now," Luna remarked.

"I'm sorry. Jonathan was a great man," I whispered as I embraced Luna.

"I'm truly sorry for your loss, Ms. LaGrange. I know what it feels like to lose a father," Sara said to Luna in a weeping tone and then quickly embraced her.

"You remember Sara from the Rosewood Inn?" I said to Luna.

"Of course, thank you both for coming. It means the world to me," Luna proclaimed as her smiling visage quivered with sorrow.

"I'm sorry for your loss, Daisy. Your father was a great man," I said to Daisy as I embraced her form, which quivered in sorrow.

"Luna told me your father died in your arms," Daisy said, in a weeping tone.

"Yes, he did. If there's anything you need, remember I'll always be there for you and Luna," I said to Daisy in a somber tone.

"Everything looks so beautiful," Sara said to Luna.

"Thank you, dear. Daisy and I arranged every detail according to Father's requests," Luna said to Sara.

"I know he would be so proud of everything. We should take our seats now," I said to Luna.

"I would love for you and Sara to sit with us on the stage," Luna said.

Sara then nodded at me as I stared at her. "Then we will sit with you," I said to Luna. I then took my seat betwixt Luna and Sara as the band stopped playing.

An elderly man of the cloth then slowly walked up to the rostrum with a warm smile directed towards everyone seated on the stage.

"That's Father Dillion. He married my father and mother," Luna leaned in close and whispered.

"Good morning, friends and family. Let us pray. Oh, Holy Father, we ask that you welcome your son Jonathan back into your kingdom, and may your divinity shine down upon us so we may always find our way in the dark…amen. We are gathered here to honor the life of Jonathan LaGrange, husband of Adelaide and father of Luna and Daisy. I remember when I first met Jonathan backstage during a play he was performing in. He told me that he was having trouble remembering his lines because his mind was so fixated on one woman in particular, that woman being his future wife, Adelaide Carlisle. Jonathan was a man of passion. You could tell by the sparkle in his eyes whenever he talked to you. So after Jonathan and Adelaide were married by me, he asked me if it was possible to have more than one purpose on this earth. I told Jonathan that we children of God were not created for one sole purpose but to find purpose in many walks of life and look upon that life with sanguine eyes, and that's what Jonathan did. He looked upon life with sanguine eyes.

"Jonathan soon found himself with four purposes in life—his thespian art, his wife, and now his two daughters. In times such as these, we ask ourselves why God would call a beloved man such as Jonathan back home. Well, my children, it's quite simple. Jonathan served his purpose on earth, and now God has awarded him eternity in the kingdom of heaven. Let it be known that Jonathan's spirit has not vanished from this earth. If you need proof, just look upon his beautiful daughters, for they carry his light within their souls. I consider it a privilege to have known Jonathan, and I know he is smiling down upon us right now, as is the grace of God," Father Dillion pronounced and then exited the stage with a warm smile.

An elderly man wearing a black suit and ornate amber scarf then stood up from his seat on the stage and walked over to the rostrum.

"That's Daniel Briar. He's a senior member on the board of thespians and my father's oldest friend," Luna leaned in close and whispered.

"John was my closest and most loyal friend. We grew up neighbors with barely two cents to our names, but John always found a way of seeing light amidst so much darkness. When John and I decided to pursue our passions and became thespians together, we didn't even have the support of our own families at the time, but we still had each other. There was this one play in particular that John and I were performing in alongside each other called *Lord Ashbury's Retribution*. During the rehearsal of that play, John gave me a poignant piece of advice, which I hold dear to this very day. John told me if I didn't believe my character to be true, neither will the audience. Even in his early days, John spoke with the wisdom of a seasoned thespian, and I knew he would achieve a revered status among all thespians.

"Even though my reviews paled in comparison to John's exalted praise from the many critics, I felt it a privilege to share the stage with a man of his immense talent. During another play, John and I were performing in alongside each other called *The Pauper's Grand Illusion*, I had a wardrobe malfunction just minutes before the curtain would rise. The entire backside of my pantaloons was torn exposing my pale behind. John then told me to embrace that obstacle, which struck me with fear and channel that fear into my performance, and sure enough, John was right, for I would later receive the most shining reviews for my performance in that play. Father Dillion is right. John's daughters have indeed inherited his light, for I see him so clearly in each of their eyes. Luna and Daisy, you two are your father's beautiful legacy to this world. So now I bid you adieu, my dearest friend, and like you always told me, the show must go on. So may you now spend the rest of your days in the grandest of company, performing for the angels," Daniel Briar pronounced as a tear streamed down his grizzled visage, and he then sat back down in his seat on the stage.

Daniel's eulogy was a beautiful testament of how one person could have such a profound and uplifting effect on another. By this point in the wake, Luna had her arm draped around Daisy in consolation as she wept, but Luna had surprisingly not shed a tear yet. A couple more thespians then gave their heartfelt eulogies of Jonathan before Luna slowly stood up from her chair and walked over to the rostrum. At that moment, everyone seated in the Thespian Pavilion fell silent as Luna began to speak.

"Thank you all for coming and your beautiful words about my father. Ever since I could remember, my father has been there to nurture all my hopes and dreams. During my debut play in the Thespian Pavilion, I was petrified as I stared at all the attendees from behind the curtain until my father arrived backstage. His mere presence provided me with a sense of solace, which gave me the strength to perform. Whenever I rehearsed lines with my father, he would stare at me with such warmth. He told me that I shone with my mother's grace and beauty whenever I performed, which is why I ultimately chose to become a thespian so that I could feel closer to my mother, whom I never knew. During one of my performances, I received scathing reviews from many critics. My father then told me those critics will soon choke on their words when I become the most-renowned thespian in the Fray. To this day, I don't consider myself a renowned thespian, but in the presence of my father, I felt like I could accomplish anything.

"When we were children, my sister, Daisy, and I couldn't wait to get home from school to the sight of our father rehearsing for a play in the courtyard, and even though we didn't fully comprehend the magnitude of the verses that he recited, he would invite us to rehearse with him. I would now like to recite a poem by Saint Thia Lynsetta, for I feel it speaks for my heart. 'If death shall claim you from my life, your saccharine spirit shall endure. Amid the sorrow and the strife, I shall love you, evermore.' I invite you all now to join me at Mourning Dove Cemetery, where my father will be laid to rest," Luna pronounced and then walked back to her chair with a sorrowful visage as the band then began to play.

"That was beautiful," I remarked in a somber tone as I warmly embraced Luna.

"There's a procession of carriages ready to take us to the cemetery," Luna said.

"All right, we'll see you there," I said to Luna.

Sara and I then exited the Thespian Pavilion and searched for a vacancy in the procession of carriages that filled the streets.

"Over here," I said to Sara as we then entered a vacant procession carriage. Sara sat beside me wiping tears from her sorrowful visage as I took out my knife and began to sharpen it upon the whetstone.

"Vincent, how do you picture your funeral to be?" Sara inquired.

"I'll be dead, so it doesn't matter," I replied.

"I'm serious. Do you ever wonder who would give your eulogy?" Sara inquired.

"I never thought about it. Perhaps it's better that way," I replied with a sigh.

The coachman's bell then signaled our arrival at the Mourning Dove Cemetery. Sara and I then exited the carriage and entered through the broad black iron gate of the cemetery. We followed the rest of the funeral congregation to the seating area where Jonathan's grave was. Sara and I then sat down in the chairs lined up in rows in front of Jonathan's grave. Luna then gestured for me to join her up front.

"Sara, do you want to stay here or join Luna up front?" I inquired as I stood up from my seat.

"I want to join Luna," Sara replied and then followed me to Luna.

"How are you? Can I get you anything?" I inquired as I sat down beside Luna.

"Your presence is all I need right now," Luna said in a somber tone as she took my hand.

The cemetery was decorated just as lavish as the Thespian Pavilion was, with roses and banners. Luna then stood up after everybody was seated and walked over to an ebony harp beside Jonathan's grave. Luna then sat down with a somber visage and began to play. The melody of the song Luna played on the harp was uplifting yet still mournful; perhaps, that was the message she was trying to convey to everyone at the cemetery. A single tear then began to stream down Luna's cheek, but that didn't distract her from playing such a beautiful song, so she continued. It appeared now that Luna could no longer suppress her sorrow, and it poured out of her as she played the harp, which was a beautiful and heartbreaking sight to behold. Luna then finished playing the harp to a quiet applause and then sat back down beside me.

"That was beautiful," I remarked as I took Luna's hand.

"That song is called 'The Nightingale's Lament,'" Luna said in a somber tone as she wiped the tears from her sorrowful visage with a black handkerchief.

Father Dillion then walked up to the rostrum beside Jonathan's grave and began to give the eulogy. Father Dillion's eulogy for the burial of Jonathan was based more in the gospel than it was at the wake. So many people find solace in the words of priests. Even those who have renounced their faith still yearn for those words, like medicine for the soul. When Heather, Audrey, and my father died, I spoke no such words of God at their funerals. My father never taught me the gospel when I was a child, only academics at the behest of my mother's dying words. I wondered if I would have grown into a different man if I was raised on the teachings of the gospel. Everyone found a semblance of hope and comfort in the teachings of the gospel, but I was taught to have faith in my own strength and abilities, for they're the reason why I'm still alive.

Eight pallbearers then slowly came walking down the path carrying Jonathan in his coffin adorned with roses. The pallbearers then placed the coffin upon the lowering device, and Jonathan then began to slowly descend. Luna then stood up from her seat and walked over to Jonathan's grave while everyone else formed a line behind her to express their final farewells to Jonathan. Luna and Daisy were attached to each other in consolation as they wept at the sight of their father being lowered into the grave before they sat back down in their seats.

"You were a great man. I wish I could've gotten to know you as well as the rest of these people have, and you need not worry. I'll take care of Luna and Daisy. Goodbye, Jonathan." I spoke aloud in a somber tone and then took out the rose from my jacket and tossed it upon Jonathan's coffin. What was written on Jonathan's gravestone evoked a smile from me, for it was profound and uplifting. His gravestone read, "The show must go on," engraved in bold letters. I then sat back down beside Luna with a sigh.

*****

"Vincent, I read in the *Daily Rosette* about the Scarlet Hunt. Are you going to enter it?" Luna inquired with a sniffle.

"Many have already asked me that question, but I feel my place is beside you," I replied.

"No, Vincent, you can't pass up this opportunity. Daisy and I will be fine. It will be good for you," Luna said

"Sara told me the same thing. All right…I'll enter, but I haven't fired a gun in months," I said to Luna.

"Hunting is in your blood. I have faith in you," Luna said with a warm smile.

"I'll be thinking of you when I'm in Vilkswood," I said to Luna.

"Goodbye, Vincent, and good luck," Luna said as we then bid farewell with a kiss.

A ray of light then pierced through the gray veil of clouds as the funeral services of Jonathan LaGrange had concluded.

"Sara, I'm going to town hall to enter the Scarlet Hunt. Do you want to come with me, or we could go straight back to the inn to drop you off?" I inquired.

"I'll go with you. It's been awhile since I've been to the town hall," Sara replied.

"To the town hall," I said to the coachman.

Sara and I then entered the carriage in a weary manner.

"How are you feeling?" I inquired.

"I'm just exhausted," Sara replied as she covered her yawning mouth.

"I know funerals have a way of draining one's energy," I said to Sara.

"I'm glad you're entering the Scarlet Hunt, Vincent. I thought of you as soon as I read that article in the *Daily Rosette*," Sara said.

"I thought of my fellow hunters residing in Thianor and their skill levels," I said to Sara.

"I wouldn't feel intimidated by them. You're not in the hunter's town of Bleakton after all," Sara said.

"That's true, but times are tough, and man is hungry. Never underestimate the abilities of a desperate man," I said to Sara in a stern tone.

"Are you talking about yourself or your fellow hunters in Thianor?" Sara inquired.

"Both. I was very desperate as I fought this wolf, not only desperate to survive, but also desperate to end its life," I replied as I pointed to the black wolf fur on my jacket.

"It must have been a fierce fight. I'm glad you're still here to tell me about it," Sara said.

"Indeed it was, but as I wear her black fur upon me every day, I also wear this scar—her final bout before she died," I said to Sara as I displayed to her my scarred right hand.

"That looks bad. Does it still hurt?" Sara inquired as she quickly took my hand betwixt her soft and delicate hands.

"I feel a slight twinge occasionally but nothing painful enough to inhibit me," I replied as Sara examined the scars on my right hand.

“We’re here,” I said to Sara as the carriage came to a halt in front of a white stone building with columns adorning it and an emerald dome, which glimmered in the sunlight. I then paid my fare to the coachman and exited the carriage.

“Oh, they painted the dome a different color,” Sara remarked as she exited the carriage.

“Oh, really? What color was the dome before?” I inquired as Sara and I stood at the entrance of the town hall staring up at the emerald dome.

“It used to be gold, but I fancy this emerald color much more,” Sara replied.

“Is that Thia?” I inquired as Sara and I entered the town hall to the sight of a bronze statue of a woman holding a rose against her chest and smiling.

“Yes, that’s Thia Lynsetta. She’s more beautiful than I remembered,” Sara replied with a smile as we stared in reverence at the statue.

“So this is the statue in which Thianor was built around,” I remarked as I walked around the statue. Underneath Thia’s statue was a plaque that read “Saint Thia Lynsetta, 1466 AD–1498 AD.”

“She died young, same age as me,” I remarked.

“She will live in our hearts forever,” Sara remarked with a warm smile as she reached out and touched the statue.

Sara and I then walked over to the front desk of the town hall where a line of people stood. I immediately detected two hunters standing in line ahead of Sara and me with rifles strapped to each of their backs. I had no doubt that those two hunters were here to enter the Scarlet Hunt. After a few moments of waiting in line, Sara and I finally stood at the front desk.

“Good afternoon. I would like to enter the Scarlet Hunt,” I said to the woman sitting at the front desk who then rifled through a stack of papers in a frantic manner.

“You’re in luck, sir. There’s one entry spot left, just sign here,” the woman said as she pointed to the entry form. I then quickly signed the entry form as Sara stood behind me staring over my shoulder.

“All right, am I officially entered?” I inquired.

“Yes, right after you pay the entry fee of fifty dollars, then you’re officially entered in the Scarlet Hunt,” the woman replied.

“A fifty-dollar entry fee? That wasn’t posted in the newspaper article,” I said to the woman in a vexed tone.

“Sir, these are the rules in which Mayor Crane has formulated for the competition,” the woman said.

“Very well,” I said to the woman as I took out fifty dollars from my wallet and smacked it down upon the ornate mahogany desk.

"Very good, sir. You're now officially entered in the Scarlet Hunt. Take this coin and present it as a token of admission during the start of the competition," the woman said.

"That's the mayor's insignia," Sara said as she pointed at the coin.

The coin had a smiling and frowning mask engraved on one side and two doves engraved on the other side.

"Fifty-dollar entry fee for a competition in which the prize remains a secret—that's bullshit," I remarked with a scoff as Sara and I exited town hall. "All right, let's go home," I said to Sara as I flipped the entry coin. The carriage ride back to the Rosewood Inn was quiet as Sara fell asleep within a few moments with her head resting against my shoulder.

"Sara, wake up. We're home," I said to Sara as I gently jostled her.

"Oh, how long was I asleep?" Sara inquired as she sat up right.

"About twenty minutes," I replied as I paid the coachman his fare and then exited the carriage.

It was 6:35 PM.

"How was the funeral, Vincent?" Roselyn inquired as Sara and I entered the Rosewood Inn and walked up to the front desk. Sara then immediately walked up the stairs in a weary manner without acknowledging Roselyn.

"She's really tired. The funeral was beautiful. Luna gave a heartfelt eulogy at the wake and played the harp at the funeral," I replied.

"I hope she and her sister will be all right. I know how devastating it can feel not to have your parents to comfort you any longer," Roselyn said.

"She knows we're there for her," I said to Roselyn.

"Vincent, how was the funeral?" Beatrice inquired as she walked down the stairs while carrying a basket of laundry.

"It was beautiful. Luna's father would've been proud of how she honored him," I replied.

"I wouldn't expect anything less from Ms. LaGrange. She's a true class act," Beatrice said with a warm smile and then entered the laundry room.

"Any work for me, Roselyn?" I inquired.

"Just help Beatrice with the laundry," Roselyn replied as she wrote in the ledger book.
"Yes, ma'am," I said to Roselyn as I walked over to the laundry room.

After an hour of telling Beatrice all about the details of the wake and funeral over laundry, I then retired to my room in a weary daze. To my surprise, I entered my room to the sight of Sara in her nightgown sleeping in my bed. I then took a profound sigh and began to get undressed.

"Sara, Sara, wake up," I said to Sara as she continued to sleep placidly beneath the scarlet quilt. I then put a log into the fireplace and stoked the flames before I sat down in the armchair with a sigh. I felt drained, whether it be from the funeral or the white plague.

I desperately needed rest. I knew not what the Scarlet Hunt would entail, but there was a flicker of excitement within me that seemed to grow as time neared towards the start of the competition. Sara then turned over in a muffled moan as her slumbering visage stared at me. I then began to sink down into the armchair with heavy eyelids as the events of the day bared down on me in a warm haze.

At 8:05 AM, I awoke in the armchair with a pillow behind my head and the scarlet quilt draped over me.

"Good morning, Vincent. I'm so sorry I fell asleep in your bed last night. I was so tired, and your bed is bigger and more comfortable than my bunk downstairs," Sara said as she entered my room with a tray of rose blossoms and a pot of coffee.

"It's all right. I've fallen asleep in worse places," I said to Sara with a grin as I rubbed my bleary eyes.

"How are you feeling?" Sara inquired as she poured me a mug of coffee.

"I'm fine. I'm going to visit Luna today to see how she's coping," I said to Sara as I got dressed.

"Oh, will you return here before the Scarlet Hunt?" Sara inquired.

"Yes, of course. I need to gather my guns along with enough provisions to last me the four days of the competition," I said to Sara and then took a bite of a rose blossom.

"I wish you all the luck in the world," Sara said in a timid tone and elfin smile.

"Thank you. I'll see you downstairs," I said to Sara and then exited my room with a mug of coffee in hand.

"Vincent, how was the funeral?" Francesca inquired while twirling her hair as I walked up to the front desk.

"It was a poignant tribute to a great man," I replied.

"That's nice. I need you to restock all the firewood in rooms 1 through 4," Francesca said.

"All right, after I'm finished, may I take Sigmund for a ride to visit Luna?" I inquired.

"Yes, you may. Just make sure he's well fed," Francesca replied.

I then began collecting five pieces of firewood from the large black iron rack in the lobby to restock each room's fireplace with. Francesca seemed like she was warming up to me more now than ever. Out of all the Merchant sisters, she had always been the most detached emotionally when it came to me, but I fully understood. It was not easy to accept a stranger into your home after all, and I no longer felt like a stranger to Francesca anymore. I then noticed a peppering of gunpowder on the nightstand as I was restocking the firewood in room 4. Another hunter must've checked into the inn for the Scarlet Hunt. I wondered how many hunters currently residing in the Rosewood Inn were also competing in the Scarlet Hunt.

"All right, I'm finished," I said to Francesca and then exited out the back of the Rosewood Inn with four carrots and an apple in hand. I then stored the produce in Sigmund's saddlebag. "All right, let's go see Luna," I said to Sigmund as I mounted him. I then trotted down the main thoroughfare of Thianor to the faint sound of bells ringing in the distance.

"The rapture is nigh. The white plague is God's wrath upon this earth. Only the penitent shall survive. If you seek salvation, then come to the church to absolve your soul!" a man shouted on a street corner while ringing a bell as I trotted into the White Stone district of Thianor.

What an ignorant statement to be shouting. These fire-and-brimstone revivalists claimed to have an end-all-be-all cure to the white plague in the form of penance. If only life were that simple, to be able to pray away any affliction, but history had shown us that praying accomplishes nothing. It's merely a desperate act from a pitiful soul that had exhausted all their options.

My mood was instantly uplifted as I noticed the vines of Luna's flat just over yonder. I then tied Sigmund to the streetlight and fed him two carrots before entering the courtyard. I then carefully sat in the crimson hammock and stared up at the second-story window, hoping to see Luna's shining visage. Two crows then landed in a flurry of black wings upon the white stone table and then stared at me, as if to wonder who I was and why I was here.

"What do you want?" I inquired as I intently stared back at the crows.

"Vincent, I'll be right down!" Luna shouted from the second-story window as the two crows flew away.

Luna then entered the courtyard from the back door of her flat holding a pot of coffee and a silver tray of pastries. Luna's flaxen hair was braided into a single ponytail, and she wore a black frilled gown with two white doves embroidered on each side of her slender waist.

"It's good to see that you've kept up the courtyard," I said to Luna.

"It keeps my mind busy," Luna said as she placed the pot of coffee and pastries upon the white stone table.

"You look beautiful. How have you and Daisy been fairing?" I inquired.

"Thank you. My father bequeathed us all his earthly possessions and savings in his will," Luna replied as she poured each of us a cup of coffee.

"That's good that he had the foresight to support you financially even in his death," I said to Luna.

"Yes, Daisy and I are well-off when it comes to money, but I care not about such material possessions. I just miss him so much," Luna said in a somber tone.

"Luna, when Heather and Audrey died, I thought about ending my life, for their absence was too painful to bear alone. You're not alone though. You have your sister and me," I said to Luna, as her visage quivered with sorrow.

"I am truly grateful for you and Daisy. I don't know how strong I could be without you two," Luna said and then dabbed her cheek with a white handkerchief.

"Not just Daisy and I, but the Merchant sisters as well. If you should ever need their support, they will be there for you. It's in their blood to care for others," I said to Luna and then took a sip of coffee.

"They are lovely women. So are you preparing for the Scarlet Hunt?" Luna inquired as she took a bite from a lemon pastry.

"Yes, that's why I'm here now, so I can spend the day with you before the competition begins tomorrow morning," I replied.

"That's sweet…stand up," Luna said with a smile as she stood up and walked over to me. I then stood up as Luna detached a pin from her gown. "This white dahlia pin was my mother's. I want you to wear it for good luck in the Scarlet Hunt," Luna said as she attached the pin to the black wolf fur on my jacket.

"No, I couldn't—"

"No, no, I want you to wear it as a memento to all those who are no longer with us," Luna told me with a warm smile.

"Where's Daisy?" I inquired and then took a bite of a cinnamon-dusted pastry.

"She's at the market. I told her to keep busy lest she sinks deeper into despair," Luna replied.

"That's good advice. When my father died, I felt imprisoned by my thoughts of him, and then I went for a hunt in Vilkswood, which liberated my mind," I said to Luna.

"Oh, it's raining. Let's continue this conversation inside," Luna said as she grabbed the tray of pastries and pot of coffee from upon the white stone table.

"I'll get the door," I said to Luna and then opened the back door entrance to her flat. I then saw the same pair of crows return to the courtyard, just as I entered Luna's flat.

"I'm not bothered by the rain. I actually find it soothing," I remarked as Luna and I entered her flat.

"Oh, so do I, but I dare not sodden this gown. It's one of my favorites," Luna said. Luna then proceeded to light all the oil lamps and candles in the great room.

"What do you suppose the prize will be for the winner of the Scarlet Hunt?" I inquired as I sat down on the emerald sofa with a sigh.

"I haven't a clue, but considering the mayor's secrecy on the matter, it must be quite a covetous prize. Mayor Crane has never been a conventional mayor. He operates in the manner of a king, holding competitions every so often to arouse excitement and curiosity in the hearts and minds of all Thianorians," Luna said.

"I'm home," Daisy pronounced as she entered the flat.

"Let me help you with those bags," I said to Daisy as I grabbed a couple bags of food from her and took them to the kitchen.

"It's good to see you again, Vincent," Daisy said to me.

"It's good to see you too. How have you been faring?" I inquired as Daisy began stirring a pot of stew on the wood-burning stove.

"Keeping busy," Daisy replied with a sigh.

"You're back so soon," Luna remarked as she entered the kitchen.

"I saw a beautiful dress displayed in the window of a boutique," Daisy said to Luna.

"Well, then why didn't you buy it?" Luna inquired.

"No, I can't squander all the money bequeathed to us from Father's will," Daisy replied.

"No, Father would've wanted you to be happy. Besides, when was the last time you bought yourself something special?" Luna inquired.

"I don't know. I feel no need for such ostentations anymore," Daisy replied in a somber tone.

"Daisy, the next time you go to the market, I want you to buy something, anything you want at a boutique. If you don't, then I will buy you something myself because you deserve it," Luna said to Daisy with a warm smile.

"That smells good," I remarked and then sat back down on the emerald sofa.

"Will you stay for dinner, Vincent?" Daisy inquired as she entered the great room.

"It would be my pleasure," I replied with a smile.

Luna and Daisy were faring quite well in the wake of their father's death. Grieving alone was all I knew in my life, but now I see the strength in grieving with another. It was evident in Luna and Daisy. I might have grown into an entirely different person if I had a sibling to grieve with in the cabin. During my short encounter with Jonathan LaGrange, I could immediately sense his strength of character. He raised his daughters to the fullest extent of his heart, and now they carry that strength in his absence. I then drew my pistol and aimed it betwixt the bison horns hanging on the wall in the dining room. I knew not how I would far in the Scarlet Hunt tomorrow, but I had the support of six great women in my life, which gave me an unassailable resolve.

"Oh, you startled me. Dinner will be ready soon," Luna said as she placed her hand over her chest.

"I'm sorry. I'm just trying to sharpen my aim," I said to Luna as I holstered my pistol.

"I wish I could help you train for the competition," Luna said as she set the dining room table.

"There's no need for training. You can't teach an old wolf new tricks," I said to Luna with a grin.

"You're not old, and I thought wolves were untamable," Luna said with a smile.

"True, but I've learned everything there is to know about hunting from my father. My skills are complete. It's the other hunters I wonder about," I said to Luna.

"Dinner's ready," Daisy pronounced as she entered the dining room carrying a large steaming pot.

"Oh, I set the table for four people," Luna remarked in a somber tone.

"It's all right. I keep doing that too," Daisy said to Luna in a somber tone as she wrapped her arm around her shoulder.

"I would like to say grace. Dear God, we thank you for the food we're about to receive. We ask that you grant us strength during these dark and trying times and may we live with a love in our hearts that purges away all fear, in the name of Jonathan LaGrange, amen," Luna proclaimed.

I then began to pour everyone at the table a bowl of stew as Luna wiped tears from her sorrowful visage with a white handkerchief.

"Is this duck?" I remarked.

"Yes, it's stewed duck. Father always loved this recipe," Daisy replied as she poured Luna and herself a glass of merlot.

"I can see why. It's a very hearty and savory dish. I could eat this every day," I said to Daisy with a mouthful of stew.

The afternoon carried on into the evening as Luna and Daisy told stories of their childhood and their father at the dining room table.

"I bought an apple pie from the corner bakery if anyone wants dessert," Daisy pronounced as she cleared the table.

"I'll have a piece. Thank you," I said to Daisy as Luna echoed my sentiment. "Oh, I'll be right back. I have to go feed Sigmund," I pronounced and then exited the flat.

*****

"I didn't forget about you," I said to Sigmund as I scampered over to him. I then reached into the saddlebag and began feeding Sigmund carrots and an apple. "What do you think, Sigmund? Would you like to live here with the LaGrange sisters? I know you live a content life with the Merchant sisters, but if you were me, where would you go to live out the rest of your days?" I inquired as I petted Sigmund. "All right, we'll talk later," I said to Sigmund as he snuffled.

*****

"I'm back," I proclaimed as I entered the flat to the sight of Luna and Daisy embracing each other. I then walked over to the dining room table and finished the rest of my pie in a somber silence.

"Luna, play us a song, please. I would love to hear 'The Frolicking Gypsy,'" Daisy said to Luna with a smile as she sat down beside me on the sofa.

"Oh, all right, but I haven't played the flute in ages, so be kind," Luna said to Daisy and then exited the great room.

"Heather used to play the violin," I said to Daisy as she took a sip of coffee.

"Was she as talented a musician as Luna is?" Daisy inquired.

"She didn't play that often, but when she did, she poured her heart into every note," I replied.

"Let's see if I remember the melody…oh yes, of course," Luna pronounced as she entered the great room with a silver flute in hand. Luna then sat down in the fireside armchair and began to play the song at her sister's behest. It was a cheerful song, the kind of melody you would hear at a festival or any gathering of merriment.

"That was the first song I learned to play on the flute," Luna said with a smile.

"It's nice and bright. Have you ever thought of joining a band of minstrels?" I inquired.

"She did when she was sixteen years old," Daisy replied.

"That was when I was still searching for my true calling. I love playing the harp and flute, but performing is in my blood," Luna said as she placed the silver flute down upon the ebony coffee table.

"Don't feel pressured to perform in a play again, Luna," Daisy said to Luna.

"Don't worry. I will be taking it easy for at least a month. In the meantime, I told my troupe to begin auditions for a substitute," Luna said to Daisy.

"It's getting late, and I need to wake up early tomorrow," I pronounced as I stood up from the sofa.

"You're leaving so soon," Daisy remarked.

"Vincent needs his rest for the Scarlet Hunt beginning tomorrow," Luna said to Daisy.

"I know, I know. Farewell and good luck, Vincent," Daisy said with a smile. Daisy then exited the great room, leaving Luna and I standing in the doorway.

"Good luck, I'll miss you," Luna said as she adjusted the white dahlia pin attached to my jacket.

“I’ll miss you too. If you need anything, don’t hesitate to go to the Rosewood Inn. The Merchant sisters will take care of you in my absence,” I said to Luna.

“That’s good to know,” Luna said and then kissed me in a longing manner as if I wouldn’t return to her in four days.

“Goodbye,” I said to Luna and then exited the flat.

“All right, Sigmund, let’s go home,” I said to Sigmund as I untethered him from the flickering streetlight. The White Stone district was peaceful as I rode Sigmund down the main thoroughfare and passed the Wishing Well. I then arrived at the Rosewood Inn and dismounted Sigmund with a sigh. I then noticed that the banner welcoming all those infected by the white plague no longer hung above the entrance of the Rosewood Inn.

“Francesca, what happened to the banner welcoming those infected by the white plague?” I inquired as I entered the Rosewood Inn and walked up to the front desk.

“Someone stole it,” Francesca replied in a contemptible tone.

“Why would anyone do such a thing?” I inquired in a vexing tone.

“The white plague has divided the people of this town, Vincent, and perhaps all towns in the Fray. There are now those who seek to condemn and abandon those infected by the white plague,” Francesca replied.

“Don’t worry. I’m sure Roselyn won’t let this act of hatred stand. Good night,” I said to Francesca as I walked up the stairs to my room.

At 8:00 PM, I coughed sporadically as I entered my room. It was my first cough in weeks, but I worried not. I then loaded my satchel with my coffee pot, a tin of ground coffee, a hatchet, twenty-five feet of rope, a sage blanket that was stored under the bed, my last ashen-gray wolf fur, a box of matches and two pounds of venison jerky. Four days in the wild was a blink of an eye to a hunter, but I still had to be prepared for any danger that could arise in Vilkswood. I would be taking my father’s rifle and a pistol with me, and that was all. I then got undressed and slipped between the bed quilt with a sigh. I was now ready to compete against any hunter tomorrow no matter how fierce their resolve is. A few moments of restless thoughts of the competition raced throughout my mind before my bleary eyes closed.

*****

At 7:02 AM, I awoke to the grating call of crows outside my window and then sat upright in bed and rubbed my bleary eyes.

“Oh, good. I didn’t miss you. I wanted to bid you farewell before you left,” Sara said as she entered my room with a pot of coffee and tray of rose blossoms in hand.

“Good morning,” I said to Sara.

“How are you feeling?” Sara inquired as she sat down on the bed.

"I'm excited," I said to Sara and then I took a sip of coffee.

"I'll see you downstairs. Take those leftover rose blossoms with you," Sara said and then exited my room. I then stored a couple of rose blossoms in the pocket of my jacket as Sara suggested. I then counted my rifle and pistol ammunition, which amounted to an excess of thirty-two rounds, more than I needed for this competition. I then slung my loaded satchel over my back along with my father's rifle and exited my room.

"Roselyn, take this as compensation for my four-day absence," I said to Roselyn as I took out one hundred dollars from my wallet and handed it to Roselyn.

"Oh, Vincent, you don't—"

"I don't want to hear it, just take it. It's the least I could do," I said to Roselyn.

"Thank you, Vincent. Good luck and be safe out there. Your room will be waiting for you when you get back," Roselyn said with a warm smile.

Sara then scampered from the back room and firmly embraced me. I'll miss you," Sara said.

"I'll miss you too," I said to Sara.

Beatrice then embraced me from behind while Sara continued to hold on tight to me.

"Farewell, Vincent, and good luck. Show those other hunters what you're made of," Francesca said with a smile as she exited the kitchen.

"Don't let those other hunters intimidate you," Beatrice said.

"All right, you two let him go. You're going to make him late," Francesca pronounced.

"Goodbye," I pronounced with a smile and farewell wave. All the Merchant sisters then waved back as I exited the Rosewood Inn.

"To the town hall," I said to the coachman as I entered the carriage.

"Good morning," a finely dressed man sitting across from me holding a black cane said.

"Good morning," I said to the man as I examined my pistol.

"You wouldn't by chance be taking part in the Scarlet Hunt, would you?" the man inquired.

"I am," I replied.

"I'm Joshua Colt. My brother is also taking part in that competition," the man said.

"I'm Vincent," I said to Joshua as I continued to examine every part of my pistol.

"It should be a grand competition. Mayor Crane has never held a hunting competition before, which leads me to believe that he has something special in mind for the winner," Joshua said.

"Do you have any idea what the prize is?" I inquired.

"No. Nobody but Mayor Crane knows that information," Joshua replied.

"Tell my brother I said good luck if you happen to cross paths with him in Vilkswood," Joshua said as the carriage came to a halt in front of the town hall. I then paid the coachman my fare and exited the carriage without responding to Joshua.

"I'm a hunter. I'm here for the Scarlet Hunt," I said to the woman at the front desk.

"Very good, sir. The competition will commence momentarily. Around the corner are five wagons waiting to take you and the rest of the hunters to the border of Vilkswood," the woman said while pointing toward the wagons.

"Thank you," I said to the woman and then exited the town hall. I then spotted the five covered wagons detailed with the mayor's insignia in scarlet and gold.

"I'm a hunter. I'm here for the Scarlet Hunt," I said to one of the seven constables standing in front of the wagons.

"Your name?" the constable inquired as he took out a slip of paper.

"Vincent Belmont," I replied in a stern tone.

"All right, and your token of admission?" the constable inquired.

"Oh, right…here," I replied as I reached into the breast pocket of my jacket. I then handed the silver coin with the mayor's insignia engraved on it to the constable.

"All right, Mr. Belmont, all is in order. You may now take your seat. Mayor Crane will be joining us momentarily," the constable said as he pointed at the middle wagon.

"Well, look what we have here. It's been quite some time since I've seen a hunter adorned in wolf fur," a hunter remarked as I boarded the wagon.

The hunter sitting across from me in the wagon smoked a black bulbous pipe while he sharpened a large buck knife upon a whetstone.

"Why do you suppose that is?" I inquired.

"Mainly because they're incredibly difficult to kill, and also it's considered bad luck. It's an ill omen to wear the fur of the wolf," the hunter said.

"I've killed four wolves, and I'm not a child, so I pay no mind to such omens," I said to the hunter with a scoff.

"Ready!" the constable shouted and then boarded the wagon.

The caravan of wagons then began to make their way northeast down the main thoroughfare of Thianor.

"I'm Corbin…Corbin Graves," the hunter said in a raspy tone while extending his hand in salutations.

"I'm Vincent," I said to Corbin as I shook his hand with an iron grip. Corbin and I then sat in silence during the remainder of the ride to Vilkswood.

The caravan of wagons had now passed through the northern gates of Thianor, and I could see the borders of Vilkswood in the distance. The caravan of wagons then came to a halt, and the constable gestured for us to exit. I and the rest of the hunters gathered in a huddled mass in front of the wagon, where the mayor was about to exit. Then after a few moments, Mayor Crane appeared.

"Welcome, hunters, to my first hunting competition known as the Scarlet Hunt," Mayor Crane pronounced in a jubilant tone.

Mayor Crane looked exactly how I imagined. He wore a black and crimson striped vest underneath a black three-piece suit. He had a sharp, bold mustache and stripes of gray slicing through his slicked-back black hair. Upon his dapper suit, Mayor Crane wore a pin of his insignia, along with a crimson pocket square and a gold chain leading from the breast pocket of his suit to his pants pocket. Mayor Crane also wore black gloves, as if he was going to do any strenuous labor.

"Now I know you all have many questions for I've kept the bulk of this competition shrouded in secrecy. Let me now disclose the objective and rules to which you gentlemen will abide by. I managed to capture a prominent twelve-point buck that I've attached a scarlet ribbon to its antlers. Attached to that ribbon is a key, which will open a strongbox at my estate. Within that strongbox is your prize. An hour ago, I've set that buck free into Vilkswood to give it a head start. All that matters is that you retrieve that scarlet ribbon and key, whether or not you have to kill the buck to do so is your choice. Once one of you hunters have retrieved the ribbon and key, you will then come right here where six constables will be camped out during the four-day duration of the competition. You will then present the key and ribbon to a constable. Upon confirmation of the ribbon and key, the six constables will then blow these horns six times in unison to alert the rest of the hunters that the competition has concluded and a victor has emerged. Any questions, gentlemen?" Mayor Crane inquired with outstretched arms.

"What if none of us retrieve this ribbon and key during the four-day duration of the competition?" a hunter wearing a tan leather bycoket hat inquired.

"Well, then I've made a terrible mistake, and you shall all receive a refund in the amount of your entry fee, but I have faith that you gentlemen won't disappoint me," Mayor Crane replied.

"What if one of us gets injured?" a gangly hunter holding two steel spring traps in his hands inquired.

"Two of the six constables camped out here are fully trained in first aid and will attend to your injury…if you can make it to them, for they're not allowed to enter Vilkswood. Oh, you may form alliances and team up however your heart desires, but know that only one hunter will receive the prize locked in the strongbox at the town hall," Mayor Crane replied. The rest of the hunters then argued among themselves while I stood behind them all in silence. I then spotted Corbin staring intently at me from the corner of my eye.

"Now that all the details are in order," Mayor Crane pronounced and then pointed to the six constables who each held horns. The six constables then played a short triumphant call-in unison on their horns.

"Let the Scarlet Hunt commence!" Mayor Crane shouted.

Three hunters immediately began to run into Vilkswood as Mayor Crane shouted his declaration. I knew my plan. We were hunting a buck, and they mainly live on the eastern side of Vilksridge, so that is where I would set up my base camp. No hunters appeared to be following me as I made my way northeast, or maybe they were, and I just didn't notice them.

An hour had passed when I crossed the bridge that arched over the Murk River arriving at the eastern side of Vilksridge. I needed the highest vantage point possible if I was to find this buck, so I climbed as high as I could up Vilksridge. I then felt a sudden sense of awakening, as if a part of me had been dormant for four months, and now I was truly in my element once again as I climbed the rocky outcrops. I knew the exact spot I had in mind to set up my base camp. I just had to get there before the other hunters.

I found it—the spot I had camped at during Gideon's Run. It was an overhanging ledge amidst a grove of birch and hazel. I then began collecting firewood and strips of birch bark in a prudent manner. Within a matter of a couple of hours, I managed to chop down twenty small birch trees into logs where I would place underneath the overhanging as my bed platform. I was sweating profusely, so I undressed down to my undershirt and then built a fire beside my bed. Vilkswood was peaceful in the spring, for there were no signs of suffering or death among the bloom. I then heard the first gunshot of the competition resonate throughout Vilkswood just as I lit a fire with the strike of a match. Did a hunter already find the buck, or was he just foolhardy and trigger happy? Time would tell. Only if I hear those horns being blown six times would it signify the end of the competition. In the meantime, I gathered leaves and spread them over my bed platform to provide more warmth and comfort.

At 2:14 PM, it was still early in the afternoon, which meant that the buck would either be grazing or resting. I brought no traps with me, for I would be actively hunting this buck, not passively waiting for it to fall victim to a trap. After a quick lunch of venison jerky and rose blossoms, I built up my fire, put my jacket back on, and then set out north with my rifle in hand. If that buck were to graze anywhere in Vilkswood, it would be right here in this patch of hazel thickets. I knew not the hunting strategy of the other hunters, but I had all the confidence in mine. So I continued north along Barden Pass while observing every animal that crossed my path with intent eyes. Gideon's Run was a much more open-hunting competition compared to the Scarlet Hunt, which focused on hunting one individual animal. I now had to take into account that if I spot that buck, then there was a good chance that another hunter had also spotted it. A buck's hearing is very sensitive, almost as sensitive as a wolf's hearing. Bucks can feel the rhythmic pattern of footsteps upon the ground from as far as a mile away, so I would have to rely on my sight to gain an advantage. I then took a rest upon a large rock when I spotted something promising.

There were deer tracks on the ground leading west. Although the tracks weren't fresh, this was still a positive sign, so I prudently followed the tracks until they disappeared, leading me to a patch of pine trees. There was a murder of crows staring down at me from the pine trees they were perched upon, if only I had their vantage point. I now had to treat every sign of a deer as if it were the buck with the scarlet ribbon and key attached to its antlers. So I then laid myself down flat upon a rock that overlooked a patch of tall grass and dandelions, and then covered myself with shrubbery. This strategy was successful for me in killing a fox and boar while I was competing in Gideon's Run, so I decided to adopt it once more.

After an hour of inactivity had passed, I was ready to hike back to my base camp, and that was when I noticed movement over yonder! A buck suddenly emerged and began grazing on the tall grass no further than one hundred feet away from where I'd lain.

"Damn it," I whispered in vexation at the sight of no scarlet ribbon attached to the eight-point buck's antlers. I had a clear shot of the buck, but I decided to let him go. I still had plenty of food left for two days, and I didn't want to scare away any other deer from grazing at this spot. So I then hiked back to my base camp to rest and regroup my weary body.

There was still two hours of daylight left, but I felt no need to venture out from my base camp to track more deer. My heart had missed Vilkswood. I no longer felt the stress and anxiety that I felt on a daily basis when I was living in the Rosewood Inn.

"Good evening. Mind if I join you for a short respite?" Corbin inquired as he walked over to my camp.

"I do mind actually," I replied in a stern tone as I grabbed my rifle.

"Very well, I'll leave you alone then," Corbin said to me and then continued north along Vilksridge until he was out of my sight. I wasn't expecting to run into another hunter this early in the competition, and I had no desire to make friends with them. Was Corbin following me, or did he have the same strategy to gain the best vantage point when hunting the prized buck? I sensed something sinister in the eyes of Corbin Graves, and although I may not know him personally, I still didn't trust him. My father told me that you could tell how trustworthy someone is by how they stare back at you. I used to think that was a superficial belief, but now I saw the truth that lies in someone's eyes.

At 7:20 PM, nightfall had slowly begun to veil Vilkswood, like a black sheet draped over the sanguine eyes of a sleeping child. I then heard another gunshot ring throughout the calm darkness of the night, followed by a rustling and cawing of crows. Gunshots were of no significance to me; only the sounds of horns being blown would make my ears perk up. I then laid my sage blanket upon the bed platform of logs and leaves and rolled up my wolf fur to serve as a pillow. My spine wasn't acclimated to the wild, for it was too used to sleeping upon the comfort of a soft mattress. After moments of restless discomfort, my weariness succumbed to the log-and-leaf bed, and I began to drift off with the help from the fire's warmth and hypnotic glow.

*****

At 6:50 AM, I awoke with a profound sigh as I sat upright upon the bed platform and put another log into the dwindling flames of the fire. It was a cloudy and frigid morning in Vilkswood as I began to brew a pot of coffee over the fire. My plan for today was simple; I had the best vantage point in all of Vilkswood for hunting deer, so I would use that to my advantage and monitor the patch of hazel, which lay below me for the entire day.

The dreariness of the morning clouds soon diminished, giving way to a vibrant cerulean sky as I remained perched upon a rock at my camp on Vilksridge. It was day 2 of the competition, and still no horns were yet blown. I was actually quite surprised that such a prominent twelve-point buck with a scarlet ribbon and jangling key attached to its antlers hadn't been spotted yet by any hunter. Perhaps that buck was wiser and more cunning that I gave him credit for. I then walked over to my camp and grabbed a scrap of venison jerky out of my satchel when I heard a disconcerting noise resonating from my bed platform.

It was a black snake, but not just any common black snake; it was a peridot phantom! The phantom was about three feet long and hissed aggressively at me as it slithered upon my bed platform. This was my first ever encounter with the most poisonous snake in the Fray, and I was not about to take it lightly. The phantom's peridot eyes glowed like Luna's as it stared at me, only the phantom's eyes were cold and vicious and fixed upon me with deadly intent. Both the stories I'd read and heard from people about this snake were cautionary tales, so I kept a breathing room distance of at least ten feet between the phantom and me, which was now slithering over my satchel. So I broke an overhanging branch off a birch tree and used it to push the phantom away from my satchel. The phantom then quickly slithered away from the burning heat of the fireplace towards me in a sinister manner, but I kept it at bay with the birch branch until I grabbed my hatchet from my satchel. My peace of mind was now shattered. I couldn't share this camp with the deadliest of snakes. So I then pinned the phantom down upon the ground as it continued to viciously hiss at me. I had to be precise at this dire moment, for the phantom could strike with lightning speed delivering such a venomous bite from its needlelike fangs, which could end my life in one minute. I then raised my hatchet, and in one swift motion, I chopped the phantom's head off. I then took a profound sigh as my heart raced with fear. I then lifted the phantom's head with a stick and tossed it into the fire. The rest of the phantom's body was still slithering as I held it firmly in my hand. Even though I wasn't hungry, I proceeded to skin and gut the snake in a hasty manner. The phantom was still slithering as I peeled back its skin and tore out its heart and intestines.

"Remarkable." I spoke aloud as I stared with awestruck eyes at the decapitated, skinned, and gutted snake, which still continued to move even as I then began to skewer it with a stick! "Now I know why you're called a phantom." I spoke aloud. I then held the skewered snake over the fire, and after a short moment, it finally stopped moving.

The snake was bony and tough as I bit into it, but I still devoured the white meat in a ravenous manner. I kept the phantom's glassy black skin stored in my satchel as a token reminder of my encounter with such a remarkable creature, and I could also tan the phantom's skin once I acquire a phial of tannic acid. I was out of water, so I grabbed my rifle and began to hike west down Vilksridge to Fox Creek, where I could fill up my canteen. I then spotted a doe as I was carefully climbing down the moss-covered rocks of Vilksridge. The doe stared intently back at me with curious chestnut eyes. It was very frustrating to encounter deer after deer but not the prized buck. The doe then sveltely ran off as I slid down a slope riddled with mushrooms into a crimson king maple tree. I could hear the tranquil sound of flowing water, which was an indication that I was close to Fox Creek.

I arrived at Fox Creek to the sight of a murder of crows feasting upon what appeared to be a dead boar on the creek bed. The crows were just as ravenous as any wolf as they picked apart the boar carcass in a savage manner. The entire murder of crows then abruptly stared at me in unison as I kneeled down to fill up my canteen with water from the creek. The black crows' beaks were stained in the blood of the boar as they stared at me with sinister black eyes before swiftly flying away in unison, like a gust of black smoke blowing through the trees. I didn't know why I never harbored fear in my heart for the crows. As a child, a crow may appear as a harbinger of darkness, but I've always had a fascination with them since my childhood to present day.

The skies quickly turned sullen, so I hiked east down Vilksridge back to my camp lest I get caught in the rain.

"Better keep your gunpowder dry. A storm's coming!" a voice shouted.

"Who's there? Show yourself!" I shouted as I pointed my rifle towards the source of the voice. I then heard laughter resonating from behind me, so I quickly spun around and pointed my rifle at a withered gray oak tree, which resembled a huddled mass of impoverished people clawing and scrapping over one another in a desperate struggle for survival.

The storm had begun with thunder and lightning as I arrived at my camp and put another log into the fire. The overhanging kept me, all my provisions, and the fire dry from the downpour of the thunderstorm. That voice and sinister laugh warning me about the storm sounded like Corbin, although I couldn't be certain, for there were eight other hunters currently in Vilkswood. Whether they were tormenting me or genuinely trying to help, I wanted nothing to do with them. I didn't win Gideon's Run two years in a row by making friends with the competition.

At 7:35 PM, the thunderstorm continued to rage on as nightfall fell upon Vilkswood. There would be no hunting as long as the thunderstorm continued with such ferocity, for the conditions were far too dangerous. All the animals that dwelled in Vilkswood would be taking refuge from the thunderstorm just like I was now. I just hoped that this storm would end before the competition did, or else I would have no choice but to brave the storm and hunt in the thunder and lighting, which was something I'd never done as a hunter. Lightning continued to strike every so often, briefly illuminating Vilkswood in a flash as I sat upon my bed platform, contemplating a strategy to hunt the prized buck. It was at times like these where I envy those passive hunters who set up traps, for they now had the advantage of simply waiting for the prey to spring the trap without having to put themselves in danger during the storm. Although, I'd learned by trial and error to never underestimate the opportunistic mind of a wolf. That one evening I went to check the four steel spring traps that I set in Vilkswood only to find that the wolves had gotten to them before me was devastating. I then laid myself down upon the bed platform as a familiar creature had joined me underneath the warmth and safety of the overhanging.

"Oh, it's you again. Where have you been all this time?" I inquired as the silent crow entered my camp in a curious manner. "I'll let you stay here as long as you don't bring the rest of your friends," I said to the silent crow with a grin. I then reached into my satchel and tossed a scrap of venison jerky at the feet of the silent crow. "If you're not hungry, then why are you here? Just to share my company?" I inquired as the silent crow took a brief glance at the scrap of venison jerky before walking towards my bed platform. "Maybe you could help me hunt this prized buck," I said to the silent crow as it continued to stare at me with a childlike curiosity glimmering in its black eyes. "You sure are different. I wonder how your family and friends treat you," I said to the silent crow with a yawn. It was strange how the silent crow always had a way of finding me wherever I was, almost as if we were drawn towards each other or connected by some imperceptible force. "Well, I need to rest. So if you spot a buck with a scarlet ribbon attached to its antlers, just peck me on the shoulder," I said to the silent crow. My eyes then slowly closed to the sight of the silent crow scampering around the fire.

*****

At 9:43 AM, I awoke late to the soothing sound of gentle rainfall as I stood up from my bed platform. I then put another log into the fire and began to brew a pot of coffee. It was day 3 of the Scarlet Hunt, and I had yet to spot the prized buck. The thunderstorm from last night had subsided but not completely.

At 5:50 PM, eight hours had passed before the rainfall had finally ended. The ominous clouds began to break, and rays of twilight shone down upon the glistening trees, and that was when I spotted it. The prized buck was discreetly feeding on hazel in the twilit grove below me. There was no mistaking it this time. The twelve-point antlers, scarlet ribbon, and key were all evident. My heart raced, and my eyes widened as I slowly kneeled down and took aim at the prominent buck. I then prudently waited for the buck to take another bite of hazel, so its attention would be directed downward for a brief moment, thus not spotting me from above. I now had a clear shot at the buck's head, so I held my breath and then slowly squeezed the trigger.

The shot resonated like thunder throughout Vilkswood, causing a murder of crows perched nearby to flee in unison. "Yes," I whispered while gritting my teeth as the buck dropped to the ground. I then grabbed my hatchet and hastily slid down the slope into the grove where the buck lay. I then noticed something sticking out of the buck's chest as I walked closer.

"Was that your gunshot?" a hunter inquired as he walked over to the buck from behind a thicket of hazel where he was hidden.

"Yes, is this your…arrow?" I replied as I kneeled down and examined the buck.

"It's a bolt…and yes," the hunter replied.

I noticed out of the corner of my eye the hunter was pointing a strange-looking weapon at me.

"What is that weapon you wield?" I inquired.

"It's called a crossbow," the hunter replied.

"You made a direct shot to the buck's heart," I said to the hunter as I pulled out the bolt from the buck's heart.

"Yes, but you made a direct shot to the buck's head," the hunter said.

"If I aimed anywhere else on this buck's body, the scarlet ribbon and key would be yours now," I said to the hunter. I then grabbed my hatchet and began to chop the buck's antler off where the ribbon and key were attached.

"I understand a headshot is instant death, thus making the buck kill yours," the hunter said as he lowered his crossbow.

"I'm Vincent," I said to the hunter as I extended my hand in salutation.

"Baxter Colt," the hunter said as he shook my hand.

"I met your brother in a carriage this morning. He told me to tell you good luck," I said to Baxter as I hooked the buck antler onto my belt.

"Oh, really? I didn't think Joshua cared," Baxter said.

"Well, farewell," I said to Baxter.

"It's a shame, isn't it, having to end the life of such a beautiful, majestic beast all for the promise of a mystery prize?" Baxter said in a somber tone as he placed his hand upon the buck.

"It is indeed," I said to Baxter in a somber tone and then ran back to my camp.

After hastily putting out my fire and storing the sage blanket, wolf fur, and coffeepot away in my satchel, I ran southeast to where the constables were camped at on the border of Vilkswood. Dusk was upon me, and the light was quickly fading as I arrived at the southeast border of Vilkswood. I could now see the campfire of the six constables glowing in the distance as I ran to them.

"I've got it…I've got it!" I shouted as I ran to the constables while waving the scarlet ribbon and key attached to the buck's severed antler in the air.

The six constables then stood up in unison as I approached them, gasping for breath. I then presented the scarlet ribbon and key to one of the constables.

"What's your name, hunter?" the constable inquired as he examined the scarlet ribbon and key.

"Vincent Belmont," I replied in a gasping tone, followed by a series of sporadic coughs.

"Congratulations, Mr. Belmont," the constable said. The constable then gestured to the other constables, who each grabbed a horn in unison. The six constables then blew their horns six times, signaling the end of the Scarlet Hunt and my triumphant victory!

"I will now escort you to Mayor Crane's estate, where you will receive your prize," the constable said as he pointed to one of the wagons. My mind raced with thoughts of what the mystery prize could be as the wagon passed through the northeast gates of Thianor. The wagon had now passed by the Wishing Well, which was bustling with townsfolk, and entered the wealthy Black Marble district, which was where I presumed Mayor Crane's estate to be located. The wagon then came to a halt in front of a gated black brick estate house. The constable then exited the wagon and walked up to the front entrance of the mayor's estate.

At 9:09 PM, I was left waiting in the wagon for an hour before the constable finally exited the estate.

"Mayor Crane is ready for you now. Leave all your weapons in the wagon and follow me, sir," the constable said.

So I followed the constable down the scarlet brick-laid pathway to the front entrance of the mayor's estate.

"Welcome, sir. May I get you something to drink?" a housekeeper inquired with a smile as I entered the mayor's estate.

"No, thank you," I replied.

My eyes widened as I stared at the abundance of luxury that decorated every inch of the mayor's estate. One prominent staircase covered by gold and scarlet runners diverged up to the second story of the estate, where I could see an array of sculptures and painting lit by the warm glow of several gilded oil lamps. At the diverging point of the staircase hung a prominent portrait of the mayor and what I presumed to be his wife and son.

"Right this way, sir. Mayor Crane is waiting for you in the parlor," the housekeeper said after I had been waiting a few moments in the fireside armchair of the lobby with the constable standing over me.

I was then surprised to see dozens of people sitting in the parlor as I entered in a timid manner. All the hunters who participated in the Scarlet Hunt, including Baxter Colt and Corbin Graves, along with the press and various finely dressed dignitaries were seated in the parlor.

"Ah, there he is—Vincent Belmont," Mayor Crane pronounced as he outstretched his arms towards me.

Mayor Crane was dressed in a black and crimson robe with his insignia embroidered on the chest. The mayor's attire, although leisurely, probably cost more than one month's rent in any flat in Thianor. The mayor stood in front of the parlor fireplace along with two constables and his wife.

"Good evening, sir," I said to Mayor Crane with a smile as I walked up to him and shook his hand.

"Sorry to keep you waiting, Vincent. I had to tuck my son, Jack, into bed and then gather all these people to bear witness to the prize you're about to receive," Mayor Crane said as he placed his hand on my shoulder.

"It's more of a reception than I'm used to," I said to Mayor Crane.

"Ah, don't be modest, Vincent. Your hunting skills deem you worthy of such a reception. Now…is that the buck's antlers sticking out of your belt?" Mayor Crane inquired.

"No, he's just happy to see you!" a voice shouted from the array of people seated in front of me.

Everyone in the parlor, including Mayor Crane, then burst out in laughter at the facetious remark, while I scowled silently in disgust.

"Yes, I chopped it off the buck after I killed it with a headshot," I replied as I held out the buck's antler with scarlet ribbon and key dangling from it.

"How long have you been a hunter, Vincent?" Mayor Crane inquired.

"Ever since I was twelve years old. My father taught me all I know," I replied.

"Yes, fathers can be pillars of wisdom. My father taught me to never settle for anything less than what my heart yearns for," Mayor Crane said.

"I know he would be proud of my victory today," I said to Mayor Crane.

"He would indeed, Vincent, as am I. Now without further ado, let us get to your prize," Mayor Crane said as he gestured to the constable that stood beside him. The constable then exited the parlor and quickly returned carrying a black strongbox.

"Well, go on, Vincent. Open it," Mayor Crane said as he gestured towards the strongbox.

It was now time to see whether entering this competition was truly worth it or not. So I took the golden key attached to the buck's antlers and slowly inserted it into the lock of the strongbox.

"Take your time. We have all night!" a voice shouted from the array of people seated in front of me.

"Now, now, don't hasten Vincent. He just wants to savor this moment," Mayor Crane pronounced.

I then slowly turned the key until a definitive click resonated.

"What is this?" I inquired as I opened the strongbox to the sight of a folded document.

"Read it out loud if you would be so kind," Mayor Crane said.

"Congratulations, victor of the Scarlet Hunt! I, Salvatore Crane, hereby award thee with a position of the utmost honor and importance to be my personal bodyguard. You will immediately move into my estate and have your own room with full amenities the likes of which only my wife, son, and I have access to. You will accompany me wherever I may go in public and take all precautions into consideration for the well-being of my wife, son, and me. You will be paid handsomely for your services at the end of every month. You may now be asking yourself why me instead of a constable? Well, the answer is quite simple. Although I have the utmost respect for all the constables who have ensured the safety of my wife, son, and me up to this point, I now require a bodyguard with the diligence and forthrightness that only a hunter possesses. This world has grown increasingly dark and violent, and civil unrest runs rampant among the townsfolk of Thianor. I want them all to know that I bleed their blood every day, and I will never disregard their suffering, which is why I need to ensure the safety and security of my wife, son, and me so that I may continue to serve my fellow Thianorians," I pronounced.

"'Tis a great honor," Mayor Crane pronounced as he held up a glass of wine.

I stood in a silent stupor as I stared at Mayor Crane and the array of people seated in front of me reacting to the prize with a mix of vexation and reverence. I would've never expected the prize of the Scarlet Hunt to be one of such a personal matter. I then noticed Corbin Graves sneering at me from the back row of seats in the parlor.

"This is a contract," I remarked.

"Indeed, it is, Vincent. I believe you are the perfect caliber of man to ensure the safety and security of my wife, son, and me. So...what say you, Vincent?" Mayor Crane inquired with a smile as the array of people seated in front of me awaited my decision with bated breath.

CHAPTER 13

A Heart Divided

To whom doth the heart decide, isn't quite so simplified.

"It gives me so much joy I just have to read it aloud once more.

> Vincent Belmont, age thirty-two, won Mayor Crane's illustrious competition last night known as the Scarlet Hunt, but to everyone's astonishment, he then rejected the mayor's generous proposal to be his personal bodyguard who would live with the mayor at his estate in the Black Marble district and ensure his safety and of his family. Mr. Belmont then told the mayor to give the prize to Baxter Colt, 'For he's just as capable of a hunter, as I am, if not more.' Mr. Colt then graciously and without hesitation accepted the mayor's proposal. When asked why he would turn down such a coveted prize, Mr. Belmont replied, 'I still have important matters that need to be resolved in my life and important people that need me. I'm sorry," Beatrice pronounced.

"We're just happy you're back, Vincent," Sara said with a warm smile as she poured me a mug of coffee and then sat down in a chair beside me at the lobby dining table.

"Vincent Belmont rejecting Mayor Crane's illustrious proposal for us," Francesca pronounced with a smile as she placed her hand upon her chest.

"Vincent never said it was because of us. Read the article carefully, Ms. Conceited," Beatrice said to Francesca.

"Why did you turn down such a proposal, Vincent?" Roselyn inquired.

"Well, it's just as I said in the article. Also I could never risk my life for a man I didn't know personally. Furthermore, a man of such wealth and privilege like Mayor Crane … besides, where would the four of you be without me?" I replied in a facetious tone and grin.

"We would be so heartbroken we wouldn't be able to carry on in this world anymore," Francesca said in a facetious tone as she playfully shoved my head on her way to the kitchen.

"Maybe the inn will get more publicity now because of Vincent rejecting the mayor's proposal. All right, everyone, let's get back to work. This inn isn't going to run itself," Roselyn pronounced, as she, Beatrice, and Sara stood up from their chairs in unison.

It was good to be back in the Rosewood Inn. I truly missed the Merchant sister's idiosyncratic charms and warmth during the three days I spent in Vilkswood. I had no regrets over rejecting Mayor Crane's proposal. If I had known from the beginning that the prize of the Scarlet Hunt was being the bodyguard for the mayor and his family, then I would've never entered the competition. I wouldn't deny that Mayor Crane is a good man who wants to serve the people of Thianor with all his heart. I just couldn't bring myself to risk my life for a man I hardly knew. Mayor Crane reacted respectfully towards me when I rejected his proposal unlike the array of people who sat in the parlor of his estate. Judging by their reaction, you would've thought the world was coming to an end. For the first time in ages, I felt like I was part of a family here in the Rosewood Inn, and I didn't want to abandon the Merchants at the mayor's behest, for I am forever in debt to them.

"Oh, so the mayor still let you keep the buck antler and the scarlet ribbon and key even though you rejected his proposal?" Sara inquired as we cranked the washing mills full of laundry.

"Yes, he did. I can show you when we're finished with the laundry," I replied.

"So what's it like out there in the wilds of Vilkswood?" Sara inquired.

"Well, Vilkswood isn't for the faint of heart. There are times where those woods can be the most beautiful place on earth, filled with such warmth and harmony, and then within the blink of an eye, those woods can turn into a cold and unforgiving place filled with terrifying predators, but then again, that's pretty much how the rest of the world is," I replied.

"I could never be brave enough to enter those woods. I'm not tough enough for such wilds," Sara said in a timid tone.

"You could be. Never doubt yourself," I said to Sara with a smile.

After an hour, Sara and I finished washing the laundry and then went to my room so I could show her the prized buck antler with the scarlet ribbon and key.

"Incredible," Sara remarked with widened eyes as she held the buck's jagged antlers in her slender, delicate hands.

"It was one of the most impressive bucks I've ever laid eyes on," I said to Sara as I combed my hair while staring into the bureau mirror.

"It must have been quite beautiful," Sara said, as she placed the antlers down upon the nightstand.

"Indeed, it was. Well, I'm off to visit Luna now" I said to Sara.

"Goodbye and give her my best wishes," Sara said and then exited my room.

"I'll be back in a couple of hours," I said to Francesca as I walked up to the front desk. "Farewell," Francesca said as she twirled her hair with her finger while studiously writing in the ledger.

"White Stone district, flat *A*-2," I said to the coachman as I entered the carriage.

"Can you believe this—a lowly hunter Vincent Belmont rejecting Mayor Crane's grand offer?" an elderly man sitting across from me remarked with a scoff as he pointed at the article written about me in the *Daily Rosette*.

"Yes, I've heard about that, but I'm sure he had his reasons," I said to the elderly man.

"What reason could there possibly be to reject Mayor Crane? What a fool!" the elderly man said.

"Maybe he found a purpose more meaningful than to risk his life for a man he hardly knows," I said to the elderly man.

"Such pride and arrogance from such a lower class of man in the presence of our great mayor," the elderly man said with a series of sporadic coughs.

I then quickly covered my nose and mouth with the white handkerchief from my breast pocket. The carriage then halted in front of Luna's flat as the bell rang.

"You know what? I don't have to prove myself to people like you," I said to the elderly man in a contemptible tone and scowl as I paid my fare and then stormed out of the carriage. I was then greeted by a heartwarming sight as I entered Luna's courtyard. A scarlet banner with gold trim prominently hung on the back facade of the courtyard that read, "Welcome back, Vincent!" in gold letters. I was flattered to say the least by this gesture. Luna made me feel like a king who had returned from a perilous journey. I cared not about all the scornful remarks circulating throughout Thianor about me rejecting Mayor Crane's proposal now, for Luna had a way of making the rest of the world disappear.

"Vincent, you're back!" Luna shouted from the second-story window with an angelic smile and wave.

"I don't deserve all of this," I said to Luna as I pointed to the banner.

"You most definitely do, my dear. I'll be right down," Luna said.

After a few moments, Luna then entered the courtyard and scampered over to me with her arms wide open. Luna was a sight to behold as always. She wore a lacy, sleeveless gold dress with a black corset.

"I missed you," Luna said as she placed both her hands upon my cheeks with a warm smile.

"I missed you too," I said to Luna as we embraced each other like a flower embracing dawn's first light.

"I'm so proud of you. I knew you would be victorious," Luna said with a smile.

"Congratulations, Vincent," Daisy said as she entered the courtyard holding a newspaper.

"Thank you," I said to Daisy with an elfish smile.

"Can you believe it, Luna, Vincent rejecting the mayor's proposal for us? You make us feel truly important," Daisy said to Luna and then embraced me with arms tightly wrapped around my neck.

"Come now, don't be conceited. We cannot take the credit for Vincent's decision," Luna said to Daisy.

"Déjà-vu," I whispered.

"What's that, Vincent?" Luna inquired.

"Nothing, I'm just happy to be back," I replied with a smile.

"We're happy to have you back. Our home isn't the same without you," Luna said.

"Please tell me you'll stay for lunch?" Daisy inquired with a wide-eyed stare.

"Well, I actually have to be—sure, of course, I'll stay," I replied with a smile.

"Splendid! Shall we eat in the courtyard or inside?" Luna inquired.

"Let's eat out here. It's a beautiful day," I replied.

I had responsibilities to the Merchant sisters and the Rosewood Inn, but unlike Mayor Crane, I just couldn't deny Luna's offer. I wanted nothing more than to spend the afternoon with Luna and Daisy in the courtyard, for I couldn't picture anything more idyllic.

"Oh, I should give this back to you," I said to Luna as I began to detach the white dahlia pin from my jacket.

"No, it was a gift. Please keep it," Luna said as she placed her hand over mine with a warm smile.

"Very well, I have a gift for you too. I'll show you after lunch," I said to Luna with a smile.

"Oh, I can't wait. I'll be right back. I just have to help Daisy with lunch," Luna said as she hopped up and down on the tips of her toes in a zealous childlike manner and then entered the flat.

"If it's good enough for sailors, then it's good enough for me." I spoke aloud as I carefully sat in the scarlet hammock. This hammock would've come in handy while I was camping in Vilkswood.

"Are you beginning to warm up to the hammock?" Luna inquired as she entered the courtyard carrying a chair.

"It is quite comfortable once you maintain your balance," I said to Luna as I lay back in the hammock with my hands behind my head.

"I told you so. I actually fell asleep in that hammock one afternoon," Luna said with a smile and then entered the flat.

Indeed Luna fell asleep in this hammock, for I could smell her saccharine scent upon the material.

"Vincent, catch!" Daisy shouted as she tossed a white object down to me from the second-story window.

I nearly fell from the hammock, but I managed to catch the object that Daisy threw so abruptly to me. My eyes widened upon further examination of the white object, for it was the skull of a wolf cub. *How did Daisy acquire such an oddity?* This I wondered as I gazed upon the skull with a sense of profound enthrallment.

Daisy and Luna then entered the courtyard carrying platters of roasted meats and vegetables and a jug of cider.

"Where did you get this?" I inquired as I stood up from the hammock and walked over to Daisy, who was setting the table.

"That wolf skull belonged to our great-grandfather Cyrus. He found it while he was hunting in Vilkswood," Daisy replied.

"You're giving this to me?" I inquired.

"It's yours if you want it, Vincent. We don't exactly have any need for animal skulls," Luna said with a giggle.

"Well, neither do I," I said to Luna.

"I thought hunters collected these sorts of things," Daisy said.

"We do…thank you. I'll put it to use," I said to Daisy with a smile.

Luna, Daisy, and I then began to eat after Luna said grace and paid tribute to Jonathan's memory.

"If you don't mind me saying, I respect and fully understand your decision not to be Mayor Crane's bodyguard," Daisy said as she filled my plate with herb-roasted chicken and pork.

"Thank you. I seem to have upset a lot of people in Thianor with that decision," I said to Daisy.

"They can all shut their gobs. It's your life, and they have no right to tell you how to live it," Daisy said.

"Daisy's right. It's your life, Vincent, and I'm so happy you denied Mayor Crane's offer, for we wouldn't be able to see you anymore if you chose to live with him at his estate," Luna said and then took a sip of coffee.

"Mayor Crane is a good man. I just couldn't bring myself to risk my life for him," I pronounced with a mouthful of chicken.

"Why do all men in power have the delusion that everyone is beholden to them?" Luna inquired and then took a small bite of chicken.

"Mayor Crane reacted respectfully towards my decision. The same cannot be said for the other people seated in his parlor, for they were gasping and aahing."

"Pay no mind to those ignorant dignitaries, Vincent. Those people only understand privilege, which is bestowed upon them by men they don't even admire. They're two-faced sycophants," Luna said while primping her hair.

Lunch with Luna and Daisy had carried on for hours as the two shared stories of their father and childhood, which I took great pleasure in listening to. Despite her growing fame in Thianor, Luna didn't possess a shred of vanity or arrogance. I could listen to Luna talk for hours and just become captivated by her radiant beauty and grace.

"All right, here's your present. I figured you have enough roses already," I said to Luna as I grabbed the buck antler with the scarlet ribbon and key out of my satchel.

Luna then giggled with a wide-eyed stare as she held the buck antler in her hands. "Is this from the Scarlet Hunt?" Luna inquired.

"Yes, it's the prized buck antler along with the scarlet ribbon and key attached," I replied.

"Oh no, you worked so hard for this. I cannot accept it," Luna said.

"It has no significance to me. Please I want you to have it," I said to Luna.

"Well, I suppose I could use this beautiful ribbon to tie my hair up," Luna said.

"Oh, we could use the antler as a coat hanger. We just need to attach it to the wall," Daisy said to Luna.

"That's very creative," I remarked with a smile.

"Could you do that for us, Vincent?" Luna inquired with a wide-eyed stare and smile.

"Sure, it's a simple enough job," I replied.

"For you, maybe. Last time I used a hammer I nearly took my finger off," Luna said.

"It's no problem. I'll do it right now," I said to Luna with a smile as I grabbed the buck antler from her.

"All right, where on the wall do you want the antler?" I inquired as I entered the flat.

Luna and Daisy then stared at each other in contemplation before agreeing on a spot on the wall beside a landscape painting of a golden meadow with a young girl wearing a cerulean dress to attach the antler.

"All right, I just need a vice, two nails, bolt cutters, and a hammer," I said to Luna.

"I'll be right back," Luna said and then went to go search for the tools I needed.

"This is a nice painting," I remarked. "I love it."

"My father said he bought this painting because the little girl in the meadow reminded him of Mother," Daisy said.

"Here you go, Vincent," Luna said as she placed the tools upon the ebony coffee table.

"Great, you should take this painting down so it doesn't fall off when I'm hammering the nails into the wall," I said to Luna.

Luna then took the painting off the wall and gently placed it down upon the emerald sofa.

I then secured the antler in the vice and began to carefully hammer in the first nail. It was more difficult than I expected, but I managed to hammer in the two nails into the base of the antler without it splitting it in twain. I then cut off the keys and scarlet ribbon from which were attached to the antler with a steel ring with the bolt cutters. I missed doing these small home decor jobs over the past five months, which I used to do for Heather in the cabin, so I took special care when doing this job for Luna and Daisy.

"All right, done," I pronounced as I hammered in the last nail, which firmly attached the antler to the wall.

"Thank you," Luna said with a smile and then kissed me on the cheek.

"I like it. There's something graceful about the shape of the antler," Daisy remarked.

"Let's test it," Luna pronounced as she took off my wolf fur jacket and hung it upon the antler.

"It's wonderful. Thank you, Vincent," Daisy remarked with a smile.

"You're welcome," I said to Daisy and then hung the landscape painting back upon the wall. I felt at home in Luna's flat just as I did in the Rosewood Inn with the Merchant sisters, but can a man have two places which he calls home?

"You chased that chicken throughout the market before falling into a puddle and staining your white dress that father bought you the day before," Daisy said to Luna with angelic laughter.

"Father found it just as amusing as you do now when he found me," Luna said to Daisy as she shared in her angelic laughter.

"So who won the bet?" I inquired with a smile and then took a sip of coffee.

"I did. Luna wasn't swift enough to catch that chicken, and she owed me her white pearl bracelet, which I gave back to her, of course," Daisy replied.

It was great to see a smile grace Luna's visage again. During Jonathan's funeral, she was in the depths of despair, and it hurt me to witness her pain. I wondered how my childhood would have been if I grew up in a town such as Thianor. Would I have made friends with other children in this town, or would I still isolate myself from the rest of them? I wish I knew Luna when I was a child. I might have grown into a different person if I had her in my life during those innocent years of wonder and discovery. My childhood consisted of day after day of being taught curriculum by my father in the cabin. At times, I felt like he and I were the only two people left in the world. The only times he every showed me affection was when I was near death from the scarlet fever and during our hunts in Vilkswood. No matter where I go and what I do, I could still hear his voice in my ear guiding me. At certain times, my father's voice was louder, like the times when I'm hunting. He told me I must be prepared to face the world in a steadfast manner when he's gone, but he never taught me about the strength of love and compassion.

"Vincent, what was your childhood like?" Daisy inquired.

"Dismal. I also grew up without a mother. It was just my father and me in the cabin, and I often wondered about the lives of other children," I replied.

"Do you think your father would have been friends with our father if they crossed paths?" Luna inquired.

"Jacob…well, he didn't understand thespians. He stayed in his own world, which he was the master of. Those times when he made trades to thespians, he became vexed quite easily at their overall personality," I replied.

"I'm sure your father would have warmed up to our father. Our father had a way of appeasing any class of man," Luna said as her visage quivered with sorrow.

"Just like you," I said to Luna as I draped my arm over her shoulder.

"I hear his voice in my head all the time," Luna said as she began weeping quietly.

"So do I," Daisy said to Luna in a somber tone as she sat down beside her on the emerald sofa and gently grabbed her hand.

"I'm all right. I'm just tired. Excuse me for a moment," Luna said to Daisy as she stood up from the sofa and exited the great room.

"I should go—"

"No, give her a moment," Daisy said as she held her hand out in front of me.

"How have you been handling everything?" I inquired.

"Every day is a battle, and Luna has been so strong, but I feel the void that Father left is eating away at her," Daisy replied in a somber tone.

"I'll always be there for her," I said to Daisy.

"I know, Vincent. You're a good man, and Luna is lucky to have you," Daisy said.

Luna then entered the great room a few moments later, dressed in a white nightgown with her hair tied up with the scarlet ribbon I gave to her. Daisy then stood up from the sofa and placed her hand on Luna's shoulder as she walked past her.

"Oh, are you going to sleep?" I inquired.

"Yes, I'm so fatigued I just can't keep my eyes open," Luna replied.

"I should get back to the Rosewood Inn to retire as well," I said to Luna.

"Or you could stay here and sleep…with me," Luna said, as she placed her hand on my leg while gazing intently at me with her bleary peridot eyes glistening from welled-up tears.

"Luna, I have responsibilities to—"

"I know. I'm sorry. That was selfish of me," Luna interjected.

"No, it's all right. I'll visit you as often as I can. In the meantime, spend time with Daisy. You two are stronger together," I said to Luna as I stood up from the sofa and grabbed my jacket off the antler.

"Goodbye, give the Merchant sisters my love," Luna said to me and then kissed me before I put on my jacket and exited her flat.

Perhaps Daisy wasn't enough emotional support for Luna right now. I felt that she needed me to be there for her in a way that Daisy couldn't. There was a part of me that almost spoke out and accepted Luna's invitation to stay the night, but then another other part of me remembered the responsibilities I have to the Merchant sisters and the Rosewood Inn. I felt torn and conflicted, for I didn't want to hurt either Luna or the Merchant sisters. So I contemplated deeply on these two paths in my life during the quiet ride back to the Rosewood Inn.

"Vincent, where have you been?" Roselyn inquired in a stern tone as I entered the Rosewood Inn and walked up to the counter with a sigh.

"I was visiting Luna. I'm sorry. Time got away from me," I replied.

"Vincent, Sara and Beatrice need your help attending to a hostile man in room 13," Roselyn said as she pointed upstairs.

"I'll be right there," I said to Roselyn as I raced up the stairs to room 13.

"Vincent, thank God you're here," Sara pronounced in a distressed tone as I walked down the corridor to room 13.

"He won't leave. He says he has a gun," Beatrice said in a distressed tone.

"Did you tell him you would alert the constables?" I inquired as I gestured for Sara and Beatrice to move away from the door.

"I did, and he's barricaded the door," Beatrice said.

"Sir, it's time for you to check out. We need the room," I said to the man in room 13, as I grasped my holstered pistol.

"Whether I die by bullet or the white plague, I care not!" the man shouted through the door.

"He means to die in there," Sara remarked in a distressed tone and visage.

"Sir, we all want to resolve this in a peaceful manner, but you must know that if you pose a threat to any of my fellow workers, I will not hesitate to defend them by any means necessary," I said to the man.

"I have nothing left to lose anymore, so spare me you negotiation tactics!" the man shouted.

"Sir, I swear if you let me in, then I will try my best to help you. If not, then you can shoot me where I stand," I said to the man.

"No, no, Vincent, you can't," Sara and Beatrice pleaded in unison as they grabbed onto me in a frantic manner.

"Fine, you may enter, but nobody else," the man said.

"Don't worry. I'll be all right," I pronounced as the man began to move the furniture away from the door.

The door to room 13 then opened, and I could see a sliver of the man's visage through the crack staring back at me with sorrowful eyes.

"It's all right. I'm not going to hurt you," I said to the man as I entered the room with my hands in the air.

The man then frantically took my pistol from the holster while he pointed his own pistol at me and then began to barricade the door again.

"May I sit down?" I inquired.

"Go ahead," the man replied.

I then slowly sat down in the fireside armchair and lowered my hands with a profound sigh.

"You told me you have nothing left to lose. I wanted to talk to you because I used to share that exact same mentality," I said to the man as he paced back and forth in front of me.

"A fortnight ago, I found out I had the white plague. As devastating as that news was to me at the time, I knew the love of my daughter would give me the strength to endure, but when I told her the news, she treated me like a monster. I then tried to contact her, but she left Thianor without so much as informing me of where she would reside, all because of the fear of me infecting her with the white plague," the man said in a distressed tone as tears began to well up in his eyes.

"What's your name?" I inquired.

"Raymond," the man said.

"I'm Vincent. I'm sorry, Raymond. I truly am. I too am infected with the white plague, so I understand the stigma. As for your daughter…she was indeed afraid. Everyone is so afraid in this day and age, so they react drastically. Let me tell you something. My wife and daughter died right before my eyes, and soon after, I was ready to end my life, for I saw no reason to live in a world devoid of their love," I said to Raymond in a somber tone.

"How could you continue living after such a loss?" Raymond inquired in a somber tone as he sat down on the bed across from me.

"It was the most difficult thing I've ever had to do, but I found a purpose that kept me alive," I replied.

"What was it?" Raymond inquired.

"My wife's dying words were for me not to be afraid. To take my life would be an act of cowardice, and at that moment, I vowed not to fail her in death as I failed to protect her in life, so I carried on living. You may feel like you're all alone in this world, as have I, but those two women outside the door listening to our conversation are part of my purpose for living. You just have to find that purpose even as death peers over your shoulder. I sense you're a good man, Raymond, and bad things sometimes happen to good men. It's not fair, but know that you're not alone," I said to Raymond.

"I don't want to hurt anybody. I just have nowhere else to go, so I came here because word caught my ear in the Wishing Well that this inn welcomes the infected," Raymond said.

"We do, Raymond, but you have to pay, and you cannot pose a threat to us," I said to Raymond.

"Like you said, fear makes a person act drastically, and I haven't any money to pay you now," Raymond said.

"Here…this should be enough for you to stay here another week, just enough time for you to find a job and flat to live in," I said to Raymond as I handed him forty dollars.

"Why would you help me?" Raymond inquired.

"I'm only doing for you what I wish someone had done for me when I was in the depths of despair," I replied.

"Thank you, Vincent," Raymond said in a weeping tone.

"I'm going to need my pistol back now," I said to Raymond.

"Of course," Raymond said as he handed me my pistol.

"I want you to go out there and apologize to those two women you've frightened and then pay the woman at the front desk," I said to Raymond in a stern tone as I holstered my pistol and began moving the furniture away from the door.

"Yes, of course," Raymond said.

I then exited Raymond's room with a sigh. I had lied to Raymond when I told him that Heather's dying words were what kept me from ending my life, but I couldn't tell him the true reason being vengeance on White Bane. He needed to hear an uplifting message, and I was glad I resolved the issue without any of the Merchant sisters getting hurt. What would have happened though if I stayed the night at Luna's flat? It felt good to be needed once again in life, but it felt terrible to disappoint the ones who depend on you. I took out the peridot phantom snakeskin from my satchel and then exited my room.

"Roselyn, do we have any tannic acid?" I inquired as I walked up to the front desk.

"There might be a little left in a small amber phial in the kitchen. Sara told me what you did for that man in room 13," Roselyn replied.

"Yes, he wanted to end his life," I said to Roselyn in a somber tone.

"You have such a good heart, Vincent. I wish every man in this town cared for others the way you do," Roselyn said.

I then searched through the pantries of the kitchen for the small amber phial of tannic acid. "Where is it—ah, there it is." I spoke aloud as I grabbed the phial of tannic acid. I then laid the peridot phantom skin down upon the kitchen table and began to brush a thin layer of tannic acid over it with a cotton ball.

"What's that, Vincent?" Beatrice inquired as she entered the kitchen.

"Peridot phantom skin," I replied.

"It's beautiful. Where did you purchase it?" Beatrice inquired with a wide-eyed stare.

"I purchased it in Vilkswood," I said to Beatrice with a grin.

"So you killed this snake?" Beatrice inquired as she pointed at the splayed snakeskin.

"Yes, I did. You know this is the most deadly snake in the entire Fray. Its venom can kill a man in one minute. I found it in my camp during the Scarlet Hunt," I replied.

"My lord, those woods are just filled with deadly creatures. So what are you going to use that skin for?" Beatrice inquired.

"I was thinking a belt or maybe a strap for my rifle, or I could sell it, I don't know yet," I replied. I then walked up the stairs to my room with the peridot phantom skin in hand.

"Good evening, Vincent. How are you feeling?" Sara inquired as she quietly entered my room.

"I'm feeling well," I replied as I laid the peridot phantom skin down upon the hardwood floor in front of the fireplace for the tannic acid to dry.

"I'm glad you resolved that stressful matter with Raymond," Sara said.

"Did he apologize to you and Beatrice?" I inquired as I took off my jacket and boots.

"He did. I was afraid he would hurt you when you were in the room with him," Sara said as she sat down upon the bed.

"You need not worry about me. I've been through more dangerous scenarios in my life. Raymond was just a man in the depths of despair who needed someone to confide in," I said to Sara as I sat down upon the bed beside her.

"I heard what you told him—about Beatrice and I being your purpose in life. Did you really mean that or were you just trying to protect us?" Sara inquired in a timid tone.

"I meant it with all my heart," I replied with a smile as I draped my arm around Sara.

"I love you," Sara said in a timid tone and then kissed my cheek, but she then quickly exited my room before I could respond back to her. So I sat there stunned upon my bed for a few silent moments of contemplation.

It had been so long since a woman spoke those three words to me, and it felt almost surreal, as if I was dreaming. I cared for the Merchant sisters, but I felt a strong bond with Sara in particular. Had my heart really grown so cold to where I could not acknowledge love when it's professed to me? The truth is, I was afraid at that moment with Raymond, afraid of losing Sara or Beatrice. So without hesitation, I sacrificed myself to protect them. I couldn't let it happen again, and images of Heather and Audrey lying motionless on the floor of the cabin flashed in my mind at that moment Raymond shouted through the door. I now had six beautiful reasons to live in this world, six reasons that I thought fondly of as I lay here in bed. I wanted to give myself fully to all of them for the fear of losing any of them, but a heart divided cannot beat at its fullest capacity.

*****

At 7:20 AM, I awoke with a headache as I sat upright in bed. The peridot phantom skin was tanned perfectly as I grabbed it off the hardwood floor and laid it down upon the table. I decided to turn the snakeskin into a belt, which I could wear, gift, or sell. So I began cutting as straight a line as I could along the length of each side of the snakeskin with my knife.

"Good morning," Sara said as she entered my room carrying a tray of rose blossoms and a pot of coffee.

"Good morning," I said to Sara as I began to meticulously cut a thin strip for the loop of the belt.

"What is that?" Sara inquired.

"It's tanned snakeskin. I'm making a belt out of it," I replied as I poured myself a mug full of coffee.

"You're a man of many talents, Vincent," Sara remarked with a warm smile as she sat down upon the bed.

"I'm not a tailor, but I do what I can," I said to Sara with a grin.

"I'm sure you will look just dashing wearing it," Sara remarked with a warm smile.

"Oh, I don't know if I'm going to wear this belt yet. We'll see. I might be able to get a sizable amount of money selling it in a boutique," I said to Sara with a mouthful of rose blossom.

"I wish I knew more about fashion so I could help you," Sara said to me.

"I'll finish this later. Let's get to work," I said to Sara.

"Good morning…all right, you two, rooms 7 through 10," Roselyn pronounced. Sara and I then walked up the stairs and began our morning rounds.

"I would've been frozen in fear," Sara said as we gathered the sheets and quilts from room 7.

"I was afraid. The peridot phantom's venom can kill a man in one minute, and I've never encountered that deadly snake before," I said to Sara as I put another log into the fire and stoked the flames.

"You never appear as a frightened man. Your demeanor is always so calm," Sara remarked.

"Not always," I said to Sara.

"All right, on to room 8," Sara said.

Sara and I then moved on to make up room 8. Room 8 appeared pristine as if someone made up the room before they checked out, and then I noticed something alarming in the bedpan.

"Are those teeth?" Sara inquired as she stared into the bedpan filled with four bloody teeth in disgust before quickly averting her eyes.

"It appears so," I replied.

"Believe it or not, that's not the most revolting thing I've found in a bedpan," Sara said. "Really? Do tell," I said to Sara with a grin.

"I once found a severed finger in a bedpan. The very sight of the bloody finger made me so sick I instantly vomited," Sara said.

"It's good that you had a bedpan right there to vomit in," I said to Sara with a grin. Sara then giggled as we moved on to make up room 9.

"That's remarkable. So she trained all those doves?" I inquired as we gathered the sheets and quilts from room 9.

"Yes, ever since she was sixteen years old. Roselyn has had an affinity with doves. She finds their songs and white feathers to be heaven-sent," Sara replied as I put another log into the fire and stoked the flames.

"I often see her talking to those doves at the front desk," I said to Sara.

"It's adorable. She talks to those doves like a mother would talk to her baby," Sara said with a smile.

"Doves are nice, but I've always been more fascinated with crows," I said to Sara.

"Oh, Roselyn hates crows. She calls them little devils," Sara said.

"They may appear sinister, but once you get to know them, you will see how intelligent and gentle they truly are," I said to Sara as we then moved on to make up room 10.

"So you relate to the crows?" Sara inquired as we gathered the sheets and quilts from room 10.

"I wouldn't say I relate to them, but I do understand them," I replied as I put another log into the fire and stoked the flames.

"I find deer to be the most beautiful and graceful animals on this earth," Sara said.

"Deer are graceful indeed, and they stare at you with such kind eyes," I said to Sara.

"Like you," Sara said with a smile as we walked to the laundry room.

"She sounds so precious. I wish I could've met her," Sara said as we cranked the washing mills.

"No matter how distraught I was, Audrey's voice would always uplift my spirits," I said to Sara.

"Keep her voice alive in your heart, Vincent, as I do with my father," Sara said.

After an hour had passed, Sara and I hung the laundry out on the clotheslines in the back alley. I then grabbed a needle, a spool of white thread, and a small bottle of oil from the stock room and walked up the stairs to my room to finish crafting the snakeskin belt. After two meticulous hours of stitching, I was finally done crafting the snakeskin belt. I then treated the belt with a fine coat of oil to make the snake scales shine like a moonlit river. I then walked downstairs and laid the snakeskin belt upon the front desk.

"How does this look?" I inquired.

"Oh, this is very striking. Is this snakeskin?" Francesca inquired as she grabbed the belt with both hands.

"Yes, it is, from the deadliest snake in the Fray—the peridot phantom," I replied as Francesca examined the belt.

"It's marvelous. Are you selling it?" Francesca inquired.

"Perhaps, I'm still weighing my options for the time being," I replied.

"Very well, your betrothed is here," Francesca said with a grin as she pointed to the lobby.

I then smiled to the sight of Luna playing the ebony harp in the lobby. Luna was radiant as always; she wore a lacy lavender dress with long hanging sleeves that fell like royal drapes in a king's chamber. Luna's hair was wavy with a few strands braided on either side of her lucent visage. So I stood there and watched her play the harp in silence for a few moments.

"I like that song," I said to Luna with a smile as I walked up to her.

"Thank you. It's called 'A Tranquil Breath,'" Luna said.

"What are you doing here?" I inquired with a smile as I embraced Luna.

"Oh, I arrived here an hour ago, but Francesca told me you were working and that I could wait in the lobby. I then asked her if I could play the harp while I waited for you, and she said that would be lovely. I was wondering if you would like to accompany me to the thespian garment fair in the central market," Luna replied with a smile.

"Oh, what is a garment fair exactly?" I inquired.

"The thespian board is selling a glorious array of garments from plays of yore to raise money to fund research for the white plague," Luna replied.

"That's great. How fortuitous that I just finished crafting this," I said to Luna as I grabbed the snakeskin belt out of my satchel and displayed it to her.

"Oh, Vincent, it's beautiful," Luna said as she quickly grabbed the belt from my hands and wrapped it around her waist.

"You're wearing the deadliest snake in the Fray around your waist," I said to Luna with a grin.

"It's gorgeous. I love the contrast of white stitching against the black scales," Luna said with a smile.

“Thank you. I took a risk,” I said to Luna with an elfish smile.

“You could sell this belt at the garment fair in the central market. Will you accompany me?” Luna inquired with a warm smile and wide-eyed stare.

“Absolutely,” I replied.

“Wonderful, then let us be off,” Luna said as she handed me the snakeskin belt.

“Stay out of trouble, you two,” Francesca pronounced in a facetious tone as Luna and I exited the Rosewood Inn hand in hand.

“To the town square, sir,” Luna said to the coachman.

I then opened the carriage door for Luna and entered the carriage behind her.

“So how is Daisy?” I inquired.

“She’s out with a gentleman right now who goes by the name of Gregory Hastings. He’s a florist exporter who works at the Sanguine Solarium. He just moved into the flat above us,” Luna replied.

“Good for her. Perhaps she will get free roses from him,” I said to Luna.

“I’m happy for her. She deserves a man who would lavish her with love and bouquets of roses every waking moment,” Luna said with a smile.

“Maybe we’ll see her at the garment fair,” I said to Luna.

“Perhaps, but I want this day to belong to us and us alone,” Luna said with a smile as she hooked her arm around mine.

Luna then paid the fare to the coachman as the carriage bell rang. Luna and I then exited the carriage to the sight of a bustling market of garment vendors selling vibrant stage clothing.

“So where shall we begin?” I inquired as I stared at all the vendors spread throughout the town square.

“Let us begin with the dresses from the Thia Lynsetta era,” Luna replied with a smile.

“Lead the way,” I said to Luna with a smile as I gestured for her to walk ahead of me.

“Let’s go,” Luna said with a smile as she took my hand.

“This dress was worn by Thia when she performed in *Eloise: The Maiden’s Cotillion*,” Luna said in a gasping tone as she held the dress up to her slender form in a zealous manner.

“So much gold,” I remarked.

“It’s as if I’m wearing pure sunlight. How do I look?” Luna inquired with a smile.

“Like a goddess,” I replied with a smile.

“Thank you, darling. Excuse me, ma’am, how much is this dress?” Luna inquired.

“Twelve hundred dollars,” the woman replied.

“Oh my,” Luna pronounced as she hung the dress back on the rack with a frown.

“Sir, I will pay you eight hundred dollars for that gallant wolf-fur jacket you’re wearing,” the woman said.

"Thank you, but it's not for sale," I said to the woman.

"Wolf fur is so coveted throughout the Fray," Luna said as we walked hand in hand.

"Indeed, deadly animals are often coveted for their fur and skin," I said to Luna.

"These are all stage garments. I'll bet you that at least two other garment vendors will make an offer for your jacket," Luna said with a grin.

"I dare not take such a bet. This is your world after all," I said to Luna with a smile.

"Oh, Vincent, look at this shawl!" Luna said as she draped a scarlet and gray shawl around her shoulders with a smile.

Upon closer examination, I noticed the shawl had a design of two gray wolves kissing each other printed so prominently on the fabric.

"So do wolves really kiss like this?" Luna inquired as she pointed at the shawl.

"Not in the manner that we humans kiss. They just lick each other. The *kiss of the wolf* though is a term for how the wolf clamps down on the neck of its prey first, thus rendering the prey incapacitated," I replied.

My visage then grew somber as visions of those two wolves clamping down upon Heather's and Audrey's necks flashed in my mind.

"Vincent, are you all right?" Luna inquired.

"Yes, I'm fine. Let's continue," I replied.

"Excuse me, miss…aren't you Luna LaGrange?" a little girl about Audrey's age inquired as she lightly tugged on Luna's dress.

"Yes, I am, and who might you be, sweetheart?" Luna replied with a warm smile as she kneeled down in front of the little girl.

"I'm Clara. I just wanted to say that I want to be a thespian like you when I grow up," the little girl said to Luna in a timid tone.

"Clara, that's a beautiful name, and I have no doubt you will be," Luna said to Clara with a warm smile and embrace before Clara scampered away.

"You're very popular," I remarked with a smile.

"What a precious angel. To tell you the truth, I'm quite surprised people recognize me, for I haven't performed in over two months," Luna said with her hand against her chest.

"You're radiant. Don't ever expect to blend in with the common crowd," I said to Luna while I perused through a rack of lordly attire.

"Oh, that looks very becoming of you," Luna remarked with a smile as I held a crimson robe with black-and-white striped fur covering each breast.

"Sir, I'll pay you nine hundred dollars for that remarkable wolf-fur jacket you're wearing," a man said.

"It's not for sale," I said to the man as Luna smiled.

"You're popular too, my darling" Luna said with a smile.

"Heather sewed the black wolf fur onto this jacket. I couldn't part with it for any amount of money," I said to Luna.

"I understand. We all need those physical mementos of the ones we love. Sometimes memories just aren't enough," Luna said.

A few hours had passed as Luna and I continued to peruse through the vast array of stage garments until we happened upon a vendor selling various accessories.

"Good afternoon," I said to the man sitting behind the stand who wore a maroon tailcoat and slacks.

"Good afternoon, sir, interested in my wares?" the man inquired.

"Perhaps, but I have something you might be interested in," I replied as I grabbed the snakeskin belt from my satchel and placed it down upon the stand the man stood behind.

"Ah, a snakeskin belt," the man remarked and then began to closely examine the belt.

"Not just any snakeskin, peridot phantom—the deadliest snake in the Fray," I said to the man.

"How much do you want for this item?" the man inquired as he splayed the belt out with both hands.

"Twenty dollars," I replied.

"I'll pay you twelve dollars," the man said.

"Are you aware that this snake is the deadliest—"

"I'm fully aware of the deadliness that this snake used to possess, sir. I'm also aware of the uneven stitching along the border of the belt and blotchy tanning on the inside," the man said.

"All right, fifteen dollars then," I said to the man.

"Twelve dollars is my final offer. Take it or leave it, but that jacket you're wearing is an absolute triumph. I will pay you eight hundred dollars for it," the man said with a wide-eyed stare.

"My good man, this belt is gorgeous. Any thespian would die to wear it," Luna said to the man.

"The jacket's not for sale, good day," I said to the man in a stern tone.

"Pay no mind to that stage snob, Vincent. He wouldn't know true beauty if it smacked him in his pompous gob," Luna said with a grin.

Twelve dollars for that snakeskin belt was actually a fair price, but I just couldn't bring myself to sell that belt after risking my life acquiring the material that it's made of. The garment fair was now in full efflorescence as bands of minstrels began to perform throughout many stands of attire. Luna and I continued to walk hand in hand before sitting down upon a stone bench beside a familiar man wearing a top hat and waving a cane.

"That game is much more difficult than it appears to be," I said to Luna as I pointed at the shooting gallery game.

"You mean to tell me you failed to shoot the wolf among doves?" Luna inquired in a facetious tone and grin.

"I did. When I first arrived here in Thianor, I played that game and missed the wolf, but I have no desire to prove my aim now. I already won the Scarlet Hunt," I replied as a stripling boy fired and missed the wolf portrait.

"Indeed, you have nothing to prove to anyone, but yourself. I used to feel pressured by the board of thespians to begin performing again soon after my father died, but I told them my heart is not ready for such an endeavor," Luna said.

"Oh, you bought that shawl. I didn't notice," I said to Luna as she draped the scarlet and gray shawl over her shoulders.

"Yes, the colors are exquisite," Luna remarked with a smile.

"It looks nice on you," I remarked.

Luna then wrapped the shawl around my neck and pulled me in close for a kiss.

"I'm spent. Do you want to go to the Wishing Well for refreshments?" Luna inquired with a sigh.

"Lead the way," I said to Luna with a smile.

Luna then took my hand as we walked through the garment fare to the Wishing Well.

"It's awfully crowded. I hope we can get a table," Luna remarked as we entered the Wishing Well.

"There's an empty table," I said to Luna as I pointed at the corner table just over yonder. I then sat down at the table as Luna sat down closely beside me.

"Good evening," the serving wench pronounced as she walked up to our table.

"We'll have coffee for now. Thank you," Luna said to the serving wench with a smile after a permissive glance towards me nodding my head.

"I know just what to do with this belt," I said to Luna as I grabbed the snakeskin belt and laid it down upon the table.

"What may that be?" Luna inquired while primping her hair.

"Here…it's yours, if you want it," I said to Luna as I handed her the belt.

"I've wanted it ever since I first laid eyes on it at the Rosewood Inn. You're such a sweetheart, Vincent," Luna said and then kissed my cheek. Luna then grabbed the belt and wrapped it around her waist with childlike glee.

"I could tell," I said to Luna with a smile as the serving wench placed a silver pot of coffee and two small mugs down upon the table.

"I hope doctors find a cure for the white plague soon," Luna said and then took a sip of coffee.

"Dr. Hadden told me that science hasn't caught up to this disease yet. In the meantime, I just have to continue not to drink. It's all I can do to lessen the symptoms. It's difficult not to drink, but I have no choice," I said to Luna as I took a sip of coffee.

"I'll be there for you every step of the way, just like I was with my father," Luna said.

"This was nice. I'm glad I joined you today. I would've never taken part in an event such as this before I met you," I said to Luna with an elfish smile.

"I can't think of anyone else I would rather spend the day with more than you," Luna said with a smile.

"Thianor is beautiful in the spring," I remarked as I stared out the window of the Wishing Well at the town square lit in the glow of warm streetlights.

"It is indeed. My parents were first acquainted in the spring. I dare say Thianor is the envy of the Fray during springtime," Luna said with a smile.

"So you've never been to Bleakton or Shors End?" I inquired as a band of minstrels set up right outside the window of the Wishing Well.

"No, I haven't. I would love to immerse myself in the culture of those towns someday, but for the time being, I have responsibilities here in Thianor," Luna replied.

"That reminds me. I should be getting back to the Rosewood Inn," I said to Luna as I took a glance at my pocket watch.

"Oh, the night is still young. Let's go to my flat," Luna said with a wide-eyed stare and then quickly paid for the coffee.

"All right," I said to Luna with an elfish smile. Luna and I then waited beside the band of minstrels for a few moments before a carriage arrived.

"White Stone district, flat *A*-2," I said to the coachman.

Luna then tossed a few coins into the opened violin case in front of the minstrels with a warm smile before entering the carriage. Luna then rested her head upon my shoulder with a bantam sigh as the carriage departed the dulcet melodies emanating from the band of minstrels.

*****

"We're here," I said to Luna with a gentle nudge as the carriage bell rang. I then paid the fare to the coachman and exited the carriage while holding Luna's hand.

"I must've fallen asleep for a brief moment in the carriage," Luna said.

"You did. I didn't want to wake you though," I said to Luna as we entered her flat.

"Daisy, I'm home," Luna pronounced as we entered her flat.

"She must still be out with that man you spoke of," I said to Luna as I entered her bedroom.

"It appears so," Luna said.

"Your bedroom is very…serene," I remarked as I stared at the emerald drapes and matching quilt.

"I'm glad you think so. I want people to feel at peace in this room," Luna said as she stared into her bureau mirror.

"Oh, sorry, it's a force of habit from working at the Rosewood Inn," I said to Luna as I stoked the flames of her bedroom fireplace. Luna's bedroom resembled Vilkswood, only there were no vicious beasts, only her standing there with such a warm and inviting demeanor.

"Please sit down. I want to show you something," Luna said as she gestured towards the bed.

I then sat down upon the bed while Luna was searching through her jewelry box upon the bureau.

"My father gave this necklace to my mother the night they pledged their love to each other," Luna said with a wide-eyed gaze as she attached the heart-shaped ruby necklace around my neck.

"Why give this to me now?" I inquired with a smile.

"It's because I love you, Vincent…and I want to give all of myself to you," Luna replied and then began to slowly disrobe from her lavender dress until her silken ivory body was fully bared before me. Even though that moment was quiet, my heart was beating so loudly at the sight of Luna's ravishing body. Luna then sat down upon my lap and kissed me while her nimble hands unbuttoned my vest and collared shirt. Luna's warm, sanguine skin enticed me with such fervor as it pressed up against mine.

"I feel so safe in your arms," Luna whispered as the pace of her breathing deepened from me kissing her neck down to her heaving chest. I then rolled over as Luna's legs wrapped around my waist and her hands clasped my cheeks as we gazed salaciously into each other's eyes. At that moment, every part of my body yearned for Luna with such a rapacious hunger, but my responsibilities to the Rosewood Inn and the Merchant sisters crept back into my mind.

"Luna…the Merchant sisters—"

"Shhhh," Luna said.

"They need me," I said to Luna as she held me firmly against her smooth, flushed chest.

"Do you love me?" Luna inquired with a quivering visage.

"I do," I replied as I placed my hand on Luna's cheek.

"Then please…be with me tonight, for I desire nothing more than your touch," Luna told me in a hush tone.

*****

At 7:30 AM, I awoke to the feel of Luna's soft breath against the back of my neck. The drapes filtered the morning's light into a shade of emerald, which was cast all throughout Luna's bedroom. So it wasn't a dream. I fully gave myself to Luna last night, and if this was a dream, then I didn't ever want to awaken from it. Luna then reached out and draped her arm over my bare chest with a faint sigh. I never imagined I could feel this way again. Luna was my world now, and in her presence, there was no pain or suffering, only happiness.

"Good morning," Luna said with a smile as she rested her head upon my chest.

"Good morning, did you sleep well?" I inquired as I stroked Luna's flaxen hair and kissed the top of her head.

"Yes, like a baby," Luna replied in a yawning tone.

"Shall I make coffee?" I inquired.

"Yes, but let's just lie here for a little longer," Luna replied as she turned away from me while pulling my arm over her shoulder like a quilt. I then noticed a two-inch-long scar on Luna's hip, which I failed to notice last night.

"What happened here?" I inquired as I gently traced my finger along the scar on Luna's hip.

"Oh, when I was fourteen years old, a man robbed me while I was walking home from the Thespian Pavilion at night. He ripped the opal pendant necklace from my neck and my reticule, but he didn't stop there. The man then pinned me down upon the ground and tried to rape me. I struggled against him, but my strength paled in comparison to his. The man then pulled out a knife and stabbed me, but a nearby coachman then heard my cries and chased the man away into the back alley. The coachman then lifted me off the cold stone of the alley where I was bleeding and carried me into his carriage. If it wasn't for that coachman driving me to the infirmary that night, I might have perished…I was only a young girl after all," Luna replied in a somber tone.

"We all have scars, whether they be mental or physical. I like to think of them as reminders of what we've overcome in our lives," I said to Luna and then gently kissed the scar on her hip.

"What happened to your shoulder?" Luna inquired, as she turned over and lightly touched the scar from my bullet wound. "I'm sorry, you don't have to tell—"

"No, it's all right. I trust you. One bleak morning at the cabin, a grave robber happened upon Heather's grave. When I discovered his intentions to steal the jewels from Heather's body, I became enraged. We then both drew our pistols and fired upon each other. He shot me in the shoulder, and I shot him in the heart. The man died instantly, and I dragged his body into Vilkswood so the wolves would devour any last shred of his miserable existence. I then cauterized my shoulder wound with a burning hot fire poker. I've never told anyone about this in fear of any constables or relatives of the grave robber who could be searching for me. It's why I came to Thianor," I replied.

Luna then leaned in and kissed the scar on my shoulder with sorrowful eyes. "I love you, and you had every right to do what you did that morning, Vincent. Every scar tells a story. I'm just grateful this scar brought you to me," Luna said as she placed her hand upon the scar on my shoulder.

"I love you too. I don't want to leave this bed," I said to Luna as I placed my hand upon the scar on her hip.

"Then don't," Luna said with a smile.

*****

It was 10:15 PM.

"Roselyn, what's wrong?" I inquired as I entered the Rosewood Inn to the sight of Roselyn weeping at the front desk.

"Othello died," Roselyn said with a sniffle.

"I'm sorry, who's Othello?" I inquired.

"He was my oldest dove. The first dove I took in and trained when I was sixteen years old. I loved him like a son," Roselyn replied.

"It's good to see you have the banner welcoming the infected hanging back up outside the entrance to the inn," I said to Roselyn.

Francesca then walked up to Roselyn from the kitchen and embraced her firmly.

"I'm sorry, honey. He was a darling dove," Francesca said to Roselyn as she gestured me away with a dismissive wave.

So I then walked upstairs and entered my room with a sigh. I could still feel Luna's soft touch lingering on my skin as I took off my jacket and boots and sat down in the fireside armchair.

"Roselyn is heartbroken," Sara said as she entered my room with a sigh.

"I know, I heard," I said to Sara.

"We could've used your help today hanging up that banner outside the entrance to the inn. Beatrice almost fell off the ladder hanging it up," Sara said as she sat down upon the bed.

"I know I have responsibilities to this inn, but I was spending the day with Luna," I said to Sara as I began to sharpen my knife upon the whetstone.

"You love her. I can see it in your eyes and hear it in the tone of your voice," Sara remarked.

"I do," I said to Sara.

"I see you've chosen her over us," Sara said in a distressed tone.

"I care for you all. Why are you talking this way?" I inquired as I abruptly stopped sharpening my knife upon the whetstone and stared at Sara with vexation.

"You're devoting more and more of your time with her. Soon you will forget all about us," Sara said in a somber tone and visage.

"Sara, you and your sisters have done a great deal for me. I will never forget about you and them," I said to Sara as I stood up from the armchair and sat down upon the bed beside her.

"First my father, then Isaac, and now you. Everyone I love leaves me," Sara said in a weeping tone as her eyes began to well up with tears.

"What about your sisters? They'll always be there for you, so don't take them for granted," I said to Sara.

"You don't understand," Sara said as she wiped tears away from her cheeks with a white handkerchief.

"I understand you have a family. I work and live here, Sara, by the good grace of Roselyn, but the rest of my life isn't beholden to you and your sisters, so don't make me choose between you and your sister and Luna," I said to Sara in a stern tone.

"Vincent, you've already made your choice. You just don't realize it yet. Good night," Sara said and then stormed out of my room.

CHAPTER 14

Scars of the Past

With no more guises, a shadow arises.

Sara and I made up rooms 1 through 4 with a detached silence. Was I too harsh with her the night before? Her once warm eyes now wouldn't so much as even glance at me as we washed the laundry. I hurt Sara, but the truth was often difficult to hear when the outcry of the heart drowns out all reason. A little over a month ago, Luna's letter stated her desire for me to move in with her, but she also took into consideration my responsibilities to the Rosewood Inn. So much had changed since then between Luna, the Merchant sisters, and me. I would now desire to be with Luna every waking moment and have her in my arms any chance I can get. I had never shared my heart with someone so fully the way that I had with Luna, and because of that, I needed her to stay in my life. Maybe it was time for me to live with Luna in her flat, for she's all I desire in this world.

"How are you, Vincent?" Beatrice inquired as she entered my room.

"I'm fine. I'm heading out soon, so if there's any work to be done, let me know now," I replied as I combed my hair in the bureau mirror.

"I heard you talking to Sara last night, and I just want to say, you don't have to feel any guilt from us for being with Luna. We adore Luna. Sara is just afraid," Beatrice said with a sigh.

"Afraid of what exactly?" I inquired.

"She's afraid of losing a father figure such as you. You really do resemble our father. Roselyn and Sara were right to make such a remark. Did Sara ever tell you how our father died?" Beatrice replied.

"No, I figured it was too painful for her to disclose," I replied.

"Our father died one evening on his way to the Sanguine Solarium to buy roses for Sara. He was hit by a stray bullet during his ride home upon Sigmund by a man who had just robbed a boutique and was fleeing the town on horseback. The constables quickly caught up with the man on horseback and shot him dead, but not before he took the life of our dear father. Sara told me our father's last words to her were 'Not to fret, princess, for I'll return with something that will make you smile.' This is why roses adorn our inn, Vincent, to honor the memory of our father, as he died with dozens of roses surrounding him," Beatrice said in a somber tone.

The death of the Merchant sister's father was a tragic story, which gave me more insight into Sara's emotional state and why she felt like she was losing me. We depend on people in our lives so strongly to the point that when they're no longer around, we feel empty, like a part of us died along with them. When Heather and Audrey died, I lost everything. I thought I buried the best part of me along with them, six feet below, and I never thought that part of me could ever arise again from the grave until Luna bestowed a newfound sense of hope within me. Any lesser man would've fallen to pieces at the death of his wife and daughter and remain forever shattered. Although that part of me remains shattered, like broken glass upon the floor. I no longer desired to gaze into the reflection of those shattered memories, but to create new, unhallowed memories with Luna. These thoughts weighed heavy on my mind during the carriage ride to Luna's flat.

I then paid my fare to the coachman as the bell rang and the carriage halted in front of Luna's flat. The courtyard was our sanctuary. I wondered how long it would take for Luna to notice me in the courtyard from her second-story window. So I sat down upon the white stone bench awaiting my dear Luna as the clouds began to break bringing forth a ray of sunlight, which lit up the courtyard.

"Surprise!" Luna shouted with glee as she wrapped her arms around my neck from behind.

"I didn't hear you come through the gate," I remarked with a smile.

"That's because I'm barefoot. I wanted to sneak up on you to test your hunter senses," Luna said with a smile as she sat down upon my lap and kissed me.

"If you were a bear, I would be dead right now," I said to Luna with a grin as I held her waist firmly against me.

"I'm glad your defenses are down when you're around me," Luna said. Luna wore a white chiffon nightgown with embroidered roses upon her chest and shoulders. "I have to go get dressed. Do you want to come up or wait in the courtyard?" Luna inquired.

"I'll come up. I could use another cup of coffee right now," I replied.

"Daisy, Vincent's here," Luna pronounced as we entered her flat.

"Oh, how are you, Vincent?" Daisy inquired with a warm smile as she entered the great room holding a pot of coffee and tray of pastries as Luna scampered to her bedroom to get dressed.

"I'm doing well," I replied as I sat down upon the emerald sofa.

"So what do you and Luna have planned for today?" Daisy inquired with a smile as she poured me a cup of coffee and sat down upon the sofa beside me with a sigh.

"I don't know yet. Your sister is the one who knows about all the events taking place in Thianor," I replied and then took a sip of coffee.

"That's true. Luna always has her ear to the pulse of this town," Daisy said.

"What are these?" I inquired as I grabbed one of the pastries from the tray.

"Those are cranberry scones. I made them this morning," Daisy replied.

"Very good," I remarked with a mouthful of the tart and moist scone.

Luna then entered the great room wearing a crimson dress underneath a black corset. Her hair was done up in a bun with two wavy strands hanging down each side of her lucent visage.

"There's an outdoor gallery exhibition in the town square of the works of Gabriel Cavalli. I thought we could browse his beautiful artwork," Luna said while primping her hair.

"Sure, who's Gabriel Cavalli?" I inquired.

"He painted that," Luna said as she pointed at the painting of the little girl in the golden meadow hanging on the wall beside the antler.

"Oh, does he live in Thianor?" I inquired as I stood up from the emerald sofa and closely examined the painting of the little girl in the golden meadow.

"No, he lived in Shors End but was born in *Somerland*. He died ten years ago, and ever since then, his artwork has proliferated in price and popularity throughout the Fray," Luna replied.

"Shall we go then?" I inquired with a smile.

"Yes, darling," Luna replied with a smile.

"Have fun, you two," Daisy told us as we exited the flat with a farewell wave.

"How grateful am I to be with the most beautiful woman in Thianor," I said to Luna as we waited on the street for a carriage.

"I'm grateful to be with you as well, my love," Luna said with a warm smile and then kissed my cheek. After a few moments of affectionate whimsy, a carriage halted in front of us.

"After you," I said to Luna as I took her hand and opened the door of the carriage. "Believe it or not, but I've never been to a gallery before," I said.

"I shall be your guide, my dear. Cavalli's work is coveted all throughout the Fray, so expect to see a vast array of people at this gallery," Luna said.

"I'm always ready for new experiences as long as I share them with—" A series of sporadic coughs abruptly cut my voice short as I turned away from Luna with my handkerchief over my mouth.

"Sweetheart, are you all right?" Luna inquired as she rubbed my back.

I then slowly looked at the white handkerchief, but there was no bloodstain upon the white fabric. "No blood. I'm fine," I said to Luna in a raspy tone and then took a long swig of water from my canteen.

"If you begin to feel weak, please tell me so that we can go back to my flat, and I can take care of you," Luna said in a distressed tone and wide-eyed stare.

"I'm fine…I'm fine," I said to Luna with a dismissive waive.

"Very well, just as long as you don't play the martyr role with me. I'm here for you. Don't forget that," Luna said as the carriage came to a halt at the town square.

Luna and I then exited the carriage to the sight of numerous works of art being displayed all throughout town square.

"So where shall we begin?" I inquired.

"Wherever the artwork takes us," Luna replied as she took my hand.

I was by no means well-educated in the art world, but even I could tell Cavalli had immense talent. There were many constables standing guard beside Cavalli's artwork to dissuade any attempts at theft.

"Look at this one," I said to Luna as I pointed at a landscape painting of a woman in a crimson dress standing at the edge of a cliff with her arms spread out.

"You notice how a woman is the center point in all of Cavalli's oil landscapes?" Luna remarked as she pointed at the painting.

"I do, and I notice how the landscape compliments the woman's mood and vice versa," I remarked as I stared intently at the painting.

"That's a very keen observation," Luna said.

Luna and I then moved to a collection of sculptures displayed in a line, as if they were all part of one collective piece of art.

"Cavalli was a sculptor too?" I inquired as I stared intently at the four sculptures before me.

"Yes, he dabbled in various mediums, but his paintings are his most renowned works of art," Luna said. The four sculptures depicted the same woman carved from four different types of stone and holding four different objects in her hands. "That's Thia Lynsetta," Luna said as she stared intently at the four sculptures. One black marble sculpture of Thia was holding a heart. One limestone sculpture of Thia was holding a sword. One granite sculpture was holding a rose, and one ivory sculpture of Thia was holding a frowning mask. "Cavalli is depicting Thia in these four sculptures as a saint of malice, love, sorrow, and nature. His message is that she's all encompassing," Luna said.

"That's one interpretation," I said to Luna.

"What's your interpretation?" Luna inquired.

"I see these four sculptures of Thia as four choices. We choose which sculpture of her that we identify with the most thereby we choose our path in life," I replied.

"I wish Cavalli were here now so we could ask him the true meaning of his art, but I suppose he would've wanted people to draw their own interpretations of his art, as most artists do," Luna said as she stared intently at the four sculptures with hand upon her chin in contemplation.

"Let us start the bidding at one hundred dollars. Do I hear one hundred dollars?" a man wearing a tailcoat and top hat pronounced from behind a rostrum upon a small stage.

"Oh, I didn't know Cavalli's work was being auctioned off as well," Luna said.

There were dozens of finely dressed men and woman sitting in front of the stage with paddles in their hands waiting for the right time to cast their bid.

"Come now, ladies and gentleman, this painting is in mint condition. It would look breathtaking in any parlor," the auctioneer pronounced with a smile.

"One thousand dollars!" a man shouted triumphantly as he raised his paddle.

"One thousand going once…twice…sold to the gentleman with a fine taste in art," the auctioneer pronounced.

"Art is what funds this town. It's the very blood that courses through the streets. I shudder to imagine where Thianor would be devoid of art," Luna said.

"I think that Thianor would be all right devoid of art, but no longer remarkable," I said to Luna as we watched the auction for a few more moments before moving on throughout the gallery.

Luna and I then slowly walked past a sculpture of a corpulent gold pig standing on its hind legs, which a group of children stood in front of, pointing and giggling. One of the children then tried to sneak underneath the scarlet rope, which blocked off all the artwork from the people's touch, but a constable immediately noticed and shouted at the child while aggressively waving his baton, which sent the mischievous child fleeing away from the golden pig sculpture.

"Children are always so curious. They see walls, and their first instinct is to find a way to get on the other side of them. I admire that mentality," Luna remarked with a smile. Luna and I then entered a large crimson tent where a collection of paintings was displayed in the dim glow of several oil lamps hanging from above the center of the tent.

This collection of paintings underneath the crimson tent was different from the rest of Cavalli's artwork, for the paintings evoked such raw and sinister emotions.

"Oh my, Vincent, look," Luna said as she pointed to a large gilded portrait just over yonder.

The portrait depicted a flaxen-haired woman smiling with roses sprouting from both her eyes.

"Is that blood?" Luna inquired as she pointed at the portrait.

"Yes, she's crying tears of blood," I replied as I stared intently at the grim portrait.

"She's smiling though," Luna remarked in bewilderment as she placed her hand upon her chest.

I stood staring at the portrait just as awestruck, as Luna was, for the message of this grim portrait confounded yet intrigued me. I then felt a sudden force upon a frigid breeze beckoning me just over yonder. So I turned away from Luna who was still captivated by the grim portrait of the smiling woman bleeding from her rosebud eyes, and began to slowly walk across the crimson tent, and that's when I saw it.

It was the wolf, White Bane, depicted in a large ebony-framed portrait. He stared at me with those malevolent amber eyes and bloodstained white fur around his snout, just as he did when he killed Heather and Audrey. My body was frozen at that moment, yet my heart beat at a frenetic pace as I gazed at the portrait with wide eyes burning with rage.

"Magnificent, isn't it—the fabled white wolf of Vilkswood?" a man wearing a black cloak remarked in a raspy tone as he walked up to me with crossed arms.

"What's so magnificent about it exactly?" I inquired with a scornful glance towards the man.

"Cavalli thought he was magnificent, and that's all that matters to me," the man replied and then slowly walked out of the crimson tent with a smirk. I then found myself grasping my holstered pistol as I continued to stare intently into the menacing portrait of White Bane.

"Vincent, are you all right? Vincent…Vincent?" Luna inquired in a distressed tone. She then grabbed my face with both hands and directed my gaze from White Bane's burning amber eyes to her serene peridot eyes.

"I'm fine," I replied.

"That's White Bane, isn't it?" Luna inquired with her hand upon her chest.

"Yes," I replied.

"Let's leave from this tent of horrors, Vincent," Luna said as she took my hand and pulled me towards the entrance of the crimson tent. Did Cavalli encounter White Bane as well, and if so, what grim effect did the white wolf have upon his life?

"This was all quite illuminating," I said to Luna.

"Indeed, but that's enough of the gallery for today. Would you care to join me for a stroll through the *Scarlet Commons*?" Luna inquired.

"Lead the way," I replied with a smile.

"To Scarlet Commons, sir," Luna said to the coachman as a carriage slowly halted in front of us.

"Luna, do you know how Cavalli died?" I inquired as we both sat down beside each other in the carriage.

"It was a heart condition, but I heard that he died halfway through painting someone's portrait," Luna replied while primping her hair.

"Just imagine what that person felt. First, being the subject of Cavalli's muse and then witnessing his death firsthand," I said to Luna.

"Whoever the person was, I would feel such guilt knowing that Cavalli died while painting me," Luna said.

"Does Cavalli have any family in Thianor?" I inquired.

"I'm afraid not. He has a younger sister, but last I heard, she resides in Shors End," Luna replied.

"Does she live off the residuals from her brother's art?" I inquired.

"I don't know, Vincent. I suppose that her brother's art supported her financially to a certain degree, but not for the rest of her life. After all, none of us want to live in someone else's shadow, even if they're family," Luna replied.

"I've lived here in Thianor for six months now and haven't been to these Scarlet Commons you speak of," I said to Luna.

"They're beautiful, especially now during spring's awakening. I remember one picturesque morning, Daisy and I had lunch at the Scarlet Commons while a group of four harlequins were rehearsing for a play. Daisy and I watched the harlequins with wide eyes as they began to juggle knives. Then without hesitation, Daisy walked up to the harlequins and requested for them to teach her how to juggle. The harlequins kindly accepted and began to teach Daisy how to juggle, but not with knives, thank God. I watched as Daisy dropped ball after ball trying to follow the harlequins," Luna said with a giggle.

"So did she give up or continue until she mastered juggling?" I inquired with a smile.

"No, Daisy continued until she mastered juggling. It actually consumed her to the point where she would juggle all the time in our flat just to impress Father," Luna replied with an elfish smile.

"We're here. Oh, look, Vincent," Luna pronounced as she paid the fare to the coachman and exited the carriage while pointing to the cerulean sky. I then exited the carriage to the sight of several kites being flown by a group of children.

"How delightful," Luna remarked as we slowly walked hand in hand down the thoroughfare of the Commons before sitting down upon a bench overlooking a small, placid pond.

"Vincent, what was it like living amidst the wild for most of your life?" Luna inquired.

"At times, it was peaceful, but there was always an underlying sense of danger, which my father instilled in me in order to keep me safe. By the time I grew into a man and my father died, that danger had become so familiar to me, but there's one thing that was missing from my life in the cabin," I replied.

"What would that be?" Luna inquired.

"You," I replied with a smile and then leaned and kissed Luna.

"I wish I met you sooner, Vincent. I shudder to think where my life would be without you," Luna said as she rested her head upon my shoulder.

"Let's not let such thoughts cast a shadow upon us," I said to Luna.

Luna and I sat there quietly upon the bench overlooking the small pond while songbirds began to sing in a dulcet harmony of nature, surrounding us in their vibrant tribute to spring.

"Excuse me, miss, could you hold my kite while I tie my shoes?" a little boy inquired as he walked up to Luna.

"Why, certainly," Luna replied with a smile as she took the spool of the kite in hand from the little boy. The little boy then began to tie his shoes with haste lest Luna lose her grasp on the spool or crash his kite. Luna then stood up from the bench and walked towards the edge of the pond, with a wide-eyed stare intently fixed upon the white dove-shaped kite.

"All right, thank you, miss," the little boy said to Luna as he took the spool from her and then scampered away.

"Just when I was beginning to have fun," Luna said with a cherub's frown. Luna and I then continued to stroll hand in hand down the thoroughfare of the Scarlet Commons.

"Children seem to always be attracted to you," I said to Luna with a smile.

"I welcome them. You can learn a great deal from the eyes of a child. Children's perceptions are clear unlike adults who tend to see the world through a dark veil," Luna said.

"When I was a child, I had such a fascination with only the most dangerous animals in Vilkswood," I said to Luna as I grabbed a stone and skipped it across the pond.

"How did your father react?" Luna inquired.

"He respected my fascination but taught me not to let curiosity be my downfall. Once again, he was wrong. After all, I owe meeting you to my inquisitive nature," I said to Luna.

"Daisy often tells me to take more risks, like I'm turning into an old woman set in her ways," Luna said with a grin.

"Was she just being facetious?" I inquired with a grin.

"No, there was a hint of sincerity in her voice. Perhaps she's right. I'm not as daring of a woman as I once was…ever since I was attacked by that man when I was fourteen years old, I began to see the world through a dark veil," Luna said in a somber tone.

"That's understandable, but you kept performing despite that horrible incident. That's pretty damn daring in my book," I said to Luna as I draped my arm around her.

Luna and I continued to stroll throughout the Scarlet Commons, passing by a vibrant rose garden in full bloom.

"Vincent, look," Luna said in a gasping tone as she pointed at a man and woman in the rose garden.

The man was on one knee proposing to the woman as she stood over him with her hands over her mouth. Luna and I were too far away from the couple to hear them, but judging by their body language, it appeared that the woman said yes. Luna then began to shed tears of joy for the engaged couple as they kissed in a full embrace.

"That's so beautiful. What a perfect setting to profess your love, just like a fairy tale," Luna remarked.

"I suppose," I said to Luna with a grin.

"Congratulations!" Luna shouted with a smile as she waved at the couple in the rose garden. The couple then waved back in unison with radiant demeanors.

When I proposed to Heather, it was nowhere near as romantic as the couple in the rose garden. I proposed to Heather during a thunderstorm one summer afternoon, but she said yes, and that was all my heart yearned for at that moment. Luna was a talented thespian, so she had an affinity for lavish settings and prominent emotions.

"I'm exhausted. Could we go back to my flat?" Luna inquired with a smile.

"Sure, I could use the rest as well," I replied.

"To the White Stone district, flat *A*-2, sir," Luna said to the coachman. "I've been receiving letters from the thespian board, beseeching me to perform again," Luna said as we sat down beside each other in the carriage.

"Do you feel like you're ready?" I inquired.

"I do miss performing, but I feel like the board only wants me to perform because of the revenue my plays bring in," Luna replied.

"You're a captivating performer, Luna. I'm sure money isn't the sole reason for their request for your return to the stage," I said to Luna.

"Do you really think the townsfolk miss me performing?" Luna inquired.

"Absolutely, but only when your heart and body are ready," I replied with an elfish smile.

"Thank you, dear. Perhaps I will take to the stage in the near future," Luna said with a smile and then rested her head upon my shoulder.

"We're here," I said to Luna as I paid the fare to the coachman.

Luna and I then exited the carriage and entered her flat.

"Well, excuse you," Luna pronounced as the familiar amber cat crossed her path.

"Whose cat is that exactly?" I inquired as Luna and I walked up the stairs to her flat.

"Oh, that cat belongs to Eleanor. She's a quiet, kind old woman who lives below us," Luna replied. "Daisy, I'm home," Luna pronounced as we entered her flat. "Oh, good evening, Gregory," Luna said to a man sitting down upon the emerald sofa.

"Good evening, Luna," Gregory said to Luna with a smile as he stood up from the sofa and extended his hand in salutation. Gregory was a thin man around my build. He had copper hair and was dressed rather dapperly with a rose pinned to his three-piece suit.

"This is Vincent Belmont," Luna said to Gregory.

"Ah, yes, of course. I've read about you in the *Daily Rosette*, Mr. Belmont, and how you turned down Mayor Crane's proposal," Gregory said with a smile as I shook his hand.

"It was my choice, and I stand by it," I said to Gregory.

"As do I," Luna said with a smile as she grabbed my arm.

"You don't have to prove anything to me, Mr. Belmont. I respect a man who makes his own path instead of one that's laid out before him by a man of great authority," Gregory said.

"I'm ready," Daisy said to Gregory with a smile as she entered the great room wearing a gold shawl and frilled black dress.

"You look beautiful," Luna remarked with a warm smile.

"You took the words right out of my mouth, Luna," Gregory remarked with a smile.

"So where are you two off to?" Luna inquired with a smile.

"To the Wishing Well, then Cavalli's gallery exhibition if we have the time," Daisy replied.

"That sounds wonderful. Have a good time, you two," Luna pronounced as Daisy and Gregory exited the flat hand in hand.

"I like him," I said to Luna with a grin.

"Yes, Gregory is a good man. I'm so happy for Daisy," Luna said.

I then sat down upon the emerald sofa with a sigh and began to sharpen my knife upon the whetstone.

"Are you planning on skinning an animal, my dear?" Luna inquired with a giggle as she entered the great room with a pot of coffee and two mugs.

"Oh, this is just a force of habit. My father always taught me to keep my blade sharp even when I'm not hunting," I replied as Luna poured me a cup of coffee and sat down beside me upon the emerald sofa with a faint sigh.

"Vincent…I saw what happened to you when you laid eyes upon that portrait of White Bane at the Cavalli gallery," Luna said.

"What of it?" I inquired in a stern tone and then took a sip of coffee.

"If a mere portrait of that white wolf can evoke such rage within you, then I fear for the fragile state of your soul," Luna replied in a distressed tone.

"How do you expect me to react? That monster killed Heather and Audrey," I said to Luna in a stern tone as I stood up from the sofa.

"Vincent, I found solace in my father's death with you. Can you not find the same solace with me in your family's death?" Luna inquired in a distressed tone.

"Don't compare the two. Your father's death was imminent. Therefore, your heart had time to prepare for such a loss. Heather and Audrey were taken from me in such a swift and vicious manner," I replied as I began pacing back and forth in front of the fireplace.

"You're right…I did have time to prepare for my father's death, but that didn't lessen the pain of losing him," Luna said with sorrowful eyes. Luna then stood up from the sofa and quickly embraced me.

"I'm sorry. I wish I could see the world with eyes unclouded by that demon," I said to Luna.

"You have nothing to apologize for. I love you," Luna said and then took my hand as we slowly walked to her bedroom.

"Every time I lie here with you, I feel as if I'm dreaming," I said to Luna as my hand slowly traced the smooth contours of her bare body.

"You're still wearing the necklace," Luna remarked with a smile as she grasped the ruby heart necklace betwixt her slender flingers.

"Of course, I dare not part with it," I said to Luna with an elfish smile.

There was no sorrow, suffering, or pain, as I lay in bed with Luna. The warmth of her skin against mine was more comforting than a fire on a frigid winter's night.

"She cares for you. I could see it in her eyes when I saw her at my father's funeral," Luna said.

"Sara feels like I'm abandoning her for you, and that tears me apart," I said to Luna with a sigh.

"She's a sweet girl with a fragile heart," Luna said.

"She sees me as a father figure. She says I remind her so much of her father who died when she was twelve years old," I said to Luna.

"How did he die?" Luna inquired.

"He was shot on his way home from buying roses for her," I replied.

"That's so heartbreaking," Luna remarked in a gasping tone.

"I don't want to abandon Sara, but she'll always have her sisters for emotional support," I said to Luna.

"Vincent, you see Audrey in Sara's eyes, don't you?" Luna inquired as she placed her hand upon my cheek.

"I do. I see Audrey in the eyes of all children," I replied and then reached down and grabbed Angie from the breast pocket of my jacket.

"Sara and her sisters are a godsend to Thianor. The comfort they provide to the infected is reminiscent of Thia Lynsetta's benevolence," Luna said.

"They have a business to run, and I don't want to be a hindrance to their productivity," I said to Luna.

"My love, nobody sees you as a hindrance," Luna said.

"Do you think my feelings for Sara are misplaced?" I inquired as I stared at Angie.

"No, the feelings you and Sara have for each other are pure. Death has a way of forming new bonds where previous bonds were severed. Just don't hurt her," Luna said.

"Her older sister told me the same when she first took me in six months ago," I said to Luna.

"You carry a heavy heart, Vincent. Some people say it's a burden, but I believe it's a trait more people in this world should possess. Just imagine if everyone in this world loved with a heart so heavy that it shielded everyone around them. That's the world I want to live in," Luna said and then grabbed Angie and pressed her against her bare chest.

"Are you reciting another play?" I inquired with a grin.

"No, I'm simply reciting the beating of my heart," Luna said with a playful shove.

"You're so beautiful," I said to Luna as I brushed a strand of hair away from her gleaming eyes.

Luna then kissed me and rolled over as she pulled my arm over her like a quilt.

"All will be clearer in the morning. Good night," Luna said.

"Good night," I said to Luna. I then kissed Luna's shoulder as my bleary eyes began to slowly close to the sight of her chest slowly rising and falling with each tranquil breath.

It was 4:05 PM.

"Be careful unloading that wine, Vincent. It cost us a fortune," Francesca said.

"Don't worry, Francesca," I said to Francesca with a smile as I carried a crate full of twelve bottles of wine to the kitchen.

"Well, then why don't you help us then, Ms. Priss?" Beatrice inquired as she entered the kitchen carrying a crate of wine bottles.

"I am going over our monthly revenue right now," Francesca replied.

"Why does the inn need such expensive wine to begin with?" I inquired as Beatrice and I unloaded the last crates of wine from the wagon.

"Oh, that's Francesca's idea. She thinks this Pinot noir will attract more upscale business to the inn," Beatrice said.

"I didn't know the inn was looking to attract that class of people," I said to Beatrice as I stored the bottles of Pinot noir in the wine cellar.

“Well, before the dreadful white plague, the Rosewood Inn was well-known throughout Thianor for accommodating wealthy dignitaries. That was back when our mother Gloria ran the inn and ordered all of us around like a general,” Beatrice said with a smile.

“If you don’t mind me asking, how did your mother die?” I inquired.

“She died only a year after my father died from the scarlet fever,” Beatrice said in a somber tone as she washed the counters of the kitchen.

“I was stricken with the scarlet fever as well. That was back when I had Heather and Audrey to aid me back to health,” I said to Beatrice as I helped her wash the kitchen counters

“Our mother wasn’t as strong as you are, Vincent. Well, not physically at least. My sisters and I waited on her hand and foot as she lay sickly in bed. The scarlet fever ate away at her day by day until she resembled a corpse. The most difficult part for me was accepting the inevitable fact that I would no longer have my mother to talk to. Sara and I wept the entire night our mother died, but Roselyn and Francesca knew what had to be done thereafter. Roselyn told me that Mother’s last words were to keep the inn running, and I love you,”

Beatrice said in a somber tone.

“She would be so proud of you all,” I said to Beatrice.

“Sara, can we talk please?” I inquired as Sara walked past me in a cold, detached demeanor and began watering the roses, which decorated the third-floor corridor. Sara didn’t respond to me. She just continued to water the roses as if I wasn’t even there.

“All right…you don’t have to respond, just please listen. I’m forever in debt to you and your sisters. You four have given me a new life in the wake of my family’s death. I don’t want to hurt you, and I don’t want you to feel any resentment towards Luna, for she brightens my life in a way that makes me forget that I have an incurable disease. I’d like to think that if Audrey was still alive that she would’ve grown into a beautiful young woman like you,” I said to Sara and then opened the door to my room. Sara then quickly wrapped her arms around my chest from behind, just as I was about to enter my room.

“I don’t want to be angry with you, Vincent. I just don’t want you to leave us. My heart couldn’t bear it,” Sara said in a somber tone.

“Please sit down,” I said to Sara as we entered my room.

“Tell me you’re staying with us, please,” Sara said as we sat down upon the bed.

“Sara, I know not what my future entails, but ever since I was diagnosed with the white plague, I’ve learned to not suppress my emotions, for my days are now numbered,” I said to Sara.

“Don’t talk like that,” Sara said in a distressed tone.

“Whether I remain here with you and your sisters or circumstances take me somewhere else, you must know that my choice is my burden, and I will always care about you and your sisters.

"So you don't want to make a long-term commitment to us?" Sara inquired with her head hanging low.

"Long-term…I'm afraid I can't see that far ahead in my life right now. I'm living every day to the fullest thanks to you and the good graces of your sisters. Beatrice told me how your parents died. A loss such as those is unbearable, but these past six months of living with you and your sisters has taught me one valuable lesson," I said to Sara.

"What lesson is that?" Sara inquired as she stared at me with a sorrowful visage.

"To never take love for granted, for it can pull you out of any misery the world buries you under," I said to Sara with an elfish smile as I draped my arm around her and rubbed her shoulder.

I hoped Sara and I reconciled our feelings. I told her the truth of my life, and that was all that could be said to someone in that situation.

"What are you reading, Vincent?" Beatrice inquired as she sat down beside me on the lobby sofa with two knitting needles and scarlet yarn in hand.

"The *Daily Rosette*, Mayor Crane is on a goodwill trip to Bleakton at the moment," I said to Beatrice.

"Vincent, accompany Francesca!" Roselyn shouted from the front desk.

"Yes, ma'am!" I shouted. I then stood up from the lobby sofa and followed Francesca as she exited the inn wearing a rose jacket with crimson stripes.

"So where are we off to?" I inquired as Francesca fed Sigmund a carrot.

"To *Thianor Emporium*. it's an indoor trading market filled with everything one's heart could ever desire. It's one of the first of its kind in the Fray. It's located in a large warehouse on Thirteenth Street, in the Black Marble district," Francesca replied.

"Oh, I don't believe I've ever been—"

"Don't worry. I'll drive. I know the way by heart. So much for your hunter's keen sense of direction," Francesca said with a smirk as she sat down in the wagon beside me and took the reins. I then shook my head with a scoff as we drove north down the main thoroughfare of Thianor.

"The inn needs new bedsheets for all the rooms. The old ones are too dull and not to mention frayed and stained with blood from the infected," Francesca said.

"Do you have a particular design in mind?" I inquired.

"I'll know it when I see it, but it will look fabulous and add a new sense of flair and sophistication to the rooms," Francesca replied.

"I'll leave it to you then. I've never had much of an eye for fashion," I said to Francesca.

"I could tell judging by that jacket you constantly wear," Francesca said with a smirk.

"What's wrong with my jacket?" I inquired with a scoff.

"Let's just say it's bleaker than a November morning," Francesca replied with a giggle.

"I'll have you know that vendors were clamoring over my jacket when I was at the garment fair with Luna," I said to Francesca with a smirk.

"Only because wolf fur remains so coveted throughout the Fray. This white dahlia pin is marvelous though," Francesca remarked as she pointed at the pin attached to the wolf fur on my jacket.

"Luna gave me this pin," I said to Francesca.

"Ah, of course, only a thespian would have such a sense of flair to liven up your jacket with a vibrant accoutrement such as this pin," Francesca said with a smile.

"Everything about Luna is vibrant," I said to Francesca, with an elfish smile, as we entered the Black Marble district.

"Do you think the white plague affects all these wealthy dignitaries living in the Black Marble district the same way it affects everyone else in Thianor?" Francesca inquired as we drove past luxurious estate houses with stone column entrances and black brick facades.

"As I've said before, a disease such as the white plague has no prejudices. It affects all classes of people from the impoverished to the wealthy. There's no cure after all," I replied.

"We're here," Francesca said as she halted Sigmund in front of a streetlight.

"It looks so dreary," I remarked as I stared at the large gray warehouse.

"You should know better than anyone not to judge a book by its cover, Vincent," Francesca said as she stepped down from the wagon and tied Sigmund to the streetlight.

Francesca and I then entered the warehouse to the sight of hundreds of people selling vast arrays of wares.

"Beautiful lady, interested in beautiful jewels?" a man inquired from behind a long glass-covered counter filled with jewelry, but Francesca passed him by with a flout.

"What an impressive market. So where would we find those bedsheets?" I inquired as I gazed around the perimeter of the warehouse.

"Last I recall, the garment department is located in the back of the warehouse," Francesca said as we walked past an array of products ranging from washing mills to pistols.

"How much for that gold-plated pistol?" I inquired.

"Sixty dollars," the man sitting in front of a rack with various pistols hanging from it replied.

"Come now, Vincent. We're not here for you. We're here to improve the ambience of the inn," Francesca said to me with a waving gesture in the manner of which a mother would gesture to her curious child who has strayed from her side.

"I like this place," I said to Francesca with a smirk as I scampered over to her side.

"You're like a child," Francesca remarked with an eye-rolling glance.

"What's so bad about that exactly?" I inquired with a smirk.

"Oh, you see those quilts hanging on the clotheslines?" Francesca remarked as she pointed to the varicolored hanging quilts just over yonder.

"So this is the garment department? It's not as vibrant as I expected," I remarked.

"Don't complain," Francesca said as she began meticulously searching through all the bedsheets hanging on the clotheslines and folded on tables.

"Francesca, what about this bedsheet?" I inquired as I displayed a black-and-white striped bedsheet to her judging stare.

"Heavens no. That looks like it should cover the bed of a prisoner," Francesca replied while shaking her head in disgust. "The new bedsheets must be elegant and vibrant, and not clash with the rest of the inn's motif," Francesca said.

"I wish I knew what you were looking for," I said to Francesca with a sigh as I continued to search throughout stacks of folded sheets alongside her.

"I told you I'll know it when I see it," Francesca said.

"Well, that doesn't help me now, does it?" I said to Francesca.

Francesca was pertinacious when it came to aesthetics. She was the kind of woman who would stop at nothing until she was satisfied.

"That's it. Right up there. Oh, it's gorgeous," Francesca remarked with a smile as she tried to reach a scarlet rose pattern bedsheet hanging from a clothesline. "Vincent, can you reach that for me?" Francesca requested as she jumped up and down beneath the bedsheet with her arms outstretched.

"If you damage that display sheet, then you buy it!" a man shouted from behind a counter.

I then in one swift motion pulled the bedsheet down from the clothesline, and it fell atop Francesca and I like a tent.

"We were going to buy the bedsheet anyway. Do you have sixteen of this one with the rose pattern?" Francesca inquired while primping her hair.

"I sure do," the man replied.

"Marvelous, we'll take sixteen of those bedsheets, wrapped," Francesca said to the man.

The man then began wrapping up stacks of four bedsheets with paper and string as Francesca rifled through her reticule for money.

"Your total is one hundred twenty-eight dollars," the man said to Francesca.

Francesca then paid the man and ordered me to push the cart full of bedsheets with a waving hand gesture in the manner of a queen ordering her subordinates.

"We're all finished here," Francesca said as we walked towards the entrance of the emporium.

I then began loading all the bedsheets from the cart onto the wagon while Francesca untied Sigmund and fed him another carrot from the saddlebag.

“I’m sure Roselyn will like the new bedsheets you’ve chosen,” I said to Francesca.

“Of course, she will. I’ve never let her down when it comes to beautifying the inn,” Francesca said as we drove down the thoroughfare of the Black Marble district.

“We finished earlier than I expected,” I remarked.

“Indeed, and since Roselyn is taking the night shift tonight, we can stop at the Wishing Well for a drink after we drop off the bedsheets at the inn,” Francesca said.

“All right, but you know I cannot drink,” I said to Francesca.

“Oh, come now, Vincent. Is one drink really going to inflame the white plague?” Francesca inquired.

“I’m afraid so. Believe me, under any other circumstance, I would love the opportunity to drink you under the table,” I replied with a smirk.

“Excuses, excuses will hang you like nooses,” Francesca said with a smile as we entered the town square.

*****

“We’re back!” I shouted as I entered the Rosewood Inn.

“Sara, Beatrice, go unload the wares from the wagon,” Roselyn pronounced.

Sara and Beatrice then sat up from the lobby sofa in unison and scampered to the entrance of the Rosewood Inn.

“What did you purchase at the emporium?” Sara inquired in a timid tone as she lifted a stack of four bedsheets from off the wagon.

“New bedsheets for all the rooms,” Francesca replied.

“Let’s take a look at these,” Beatrice pronounced as she ripped open one of the wrapped stacks of bedsheets. “Oh, these are very posh, Francesca,” Beatrice remarked with a smile and then carried a stack into the inn.

“What do you think?” Francesca inquired as she displayed a bedsheet to Roselyn at the front desk.

“They’re beautiful. We can donate the old sheets to Thianor Infirmary,” Roselyn replied with a warm smile.

“Vincent and I are going to the Wishing Well for a nightcap now unless you need us, of course?” Francesca inquired.

“No, Sara and Beatrice can make all the rooms with the new bedsheets. You two, go ahead,” Roselyn replied and then went back to petting her doves.

“All right then, let’s go, Vincent,” Francesca said.

Francesca and I then boarded the wagon and began to ride down the main thoroughfare as the clear spring sky shone with amber hues of the twilight hour.

*****

"One double honeyed bourbon, Carmella!" Francesca shouted as we entered the Wishing Well.

"One coffee," I said to Carmella.

"Let's just sit at the bar. There appears to be no empty tables," Francesca said and then sat down on a stool while adjusting her jacket.

"I ordered the same drink as you the first day I came here," I said to Francesca as I sat down beside her.

"It's such a warm and comforting drink, isn't it?" Francesca inquired with a grin. "Indeed, I drunk six of them that day," I replied with a snicker.

"Here you go, doll," Carmella said to Francesca as she served her the steaming glass of honeyed bourbon.

"Cheers…may our lives be full of joy!" Francesca said with a smile.

After a few short moments, Francesca had already finished her honeyed bourbon and ordered another at the same pace as I did.

"That must be the band," I remarked as I pointed to the band setting up in the corner of the tavern.

"I hope they play a song I know," Francesca said and then took another sip of honeyed bourbon.

"The only song I know from this town is the 'Bard's Ballad,'" I said to Francesca and then took a sip of coffee.

"Oh, that song has been played to death. I know it's the anthem of Thianor, but I still roll my eyes every time I hear it being played," Francesca said with a scoff and then finished her honeyed bourbon with a swig.

"Well, what's your favorite song then?" I inquired as the band began tuning up their instruments.

"'Harlot's Soliloquy,'" Francesca replied.

"Play 'Harlot's Soliloquy!'" I shouted as I tossed a coin into the empty violin case in front of the band.

The female violinist then nodded her head with a warm smile, and the band began to play.

"Oh, Vincent, you're a darling," Francesca said with a smile and playful shove. I could immediately tell why "Harlot's Soliloquy" was Francesca's favorite song, for it was brash and dramatic with soft undertones, just like her personality.

"Another one, darling, and you must tell me how you get your hair looking so lustrous?" Francesca inquired with a grin.

"It's called argan oil. It works wonders," Carmella replied as she flipped her flowing auburn hair to one side of her shoulder with a smile.

"It does indeed. You look gorgeous, honey," Francesca said to Carmella with a grin as she leaned in close over the bar.

"Are you trying to make my husband jealous?" Carmella inquired with a smile as she made Francesca another honeyed bourbon.

"He should be jealous. The men of this town get so much undeserved praise for their drab appearances and even drabber careers," Francesca said to Carmella with an eye roll and scoff.

"They're not all insufferable. I'm married to one of the few good ones," Carmella said to Francesca with a smile as she served her a third honeyed bourbon.

I was beginning to see Francesca in a whole new light as she talked to Carmella with such affection and charm. Two men just over yonder then began juggling bottles. They were no doubt harlequins judging by how flawlessly they juggled the bottles between each other. Everyone in the tavern then applauded as the two men stopped juggling and bowed with a smile.

"All right, that's all well and good, but this is a tavern, so please take your performance outside, gentlemen," Carmella pronounced.

"Dante and Corpulas?" I inquired with a smile as the two men walked past me.

"That is us. Have you seen us perform before?" one of the men inquired with a smile.

"I have. I didn't recognize you two without the masks, but your juggling refreshed my memory. When I first arrived in Thianor, you two were juggling flaming torches. It was remarkable," I replied with a smile.

"I didn't know you two were twins," Francesca remarked as she waved her finger at both of the men.

"Most people don't know that because of the masks we often wear. We must rehearse now for an upcoming play. It was a pleasure to meet you both," the man pronounced and then exited the tavern.

"What a whimsical pair. So tell me, Vincent, what's it like to…how shall I put it, be involved w-with a thespian?" Francesca inquired with a giggle.

"Oh, you're talking about Luna," I replied.

"Well, of course, my dear, w-who else would I be talking about?" Francesca inquired with a smile as she playfully patted my cheek.

"Being with Luna is…illuminating," I replied.

"That's it? Well, she does light up a room. I'll give you that," Francesca said with a smile and then took a swig of honeyed bourbon.

"Oh, excuse me," a rotund man with a sable beard wearing a tailcoat said to Francesca as he sat down beside her at the bar.

"You're excused," Francesca said to the man with a giggle and then primped her hair.

"Wait, haven't we met before?" the man inquired, as he stared intently at Francesca.

"I don't believe so. Have you stayed at the Rosewood Inn before?" Francesca inquired.

"No, that's not it. Wait…yes, yes, I didn't recognize you before without your legs wrapped around me," the man said to Francesca with a smirk.

"Excuse me!" Francesca remarked in a vexatious tone and stare.

"Is your rate still the same or have you changed it?" the man inquired.

"That's not my life anymore," Francesca replied in a stern tone.

"Come now, sweetheart, how much for a slap and tickle?" the man inquired as he waved money in front of Francesca.

"Well, darling, the slap is free. Now fuck off," Francesca said to the man as she swiftly slapped him in his bloated and flushed face. My gaze was then quickly averted from the band in the corner to the man that Francesca just slapped as he raised his cane towards her.

"You insolent wench," the man remarked in a stern tone.

"Move along before I use that flushed head of yours for target practice," I said to the man as I jolted from the barstool and grabbed his cane before it could make contact with Francesca.

"Who's this? Your husband?" the man inquired as he struggled over control of the ebony cane, which I had a firm grasp on.

"No, but he's more of a man than you'll ever be," Francesca replied with a smirk.

I then released my grasp of the man's cane as I stood betwixt him and Francesca with my other hand on my holstered pistol.

"Very well, it's beneath me to indulge in such a crass harlot anyways," the man proclaimed as he took a glance at my hand on my holstered pistol and then stormed out of the tavern with a scoff.

"I'm sorry for that pig's behavior, Vincent. There are those who wish to pull you back down to hell, even when you've fought so hard to rise from that disgusting world," Francesca said with a somber visage and then took a swig of honeyed bourbon and slapped money upon the bar.

"It's all right. I understand," I said to Francesca with a sigh.

"I-I want to go home now," Francesca said in a somber tone.

"You're soused. I'll drive us back to the inn," I said to Francesca as I helped her into the wagon.

Francesca's head swayed back and forth as her bleary sapphire eyes gleamed in the glow of the streetlights as we drove down the thoroughfare.

"Easy, Sigmund, Mommy's stomach is churning!" Francesca shouted as she leaned forward.

"Careful," I said to Francesca as I put my arm out in front of her.

"R-Roselyn's right about you, Vincent. You really do resemble our father. It's almost as if you're his reincarnation…if you believe in that," Francesca said to me with a scoff as she rested her head upon my shoulder. After a few silent moments, Francesca appeared to have fallen asleep on my shoulder in a soused slumber as I halted the wagon in front of the Rosewood Inn.

"Francesca, wake up. We're here," I said to Francesca as I gently jostled her shoulder. "Help me down, won't you?" Francesca said in a weary tone.

It was 11:35 PM.

"Why am I not surprised?" Roselyn pronounced with a sigh as Francesca and I stumbled into the Rosewood Inn.

"Go easy on her," I said to Roselyn as Francesca stumbled into the back room.

"I'm glad you were with her, Vincent," Roselyn said.

"You need not be so worried. She's a grown woman," I said to Roselyn.

"She caused a disturbance at the Wishing Well, didn't she?" Roselyn said while shaking her head.

"How did you know?" I inquired with a sigh.

"I'm her sister, Vincent. I know her nature," Roselyn replied.

"A man was harassing her. He offered to pay her for a night of pleasure. Francesca then refused and justifiably slapped the man," I said to Roselyn.

"Oh, I'm proud of her for resisting that horrid lifestyle," Roselyn said in a somber tone.

"So Francesca was a prostitute?" I inquired in a timid tone.

"Yes, for about a year after our mother died. I pleaded with her almost every day to work with us at the inn, for she's better than that lifestyle, but she shunned us and continued. Then one night, Francesca opened her eyes entirely to the misery she chose to live. She was beaten half to death by some bastard who refused to pay her. Ever since then, Francesca had renounced that detrimental lifestyle, and we couldn't be happier to have her here with us," Roselyn replied.

"She's lucky to have a sister like you. Good night," I said to Roselyn and then walked up the stairs to my room.

Francesca was a strong woman whom I respected and now understood much better. To renounce such a lifestyle and rise from such misery takes a great deal of resolve. Francesca came to that revelation with the help of her sisters' unwavering love. I now felt like Francesca's last facade had been torn down, and I could fully see her for who she truly is. We tried so hard to renounce the past, but it would always find a way to return during the most unexpected times. Although those past memories may cut us deep, they also made us stronger. The key was not to be consumed by the past, but to use the past as an education for a fearless future, just as Francesca had done with her life.

*****

It was 7:05 AM.

"Vincent…Vincent," a dulcet voice called out to me.

"Oh, good morning," I said to Luna in a raspy tone.

Luna was lying down beside me on the bed wearing a frilly chiffon dress resembling a daffodil in full bloom.

"Good morning, darling," Luna said with a warm smile as she placed her hand upon my cheek.

"Am I still dreaming?" I inquired in a yawning tone.

"If you are, then don't wake up, my dear," Luna replied as we kissed.

"I'm serious. I can't quite tell," I said to Luna.

"All right, maybe this will help you return to reality," Luna said as she pinched my stomach in a playful manner.

"All right, I'm awake," I said to Luna with a smile as I sat upright in bed with a stretch.

"It's a beautiful day," Luna said with a smile as she opened the drapes.

"Who let you in?" I inquired as I stood up and began getting dressed.

"Sara let me in. She's such a sweetheart," Luna replied as she poured me a cup of coffee.

"How did she act around you?" I inquired as I combed my hair in the bureau mirror.

"The same, kind and quiet," Luna replied.

"I talked with her yesterday. I don't want her to harbor any resentment towards you," I said to Luna.

"I could talk to her if you'd like. I doubt that girl has a resentful bone in her body. She just cares for you," Luna said.

"Let's not force the issue. Sara will talk when she feels the need to," I said to Luna as I adjusted my black collared shirt.

"I was on my way to the market this morning. Would you care to join me?" Luna inquired as she embraced me while we stared into the bureau mirror.

"Sure, I just have to ask Francesca if I can take the night shift," I replied.

"All right, dear, I'll be waiting in the lobby," Luna said and then kissed me on the cheek before exiting my room.

*****

"Good morning, Francesca. How are you feeling?" I inquired as I walked up to the front desk.

"Shhhh, not so loud, Vincent. My head is still throbbing from last night," Francesca said with her hands massaging her temples.

"I'm going to the market with Luna. Could I take the night shift tonight?" I inquired.

"Very well, Vincent. Does Luna always dress so radiantly when going to the market?"

Francesca inquired with a smile as she pointed to Luna in the lobby.

"Always," I replied with a smile. "Shall we?" I pronounced as Luna and Beatrice were talking to each other in the lobby.

"Farewell," Francesca pronounced with a wave as Luna and I exited the Rosewood Inn with our arms entwined.

"To *North Market Street*, sir," Luna said to the coachman as we entered the carriage.

"You look beautiful," I said to Luna with an elfish smile.

"Thank you, dear. I bought this dress yesterday at a boutique with Daisy," Luna said.

"The sun itself would be envious of your radiance right now," I said to Luna with a smile.

"Did anyone ever tell you that you have the soul of a poet?" Luna inquired and then kissed me.

"No, you're the first," I replied.

"Well, you do. You speak more poetically than most thespians I know," Luna said.

"You can attribute that to the many books I read when I was a child in the cabin."

"I write poetry whenever I'm distraught or in love. It's very cathartic for me," Luna said.

"Really? I would love to read some of your poetry," I said to Luna.

"I would be delighted to show you. I have a collection of sonnets stored in the nightstand in my bedroom," Luna said.

I then paid the fare to the coachman as the carriage came to a halt at North Market Street. Luna and I then exited the carriage to the sight of various produce stands lined on each side of the street, which was already bustling with people.

"Daisy and I frequent this market, for it has the best quality produce in Thianor," Luna said.

I didn't need to worry about losing Luna among the bustling crowd of North Market Street, for she shone like a firefly among the dark river of people.

"Peaches, fresh peaches!"

"Strawberries just picked them this morning!" vendors shouted as Luna and I walked past the stands filled with rubicund fruits.

"Oh, I'm going to buy some strawberries. Daisy could use them to make a pie," Luna said with a smile.

"How is your sister doing?" I inquired as Luna paid the vendor for a small basket of strawberries.

"She's happy. She's been spending more of her time at Gregory's flat. She used to tell me I could join her and Gregory, but now she offers no such invitation," Luna said.

"She wants to be alone with him," I said to Luna.

"I can relate to that sentiment," Luna said with a warm smile.

"Careful, Vincent," a man wearing a cloak said with a sneer as I walked past him.

"Wait, what?" I inquired as I quickly turned around, but the ominous man had vanished into the river of people, like a puff of smoke dispersing throughout the pines.

Luna and I continued to walk down the long and winding North Market Street while stopping every so often at a stand to buy various produce. I had bought a bag of roasted walnuts and venison jerky, for I had missed the taste of the smoked meat I used to eat on a daily basis when I lived in the cabin.

"Try some," I said to Luna as I offered her some venison jerky.

"It's tough," Luna remarked as her delicate mouth struggled to chew the jerky.

"I guess it's an acquired taste among hunters," I said to Luna with a grin.

"Try this," Luna said as she fed me a strawberry with a smile.

"That's definitely not an acquired taste," I remarked with a mouthful of the saccharine strawberry.

"All right, let's not eat all the produce before we get home," Luna said with a giggle.

"So are we done?" I inquired and then took a bite of venison jerky.

"That's everything, dear. Let's go back to my flat," Luna replied with a smile.

*****

"White Stone district, flat *A*-2," I said to the coachman as Luna and I entered the carriage holding the produce we bought from the North Market Street.

"How are you feeling?" Luna inquired while primping her hair.

"Just tired. Nothing a little rest won't solve," I replied with a sigh.

"Have you seen a doctor recently?" Luna inquired.

"Not since my diagnosis, but what would be the point?" I replied.

"The point is to know what you can do in order to live as long as possible," Luna replied.

"I'm already doing all I can by not drinking. Trust me, I'll know if my white plague becomes active," I said to Luna.

"I'm sorry. I know it saddens you when I talk about it, but you mean the world to me, Vincent," Luna said as she placed her hand upon mine.

"Then let's talk about something less grim," I said to Luna.

"All right, I've been reading the script of a new play that the thespian board mailed to me," Luna said.

"Really? Is the play intriguing?" I inquired.

"Somewhat but nothing to get too excited over," Luna said with a sigh.

"So you won't be performing in the play?" I inquired.

"I'm afraid not. I don't accept every play that's proposed to me, only ones that transcend the boundaries of convention," Luna replied.

"Like *Madam of the Crimson Manor*," I said to Luna.

"Exactly, my dear," Luna said with a smile as the carriage halted in front of her flat.

I then paid the fare to the coachman as Luna and I exited the carriage and entered her flat.

"Oh, good morning, Luna," an elderly woman dressed in a black frock and blanket draped over her shoulders said to Luna with a smile.

"Good morning, Eleanor," Luna replied to the elderly woman with a warm smile.

"Have you seen Artemis?" Eleanor inquired.

"No, I haven't seen him. I'll let you know if I do," Luna replied with a smile.

"Nice to meet you," I said to Eleanor as Luna and I walked up the stairs to her flat.

"I swear that woman's cat will be the death of her," Luna said with an eye-rolling glance as we entered her flat.

"Daisy, I'm home," Luna pronounced and then went to the kitchen to store away the produce.

"She's not here," I said to Luna as I entered the kitchen.

"It's quite all right. More strawberries for us then," Luna said with a smile and then began making a pot of coffee.

I then sat down upon the sofa with a sigh.

"Let's go to my bedroom. We'll have more privacy there," Luna said as she walked to her bedroom holding an ivory bowl of strawberries and pot of coffee with two mugs.

I then laid my weary body down upon the bed as Luna poured me a cup of coffee and then began rifling through papers in the drawer of her nightstand.

"These are a few of the sonnets I wrote in the past month," Luna said as she lay beside me on the bed and handed me the sonnets.

Shadow of You

I felt your presence on this morning.
It lingered softly and serene.
Lost in the haze of such mourning,
Although your passing was foreseen.
I felt your presence on this night
Before the tears began to fall,
Though you still comfort me despite
These mortal strains, which I befall.
You follow me as I remain
In this state of desolation.
What must I do to quell the pain
From your shadow's reservation?
Your memory's locked away in the past.
So now I'm left with the shadow you cast.

Blossom

You are my love; you are my spring.
Your mere touch satiates my soul.
Upon your chest, my heart doth cling
As we blossom as a whole.
You are the sunlight to my rose
The blood that flows throughout my breast.
Across the fields and through the meadows,
I shall journey at your behest.
I breathe you in like the sweetest breeze.
Within my heart, you blissfully dance
Like sparrows amidst the sycamore trees.
I shudder from your slightest glance.
We were meant to be together.
Let us stay in bloom forever.

"They're both beautiful," I remarked as Luna rested her head upon my shoulder while eating strawberries.

"'Shadow of You' is about my father, and 'Blossom' is about you," Luna told me with a warm smile.

"I suspected that. I've never had anyone write such beautiful words about me before," I said to Luna with an elfish smile.

"I meant every word," Luna said with a wide-eyed gaze and then kissed me.

Luna's kiss now tasted even sweeter than usual with the residuals from the strawberries coating her lips in saccharine syrup.

"Have you ever thought about getting your poetry published in the *Daily Rosette*?" I inquired.

"Oh, heavens no. I'm not that talented of a writer," Luna replied.

"You're a talented thespian and musician. I have no doubt that people will receive your poetry the way that I just did," I said to Luna.

"Thank you, dear. That means so much coming from you, but I'm no Cornelius Abbott," Luna said.

"Oh, I've heard of him. I have one of his novels back at the cabin," I said to Luna.

"He's such a prolific writer. A few of his novels have been adapted into plays," Luna said.

"Have you performed in any play adapted from Abbott's writings?" I inquired and then took a sip of coffee.

"I have. The play was called *The Claremont Syndrome*. I played Vanessa Claremont, a woman who's continuously tormented by an ominous man named Mason Reeves. Fearing for her life, Vanessa then seeks the help of the local authorities in her town for protection from Mason's torment, but to Vanessa's dismay, the constables inform her that no such man, living or dead, has ever existed in their town. Vanessa was then branded by everyone as a lunatic with an unbalanced mind until she became determined to prove that Mason Reeves did in fact exist. So Vanessa stayed at her mother Christine's house for a week, waiting for the arrival of the ominous Mason to appear before her, and sure enough, he did. Mason told Vanessa to kill her mother, for she was part of a secret society whose prerogative was to silence women like Vanessa, but Vanessa vehemently refused. Christine then caught ear of her daughter's dispute with Mason and came running into the bedroom. Christine then inquired in dismay who Vanessa was shouting at. Vanessa then told Christine that it was Mason, and he was standing right in front of her. Christine then looked upon her daughter with bewildered eyes, for there was no man in their bedroom. I read that this novel was based on Cornelius Abbott's childhood, so there is truth in the story, which makes it all the more profound knowing that this could happen to someone's mind," Luna replied.

"That's an incredible story. I'm sure you were riveting as Vanessa Claremont," I said to Luna.

"I tried my best to envelope her state of mind after I read the novel, but the play wasn't received well by the audience," Luna said with a sigh.

"Social stigmas of the mind are topics that don't relate to everyone, but I applaud you for bringing awareness to the issue. You're really ahead of your time," I said to Luna.

"I just want to be remembered as a thespian who spoke to the hearts and minds of all classes of people, so they no longer feel alone in this world," Luna said.

Whenever Luna gave me a brief summary of one of the plays she performed in, her eyes would ignite with such a passion. Luna had the instinctive ability to captivate me whenever she spoke. She was remarkable, and although her body and mind weren't ready to perform on stage again, I believed without a shadow of a doubt that she belonged on stage, for it was her true purpose in this world to perform and bring awareness to such stigmatic topics.

"I want you to have this…keep it with you, and if you should ever feel alone in this world, just read it, and remember how much I love you," Luna said as she ripped the paper that had her poetry written on it and then gave me the sonnet that she wrote about me entitled, "Blossom."

"Luna, I don't want to revert back to who I was before I met you," I said to Luna with a sorrowful visage.

"You don't have to because I'm always with you, and who you were doesn't dictate who you will become," Luna said as she placed her hand upon my cheek while gazing at me with widened eyes.

"I'm afraid of that life…the silence still haunts me," I said to Luna in a somber tone and downcast eyes.

"Look at me. It's natural to be afraid. Never suppress those feelings, for they can grow into a force that will destroy you from within. I was terrified when my father died. Knowing that I would no longer have his wisdom to comfort me in the darkest of times made me shudder, but then I thought of you, Vincent," Luna said.

"I'm afraid I'm not as wise as your father was or as charming," I said to Luna with a grin.

"Please be kind to yourself, Vincent. I've never met a man like you before. I knew on that night we shared that bottle of wine in the courtyard that you were special," Luna said with a smile.

"I knew on that night you took down that wretch in the alley beside the Wishing Well with two swift kicks that you were special," I said to Luna with a smile.

"I'll remember that night for the rest of my life and how gallant you were," Luna said as she draped her arm over my chest.

"Luna, I'm home!" a voice pronounced from the great room.

"That must be Daisy," Luna remarked.

Luna and I then stood up out of bed and reluctantly exited the comfort and serenity of the bedroom to greet Daisy.

"Good afternoon," Gregory pronounced as Luna and I entered the great room.

"Good afternoon," Luna said to Gregory with a warm smile.

"Daisy, let me show you what I purchased at North Market Street," Luna said to Daisy as they entered the kitchen, leaving Gregory and I standing in the great room.

"Mr. Belmont, you're just the man I've been meaning to see," Gregory said as I stoked the flames of the fireplace.

"Oh, really?" I inquired as I put another log into the fire.

"Yes, but we cannot talk about it here. Will you join me in my flat upstairs?" Gregory inquired with a nervous darting glance.

"Gregory needs my help in his flat," I said to Luna as she entered the great room.

"Oh, all right, dear," Luna said with a farewell kiss. Daisy and Gregory also shared a farewell kiss before Gregory and I exited Luna's flat.

"Oh, there's that cat," I pronounced while pointing at Eleanor's cat, Artemis, who sat quietly on the windowsill as Gregory and I walked up the stairs to his flat.

"That woman's cat seems to have taking a liking to me. I've seen him every day sitting on that windowsill in the corridor," Gregory said with a grin as he unlocked the door to his flat.

"Please sit down, Mr. Belmont. Can I get you a drink?" Gregory inquired as we entered his flat.

Gregory's flat was nowhere near as lavish as Luna's flat, but there was something that immediately caught my eye as I entered.

"Oh, you like that? I purchased that piece at the Cavalli exhibition gallery. It was being auctioned off to the highest bidder. It's called *Incendiary Hope*," Gregory said as he pointed at an oil painting hanging above his fireplace depicting a man and woman standing in the woods holding hands as flames surrounded them.

"How much did that painting cost you?" I inquired as I gazed at the painting with widened eyes.

"Six hundred dollars. It wasn't the star lot, but it was still rather expensive," Gregory replied, as we both sat down across from each other in black armchairs. "I need your advice on a sensitive matter, Mr. Belmont," Gregory said as he stood up from the armchair with a glass of bourbon in hand and began to pace back and forth as I often do when I'm distressed.

"You couldn't talk to Daisy, why come to me?" I inquired.

"I came to you because I'm thinking about asking Daisy to marry me," Gregory replied and then took a sip of bourbon.

"Oh, does Luna know?" I inquired.

"No, you're the first one I've disclosed my intentions to on this matter. I would normally talk to my father, but he lives in Shors End, and I shan't tell Luna of this, for you know how women cannot keep secrets," Gregory said.

"Do you love her?" I inquired as Gregory continued to pace with his hand on his forehead.

"With all my heart. Daisy is the most enchanting woman I've ever met," Gregory replied.

"Then what's the problem?" I inquired with a sigh.

"What if she doesn't feel the same way?" Gregory replied in a distressed tone.

"It doesn't matter where, when, or how you propose to the woman you love, for the very act of making the proposal is all she will care about," I replied.

"Daisy told me you were married," Gregory said as he sat back down in the black armchair.

"I was," I said to Gregory in a somber tone.

"So how did you go about proposing to her?" Gregory inquired.

"Well, it was raining one summer morning, and I could no longer keep my intentions a secret to her, so I right then and there proposed to Luna, I mean Heather," I said to Gregory with a grin while shaking my head.

"Not exactly a picturesque proposal, but she said yes and that's all that matters," Gregory said with a grin.

"Exactly, I just want to ask you two questions," I said to Gregory.

"Go right ahead," Gregory said and then took another sip of bourbon.

"What thought first enters you mind when you wake up in the morning?" I inquired.

"Daisy's beautiful smile," Gregory replied with an elfish smile.

"All right, and this question may seem rather existential, but what is your purpose in life?" I inquired.

"To make Daisy happy," Gregory replied.

"You couldn't have answered those two questions more perfectly," I said to Gregory.

"So I passed your test then, Mr. Belmont?" Gregory inquired with a grin.

"It's no test. I'm just curious. Just live your life by that painting, with hope from the woman you love as the world burns around you," I replied.

"You're really not what I expected, Mr. Belmont," Gregory remarked.

"Call me Vincent, and why is that so?" I inquired.

"I suppose it's due to all my preconceived notions that hunters are an emotionally detached class of people who can take a life with no remorse or hesitation, but I was greatly mistaken. I now see why Luna is so enthralled with you, Vincent," Gregory replied.

"Luna is the greatest thing that's ever happened to me, and I don't want to imagine my life without her in it," I said to Gregory.

"The LaGranges have such an allure about them, haven't they?" Gregory said.

"Yes, a radiance," I said to Gregory.

"*Radiance*, yes, that's the perfect word to describe them," Gregory said with a smile.

"I should be going now," I said to Gregory as I stood upright from the armchair.

"Thank you, Vincent. I shall take your advice to heart. You're welcome in my flat any time…well, unless of course I'm with Daisy. Then she and I will need our privacy," Gregory said with a grin.

"Of course," I said to Gregory with a grin.

"Perhaps you could take me hunting in the near future. Although…I don't know if I have the stomach for it. When I was a stripling boy, I vomited while I was hunting with my grandfather," Gregory said with a snicker.

"I vomited as well during my first kill with my father, just as I attempted to gut and skin a boar. My father then told me I would quickly get used to the smell and sight of blood, and before I knew it, gutting and skinning animals became second nature to me."

"We're not cut from the same cloth in that respect, my friend," Gregory said with a smile.

"Farewell, and good luck with Daisy," I said to Gregory and then exited his flat.

*****

I needed somewhere to reflect on my life and my future with Luna before I would go back to work at the Rosewood Inn this evening.

"To Scarlet Commons," I said to the coachman as I entered the carriage.

"Good evening," an elderly man said in a raspy tone as he sat across from me.

"Good evening," I said to the man.

"You wouldn't happen to be from Bleakton, would you?" the elderly man inquired.

"What makes you say that?" I replied with a grin.

"Your attire and demeanor?" the elderly man replied.

"I haven't been to Bleakton in quite some time," I said to the elderly man.

"It's a shame, isn't? What's become of that town," the elderly man said while shaking his head.

"What do you speak of? What's happened to Bleakton?" I inquired.

"This is my stop. Good day, young man," the elderly man said as he paid his fare to the coachman and then exited the carriage. I felt so at home in Thianor that I'd become blind to the rest of the Fray, and if Bleakton had changed for the worse, then it was of no consequence to me now.

I then paid the coachman my fare and exited the carriage. Whenever I would go hunting in Vilkswood, it gave me time to deeply reflect about my life. Since I couldn't go to Vilkswood for the time being, the Scarlet Commons was the next best place. I slowly walked down the thoroughfare of the Commons, passing by children and elderly couples both partaking in the bloom of spring. Gregory was a good man, and I wish him and Daisy all the happiness in the world as I'm sure Luna does as well, and talking with him gave me a pro-found insight on my relationship with Luna. I then sat down upon the same bench overlooking that small and tranquil pond that Luna and I sat down in yesterday and gazed pensively at the glassy still water.

"Never take love for granted," I whispered as I took out the sonnet Luna wrote for me from the pocket of my jacket. The sun then began to shine brightly at that moment as I reread Luna's sonnet with a smile.

"Oh, it's you again." I spoke aloud as the familiar silent crow perched upon the bench beside me. "What's it like to be voiceless in this world?" I inquired as I stared at the silent crow. "Oh, right, you cannot answer." I spoke aloud with a profound sigh. "If you're not going to help me, then why do you insist on following me?" I inquired as the silent crow stared at me with its head tilted at a rakish angle. I now knew what I must do to sustain my happiness, and for the first time in my life, I harbored no fear of what that entailed. "Farewell, my mordant friend," I said to the silent crow as I turned my head, but he was already gone. "To the Rosewood Inn," I said to the coachman as I entered a carriage.

At 10:45 PM, it appeared that Francesca's idea to attract wealthier townsfolk back to the Rosewood Inn with expensive wine and bedsheets was successful, for business was flourishing.

"These night shifts are so grueling. Why must all creatures be so lively during the night?" Beatrice inquired with a sigh as we began to crank the washing mills full of laundry.

"Not all creatures are most active during nightfall. Humans are generally dormant during the night compared to other animals," I replied with a bantam laugh.

"I suppose I should be happy. Roselyn told me this month was the most lucrative month in the history of the inn. I think that's attributed to all the events that took place in the town square the past fortnight," Beatrice said.

"You're right. Those events were lucrative for everyone," I said to Beatrice.

"You seem in high spirits, Vincent," Beatrice remarked.

"I had a revelation today while I was at Scarlet Commons," I said to Beatrice.

"Oh, a revelation, do tell," Beatrice said with a smile.

"I wish I could," I said to Beatrice.

"A secret revelation—it's not about me, is it?" Beatrice inquired with a grin.

"No, no. I just cannot disclose it yet. I will soon though," I replied.

"You're such a tease," Beatrice said with a playful shove.

"Vincent, Beatrice, hang those bedsheets on a clothesline in the kitchen. They're too expensive to hang out in the back alley to dry," Roselyn pronounced as she walked into the laundry room.

"Very well, I just hope there's enough room," Beatrice said to Roselyn. "Can you believe her? It will take ages for these sheets to fully dry indoors," Beatrice said with an eye roll.

"She doesn't want them to be stolen just like the banner was. Better safe than sorry," I said to Beatrice.

"I suppose. You know, if I close my eyes, I could swear our mother was still alive. That's how much Roselyn reminds me of her," Beatrice said as we took the four sheets out of the washing mill.

"Out of you and your sisters, who looks the most like your mother?" I inquired.

"Well, I would say Francesca resembles Mother the most, but not when she speaks, then Roselyn resembles Mother," Beatrice replied with a grin as we hung the sheets on two clotheslines strung across the kitchen.

"Beatrice, doesn't that look like a wolf?" I inquired as I pointed at the wet hanging sheet.

"I don't see a wolf. I just see roses. You need to get some rest…good night," Beatrice replied and then exited the kitchen. I then shook my head and walked up the stairs to my room.

"Good evening. I just wanted to see how you were feeling?" Sara inquired in a timid tone as she entered my room wearing a white nightgown.

"I'm feeling well. I kept up with Beatrice at every step," I replied with a grin as I stoked the flames of the fireplace.

"That's good to hear," Sara said with a sigh as she sat down upon the bed.

"How are you feeling?" I inquired as I slowly got undressed.

"I'm tired but happy that the inn is getting so much business," Sara replied.

"Yes, your parents would be so proud of how you and your sisters have run the inn," I said to Sara.

"Thank you. I often think about what Mother would say to me now," Sara said.

I then took out the sonnet that Luna wrote for me from my jacket pocket and slipped it between the pages of the only book I brought with me when I departed from the cabin entitled *A Dark Path*.

"It's really warm in here. Let me open the window. Perhaps a band of minstrels will be playing outside the inn," I said to Sara as I opened the window a crack and then sat down upon the bed beside Sara.

"Vincent, I'm sorry for how I acted about you and Luna. You deserve to be happy," Sara said with downcast eyes and an elfish smile.

"It's all right. No need to apologize. Now unless you're going to tuck me in and read me a story, I have to get some sleep," I said to Sara in a yawning tone and grin.

"All right then, good night, Vincent," Sara said with a giggle and then exited my room. Just as I predicted, I could hear the faint dulcet melodies of a band of minstrels playing outside the front entrance of the inn as I lay peacefully in bed. Tomorrow would bring forth a new chapter in my life, one which I was wholeheartedly ready to pursue.

*****

At 7:05 AM, I awoke to a gentle knock on the door, and I sat upright in bed with a stretch.

"Good morning," Sara said as she entered my room holding a pot of coffee and tray of rose blossoms.

"Good morning," I said to Sara as I stood out bed and quickly began to get dressed.

"I hope it doesn't rain today. I am planning on going to North Market Street with Beatrice," Sara said.

"Luna and I went there yesterday. You want some venison jerky?" I inquired.

"Oh, thank you," Sara replied as she delicately grabbed a piece of the jerky from the bag and took a small bite. Sara's reaction when eating the jerky mirrored Luna's as she struggled to chew the tough meat.

"Luna didn't care much for it either," I said to Sara with a bantam laugh.

"No, it's all right, just a bit tough," Sara said as I took a sip of coffee.

"Sara, I want to look my best today. Would you be willing to give me a shave and perhaps a slight trim?" I inquired.

"I'd be delighted to. Would you prefer we do that now or after we make up the rooms?" Sara inquired with a smile.

"Let's do it now if you don't mind," I replied.

"All right, sit down. I'll be right back," Sara said and then exited my room.

Sara then returned after a few moments with all the necessary tools required for shaving my beard and trimming my hair.

"Do you want me to trim your hair first?" Sara inquired with a smile as she ran her fingers through my hair.

"Shave my beard first, please," I replied.

"All right, sir," Sara said and then began to apply the soap all over my beard with a brush.

Sara then began the shaving process with one gentle straight razor stroke at a time.

"I'm glad you trust me with your beard and hair, Vincent. Even my father was reluctant whenever I wanted to prove to him that I've gotten better at shaving," Sara said as she meticulously shaved around my mouth.

"Why spend money on a barber when I can come to you?" I said to Sara with a grin.

"I'm sure a barber would do a much better job than me," Sara said.

"You've done a fine job thus far, Sara," I remarked.

"Compared to how I used to shave my father, I would agree…lift your head," Sara said with a giggle as she slowly shaved under my jawline and neck.

"Back in Bleakton, I knew this man named Gimdrick Corval. He was a hunter who had a very prominent copper beard, which was so large I swear a family of finches could nest in it," I said to Sara with a bantam laugh.

"He sounds rather imposing, like a bear," Sara remarked.

"He may have appeared that way, but his personality was very hearty," I said to Sara.

"All right, all done shaving. Now to trim your hair," Sara said with a warm smile. "How short do you want your hair?" Sara inquired.

"Not that short, just trim about half an inch off," I replied as I pointed at the top of my head.

"All right then," Sara said and then began to comb my hair with a wet brush.

"I miss how fully dark my hair used to be. I have so many white hairs now," I said to Sara.

"Don't fret, it makes you look distinguished," Sara said as she grabbed the scissors and began to cut my hair.

"Last time I attempted to cut my hair was back in the cabin. I searched the cabin for hours, but I couldn't find the damn scissors, so I just ended up using my knife," I said to Sara with a laugh.

"Oh, I bet that was painful," Sara said with a giggle.

"Oh, it was. Now I'm wiser to know when a woman's touch is needed," I said to Sara with a smile.

"All right, all finished. How does it look?" Sara inquired as she held a hand mirror behind my head.

"Are you sure you've never cut hair before?" I replied with a smile.

"Yes, you're my first," Sara said in a timid tone.

"Well, you did a great job. I feel like I should be paying you," I remarked with a grin as I stared at myself in the bureau mirror.

"Thank you," Sara said with a beaming smile.

"I'll meet you downstairs," I said to Sara with a smile.

"Rooms 14 and 15 need to be made up," Francesca pronounced.

"Oh, good, only two rooms," I said to Sara.

"You're looking rather dapper, Vincent," Francesca remarked with a grin as she twirled a strand of her hair around her finger.

"Thank you. Sara is responsible for my groomed appearance this morning," I said to Francesca with a grin. Sara and I then scampered upstairs to make up the two rooms.

"Oh, someone left a necklace on the nightstand," Sara remarked as she grabbed the necklace.

"Let's store that in the lost and found at the front desk," I said to Sara as I put another log into the fire and stoked the flames.

"Oh yes, of course, the woman who left this behind must be so distressed," Sara said as she tucked the necklace into the pocket of her gown. Sara and I then gathered the quilt and sheets from the bed and exited room 14.

"Ah, you see, now this is how everyone should leave a room," I pronounced at the pristine sight of room 15.

"Yes, but we still have to wash the quilts and sheets. Those are the inn's standards of quality," Sara said as I put another log into the fire and stoked the flames. Sara and I then gathered the quilt and sheets from the bed and exited room 15.

"Could you store this in the lost and found?" Sara said to Francesca as she handed her the diamond necklace.

"Oh my, how could such wealthy people be so careless with their valuables?" Francesca replied as she stared at the necklace before storing it away in a chest under the front desk.

"We're all human. Money can't buy an incisive memory now, can it?" I said to Francesca. Sara and I then entered the laundry room to wash the sheets and quilts. Sara and I then loaded the washing mills with the quilts and sheets and slowly began to crank them. I then grimaced with a hissing groan as the scar on my shoulder began to twinge.

"What's wrong?" Sara inquired.

"It's just the scar on my shoulder. It twinges from time to time," I replied as I switched arms to crank the washing mill.

"Oh, I'm sorry," Sara said in a timid tone.

"It's of no consequence, only during the times when I'm about to fire my guns," I said to Sara.

"Is it very painful?" Sara inquired.

"No, I now see this scar on my shoulder as a mark of what I was able to overcome. To live is to feel pain after all," I replied.

"I suppose, but scars are permanent. Some would argue that mental scars are worse than ones on the surface of our skin," Sara said.

"I know…believe me I know, but to endure the detriments of those scars is all we can do in life," I said to Sara.

After an hour had passed, Sara and I then began hanging up all the rose pattern sheets in the kitchen to dry.

"There's a man waiting to see you in the lobby," Francesca said as she pointed to the man.

"As I live and breathe, Vincent Belmont, the man who rejected Mayor Crane," the man pronounced with a scoff and smirk as he stood up from the sofa. The man wore a weathered black leather jacket and gloves and smoked a crimson pipe. His demeanor was rather suave with a domineering undertone as he extended his hand towards me in salutations.

"Have we met?" I inquired as I reluctantly shook the man's hand.

"Corbin Graves. I'm offended you don't remember me but not surprised, for our past interactions were rather brief. I competed in the Scarlet Hunt. We shared the wagon transport to Vilkswood together," the man replied as we both sat down in opposing armchairs in front of the lobby fireplace.

"Oh yes, now I remember. You were the man who told me that wearing wolf fur was bad luck," I said to the man with a grin.

"You're going to make me eat those words now, aren't you? I want to begin by saying I thought it was very funny when you rejected Mayor Crane's proposal. I don't know if you noticed, but in the mayor's parlor, I was the only one laughing when everyone else was gasping from your decision," Corbin said with a snicker and then took a puff from his crimson pipe.

"I'm glad you found it so amusing," I said to Corbin.

"Reminiscing over that night is not why I'm here though. I need your expertise on wolves," Corbin said.

"I wouldn't consider myself an expert on wolves," I said to Corbin.

"Last I recall, while we were riding in the wagon to Vilkswood, you told me you killed three wolves in your lifetime," Corbin said.

"Four wolves actually, but that still doesn't make me an expert," I said to Corbin.

"Nevertheless, I knew you were the hunter to seek counsel with. Have you heard of White Bane, the fabled white wolf of Vilkswood?" Corbin inquired.

"Yes, I've heard the fable, but that wolf has no relevance in my life," I replied in a stern tone as I stood up from the armchair and began to walk past him.

"I've acquired a patch of that wolf's fur," Corbin said.

"Impossible," I remarked in an incredulous tone as I quickly halted in front of Corbin.

"Nothing is impossible for an ambitious man. You should know that better than anybody," Corbin said.

"How did you acquire his fur?" I inquired as I sat back down in the armchair.

"Two days after the Scarlet Hunt had concluded, I went back to Vilkswood to sharpen my hunting skills. I was cleaning a pheasant in the creek when I saw the white wolf leering at me through the morning fog. I then immediately took out my rifle and fired upon the ominous beast, but I couldn't see if I shot it on account of the damn fog obscuring my vision, so I went to investigate. I then saw a patch of snow-white fur upon the creek bed where I shot upon the white wolf," Corbin replied.

"It was just the morning fog playing tricks on your mind. That's happened to me before," I said to Corbin.

"That's why I need you to verify if that patch of fur is from White Bane or not," Corbin said.

"Show me the fur," I said to Corbin.

"I keep it stored in a box at my flat," Corbin said.

"I'm meeting someone. Let's do this some other—"

"I assure you it will be worth your while. Then we could team up and go down in history as the hunters who killed the fabled white wolf," Corbin interjected.

"Very well, let's make this quick," I said to Corbin with a sigh. "I'll be back in a few hours," I said to Francesca as Corbin and I exited the Rosewood Inn.

"To the White Stone district, complex *C*-5," Corbin said to the coachman as we entered the carriage.

"How long have you lived in Thianor?" I inquired.

"My older brother Noah and I moved from Bleakton to Thianor when we were stripling boys. We were orphans raised in the Claymore House until we couldn't take the misery of that establishment any longer and departed Bleakton in search for a better life. Growing up in this cold world with no parents scarred me, but my brother always reassured me that we could overcome anything as long as we stayed together," Corbin replied as he took out his knife and began to sharpen it upon a whetstone while staring pensively out the carriage window.

"Yes, this town has been good to me as well. I've lived here for almost seven months now," I said to Corbin.

"Since when did I say this town was good to me? I simply said that my brother and I came here in search of a better life, but all we found was the same misery. There's nothing but pompous fucking thespians in this town, not to mention Mayor Crane who looks down upon people like us," Corbin said in a stern tone.

"I thought the same as you when I first arrived here, but I soon found out how mistaken I was. This town is full of benevolent people who you can trust with all your heart," I said to Corbin.

"Are you referring to those women you work with at the Rosewood Inn?" Corbin inquired.

"Yes, they took me in when I had nowhere else to go," I replied.

"How sentimental," Corbin remarked as he quickened the sharpening of his knife upon the whetstone in an aggressive manner.

"We're here," Corbin said as he paid the fare to the coachman and exited the carriage.

Corbin and I then entered his flat and walked up the dismal gray stairs to the third floor where there were no oil lamps or candles to light up the darkened complex. I noticed the third-floor window in the corridor of the complex was shattered with bloodstains upon the jagged shards of broken glass.

"So this is where you live?" I inquired as Corbin and I entered his flat. Calling Corbin's flat dismal was like calling a cave dark, for it resembled one in every aspect. The gray walls were stained in black splotches, and the hardwood floor was rough and splintered, like a wild beast had been scuffing around in a furious rage.

"It doesn't have the comfort and luxury of the Rosewood Inn, but a man makes due with what little he has in this world in order to survive," Corbin said.

“All right, where’s the fur?” I inquired.

“It’s in that box on the desk,” Corbin replied as he pointed to a small box upon a desk beside the begrimed window.

I then opened the box but was immediately disappointed by what I saw inside.

“This is rabbit fur,” I said to Corbin while shaking my head, and just then, like a bolt of lightning, I felt a heavy strike to the back of my head, which sent me tumbling to the floor. I then saw Corbin standing over me holding a rifle before all turned to black.

*****

“Wake up, Vincent,” a voice said in a stern tone as he threw a mug full of malodorous water upon my grimacing visage. I awoke with my arms and legs tightly bound to a chair with thick rope. I then slowly raised my throbbing head to the sight of Corbin smoking his crimson pipe as he sat in an armchair across from me.

“W-what is this? What do you want?” I inquired with a hissing groan as Corbin leered at me in silence.

“I just knew that wolf would lure you to me,” Corbin replied with a snicker.

“Y-you never encountered White Bane, did you?” I inquired as I could feel blood dripping from my head and down the back of my neck.

“Of course not, but I knew you couldn’t resist the prospect of killing that fabled wolf. Man is so pitifully predictable,” Corbin replied.

“Why are you doing this?” I inquired as I struggled to free any limb that was tightly bound to the chair, but the severe head trauma that I just incurred rendered me dazed and incapacitated, like a rabbit caught in a deadfall trap.

“I never told you what happened to my brother. One morning, he woke me up to join him for a hunt in the southwest region of Vilkswood. He promised me he would return in a couple of hours with fresh game, but after those hours had passed, I began to worry. Then two days had passed, and Noah had still not returned from his hunt, so I went out in search for him in the southwest region of Vilkswood. After hours of searching for Noah, I laid eyes upon something that wrenched my heart. Noah’s jacket lay torn and bloodied upon a rock at the entrance of the Crimson Cave, but something wasn’t right, for Noah always warned me to give that ominous cave a very wide berth when hunting in Vilkswood. So why did I find my brother’s jacket at the mouth of the cave? Even I know that wolves don’t drag their prey long distances. They feed upon them on sight. So I then began to search the perimeter of the Crimson Cave for any signs of Noah, but I found nothing. So I widened my search more and more until I reached the southwest border of Vilkswood, where I then discovered a cabin.

"I banged on the front door and peered through all the windows, but it appeared that nobody was home. Then I saw a sign that gave me more closure on my brother's death. Drops of blood were peppered around a gravestone on the west side of the cabin. This blood was relatively fresh, no more than a couple days old, and judging by the splatter, it was from a gunshot and not from the bite of a wolf's fangs. I then got down on all fours and examined the snow around the perimeter of the gravestone, and it appeared as if someone smoothed over a trail of footprints leading from the gravestone to Vilkswood. So I then shot through the lock of the front door and let myself into this lovely cabin. I searched throughout the cabin to discover that a hunter lived there, but not just any hunter, a hunter with shining accolades—two-time winner of Gideon's Run. *This man must be well-renowned among all hunters throughout the Fray,* I thought to myself. So I waited for him to return to his warm home in hopes to get some much-needed answers about my brother. A day had then passed and then three days and then a fortnight, before I grew tired of waiting for this man. It was clear to me now that this prized hunter named Vincent Belmont fled his home soon after he shot my brother dead and dragged his body deep into Vilkswood in hopes that the wolves would do the rest of his dirty work for him and devour the evidence that was my brother," Corbin said with a quivering visage as his eyes burned with such a malevolence that I've only seen once before from White Bane on the day he killed Heather and Audrey.

"Your brother was robbing my wife's grave. I had every right to do what I did!" I shouted, as I writhed furiously in the chair. Corbin then stood up from the armchair and slowly leaned in close to my weeping head.

"So let me get this straight. Are jewels that adorned your wife's corpse worth more than my brother's life? Answer me!" Corbin shouted as he clutched my hair and pulled my head towards his burning gaze.

"I'm sorry about your brother, but he shot at me first. I was just defending myself. I can't take back what I did that day, and it has continued to haunt me," I said to Corbin with a painful grimace.

"Thianor has indeed been good to you, Vincent. Those four kind women you work with at the Rosewood Inn, and not to mention Ms. LaGrange. You've managed to build quite a happy life from the death of my brother. So you could say that it was Noah who was responsible for all this happiness in your life because I highly doubt you would have fled to Thianor if you hadn't shot him dead that day," Corbin said.

"How do you know of Luna?" I inquired in a distressed tone.

Corbin then snickered as he put another log into the fire and stoked the faint flames. "You know I almost gave up my search for you, Vincent. I searched everywhere in Bleakton for you, but you were nowhere to be found in that town full of hunters. So then I thought to myself, *Of course, this man would never flee to Bleakton, for that would be too obvious of a town to lay low in during the wake of committing a murder.* So I came back here. Then on one night, I laid eyes on such a beautiful vision known as Luna LaGrange, and she was holding the arm of a man wearing a wolf-fur jacket as they both entered a carriage. I've never, for the likes of me, seen a *Thianorian* wear wolf fur, and then I remembered the wolf fur that lay on the hardwood floor of your cabin covering up a grizzly bloodstain. Ever since then, I've been your shadow," Corbin said as he grabbed my pistol and closely examined it while pacing back and forth in front of me.

"Wait, that was you at the Cavalli exhibition wearing the cloak, as I stared at the portrait of White Bane, wasn't it?" I inquired with widened eyes.

"Ah, I see those sharp hunter instincts have finally kicked in. Yes, that was me at the art show," Corbin replied.

"That was also you at the North Market Street, wasn't it?" I inquired.

"Right again, Vincent. You see the thing about shadows is that you never truly notice them, just as this town never truly noticed me and my brother. We were merely shadows in the bright lights of all these thespians," Corbin said in a contemptuous tone.

"You think you're the only one who's lost everything. I watched my wife and daughter die right before my eyes," I said to Corbin.

"Yes, there's no doubt that defined your life as you have defined mine by killing my brother. I know a great deal about you, Vincent. I've studied you during that fortnight I spent in your cabin waiting for your return," Corbin said.

"You know nothing about me!" I shouted as Corbin sneered at me with my pistol in his hand.

"Oh, really? I knew you were lying when you told me White Bane had no relevance in your life. Your fervid reaction, as you stared at his portrait at the art show revealed that to me. But why…why would a hunter be so obsessed with the white wolf of Vilkswood?" Corbin inquired, but I stared back at him with silent contempt.

"Oh yes, of course, I don't know why I failed to see it before. That wolf was responsible for the death of your wife and daughter, wasn't he? Corbin inquired with a snicker.

"You bastard!" I remarked.

Corbin then took out his knife as he clutched my hair and pulled my head back.

"Go on, end my life if you think it will quell your rage," I said to Corbin, as he held his knife close to my throat.

"No, Vincent. As I said, I know a great deal about you, and ending your life would be too merciful for the crime you committed," Corbin said.

"You have a life to live, as do I, and I'm sure your brother wouldn't want vengeance upon me to be your sole purpose in this world," I said to Corbin.

"Don't you dare claim to know my brother!" Corbin shouted and then struck me in the mouth with my pistol.

"You claim to know a great deal about me. Well, did you know that I have the white plague?" I inquired and then spit blood upon Corbin's furious visage.

"That's the difference between you and I. I have nothing left to lose in this world, but you…you have many loved ones in your life now. Ah, Luna LaGrange, what a beautiful creature she is. I wonder how beautiful she'll look as her blood spills upon the floor," Corbin said with a sneer and then slowly wiped the blood off his cheek.

"If you hurt Luna or any of the Merchant sisters, then you will share the same fate as your brother. This I vow," I said to Corbin as I quivered with rage at the sight of him sneering back at me. I then writhed with all my might to escape the thick rope that bound me to the chair, but my strength couldn't prevail.

"You're in no position to be threatening me, Vincent. Just look at yourself. The two time winner of Gideon's Run now trapped like a frightened rabbit in a snare. Oh, how I've waited so long for this moment," Corbin said as he paced back and forth in front of me while sneering.

"I'll notify the constables of your intentions," I said to Corbin in a stern tone.

"Oh, come now, Vincent. You know just as well as I do that the constables couldn't give a shit about the daily altercations of people like us. They only jump to attention when there's a robbery or at the mayor's behest," Corbin said with a scoff.

"People like us…I'm nothing like you. I only kill to defend, protect, and provide for my life and the people I care about," I said to Corbin.

"Noble till the end I see, but today isn't the end of your life. It's merely a departure from the love you've grown so accustomed to—the love you've built from the bones of my brother," Corbin said.

"Please…please, I've lost everything. Everything I thought which was irreplaceable in my heart, but I've now found a woman whom I want to spend the rest of my numbered days with. Please I plead to your humanity, just let me live my life," I said to Corbin in a somber tone as my eyes began to well up with tears.

"Your begging is not as satisfying as I imagined it to be, lo these many months of plotting your downfall. You know what? I've had a change of heart. Your love has inspired me, Vincent, so now I offer you this choice. You can either live a life without Luna, or you can live in a world without Luna. If you truly love her, then you will suffer for her. I trust you know what I say to you now," Corbin said.

"You think you can banish me from this town completely?" I inquired.

"I have eyes and ears all over this town. I searched across the entire Fray to find you, and unbeknownst to you, I've been your shadow for months now. I thought a man like you who's lost everything would be more cautious and take heed to the imminent death of his loved ones. Do you really want to take that chance?" Corbin inquired.

"No," I replied in a somber tone.

"Then we have an understanding. You will leave this town today before dusk, and remember, if you choose to stay here, then I will be your shadow and the ones you love will suffer and die by my hand," Corbin said as he cut the rope that bound my hands and then swung a black cloak over his shoulders as he stormed out of the flat with a snicker.

*****

I stormed up the stairs to my room as I entered the Rosewood Inn without acknowledging Roselyn at the front desk. This would be the last time I see her and her sisters, and that very thought left me cold and quivering as I began to write my farewell letter.

> Dear Merchant sisters,
>
> I'm afraid my time with you four is over. I can no longer remain in Thianor, for a very dangerous and demented man has claimed your lives if I stay, and I can't take that risk. You four are the salt of the earth, and I believe if everyone in the Fray had half the hearts that you four possess, then there would be no pain or suffering, only warmth and love.
>
> Roselyn, you took me in to work for you and your sisters when I had not a soul in this world to turn to, and I will forever be in your debt. The benevolence and leadership you bestow upon your sisters and all the people staying at the Rosewood Inn is no less than saintly. You accepted me into your family when I felt alone and undeserving of love, and I became a better person day by day as I worked for you. I know your parents would be so proud of how you've continued to run the inn and keep everyone together in the wake of their deaths. I never had any siblings, but I see you as a sister, and I love you.
>
> Francesca, we locked horns at first, but as time passed, I could see the love in your heart reveal itself to me little by little. You are a strong. Some would say obstinate woman, but I've always admired that about you, ever since the first time we met that night you offered to help me walk up the stairs when I was soused beyond all reason. You've overcome such a dark chapter in your life, and your sisters need your resilience. So please open your heart to them on a daily basis, for they love you, and so do I.

Beatrice, talking to you day by day was a joy that I cherished from the moment I awoke in the morning to the moment I fell asleep at night. I felt safe talking to you about any topic, whether it be love or death, pain or happiness. You were there for me, lending me your open heart and mind. Your blithesome spirit can warm the coldest heart. I will miss our daily talks as we made up the rooms and washed the laundry. I could always trust you even when I couldn't trust myself. Your humor and charm would always uplift my spirits even on the darkest days when the white plague sapped the life from me. You always filled me with such warmth that would get me through the day, and I love you.

Sara, I'm so sorry. During my first couple of nights in Thianor, I was in the depths of despair when you told me to find a better friend. I didn't want to open up to anyone back then, but you stood by me with such a kind and understanding heart, which pierced through the stoic armor that I have imprisoned myself in. You're such a beautiful young woman, Sara, and I considered it a privilege to have worked for you and your sisters these past seven months. I'm sorry if I hurt you, but know that your sisters will always be there for you, so don't ever take them for granted. I lost my daughter once before, and now I feel like I've lost her once again with you, Sara. When you first told me how much I reminded you of your father, I was hesitant to assume that role, for I thought it would bring forth an array of painful emotions which I felt for my daughter Audrey. I'm now grateful that you saw me in such a light, for it was more than I deserved. I'm going to miss seeing you smile as you wake me up every morning, but you must not fret over me now, for you have so much of your life ahead of you. You're a strong young woman who can overcome anything, Sara, and I love you.

I will never forget the kindness you all have shown me, nor could I ever repay it. When I needed a place to stay, you all gave me a home. I don't want to leave, and it pains my heart to write this letter, but it's the only way I can ensure the safety of you all. I will look back on my times spent at the Rosewood Inn as a ray of sunlight, a ray of hope in this dreary world. I wish you four all the happiness and success in the world, farewell.

Love,
Vincent

PS: I left one of my rifles for the four of you in my room for protection in case any of your lives should become threatened in the future. Use it well.

I couldn't say farewell to the Merchant sisters or Luna in person, for seeing their somber visages would be far too painful and make it far more difficult for me to leave Thianor, so these letters would have to suffice. My life was now under the command of a demented man hellbent on destroying all which I love in this world. Corbin was right. I wouldn't dare take that chance of anyone I love dying once more from my faulting actions. I've been through that misery with Heather and Audrey, and I won't let that happen again to the ones I love. So I then wiped the tears from my quivering visage and began to write my farewell letter to Luna.

Dear Luna,

I want nothing more than to spend the rest of what little time I have left on this earth with you, but I'm afraid I cannot. Unless I depart from Thianor by dusk today, your life, along with the Merchants, will be claimed by a very dangerous and demented man. The same man whose brother gave me the scar on my shoulder. I won't tell you the man's name, for I fear knowing his identity will only put your life in greater danger. Unbeknownst to me, this man has tracked me down across the Fray and has been following me for months in Thianor. He seeks vengeance on me for killing his brother, and I don't underestimate the lengths he will go to in order to make me suffer, for I saw nothing but pain and hatred in his eyes.

I'm so sorry I brought this upon you. I thought that chapter of my life was over, but I was wrong. On that night we shared that bottle of wine in your courtyard, you told me there was a darkness over me. You're right. There is a darkness over me, and I won't let it pass on to you, and if leaving you is the only way I can protect your life, then that's what I must do. I love you more than anything in this world, and I won't gamble your life as I did with Heather and Audrey. It may feel like I'm abandoning you, but please know that I'm fighting against every fiber of my being to stay in Thianor. I couldn't ask you to come with me, for you have a well-established life here in Thianor. I want nothing more than to kiss you and hold you in my arms right now, but I fear that if I do, then I won't leave Thianor, and your life will be in danger. You told me not to play the martyr role with you, but sometimes, you have no choice in life, and that madman knew the choice I would make before I made it.

Luna, please keep performing on stage in my absence, for I believe it's your true calling in life. I was a better person when I was with you, Luna, and I will never be the same in your absence. I told your father that you gave me a newfound purpose in life. The very air I breathed each day was made from your love, and you will always be a part of me. Tell Daisy farewell and that I wish her and Gregory all the happiness in the world. I hope that you can forgive me, for you're the last person in the world I want to hurt. Wherever life may lead me now, know that you will always remain in my heart. I love you, Luna.

Yours truly,
Vincent

PS: I left you with my rifle for protection in case your life should ever become threatened in the future. May it serve you where I cannot.

I then quickly gathered all my possessions from my room and stored them in my satchel. I had to leave the Rosewood Inn without running into any of the Merchant sisters, for my heart couldn't take such a confrontation. The Merchant sisters were my family, and now I don't know if I'd ever see them again. I then took one last look at the room I've called home for the past seven months before I exited room 16.

No Merchant sisters were in sight as I slowly walked down the stairs with my satchel and rifle slung over my shoulders. I then saw Roselyn feeding her doves with an angelic smile as I walked towards the front desk with my room key and farewell letter in hand.

"Thank you," I said to Roselyn, in a somber tone and smile, as I placed the farewell letter and room key upon the front desk, and then exited the Rosewood Inn.

"White Stone district flat *A*-2," I said to the coachman in a somber tone as I entered the carriage. I missed them already. I needed benevolent people like the Merchants in my life, and now I felt all the warmth leave my body. At that moment, the internal struggle I faced to exit the carriage and run back to the Rosewood Inn was overwhelming, but I couldn't. Sacrificing my happiness for the Merchant sisters' lives wasn't a difficult decision. It was just as Corbin said, "I will willingly suffer for the ones I love."

It was 5:56 PM.

"Wait here for a moment. I'll be right back," I said to the coachman as the carriage halted in front of Luna's flat.

"Very well, sir," the coachman said as I exited the carriage. I now stood at the front gates of Luna's courtyard with an overwhelming sense of despondency that left me frozen. This courtyard was where I first fell in love with Luna, and now it was where I must leave her. At that moment, a thought crossed my mind, a thought that could easily resolve everything. I could kill Corbin right now just as I killed his brother, and then nobody would be left to threaten the lives of the people I love. I knew where Corbin lived and his last name. I could track him down just as he tracked me down across the Fray. Corbin claimed he would be my shadow as long as I remain in Thianor. If that were true, then he most likely was watching me right now. I then stared all around me in a nervous manner for any signs of Corbin, but I saw nothing. So now I had a new choice, would I take one more life to save five? No, I won't. Taking a life has become too easy for me, and no matter how much of a demented, miserable, and consumed man Corbin may be, I will not kill him, for his death will then haunt me, just as his brother's death has. I then entered the courtyard with my rifle and farewell letter to Luna in hand.

"Vincent!" a voice shouted as I placed the rifle and letter upon the white stone table. I knew that dulcet voice by heart. It was Luna from the second-story window, but I wouldn't look up to acknowledge her. I couldn't.

"Wait, where are you going?" Luna inquired as I exited the courtyard with tearful eyes.

How could this have happened? How could my life be taken from me so swiftly once again? Luna, today I was going to ask for her hand in marriage.

The tale continues with Part II.

ABOUT THE AUTHOR

Greetings, lovers of literature. I am Robert James Allen, and ever since I was nineteen years old, the literary works of Edgar Allan Poe, William Shakespeare, Charles Dickens, and Henry David Thoreau have beguiled me. I consider those renowned writers to be the most prolific writers of all time, and I consider my writing to be wholeheartedly inspired by their work. The art of storytelling is in my blood, and I strive to write about topics that resonate in the hearts and minds of all demographics that are struggling in life and feel like they have no voice. Throughout my entire life, I've only ever felt solace within the deep recesses of my mind. I now share those recesses to the world in hopes that we may better understand and accept each other's demons, rather than stigmatize and forsake them. The past five years that it took me to write this story have given me a purpose in life. During my darkest of times, I would continue to write this story, and the dismal world around me would suddenly disappear as I began to live within the pages of this story I was creating. This is my debut novel as a published author and the most profound literature I've ever written.

CPSIA information can be obtained
at www.ICGtesting.com
Printed in the USA
LVHW052042140423
744403LV00005B/250

9 781643 148120